HOLLOW VEINS

SABRE SECURITY BOOK THREE

J ROSE

TRIGGER WARNING

Hollow Veins is a contemporary reverse harem romance, so the main character will have multiple love interests that she will not have to choose between.

This book is very dark and contains scenes that may be triggering for some readers. This includes physical and psychological abuse, torture, sexual assault and abuse, imprisonment, graphic violence, serial murder, PTSD, Trichotillomania, mass suicide and cult-worship.

If you are triggered by any of this content, please do not read this book.

Additionally, British Sign Language (BSL) is used throughout and is distinguished through the use of italicisation.

Settle in and enjoy the final chapter of Harlow's story!

J ROSE SHARED UNIVERSE

All of J Rose's contemporary dark romance books are set in the same shared universe. From the walls of Blackwood Institute, to Sabre Security's HQ, and the small town of Briar Valley, all of the characters inhabit the same world and feature in Easter egg cameos in each other's books.

You can read these books in any order, dipping in and out of different series and stories, but here is the recommended order for the full effect of the shared universe and the ties between the books.

For more information: www.jroseauthor.com/readingorder

"Better to reign in Hell than serve in Heaven."
\- John Milton

SCENE DU CRI

PROLOGUE

Michael Abaddon

God Save Me – Genosky & Promoting Sounds

With my knees pressed against the floor of the bedroom, I stare up at the hewed wood of the crucifix nailed into the wall. My hands are tightly clasped together, the gold-edged Bible laying open in front of me.

"Lord Almighty. Forgive me, for I have sinned. My flesh is weak. I have wrestled with sin and failed. Grant me your holy forgiveness, Lord."

I roll up the sleeve of my simple shift shirt that has the scent of cheap soap clinging to the fabric. Then I lift the knife that rests beside my Bible. The blade is curved into a wicked arc, the hilt glinting with rich engravings.

As steel meets flesh, the flow of hot, cleansing blood seeps from the deep wounds I inflict upon my inner forearm. Over and over. Slash after slash. Cut. Slice. Bleed. Repent.

"Forgive me, Heavenly Father. I did not mean to hurt her."

Yes. You did.

For as long as I can remember, there's been this dark, murmured voice in the back of my mind. On occasion, it escapes the shackles I've forged from fire and brimstone to keep it imprisoned in the safety of my imagination.

When it does come out, my scripture fails. The Lord's light disappears from my inner landscape, overshadowed by the cloying shadows of the devil's soldiers, preparing to invade.

Slicing deep into my arm, I repeat the words bruised and beaten into me throughout the years we spent at Genesis Home, despite the decades that have passed. The twisted symphony has accompanied my darkest hours ever since.

You are a sinful demon, Michael.

Pain cleanses us of all our sins.

Remember your scripture.

Placing the bloodstained knife down with a shaking hand, I take a strip of clean cotton from inside the hand-carved wooden box that houses my equipment. The pure-white fabric is soon soaked through with dark, sinister crimson.

It doesn't stop the memories of her voice screaming for mercy. I didn't mean to hurt her. All I wanted was to talk. The short walk home from the chapel that hosts evening prayers snakes through the depths of the city. It's impossible to ignore the walking sacks of flesh and sin.

They heckle as you pass, tempting demons in with their disgusting offers and bare legs. One shouted that she'd suck my cock for little more than the price of a newspaper. Filthy fucking whore.

I'm not sure how it happened. The world flashed in and out in shades of red, and before I knew it, her face was pummelled into a paste beneath my swollen fists. I ran before the authorities could be alerted.

Rosetta and I move regularly, adopting new names and identities. It has become second nature to us now, after we were forced to flee our previous home when a similar *incident* occurred. For that, I can only blame the devil.

"M-Michael?"

While my head stays lowered, my hands curl into fists.

"What have I told you about interrupting me while I'm praying?"

"I'm s-sorry," Rosetta stutters. "I just wanted to remind you about your meeting. The train leaves in half an hour. You're going to be late."

Seething, I push the box back underneath our plain double bed and stand. She still dares to speak to me, even through her split lips and the dark clouds of bruises that ring her eyes.

I should've broken her fucking jaw. That would keep her quiet. She's lucky to even be breathing. The Lord only punishes those who deserve it. Those who are corrupted enough to draw his wrath.

There's a reason why Rosetta lost our child—she's a sinner, like the rest of them. After years of attempting to fill her barren womb, we were finally rewarded, only for her to screw everything up. Again.

"Have you done your afternoon prayers?" I ask curtly.

Her eyes duck in fear. "Daphne called. I was on the phone."

"But you thought interrupting mine was appropriate?"

"I w-was only trying to help."

"Silence. I don't want to hear any more of your lies."

She swallows a cry of pain as my fist connects with her cheek. A spray of dark blood hits the wall and leaves a smeared imprint like one of those Rorschach inkblot tests that doctors used to make me do.

I still don't know what they were looking for. The demons within me aren't so easily discerned. They speak in shadows and the silent pauses between breaths. No one can cure my God-given right to rule.

"You're going to kneel on the floor. Now."

With tears soaking into the weathered flesh of her cheeks, Rosetta nods and follows my command. Her blue dress is tucked beneath her legs as she assumes the position beneath the watchful gaze of the crucifix.

"And you're going to pray," I spit at her. "Pray for God's forgiveness. That child's death is on your head."

"Please," she whimpers. "I didn't mean to lose our baby. I had a miscarriage."

"You think I care what you meant? This is your punishment for allowing sinful thoughts to enter your mind. Now you have to pay the price for your lustful ways."

Rosetta screams when I grab a handful of her brown hair and use it to smash her face into the wall. The quiet *crunch* of her already crooked nose colliding with the flat surface sends spikes of violence through my veins.

More.

She deserves more.

They all do.

"I'm going to go deal with this situation." I stroke a hand over her head. "God grants his hardest battles to his most dedicated soldiers. It seems I am being tested today."

She doesn't respond, her gaze focused on her laced fingers. I can see the movement of her lips forming the words I've whipped, beaten and bruised into her soul.

Rosetta must repent, like every other woman who dares to lead me astray. They must all earn God's mercy to receive it. He sees their lies and bad intentions, no matter what mockery they preach.

I leave her crying on the floorboards and head for the train station. We're currently based out of Wolverhampton, eighteen months into our latest identity. There's no telling how long this one will last.

The people who once pursued us have long since lost interest or have passed on. This was supposed to be our fresh start, along with the life God granted us.

Instead, I have a useless whore of a wife, and the demonic slut who abandoned me as a baby has dealt me another blow. Her death allowed my half-sister, Giana, to track me down.

I wasn't expecting to find a sibling when I attended to my mother's meagre affairs. Michael Abaddon's life was abandoned years ago, much like she did to me as a child, but I still kept tabs.

The train ride to the quiet countryside is a painful three hours. Leaving the stifling heat of strangers packed together like sardines, I summon a taxi then rattle off the address written on my palm.

After a short drive through the countryside, a small, cramped house nestled amidst a bad neighbourhood greets me. There's a battered, centuries-old truck parked outside the family home.

My knuckles rap against the door in a reluctant lament. The reasons for allowing this interaction are selfless. I'm trying to save Giana. Our mother was a godless cunt wrapped in the skin of a whoring demon.

My so-called sister has that bitch's blood in her veins, so she is cursed. Our whole family is. That's why the devil is buried deep in my bones and comes to me in murderous whispers. I've been cursed too.

I have to help her.

I have to save her.

When the door opens, the first thing I notice is the smattering of toys across my sister's threadbare carpet. She's short and thin, her blonde hair untidy and framing uncertain green eyes that match my own.

"Michael. You came."

"I did." Stepping inside, I peer around the messy porch. "I don't have long. I've left my wife at home."

"How is she? And the baby?"

Anger curdles in my gut. I offered Giana a smattering of details at my mother's unmarked graveside. In the handful of weeks that have passed since then, the cruel lash of fate has cut my luck short.

"Fine," I lie stiffly. "Healthy."

Giana smiles. "That's good. Those first few months are so crucial."

"Indeed, they are. Is your husband home?"

She guides me through the house towards the kitchen. "He's at work. I thought it might be best if we talked first, before I introduce you to anyone."

More lies. I can sense it. She's hiding something about her life and the people she lives with. There's no love in her voice, no pride.

"You didn't tell them about her, did you?" I guess.

Giana's gaze ducks. "You can't even say *her* name?"

"No. I refuse."

She sighs. "I left my old life behind when I was adopted as a child. After marrying Oliver and having Letty, I didn't feel the need to share my birth mother's story with them."

The children's toys were a dead giveaway, but the moment I hear her name, darkness rears its head inside of me. Glossy black wings unfurl, and hell's fires begin to burn beneath my skin.

"How old is Letty, exactly?"

"She turned eight-years-old a couple of weeks ago."

"Precious." I take a seat at her round, cloth-covered table. "Children are a blessing from God."

"Oh, well, I suppose they are." Giana hesitates, seeming doubtful. "Are you excited to become a father yourself?"

Acid slips over my tongue. "Oh, yes. We are thrilled. We've been trying unsuccessfully for many years."

"I didn't expect to have Letty. We had only been married for a couple of months when I got pregnant."

If I'm not mistaken, there's a hint of displeasure in my sister's voice. Just a whisper. The smallest grain of resentment.

"She was unplanned?" I poke further.

Her eyes lower. "Very much so."

"You should be thankful for such a blessing."

The crease between her furrowed brows deepens. I remain silent as she fills a chipped teapot and hands me a similarly damaged mug. Clearly, they don't entertain much.

"Do you go to church?"

"Church?" she repeats. "No. We aren't religious. My adoptive mother was an atheist."

Blasphemous bitch.

"The Lord grants all his children mercy, if they will only ask for it," I inform her. "You should think about that."

"Uh, well... Like I said, we're not religious."

"When the time for judgement comes, it won't matter who believes in the Lord's divine work and who does not. The sinners will be judged regardless."

Her eyes slide over to me before quickly darting away. The awkward silence is broken as she sits down and pours the tea.

"Are there moments in your life that you regret?" I question softly. "Things you wish that you could take back? Mistakes? Sins?"

"Of course," she admits.

"Are you happy, Giana?"

"I ... *ahem*. Well, I am."

"There's nothing in your life that you'd change?"

"Why are you asking me these things?" she snaps, becoming flustered.

I lean forward to bring our eyes level. "I know that you have a feeling deep inside of you. A sense that something is broken, somehow."

Her lips fall open on an unsteady breath. "I... I..."

"It's always been there. No matter where you go or what you do, the voice still whispers."

Her green eyes sparkle like pine trees draped in morning dew, and her bottom lip wobbles. There it is. The lie. The story she tells the world. I can see the deceit buried in her irises.

"How old were you when she left you?" I ask, barely above a whisper.

"Seven," Giana chokes out. "I was seven."

"So young to be left alone in the world, isn't it? I didn't make it that long. Our mother squeezed me out then abandoned me at the first children's home she could find."

"I'm sorry, Michael. She hurt us both. You know that."

"Do I? Seems to me that you had seven years of knowing one of your parents. You were cared for, however briefly. Maybe you were even loved."

"She gave me up for adoption. That isn't love."

"It's a damn sight better than being abandoned in an abusive prison."

Her chair scrapes back as she stands in an attempt to regain some futile sense of power.

"I have to pick Letty up from school," Giana blurts. "Perhaps we should talk another time."

Drawing to my feet, I reach inside my coat pocket and pull out the slim, leather-bound book I tucked inside earlier. It's a smaller version of my own Bible and well-worn from use.

Placing it down on the kitchen table, I offer my half-sister a knowing grin. The deep grooves of her frown have evaporated into a look of discomfort and almost… fear.

She looks just like that disgusting slut did last night as I prowled closer, my fists raised and ready to beat the Lord's sermon into her.

"For you." I push the book towards her. "God is willing to accept all strays, Giana. No matter how lost. Perhaps it's time for you to come home."

Turning my back on her startled facial expression, I let myself out of her home. Giana doesn't follow. When I look over my shoulder before closing the door, she's clasping the Bible in her hands and has begun to thumb through the pages.

Hook, line and sinker.

Her heathen soul is ripe for the taking.

But if my dearest sister wants me to save her from a loveless marriage and a child she never wanted, she will have to pay for her ticket into the Lord's light. No redemption is free of charge. A debt must be paid.

Rosetta will never give me a child.

I'll have to steal one for myself.

SCENE DU NO
J.ROSE

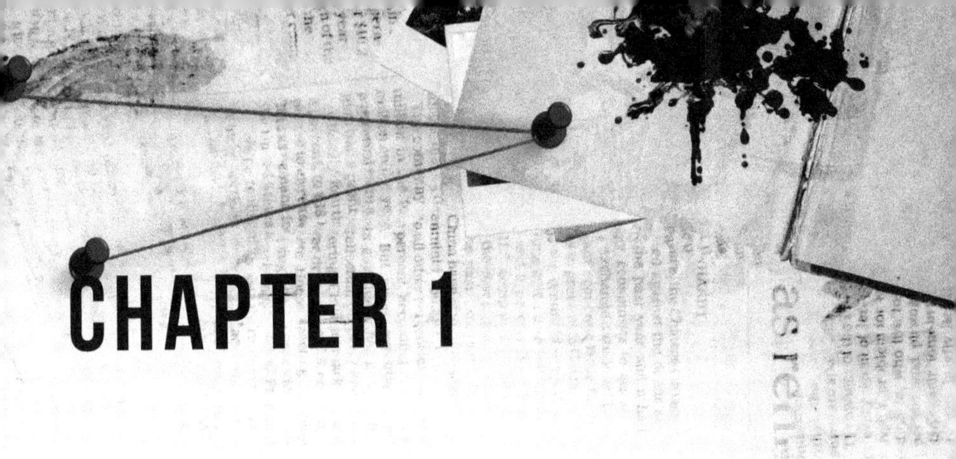

CHAPTER 1

Harlow

Who Are You Fighting For? – Gina Brooklyn

"Catch the fucking ball!"

The sound of a football whooshing over me disturbs my swelteringly hot afternoon study session. I peer down the stretch of sandy beach in time to see it collide with Leighton's lowered head.

"Ouch!" he bellows. "You asshole."

On the other side of our private beach, Enzo's golden, sun-kissed skin glows in the afternoon warmth. His shoulders look like carved trunks of oak that are painted a flawless shade of caramel.

"I warned you. What the hell are you looking at?"

"My damn mosquito bite," Leighton shouts back. "Look at the size of my leg! It looks like it's gonna fall off or something."

"Want me to amputate it for you? Free of charge."

"You'd like that, wouldn't you?"

Enzo chuckles. "Very much so."

With an eye roll, I refocus on the notebook in front of me.

Normally, Theo helps me with the algebraic formulas we're currently learning in my online maths course.

Every single day for the last two months, I've woken up to the same bubble of peace and tranquillity. They are two words I never thought I'd use to describe my life, but we've somehow found it, even if only temporarily.

I landed on these shores broken and bruised, but our break from reality has healed wounds I didn't even know existed until they were gone. Our two-week holiday soon stretched into a two-month sabbatical.

With a dramatic huff, Leighton collapses on the sand-covered beach towel next to me. Flopping onto his back, he throws a lazy hand over his face that's framed by salt-mussed brown locks.

"Who won?" I ask absently.

His warm, emerald eyes flick over to me. "Who do you think? That man needs to learn how to lose. It'll be good for his ego."

"Thought you were just letting him win?"

"Well, obviously. I'm nothing if not a gentleman."

Placing my pen down, I roll sideways on my towel to snuggle up against his bare torso. With Leighton dressed in only a tight pair of blue swim shorts, every sculpted line of his stocky build is exposed to my kisses.

My lips travel up his sand-dusted skin then over blemishes and adorable freckles brought out by the constant sunshine, until his button nose is brushing mine.

His features are handsome and symmetrical, much like his brother's model-perfect looks. Leighton's face is softer, though, clearly younger and always lit with a gleam of mischief.

"That's a very skimpy bikini you're wearing today," he murmurs appreciatively. "Looks good, Goldilocks."

"It would look even better on your bedroom floor."

Leighton's lips part. "Fuck yeah, it would. You offering?"

"My classes are done for the day."

Before our mouths can meet, the sand we're lying on almost shudders with the weight of Enzo thumping his mountainous body down on my other side, the football now abandoned.

That man could shake heaven and Earth, if he felt so inclined, without breaking a sweat. I don't think I've seen him wear a single shirt in the eight weeks we've spent in Costa Rica.

"I won," Enzo declares triumphantly.

"So I heard."

Two paw-like hands wrap around my waist from behind and drag me backwards, away from Leighton, until the press of firm abdominals meets my spine.

"Mine," Enzo growls out. "What's my prize, little one?"

"Thief," Leighton mutters.

"Shut up, little shit. She's mine to steal."

Stifling a giggle, I twist in Enzo's embrace until I'm on my back, staring up into the vivid amber depths of his irises. They're almost covered by jet-black hair so overgrown, it brushes his earlobes.

The sharp planes and strong angles of his face have been brought out by the almost glowing quality of his tan. In the Costa Rican sunshine, he's darkened to a gorgeous, bronzed colour.

Enzo's looks are too harsh to be classified as traditionally handsome, but he could rival a Viking warrior. Every ridge of muscle that carves his Herculean frame screams intimidation.

"What would you like?"

His full lips twist into a smirk. "I can think of a few things."

Trailing a thick finger over the strap of my red, halter-neck bikini, he ever so softly pushes it off my shoulder. It took me almost a month to work up the courage to wear my scarred skin so freely.

"Whoops." Enzo's smile darkens. "My bad."

"This is my favourite bikini," I protest. "Please don't wreck it like you did the last one."

"You wrecked her bikini?" Leighton repeats, sounding almost jealous. "That's it. Hand her back, you fucking caveman."

"Why don't you come and get her?" Enzo challenges. "Spoiler alert, you'll lose. Again."

"I let you win!"

"Bullshit. I declare a rematch."

"Winner gets to sleep in Harlow's bed tonight?" Leighton suggests. "Alone this time. I'm sick of you hogging the whole mattress."

"Hey! Don't I get a say in this? It's my bed."

But neither of them answers me, too busy shaking hands over my head. The idiots abandon me to resume their game, now kicking the football even more violently than before.

Left alone with my laptop, notebook and a dog-eared textbook that barely survived the international postage from England, I give up the pretence of studying. It's almost lunchtime anyway.

Thanks to Theo's daily tutoring, I was able to begin my deferred classes online and settle in with relative ease. Lounging in the sunshine quickly grew boring after the first couple of weeks.

Once I healed up and my technicoloured face was fit for live videos two hours a day, I decided to take a leap of faith. Turns out, it was the best decision I could've made.

It wasn't even that hard to catch up. After the first few classes, I surprised myself with how much knowledge I've retained, despite the almost fourteen years since I last attended a school class.

"You are such a fucking dick!" Leighton shouts as he chases after the football, now floating out to sea.

Enzo folds his arms, smirking to himself. "I'm calling it. You lost, Leigh. Loser has to go fetch the ball."

Still cursing, Leighton throws himself into the crystal-clear water lapping at the edges of our private, white-sand beach. His head disappears beneath the waves, chasing after the ball.

"That should keep him occupied." Enzo lopes towards me, full of swagger. "Finished for the morning?"

"I'm all done. Just have a pop quiz to prep for tomorrow."

"Fuck that," he declares. "Let's go out. Theo's gonna be stuck in his briefing with the intelligence department for hours yet."

Stretching, I crack my stiff neck. "He really can't bear to take a single day off, can he?"

"He lasted about a week longer than I expected without opening his laptop." He offers me a hand up. "Hunter and I placed bets."

Enzo tugs me to my bare feet. With July merging into early August, it's a pleasantly hot day on the shoreline. After never once leaving England, adjusting to this climate took some time.

"Is Hunter asleep?"

"Knocked out cold," he confirms. "Another migraine. Leighton convinced him to take one of those pills the specialist prescribed."

"Shit. It must be a bad one for him to cave."

"Not quite as bad as last week, I don't think. Hard to tell. You know how weird he is about admitting when he's in pain."

Rolling up my beach towel, I protest when Enzo steals it from me, along with my belongings, insisting on carrying them himself. His spare arm circles my shoulders to pin me against his side.

Our private villa stretches out behind the beach that we get all to ourselves. The nearest town, Quepos, is a twenty-minute drive through luscious rainforest and winding, dusty roads.

The villa is carved from glowing, stained beams of wood with thick floorboards and floor-to-ceiling windows covered in flowing, white curtains. It was an excellent call on Leighton's part.

With five individual bedrooms, a sprawling open-plan kitchen and complete isolation from other human beings, we've lived out the last couple of months in blissful peace and quiet.

"What do you want to do?" Enzo asks, holding open the billowing curtain for me.

I step inside the coolness of the villa. "How about another dirt bike lesson?"

"Keep it up and you won't be needing many more lessons from me. We'll have to get you a bike of your own at home."

The first day Enzo unveiled the slightly rusted, off-road bike he rented from a local, I was too terrified to even lay a finger on it. That soon changed after I had my first few lessons, though.

There's no feeling quite like racing along the winding, helter-skelter roads of rural Costa Rica with the warm wind in my hair and Enzo's strong arms strangling my waist as he hoots in approval.

"Go put some clothes on," he orders. "We can grab a drink in town after. I need to check the post office for a package anyway."

"Anything important?"

"Just some paperwork that Kade needs us to sign for the company. Nothing crazy important."

I circle my fingertips over my exposed sternum. The mention of home causes my heart to ache. As much as I've loved our time here, this isn't where we belong. We can't hide forever.

After snagging a pale-yellow sundress and pair of Chucks from my bedroom, I make a beeline for the small office at the back of the villa. The chatter of voices emanates through the ajar door.

I can see Theo rubbing his temples while glowering at his laptop. The black frames of his glasses are pushed up to hold his white-blonde ringlets out of his face. On the screen, his team is bickering amongst themselves.

"We've run our facial recognition software on every camera in the fucking country," Fox argues defensively. "It didn't work."

"We're doing the best we can to find him," Rayna adds.

"I don't give a fuck about what you think you're doing." Theo puts his glasses back on. "Nobody disappears off the face of the planet. Run the damn software again."

"But—"

"That wasn't a request. Call me when it's done."

Slamming his laptop shut, Theo lets loose a groan as his forehead collides with the desk. I sneak into the room on silent feet then bury my face in his head full of curls.

"I had no idea that you were so bossy," I breathe into his hair. "Poor Rayna and Fox."

His head doesn't lift. "I designed that software myself. Nothing gets around it. I'll break every last security law in the country if that's what it takes to get a lead."

Winding my arms around his neck, I pull him back against my chest and snuggle him tight. Theo relaxes into me, taking a calming breath to settle his impatience.

"He's been silent for two months," I point out. "No more victims, no messages. Not even a sighting. You're being too hard on yourself for coming up empty-handed."

"Don't mistake his silence for defeat, beautiful. This isn't over. Not by a long shot."

Savouring his scent, a tantalising blend of fresh mint and the pages of the books we both hold so dear, I ponder his words. He's right. Silence doesn't equal defeat.

We all know that Pastor Michaels—or Michael Abaddon as we

now know him—is still out there, lurking in the shadows and biding his time. He's evaded capture for far longer than any of us anticipated.

Hudson and Kade have continued the manhunt in our absence, providing us with regular updates. We've theorised that my monster has found himself allies. I think it's the only reason he hasn't been caught.

"Got any homework you need help with?"

I release Theo with a sigh. "Nope. Enzo's taking me out on the dirt bike. We're gonna go pick something up then get a drink."

"Sounds good. I've got some more work to finish up here. Will you two be okay?"

"Yes, Theodore." I plant a kiss on his cheek. "Don't worry so much. This is supposed to be a holiday, you know."

Grabbing my wrist before I can leave, Theo tugs me backwards. I topple onto his lap, almost falling over before his slim arms catch me and two pale-blue eyes stare down at my face.

The hesitant kisses he once offered have long since dissolved into hungry, bruising collisions. He's no longer afraid of breaking me, and I love it.

We've fooled around a few times but have never taken that final step. Each time, we inch a little closer to the end goal, and I'm desperate for that day to come.

My lips automatically part, allowing his tongue to slide into my mouth and tangle with mine. He tastes like the half-finished cup of coffee on the desk, mingled with something entirely Theodore.

When we break apart at the sound of Enzo shouting my name, his nose nudges mine. My legs are trembling as warmth begins to pool in my lower belly, demanding more of his attention.

"Be careful," he whispers throatily.

"Always am."

"Doesn't stop me from worrying about you. All it takes is one mistake."

"Hey." I grip his chin so our eyes meet. "Stop waiting for this to be taken away from you, because it isn't going to happen. I'm staying right here, where I belong."

The thin slice of darker blue, almost black around his irises, expands, leaking fear and apprehension. I can read him like a book after all the time we've spent together.

"I can't help it. Everyone I've ever loved has left me, and I can't lose you too, Harlow. I won't."

I press our foreheads together. "You never have to."

"Promise?"

"I fucking promise."

He smirks. "Potty mouth."

"You love it."

Slanting my mouth against his again, I brush a stray ringlet from his face before getting up from his lap and grabbing my Chucks. As I retreat from the room, his mobile phone is already ringing again.

With a final blown kiss, I head for the third bedroom down the bamboo-lined corridor. Inside, the curtains are drawn tightly shut, plunging the king-sized bed into complete darkness. There's a lump under the duvet.

I watch for the rise and fall of Hunter's sleeping form. Where his long, chestnut waves would've once spilled over the pillows, his hair is kept very short now, neatly shaved to show the grisly scar from his surgery.

It's been a trying couple of months for Hunter. Well, for the whole family. We've all been learning British Sign Language to help with communication, but it's an imperfect process, and everyone's patience has been tested.

There are some days when he doesn't leave his room or utter a single word—signed or spoken. Others, there's a glimmer of the person he used to be before the world broke him. There's no predicting which mood he will wake up in.

My fingers itch with the urge to approach him and curl up in the warm shell of his body. I want to keep Hunter safe, like he's done for me since the moment we met.

But I can't protect him from this.

Nobody can.

"Harlow! You coming?"

Closing the door, I follow the sound of Enzo's voice. He cocks an eyebrow as I slip the sundress over my bikini while walking. He's ready to go with two helmets and a shirt thrown on to cover his broad chest.

"He's still asleep." I slip on my shoes. "Maybe we should call his doctor. These headaches are so debilitating for him."

"The specialist said they're to be expected."

Enzo lifts my long hair then begins to twist it into a braid. His fingers deftly weave through the strands, lacing them together into a tight plait.

Every time he strokes the sensitive slopes of my scalp, I have to bite back a sigh of pleasure. My hair is still a no-go for almost everyone, apart from the guys and their reverent touches.

"He can't live like this forever."

"And we can't fix everything for him," he says curtly. "Hunter has to figure out some things for himself, including how to live with his injuries."

Removing the ever-present elastic from his wrist when the braid is complete, Enzo ties it off and nods to himself. Leighton has trained them all to carry elastics around when I need an intervention to stop from pulling my hair again.

Enzo positions the helmet to cover my head. I pout at him as he fastens the strap tight under my chin and declares the job done.

"He's in pain, Enz."

"I know, angel. Trust me, if I could take his pain away and have it myself, I'd do it in a heartbeat. But I can't do that."

Holding my breath to stop the frustrated tears from rising against my will, I make myself nod instead. Enzo drops a kiss on the tip of my nose and tangles our fingers together.

"Come on, let's go. Drive all the way into town without stalling the bike, and I'll throw dinner on top of those drinks."

I squeeze his calloused hand.

"You've got yourself a deal."

SCENE DU CRIME

CHAPTER 2

Leighton

Strangers – Bring Me The Horizon

Poking the strips of sizzling chicken in the pan, I slide the chopping board and knife over to Hunter. His eyes connect with mine before he tackles the pile of fresh veggies and begins to neatly slice them.

Spread out across the three-foot dining table that dominates the open-plan kitchen, Harlow is frowning down at her notebook as she works through some complicated maths problem with Theo's help.

Sliding my phone from my pocket, I shoot her a message and watch as she picks her phone up to read it with a tiny grin.

Leighton: Aren't you bored?

Harlow: To death.

I smother a laugh. Knew it. Theo's tutoring is exhausting to watch, let alone participate in.

Leighton: How haven't you murdered him yet?

Harlow: I finished my period yesterday. Feeling less stabby.

Leighton: Damn. I was hoping for more period sex.

Harlow: I can still do the latter ;)

Leighton: It's a date, princess.

"You need to carry the three over," he instructs from behind his laptop. "Like this. Then you can circle back and divide the sum by four to find the overall fraction."

The palm of her hand crashes against her forehead. "When on earth am I ever going to need to use fractions? I thought these skills were meant to be important."

"You'll never need to use fractions," I chime in. "They're just one of the many bullshit hoops the education system makes you jump through. Complete waste of time."

"That isn't true." Theo casts me a glare. "Fractions are helpful."

I point towards him with a spatula. "Name one example."

"You walk in with three pizzas, and there are five of us waiting to eat. How do we divide them up?"

"We don't, obviously. I eat all three. Fuck the lot of you. Get your own damn pizza, or starve to death. It's not my problem."

Laughing to herself, Harlow smothers her grin. "Charming."

Glowering at me, Theo's eyes narrow in annoyance. This is precisely why he's her tutor for this pointless schooling mission she's on and not me.

I did offer, though.

She laughed in my face.

"Food ready yet?" Enzo emerges from his bedroom, his black hair wet from the shower. "I'm fucking starving after that run."

He has taken to signing his words as he speaks to help Hunter's comprehension. We're trying our best to be thoughtful and inclusive, but my shit-for-brains attention span is making learning a new bloody language difficult.

"Ten minutes," Hunter mutters.

Glancing over at him, I notice he's slicing the veggies wrong. I tap his shoulder to gain his attention then freeze up, uncertain of what to say next.

"Uh, what's the sign for *dicing*? Anyone?"

"There isn't a sign for it," Theo responds like it's obvious. "You'll have to fingerspell. There aren't words in BSL for everything. The same as there aren't full sentences, just words."

"How the hell do I fingerspell?" I growl out. "And what's the point of inventing a language if you don't have all the words?"

"I didn't invent it, Leigh. Take it up with someone else."

"I intend to."

"You need to use a combination of sign language, fingerspelling, lip-reading and body language."

"All four fucking things?" I snarl in frustration.

"Yes!"

Hunter takes a swig from his beer, watching me with a grin tugging at his lips. I'm glad he's finding this situation funny. In his position, I don't know that I'd find our inability to communicate properly so amusing.

"You need to start studying more." Enzo tosses me an unimpressed look. "His hearing isn't coming back. You can't write text messages to him instead of speaking forever."

"Thanks, idiot. Like I didn't know that."

"You're the one being an idiot, Leigh. We're all making an effort to learn a new way to communicate, except for you."

"It's hard, alright?"

"Harder than what he's going through right now?"

"Guys." Harlow snaps her notebook shut to cut us off. "You're both acting like assholes, and it ends now. We're in this together."

"But, Harlow—"

"Enough, Enz. Leighton is trying his best. Back off."

Enzo mutters an apology under his breath then drops it. I cast Harlow a grateful look. She winks back at me, tidying up her school stuff before clearing the table for dinner.

Sliding behind the floating kitchen island, she cuddles up to Hunter's back. With her arms around his waist, Harlow takes hold of the knife and demonstrates dicing the veggies instead.

"All he had to do was tell me if he wanted them diced," Hunter complains, retaking the knife. "I'm not a mind reader."

Feeling like a total dickhead, I glare at the chicken while pushing it around the frying pan. It's not my fault they've all picked up sign language like it's easy. I'm trying my best here.

We're all struggling in our own ways. This whole situation is challenging, but we're doing our best to muddle through and help Hunter get back on his feet, one day at a time.

With all the food ready, we kick Theo's work-from-home setup off the dinner table then spread out everything we've made. Enzo locates a pack of cold beers from the fridge and doles out the brown-coloured bottles.

He attacks the food first, piling his plate high with chicken, salad, veggies and fresh bread from the local bakery. Hunter sticks to his second beer, gingerly poking some lettuce around his plate.

"I was thinking about taking a hike tomorrow," I announce, breaking the tense silence. "We haven't been to the national park since our first week here."

Enzo nods, chewing his mouthful. "I wouldn't mind doing some sightseeing. Why don't we all go? Together?"

Everyone's eyes automatically slide over to Hunter's slumped shoulders. I know he despises the fact that our day-to-day schedule depends on his health now.

His severe migraines and occasional dizzy spells are aftereffects of his head injury. Even months later, it's still healing, and he requires regular check-ups with his consultant to monitor his progress.

"*Hiking? Tomorrow?*" Enzo signs.

Hunter shrugs. "You guys can go."

Wiggling her fingers to gain his attention, Harlow's brows arch as she replies, "*Come.*"

My brother's chocolate-brown eyes slide back down to his plate. The scar that slashes through his eyebrow is joined by several new patches of tight, pink skin that span from his reconstructed ear.

"You don't have to include me." Hunter takes another swig from his beer. "I'm fine alone here. It doesn't matter."

"We don't have to exclude you either," I snap back, even if he can't hear me. "Someone tell him what I'm saying. This is ridiculous."

"Leigh," Harlow warns.

"He's the one pushing us away!"

"And it's your job not to let him," she argues, reaching out to touch Hunter's tattooed arm. "*Come.*"

Shrugging once more, he pushes her hand aside. His chair loudly scrapes backwards. He takes his beer to his bedroom without a word. The sound of the door slamming shut reverberates around us.

I wish I could say this was a one-off, but his intense mood swings have become normal. My brother has always been a grumpy bastard, and now he has a legitimate reason to lose his shit.

Theo spears a slice of cucumber. "That went well."

I slam my fork down. "Look, I'm trying my best here. He's not exactly making it easy to help him. That wasn't all my fault."

"It's no one's fault," Harlow corrects. "Just give him some space. He made it out of bed today, so that's an improvement."

We lapse back into tense silence until Enzo breaks it.

"He needs to go home. All this moping around isn't good for him. We should get him back to work. He needs to feel like himself again."

"How do you know what he needs?" I accuse.

"I'm trying a lot harder than you are to help him. You did what, one sign language class? Months ago?"

"Not this again." Harlow shakes her head in despair. "The pair of you need to grow up, and fast. We don't have time for this."

Pushing her plate aside, she stands then disappears through the floating curtains that lead to the back porch overlooking the shoreline.

The sun slants through the translucent material, lighting the beach beyond. My stomach twists with shame. None of us are handling this situation well, apart from Harlow.

Her patience is seemingly unlimited. I wish she could lend some of it to the rest of us. It feels like we're careening towards a cliff's edge right now, and I don't know how to stop it.

"She's right," Theo concurs. "We're supposed to be supporting each other, not bickering. Hunter doesn't need that."

Taking a deep inhale, I meet Enzo's eyes. "Look, I'm sorry. I know you're only trying to do what's best for Hunter."

"I'm sorry too," he offers. "There are no rules on how this works. We're just figuring it out. I know you're doing your best to learn."

"I should go check on her."

Enzo rises, his food abandoned. "I've got Hunter."

We both leave Theo sitting at the table alone, his gaze bouncing between us. "I'll just eat all the food, then."

As my feet sink into the cool sand, the warmth of the fading sunbathes me in burnt-orange hues. It's a beautiful evening, perfectly still and hot, the faint chirping of birds echoing with the waves.

At the edge of the ocean, Harlow stands immersed in water, her gaze fixed on the fiery ball of light sinking below the horizon. I stop beside her, letting the bathtub-like water lap at my toes.

"I'm sorry, Goldilocks."

She doesn't respond, her luminous, blue orbs locked on that sunset. I can almost see the golden flames reflected in her eyes. The light sparkles off her skin, gleaming with a healthy glow.

This trip has done her so much good. She's put on at least half a stone of weight, filling out her body with gorgeous, inviting curves that keep me up at night. Her butt and breasts have grown to healthy proportions too.

The biggest change is the thick tufts of shiny brown hair slowly reducing the bald patches that once marred her scalp. It'll take time for the hair to grow back fully, but the damage has stopped spreading now that her relapses are few and far between.

She's healing.

Growing.

Emerging from her chrysalis.

I won't lie. It was the single most harrowing moment of my life when we got the call that she'd disappeared from HQ, taking our broken hearts with her. My entire world ceased to turn.

But the longer we spend here in our private bubble, hidden from the relentless cruelty of the world, I can see that it was necessary. That baptism of fire allowed her to rise again, beaten but unbroken.

"Can you believe this is the same sun we see rise and fall in England?" Harlow murmurs. "It looks different out here."

"Maybe you're different here, not the sun."

"Maybe, but I think I like who I am here."

Tentatively, I steal her hand. "I like who you are here too. But for the record, I love every goddamn version of you."

Her head falls to rest on my shoulder. "If we can't make our relationship work here without fighting, how on earth do we do it back home?"

"We'll do it together, princess. Like we always have."

Extricating herself from my arms, Harlow steps farther into the ocean. She's wearing one of her light linen dresses, but it's quickly pulled off her body and discarded in the water.

"Uh, Goldilocks?"

"I want to swim," she calls back while wading deeper into the water in her underwear. "It's still warm."

Tearing my t-shirt over my head, I toss it back onto the beach then follow her into the waves. It feels like the world's largest bathtub, glinting with the final rays of sunshine.

Above us, the pearlescent half-circle of the moon is visible, peppered with stars growing brighter as darkness falls. Soon, we'll be under nothing but moonlight and God's all-seeing eyes.

When a soaking-wet, cotton bra floats past me, I realise that Harlow is stripping naked. Her panties bob on the surface of the water next. Fuck me. All I can see are her creamy skin and wet hair sinking into the water.

Dumping her wet clothes on the sand along with my boxer shorts, I dive beneath the water then swim fast to catch up. The sea is shallow enough for us to stand, despite being far from the shore.

Water laps at Harlow's clavicles, almost covering her shoulders. When she swims closer to me, her short legs find my waist and wrap around it to bring us flush against each other.

"If we drown out here, Enzo will kill us both."

"I don't care." She clings to me, bringing her rounded, glistening breasts to my chest. "Forget everyone else for a second."

I hold her against me, letting her feel the brush of my hardening cock pushing into her belly. "Happy to."

Her mouth clashes with mine, magnetised together beneath the enigmatic pull of the moon controlling the tide. We're equally as powerless, caught by an invisible force that ties us together.

With her lips caressing mine in languorous strokes, Harlow tastes so sweet. I can't get enough. I want more. Need more. Her touch keeps me alive amongst the chaos.

Our teeth clash as our kiss deepens, each vying for control of the other. I hold her upright in the water. We're alone with nothing but waves and silence intensifying the moment.

Even out here, at the mercy of Mother Nature, Harlow still belongs to me. Mind, body and soul. I'd take her beneath the water and drown us both before letting anyone ever take her away from me again.

When her hand disappears and slender fingers wrap around the steel of my cock, I groan into her lips. We're both completely bare and covered by nothing but the ocean surrounding us.

I grab a handful of her breast, palming the now generous swell. Her nipples are stiffened into peaks beneath the water, begging to be tasted. I break the kiss to suck one into my mouth before biting down.

"Leigh," she whimpers.

Her body is writhing against mine, undulating with each calm wave washing over us. I grasp her hips, controlling her movements to find the exact spot I want to be buried in.

"I'm so fucking glad you went on birth control," I moan into her lips. "Now there's nothing stopping me from doing this."

Harlow cries out as my cock surges inside of her at the perfect angle. Her pussy clenches around me, so damn tight it's almost painful. We fit together like lock and key.

She wasn't expecting that so soon, but I couldn't wait a second longer. Around her, my control is non-existent. She drives me wild without having to utter a single word.

"What if … someone sees?" Harlow gasps.

"Look around." I bite down on her plump bottom lip. "There isn't a soul in sight. I can fuck you wherever I want, baby. Remember that."

She slips her arms around my neck to hold on tight as I thrust into her slit, pushing my hips upwards. Water sloshes around us with each pump, easing the glide of my dick slamming into her.

Her tits are shoved in my face, and water clings to the buds of her hardened nipples. It should be illegal to look this gorgeous. How can I be expected to control myself?

"Do you like it when my cock stretches your sweet little cunt, princess?" I goad her.

"Oh God, Leigh. Yes."

The last sparks of sunlight vanish, bathing us in evening shadows. Darkness encroaches across the water, turning vivid aqua into dark and deadly blackness, broken by the moon's strobe lights.

Out here, it's hard to believe that the rest of the world still exists. This paradise feels like a self-contained universe all on its own. I'd hand my soul to the devil if it meant we could stay here forever.

Legs cinching my waist, Harlow uses momentum to draw her hips upwards and push down on me just as I thrust up into her. We meet in the middle, stroke for stroke, both gasping for air.

"That's it, princess." I palm her ass cheeks. "I wanna see you come for me in the ocean. Now there's a story."

Her breaths escape in adorable little mewls, and her voice is saturated with pleasure. Each time she bounces on my pierced cock, I feel my balls tighten, begging to spill deep inside her cunt.

I love that I can fill her up now. That little white pill she takes each morning is my new best friend. The sight of my come running down her thighs on my birthday two weeks ago was the best present ever.

"I'm gonna come inside you," I say gruffly. "Then I'll take you back inside and fuck you again, bent over the kitchen table."

"You can't do that," she squeals. "Not in front of the others."

"Can't? You really want to use that word?"

Cut off mid-moan, she yelps in surprise when I pull myself out of her. Before she can yell at me for snatching her orgasm away, I lift her from the water and throw her over my shoulder in a fireman's carry.

"Clearly, I need to prove a point." I swat my hand against her dripping ass cheek. "You should never doubt me."

"Leigh! Wait!"

"Shut it, gorgeous."

Walking straight past our sopping wet clothes, I emerge from the sea then heft her higher on my shoulder. Harlow protests the whole way up the beach until we step back inside the villa, then she stops.

Theo is still sitting at the table, his laptop now relocated in front of him as he nurses a second beer. The moment we step inside, he nearly drops the damn thing. His eyebrows shoot upwards.

We're both completely naked and leaving a trail of saltwater across the flooring. Poor Theo has no idea what's coming if this stuns him to silence.

"Leighton," Harlow scolds again. "Put me down this instant."

"Oh, I'll put you down."

Pulling her back over my shoulder, I shove discarded plates and cutlery aside, clearing a spot on the table right next to where Theo is sitting in a state of disbelief.

Harlow squeals as she lands on top of the table, her spine pressed against the wood. Grabbing her wrists, I pin them down, ensuring she can't attempt to escape the situation.

Her eyes are locked on Theo. He hasn't moved away from her sprawled out body, every naked inch glistening with drips of seawater and enticing him in.

"I'm proving a point." I yank her body closer to me. "This is what you're missing out on, Theodore."

Harlow's eyes don't tear from his as I settle back between her thighs, now at the perfect height. She's entirely at my mercy. Theo sits frozen, but he can't seem to find the willpower to leave.

I know they haven't slept together yet. He's taken months to even get this far, but their relationship is progressing, however slowly. He just needs some encouragement to take that leap.

"Looks like we have a witness to me proving my point," I tease. "You gonna show him how good my name sounds on your tongue, Goldilocks?"

Harlow swallows her complaints as I dip a hand between her legs, finding the molten heat at her core. My finger pushes inside her entrance, swirling moisture up to her swollen clit.

Strumming her bundle of nerves, I savour the high-pitched gasp that tears free from her throat. She's desperately trying to hold it in to save embarrassing Theo, but I know exactly how to please my girl.

Pushing a finger back inside her, I pump it in and out, adding a second digit to stretch her wider. She writhes on the table, her hips rising to grind against the heel of my palm.

"So wet, baby. Does Theo watching turn you on?"

"Screw you, Leigh," she groans.

"Soon, princess."

Pinching her bundle of nerves again, I remove my fingers from her pussy. She flames bright-red when I offer the glistening digits to Theo with a confident smirk.

"Want a taste?" I lift an eyebrow. "She's fucking soaked just knowing that you're sitting there, unable to move a muscle."

His lips are pursed, but the bob of his Adam's apple working overtime answers my question. If he wanted to leave, he would. Instead, he's fascinated by the sight of me finger-fucking Harlow.

"Let's give him a real show, shall we, Goldilocks?"

Grasping her narrow hips, I line myself up with her entrance then push back inside her. Harlow grips the edges of the table, crying out so loud, I wonder if we'll have even more company soon.

She still feels heavenly around me. All I can see is her luscious brown hair, spilled out around her head in a halo that complements her blue eyes.

My gorgeous girl.

All. Fucking. Mine.

Holding her hips in a bruising grip, I thrust into her with insatiable hunger. I'll tease the submission free from her throat until it spills out in a scream of pleasure just for Theo's benefit.

The table shakes with our movements, rattling plates and cutlery, all while Theo is held prisoner by his own curiosity. If this doesn't cause his resolve to break, nothing will.

"How incredible does she look right now?" I goad him between thrusts. "Sure you don't want a taste, Theodore?"

His mouth opens and shuts. "Uh."

"Leigh," Harlow mewls. "Stop it."

"Not a chance." I pump into her pussy, loving the way her walls clench tightly. "I wanna see my baby fall apart first."

Her hand slaps across her mouth, holding back a loud moan that would undoubtedly draw Enzo back out here. With a snarl, I recapture her wrist then pin it down to the table.

Her gasps break free in a whispered torment, high-pitched and so fucking adorable, it pains me. The innocent, blue-eyed slip of a girl I first met has blossomed into an incredible woman.

But deep down, past all the layers that she plasters on to fit into the world around her, Harlow's still just a lost soul looking for her home. Like us all. That's why we work… Together or not at all.

As her slick cunt tightens around me, our bodies smashing together in a frenzy of need, I feel my own release approaching. I never thought I'd have Theo as a captive audience, but a sick part of me loves it.

He's allowed to watch her juices spill over my cock, but I'm the one buried deep inside of her right now. She belongs to me and me alone for these brief, blissful moments.

When we're done, I'll surrender the rest of her heart again, but not a second sooner. When I'm fucking Harlow into a boneless puddle, she belongs to only me.

"I'm so close," Harlow whines.

"Come for me, princess. Show Theo what he's missing."

With a roar, I pound into her for a final time and feel myself explode. Harlow's clenched tight around me, and the drawn-out cry that bursts free from her mouth is music to my ears.

Watching her come will never lose its novelty. I never understood the fascination people have for admiring stupid shit like expensive artwork or a rare bottle of wine.

I get it now… the obsession.

She's mine.

I'd kneel at her feet and watch the rise and fall of her chest all day long without stopping for air. She's my addiction… my hedonistic, unjustifiably indulgent expense.

I am endlessly fascinated by this woman and everything about her. The last twenty-five years of my life cease to exist now that I know what life looks like with Harlow in it. I wasn't alive until I met her.

"That's it, baby. Louder."

"Fuck, Leigh!" she screams.

Spilling into her, I love the way her legs tighten around my waist, ensuring I fill every inch of her pussy with my seed. There's nothing like the feeling of complete and utter surrender.

Slumping between her legs, I bury my face in her neck, gasping for air. Harlow barely lets me catch a breath before she tugs my hair and guides her lips to mine.

"I can't believe you just did that," she murmurs.

"I'm not gonna apologise for taking what's mine."

"Did you have to do it in front of him?"

I hesitate for a second. "Yeah. I did."

Groaning under her breath, Harlow hides her face in my chest. She's still painfully shy at times, even when her bodily instincts take over and demand to be satisfied.

I doubt many people would ever bring themselves to even consider the possibility of vulnerability after enduring what she has. This beautiful creature is the one percent.

The survivor.

Our blessing in disguise.

Once I've caught my breath, I look back over to the silent, stammering man caught amongst our chaos. Theo's cheeks are flushed the most violent shade of red, even if his fascination is clear to see.

"I should ... g-go," he stutters.

With a nod, he abruptly stands. The bulge tenting his usual faded blue jeans is painfully obvious. I bite back a remark that would only make him blush harder. Harlow might actually kill me in that case.

He disappears into his bedroom so fast, I'm surprised he doesn't leave a trail of smoke behind him. The moment he's vanished from sight, Harlow smacks my chest, blushing beetroot-red herself.

"You two really belong together." I trail a finger over her flaming-hot cheek. "Can't even have a bit of harmless voyeurism without turning into a tomato."

"I am not a tomato."

"You should look in the mirror."

"Well, it's your fault," she complains. "You jumped on me like some kind of wild animal."

"Well, I didn't see you complaining." I push sticky hair from her forehead. "Especially not at the end there."

Before she can shove me off, the door to Hunter's bedroom slams shut, and a looming shadow emerges. Enzo takes one look around the room—plates dislodged, Harlow's bare tits, my ass on display—before halting.

"What the fuck did I miss?"

SCENE OUT
LOOSE
NOT

CHAPTER 3

Harlow

Let The Right One In – Boston Manor

"I'm in my cage, listening to the falling rain. If I concentrate hard enough, it covers the sound of her dying whimpers. I've always loved water and the cleansing power it holds. Even over death."

On the laptop screen, Doctor Richards listens to me, tapping a fountain pen against his closed lips. I set the journal down and breathe through the revulsion reading my own memories brings.

"Which victim was this referring to?" he questions.

"It was Tia. There was a rainstorm the night she died."

Jotting something down, he looks thoughtful. "You don't speak about her a lot. Why was this memory significant to write about?"

"We were close. It's still hard to think about her." I glance at the open door where sea air is leaking inside. "She loved the beach. I've thought about her a lot more since we got here."

"It's important not to erase her existence from your mind simply because it's painful," Richards advises. "You're doing well to write about her in a safe, controlled way."

"Thank you."

I still feel weird being complimented by Richards, especially after what I did to him. I never wanted to hurt him, not even when he threatened me with detainment in a mental health ward.

But after an awkward apology, we fell back into our regular weekly schedule, holding sessions over video call instead. For the first time since starting therapy, I feel like it's helping me.

"How many journals have you filled now?" Richards asks.

"This is my third. Jude supplies me with new ones." I laugh to myself. "He's particular about his stationary, and it's rubbed off on me. I can't write in anything else."

Richards shakes his head. "I have never met anyone more particular than Jude. I'm glad the writing is working out. You've come a long way in the past few weeks."

"I guess."

"You have. It's a great achievement."

Looking back down at the journal that I've spent countless hours spilling my darkest, innermost thoughts into, I allow myself a sliver of satisfaction. Just a tiny bit.

I'm working hard on myself right now, and it's paying off. I still struggle with the compulsion to pull when things get overwhelming—you can't break a deeply ingrained habit in a couple of months.

But I've now trained myself to stop, breathe and find a pen instead of falling into the familiar comfort of hurting myself. Instead, I batter the pages with ink and determination to get the pain out.

My writing isn't always chronological, nor is it exclusively memories I've pieced back together. These pages are my life. Messy, imperfect, chaotic life in all its varying extremes of good and bad.

"I had an idea I wanted to discuss with you."

His words startle me back to the video call.

"Oh?"

"You've overcome so many obstacles." Richards rests his chin on his laced fingers. "There are a lot of people out there who would benefit from hearing your story. You could do so much good with it."

"I don't understand. My story?"

"Have you considered turning these journals into something more? Perhaps a memoir?"

I frown at the screen. "You think I should write a book?"

"Something to think about," he suggests. "Words are our last unlimited resource. If nothing else, humans will always hold the ability to inspire hope with them."

Clutching the journal a little tighter, I battle a wave of anxiety. It's been the biggest challenge of my life to relive the contents of these pages, word by word, to reconstruct my past.

I don't want someone picking apart my story and writing a callous hit piece for the local newspaper to earn some measly commission. My heart couldn't take that level of rejection, even from a stranger.

"What are you thinking?" he prompts.

"It's just … being vulnerable." I gulp down the lump in my throat. "It's hard for me. This would be putting my entire life out there for the world to read and judge."

"I appreciate that it's a big step. You don't have to do it if you're not comfortable. You've been through so much. Helping others can be its own form of healing, though."

Amidst the panic, a glimmer of something lights my chest. I don't know what this feeling is, but my fingers are twitching with the urge to put pen to paper again. He's lit a tiny spark deep within me.

"That's the end of our session. Same time next week?"

"Sure. Thank you for listening," I offer sincerely. "I appreciate all the help you've given me."

His smile pulls taut the wrinkle lines beneath his spectacles. "I am so incredibly proud of how far you've come since we first met, Harlow. You should be proud too."

Throat tightening, I offer a quick wave then leave the call before I burst into tears. Richards's pride isn't something I thought I needed, but fuck if it doesn't feel good.

Stretching my arms above my head, I quickly return the journal and laptop to my bedroom. The guys are all outside, giving me some privacy. We're due to head into town for some groceries this afternoon.

Sticking my head out through the curtains, I spot them on the back veranda, sprawled out across several sun loungers. Theo's nose is buried in a well-loved copy of *Animal Farm*, lost in its crinkled pages.

On the lounger next to him, Hunter is stretched out, a pair of aviators resting on the tip of his nose as he lightly snores. He doesn't stir when Leighton squirts sun cream on his chest and begins drawing with his finger.

"Hey!" I shout.

His head snaps upwards. "What's up?"

"Stop drawing a dick on your brother. You know that'll burn onto him in this heat."

"Well, duh. That was the plan, Goldilocks."

Heading outside, I nudge Hunter's leg to startle him awake. He catches Leighton red-handed and looks down at the crooked drawing of a lopsided cock on his chest in layers of sun cream.

"Sometimes, I wish I'd been an only child," he says, wiping it away. "Try it again and you won't have a finger to draw with."

Leighton pouts at him. "Spoilsport."

"You did what?" he repeats, confused.

"Fuck, I don't know the sign for that."

"Spell it out," Theo advises. "Like I showed you yesterday."

Brows furrowed, Leighton stares down at his fingers then begins to clumsily spell out the word. It only takes a second for Hunter to catch on. He flips him the bird before stretching his limbs, now wide awake.

"Hey, Theo." Leighton holds his fingers ready to sign. "You're a *N E R D*. You know what that spells?"

"It spells *you're an awesome friend and a brilliant teacher*," he quips back. "Aw, thanks, Leigh."

"Do you just make up half the shit you're teaching us?"

"Don't like it? Find another teacher. I won't complain."

"We need groceries," I interject before they try to throttle each other. "Let's go into town."

When a massive pair of arms circle my waist to wrench me off my feet, I scream loudly. Enzo snuck up behind me," and I'm twirled in a huge circle. His breath is hot against my earlobe.

"You wanna drive, little one?"

"Not sure we can get groceries on a dirt bike," I wheeze out.

"We're going in the car. You need to start practising."

"She doesn't have her provisional licence yet." Theo sighs, folding the corner of the book page.

"Who's gonna care out here?" Enzo combats. "We're living in a damn jungle."

Theo's reply is cut off by an outstretched hand whacking him around the head. Hunter points at the folded page he just damaged to mark his place in the book.

"That is sacrilege, Theodore."

He rolls his blue eyes and signs back, *"Mine."*

"Do it again and I'll be taking that book into custody for its own protection."

Hunter wears an unexpected grin, and when he glances at me, he removes his sunglasses to wink. A miasma of butterflies explodes in my belly. I'd forgotten how much I love his smile.

Leaving Enzo to herd the troublemakers to the car, I slip inside to gather my stuff. We meet outside the villa where a dirt-streaked Jeep has been haphazardly parked in front of the palm trees.

"What kind of parking do you call that?" Enzo booms.

Leighton claps his shoulder. "You like it? I tried really hard."

"A fucking blind man could park better than that! Jesus Christ."

"You know I'm the looks and he's the brains." He jabs a finger towards Hunter. "You want better parking, get Hunter to do it."

Strolling past his brother, Hunter nabs the keys from Enzo's hands. He's behind the wheel in a heartbeat. Enzo blinks, poised to protest. I grab his hand and haul him towards the Jeep.

"If he wants to drive, let him," I encourage. "It's a miracle he's leaving his bed."

Hopping in the back seat, I scoot over Theo to slide between him and Leighton. Enzo takes the passenger seat and keeps a wary eye on his best friend, ready to intervene if needed.

Hunter peels off in a spray of gravel before we careen down the winding roads. Glossy, billowing trees, sparkling sunshine and the chirp of tropical birds accompany the music blasting from the radio.

With his sunglasses on and a tattooed arm slung outside the car, Hunter looks like his old self for the first time in weeks. That tiny smile still pulls at the corners of his mouth.

It's the best thing I've ever seen.

The old Hunter is still in there.

We return to civilisation in record time. Quepos is a bustling coastal town, humming with tourists, local business owners selling their wares and backpackers passing through.

Shopfronts are painted in vivid shades of yellow, green and red, while the nearby cruise port is filled with intimidatingly large ships docked for the day in brilliant-turquoise waters.

Arriving intact and without incident, Enzo's hunched shoulders relax as we all exit the car. While I'm relieved his overprotective attention has moved on from me, I'm not sure Hunter appreciates it.

"Let's get food," Leighton pleads, his eyes on a nearby restaurant.

"You literally ate breakfast two hours ago," Theo replies.

"Exactly. How have I not withered away already?"

"I could eat," Enzo chips in. "We can hit the market afterwards. Where's that fish place you guys tried last week?"

I point towards the boardwalk, littered with bars and cafes overhanging the pearly-white beach. "Down there."

He takes off with renewed purpose, his nose upturned like a bloodhound. I watch Leighton follow, his spirits buoyed by the prospect of food. Catching up to Hunter, I capture his hand.

"*Are you okay?*" I sign.

He nods. "Yeah."

I tap my temple and furrow my brows in question.

"No headache today," he replies. "We're good."

With a smile, I reach onto my tiptoes to press a kiss against his parted lips. His hand cups the back of my neck to trap our mouths together, dancing a symphony in front of the whole street.

"Stop worrying," he whispers. "I'm okay."

Stroking my hands over his closely cropped hair, I kiss him firmly, communicating everything I can't say. He's spent the last year worrying about me. It's my turn to look after him now.

Tucking me into his side, Hunter holds me close and leads the way into the nearby restaurant. It's busy, given the sweltering hot weather in peak tourist season.

I came here with Leighton last week when we visited the bigger, public beach for an afternoon. We're bustled over to the best table in sight, courtesy of the over-friendly waiter who recognises Leighton.

There's a perfect view of the beach, packed with sunbathers and young couples enjoying cocktails in the blazing sunshine. I love this place. It's like paradise on earth.

"I am going to order the whole menu this time," Leighton declares excitedly. "What were those weird things we ate last time, princess?"

"Mussels," I supply.

"They were so fucking good. I want a double portion."

"You can foot the bill, in that case," Enzo grumbles.

"I'll have to ask my boss for a pay raise if we stay here for much longer." Leighton sighs. "I'm all in favour of us permanently relocating. Fuck going home."

"We have to go back sometime," Theo says while studying the menu. "I'm stunned that Hudson and Kade haven't burned HQ down yet."

"Or that Brooklyn hasn't killed them." Enzo waves over the waiter. "She did not appreciate us giving them full authority in our absence."

With food and drinks ordered, we settle into a round of ice-cold beers and fresh bread dipped in oil. Hunter slings his arm over the back of my chair, lazily drawing circles against my shoulder.

In public spaces, he tends to zone out. I suppose it's his way of coping with not knowing what anyone around him is saying. He's found his own ways of dealing with the world.

After stuffing ourselves with fresh seafood and a few too many beers, Enzo disappears with Theo to visit the nearby market. I rattle off my list of requests then head for the beach with the brothers in tow.

The pearlescent grains of sand feel like velvet beneath my bare feet. Slipping and sliding over sand so white, it almost looks like snow, my toes dip into the water's edge. It's a balmy afternoon.

"Incoming!"

Leighton's yell precedes a blur of bronzed skin racing past me. He throws himself into the water headfirst, his unbuttoned blue shirt discarded. I watch him disappear beneath the water.

Stopping at my side, Hunter's eyes are fixed on the horizon. With afternoon succumbing to the tempting embrace of evening, the sun highlights his skin in rich, warm beams of light.

All I want is to curl against his chest and have one last normal conversation with no fear of upsetting him or making him feel alienated. The ability to talk and be heard is a precious commodity that we take for granted.

His arm bands around my waist, and he pulls me close for a cuddle. Even in the silence of our new reality, he still finds a way to understand the darkest, innermost corners of my psyche.

"Don't be sad," he murmurs. "Enjoy the moment."

God, how I want to.

Even as my heart shatters.

Tapping his arm, I guide his eyes down to me. One of the first signs I learned was *I love you*. His eyes crinkle with a satisfied smile as I cover my heart with both of my hands before pointing up at him.

"I love you," Hunter echoes.

"*Promise?*" I sign back.

His head dips down to secure our lips together in a soft, lingering kiss that curls my toes. "How could I not?"

Mouths locked together, the beach melts into the background. I willingly step into Hunter's lonely silence and let his darkness shroud me in shadows. We don't need anything but this moment.

His scent is different here. Gone is the spicy, peppery fragrance of designer aftershave worth more than a one-bedroom apartment.

Instead, he smells like saltwater and linen sheets.

Our lips break apart when the mumblings of discontented sunbathers shatter our peace. Leighton is still causing havoc in the water, now playing volleyball with a young kid.

But his antics haven't disrupted this oasis. It's the click of a camera lens and several hurried shouts calling for attention. Up the sandy bank, a gaggle of people are inching towards us, weighed down by gear.

A lead weight drops in my stomach. Reporters. I can spot them a mile off. Their usual casual business wear and corporate smiles have been replaced with equipment bags and sunglasses.

It's the cameras clasped in their hands that betray them, poised at the ready. I tug on Hunter's shirt sleeve and point over my shoulder. His easy smile dissolves into a horrified stare.

In two whole months of hiding out here, we haven't seen a single reporter. Our location is a very well-guarded secret. Not even Sabre's staff know where their bosses are on sabbatical.

"Maybe they're not here for us?" he guesses.

"Hunter Rodriguez! Can we get a statement?"

Fuck!

Quickly replacing his sunglasses, Hunter tightens his arm around my shoulder to hide me. I shout Leighton's name, waving like crazy to draw him out of the water. We need to haul ass right now.

"Harlow! Can you tell us what happened with Candace Bernard? Why did the killer escape? Where is he right now?"

The barrage of ridiculous questions reaches a fever pitch. All around us, interested tourists have turned their attention to us. Some are even filming on their smartphones.

"Leave us alone!" I yell at them.

"Tell us what happened." A reporter shoves a portable microphone towards me. "Why are you hiding? What about the investigation?"

"We will not be answering any questions." Hunter's grip on me reaches a bruising intensity. "Don't say a word, Harlow."

Their crazed eyes fix on him, along with the glint of recording lenses. Leighton splashes out of the sea and runs towards us as fast as he can move, but Hunter's quickly surrounded by vampires.

"Mr Rodriguez, will you apologise for allowing the suspect to escape? Is your company going to step up their search efforts for Michael Abaddon?"

The colour has drained from Hunter's face. I can feel his entire frame trembling as he holds me in a protective vice. It's all he can do to attempt to shield me and conceal his own fear.

He can't hear a word they're screaming at him right now, and it's too much. His façade is on the verge of crumbling in front of live cameras and Sabre's harshest critics.

"Get away from us," I plead, trying to drag him backwards to escape. "We won't be answering your questions."

"The public deserves to know the truth," a female reporter snarks. "You've hidden behind Sabre for almost a year now. Why won't you speak up?"

Recoiling like I've been slapped, anger spikes through me, and I snatch the camera straight from her hands. She squeals in protest as I throw it into the sea.

"I don't owe anyone an explanation," I spit in their faces. "You have no right to invade our privacy like this."

Leighton passes the bitch chasing after her expensive camera. I'm soon sandwiched between them and being hauled back up the beach, letting the cameras chase behind us.

"Where the fuck did they come from?" Leighton snarls.

"I have no idea. How did they track us down?"

"Someone must have recognised us last week and contacted the media." His voice is hard as nails. "The whole circus will be here by tomorrow."

We run towards the car, dodging more startled holidaymakers watching the fiasco with open mouths. Leighton hits speed dial then shoves me in the back to escape the onslaught of more questions.

Behind the wheel, Hunter waits impatiently, his eyes on the rearview mirror positioned on the market's swinging doors. His hands clench the steering wheel so tight, the vinyl creaks.

"We have to leave," he announces. "Tonight."

SCÈNE DU CRIME

CHAPTER 4

Enzo

The One You Loved – The Plot In You

England is fucking cold.

Even in August.

The pitiful summer temperatures don't compare to the tropical paradise we've grown accustomed to. Stepping off the private plane, cold air smacks me in the face and shouts *welcome home, idiots.*

Yeah, home.

Somewhere I would've been happy to never see again, until our secure location was leaked to the world's media. News travels fast amongst soulless newscasters and their overpaid drones.

We had half of Costa Rica's journalists and a crew of international assholes camped outside the villa within three hours. They even filmed us hurling our suitcases into the Jeep and getting the fuck out of there.

This isn't the ceremonious welcome I had anticipated upon returning home—Hudson's scowling mug smoking a cigarette while the Anaconda team guards our airstrip. Some welcoming committee.

"Enz." Hudson clasps my hand tight. "Good flight?"

"Long and uncomfortable."

"Private jet not to your liking?"

Leighton offers him a wave as he throws bags into the awaiting car. "Preferred the private beach, thanks. Where's the Mustang?"

"Phoenix spray painted the alloys bright pink." Hudson's frown is thunderous. "He's paying for it to be fixed. And I beat his ass."

"How bad was it?" I wince.

"He's fine. Got off easy, in my opinion."

Joining us on the tarmac, Theo and Harlow both offer the team tired smiles in greeting. Hudson clasps her in a quick hug before starting to load up the company SUV with our luggage.

Last to leave the aeroplane, Hunter pauses at the bottom of the metal steps. I can read the hesitation carving his features into unyielding lines from here. His shitty attempts to seem emotionless don't work on me.

He's nervous.

It's an odd sight.

Welcoming their boss with handshakes, Becket and Ethan follow the email guidance we distributed weeks ago and greet him in sign language. The narrowing of Hunter's eyes is his only response.

"All ready to go?" Hudson slams the car boot shut. "We should get moving. Got a lot to catch you up on."

Inside the blacked-out car, it's a snug fit. We follow behind Becket and his team, exiting the airport with no interference. Our passports were checked on board, courtesy of a discreet fee.

I'd rather the press doesn't know the moment we land back in the country. Clearly, two months wasn't long enough for the media feeding frenzy to move on to its next victim.

Harlow lies down across the seats, settling her head in Theo's lap. She quickly falls asleep, her arms curled inwards for protection. With her eyes shut and Hunter relegated to the back, I lower my voice.

"Any more developments?"

"We haven't had a single sighting," Hudson replies, his eyes on the road. "He's clearly gone deep undercover somewhere, aided by accomplices. We've scoured the whole country."

"Have you alerted the local parishes? I still reckon he's using their church networks to remain undercover. Those religious nutjobs think he's the goddamn saviour."

"Not everyone is a nutjob," Hudson points out.

"But you can bet your ass that the ones aiding Abaddon are."

Refocusing on the road, Hudson takes the first exit and bears down on the accelerator. We overtake the Anaconda team and tear off up the motorway, heading east.

"What about the familial connection?" I check to make sure Harlow is still asleep. "We know Abaddon is Harlow's maternal uncle. That's a direct link."

"She doesn't have any other family who could be harbouring him," Theo chimes in. "I did a thorough search in case there was a third abandoned child. Michael and Giana were the only ones."

"Speaking of, her trial has been moved up to early December," Hudson informs us. "She entered a not guilty plea at the hearing last week to charges of false imprisonment and kidnapping."

"Shit," I curse. "Harlow won't take that well."

"Yeah, Candace Bernard didn't either. She's planning to testify against Giana." Hudson gives me the side-eye. "Harlow will have to do the same."

"I want to keep her well away from that madness."

"The prosecution has to build a case against Giana," he reasons. "Establish a pattern of behaviour. Getting both Harlow and Oliver on board will ensure she rots behind bars."

"We have no choice, Enz," Theo agrees with him. "Harlow has to testify against her."

Already, a killer headache is pounding behind my eyes. We've only been back in the country for ten minutes. I was right to get us the hell out of here in the first place. Perhaps we should've stayed away.

The journey passes in tense silence until we're pulling into the familiar, quiet cul-de-sac of our new home, safely outside London's smog-covered madness.

The house is dark and draped in evening shadows. It's still weird to think of this place as home. We left before ever truly settling in. I'm not sure any of us knows what life we're returning to.

"I'll let you guys settle in and unpack." Hudson parks behind Hunter's covered convertible. "Let's debrief tomorrow. I'll bring the dog back."

"Thanks for the ride."

"Anytime. It's good to have you back."

Leaving Hunter and Leighton to unload our luggage, I pop open Theo's door. He's pinned beneath Harlow, her eyes stuck shut and lips slightly parted.

She barely stirs as I lift her from his lap and cradle her to my chest. Despite putting on some much-needed weight, she's still tiny and featherlight in my tree trunk arms.

The house is pitch-black and musty, the scent of dust thick in the air. Hunter steps inside and begins to flick on lights. It's exactly how we left it—semi-decorated, messy and impersonal.

"I'll run out for some milk," Hunter offers.

I cock my head in a silent question.

"For tea."

With that simple explanation, he snags the keys to his convertible from the dresser and vanishes back into the night. I pretend not to notice the tremble of his hands as he slams the front door shut behind him.

I'm sure that in the long run, returning to his usual routine will help to drag him out of the mental hole he's dug for himself. Before that can happen, he has to let go of the paranoia eating him up.

None of us are judging or pitying him. All we want is to help make this transition as smooth as can be. That's a little hard to do when he's constantly isolating himself and pushing us away.

"Did you instruct all the staff to learn sign language?" Leighton asks, carrying a suitcase. "The Anaconda team used it."

"It was my idea," Theo explains. "We emailed a couple of weeks ago. They've only learned the basics."

"I thought it would help ease his transition back into work."

Leighton shakes his head. "He looked pretty offended by it."

"He can be offended all he wants." I toe off my thick-soled boots. "Ignoring everyone isn't going to protect him. He needs to learn to communicate like we're all doing."

Thumping up the staircase, I leave them to continue lifting luggage inside. Harlow snuggles against me, her fingers curled in my T-shirt. Her features are slack, the grip of sleep still holding her captive.

It was a long twelve-hour flight across several time zones. We're all exhausted and jet lagged. Nudging her bedroom door open with my shoulder, I step into the welcoming darkness.

All I want right now is to collapse on her unmade double bed and hold her close for a few hours of undisturbed sleep, but the problems we left this country to avoid haven't gone away.

They just festered and grew, awaiting our return to reality. We couldn't avoid our responsibilities forever. Still, I don't regret our two-month sabbatical.

It didn't fix all the wounds this past year has inflicted. Nothing ever could. Yet I feel more confident that we can face the impending chaos now as a united front. We've rebuilt those burned bridges.

"What time is it?" Harlow mumbles sleepily.

"Almost ten o'clock at night." I ease her onto the bed, brushing hair from her face. "We're home, little one. Do you want to shower first or just get some sleep?"

"Shower. I feel so gross."

She manages to peel her lids open, revealing bloodshot eyes in the lightest shade of blue. Even half-awake and rumpled, she's still the most stunning creature I've ever seen.

I tuck tangled hair behind her ear. "Come and wash."

"Can't … move."

With an eye roll, I scoop her back up. Her face buries in the crook of my neck, lips brushing against my throat. In the darkness of the room, I can almost fool myself that we're back in our warm, cosy villa.

"Lucky?" she whispers.

"Coming home tomorrow, baby."

"I missed her."

Inside the bathroom, I place her down on the counter next to the sink basin. "I'm sure she's missed you more."

Harlow's en-suite is the nicest in the house but still a little cramped and dated. Plain cream tiles meet frosted glass, encasing the old-style, combined shower and bathtub.

The whole house needs a bit of a refresh. We bought the place practically unseen in our rush to get the hell out of London. It needs some investment and TLC to make it feel like a home.

"We seriously need to redecorate."

"It's fine, Enz."

"This place is a dump compared to home."

Harlow stretches her arms over her head. "This is home now,

remember?"

"Don't remind me."

Pressing a gentle kiss against her temple, I turn my back to heat the shower. The shuffle of Harlow pulling off wrinkled clothing causes my pulse to spike, despite being as exhausted as she is.

With steam filling the room, a flash of bare skin slips past me. Harlow's small curves and soft, sloping hips step inside the shower. Her nipples are two hard points, beckoning me in.

"You coming?" she asks over her shoulder.

"I should help the others get settled."

"They're big boys. Climb in and wash my back."

"Demanding much?" I scoff.

Her eyes burn bright with challenge. "You bet."

I fucking love it when she gets all stroppy and confident. This stronger, cheekier side of Harlow has been showing itself more often. I couldn't be prouder of her.

Stripping off my plain, black t-shirt and jeans, I flick the lock on the door then climb in behind her. It's a tight squeeze, but she shuffles farther under the spray of water so I can press up against her spine.

Arms wrapped around her waist, I plant a delicate kiss on her shoulder. The beat of hot water slips between us, melding our skin together. I love the small curves that have filled out her frame.

"Are you glad to be home?" Harlow asks.

Reaching for a bottle of shower gel, I lather the jasmine-scented liquid across my hands then begin to massage it into her skin. Her head tips back, lips parted on a sigh.

"Yes and no," I admit.

"We had to return sometime."

"I would've preferred if it was on our own terms. Now we're back on the radar, and all the bullshit will start over again."

After washing the shower gel from her skin, I take the shampoo and work it through her long, tumbling hair. Almost all the bald patches are covered in a short fuzz of hair now.

She leans back into me, her eyes semi-closed. I massage her scalp next, taking time to memorise each ridge of bone carving her skull. When her eyes reopen, she peers up at me.

"Can I run something past you?"

"Sure, angel."

"Richards had an idea," she says uncertainly. "He thinks I should write a memoir and set the story straight. I've got enough filled journals to make a whole book at this point."

Damn nosy doc.

"I don't think that's a good idea, little one."

Her face falls. "Why not?"

"We've tried to work with the media before," I try to explain. "It never goes as planned. They have their own agendas and will always find a way to fuck us over, no matter what they promise."

"This wouldn't be working with the media, though. I could publish the book with a company or even by myself. It's not like I'm giving them a direct statement or interview."

"But they'll still host round-the-clock debate sessions and analysis segments ripping apart every word you print. This book would spread like wildfire. That I can guarantee."

Washing out the bubbles from her hair, I lean over her shoulder to peck the soft slope of her throat, hoping she doesn't hate me.

I'd love nothing more than to see Harlow take control of her own life, but this would be a monumental step at a very bad time. Her story will set the world on fire and burn us all to death.

We can't track down Michael Abaddon and put an end to his reign of terror if we're too busy fighting fires on all sides to keep Harlow safe from the world's morbid curiosity.

"Maybe it was a stupid idea," she backtracks.

"No." I turn her around under the spray of water. "It's a good idea but the wrong time. We're in a sticky situation right now, and I don't want to make it worse."

Her eyes are downturned, hiding the tinge of disappointment. I slide a finger underneath her chin to raise them back up. She looks inexplicably sad. It stabs me right in my foolish fucking heart.

"Let me catch this motherfucker and break his spine first." I stare deep into her cerulean eyes. "Then you can publish whatever you want. I'll be first to cheer you on."

She summons a tiny smile. "You will?"

"Damn straight, I will."

The sharp edges of her smile slump. "But writing... Enz, it's giving me control back for the first time in my life."

"I'm not saying you have to stop writing. Write your little heart out if it helps. All I'm concerned about is keeping you safe until we can see this case through."

Nodding, Harlow stretches to kiss my lips. "I guess I can understand that. Thank you for always looking out for me."

"You don't need to thank me. It's my job."

"Your job? Still?"

"I didn't mean it like that." I shut down her presumption. "My job as your boyfriend, or whatever the fuck you call me."

"Boyfriend, huh?" she teases. "That title suits you."

"Well, I'm that first and foremost. Always will be."

"Oh, Enz."

Hitching her leg on my hip, she twines her arms around my neck and draws us together. The swell of her breasts meets my chest, causing my cock to twinge with excitement.

Grabbing her pert ass cheeks, I press my hardening erection into her, biting back a groan. I can't fucking think straight around this sexy, little vixen.

"Are you still tired?"

"A little," she admits.

"I'm gonna make you feel good, then you can sleep. My perfect angel deserves an orgasm first."

Cheeks flushed, her lips part on a sigh as I kiss my way over her neck, throat and clavicles. My tongue drags between her tits, tracing the curve of her sternum before continuing down her torso.

Lowering to my knees, I crouch down in the shower, surrendering myself to her in the most vulnerable way possible. There isn't another creature on this planet I'd kneel for—only her. My goddess.

Wrapping a hand around her ankle, I encourage her leg to rise and prop itself on my shoulder. She obeys without complaint. Her trust in me is dizzying, even after all this time.

"Let me see that perfect pussy. Are you wet for me, angel?"

"Yes," she moans.

With her leg raised and spine pressed against the tiled wall, I'm eye height with her dripping cunt. There's nowhere to hide. It's all on display, glistening and begging to be tasted.

Pressing a kiss against her mound, I drag my lips downwards, over the swollen swell of her clit. Harlow's hips buck, pushing her pussy into my face. I swirl my tongue over her bundle of nerves.

"Oh God, Enz."

Gently flicking the bud, I let my mouth traverse even lower so my tongue slides through her wet folds. She's soaked to the core, and her sweet juices burst across my tastebuds, making my cock stiffen even more.

Her innocence coats my tongue, and I lap at her core, sucking and licking in a punishing rhythm. I fucking love the way she tastes. I'd be quite content to suffocate in the slick warmth between her thighs.

Shifting her hips, she rocks against my face, encouraging me to eat her sweet cunt. I spear her slit with my tongue, lifting my thumb to rub her clit in slow, teasing circles.

"Please," she begs. "More."

Running a thick finger between her folds, I coat it in stickiness and push it inside her pussy. The moment I enter her warmth, Harlow cries out, her moans swallowed by the beat of the hot water.

"Still so tight, little one." I strum her clit again before thrusting my finger in even deeper. "Your cunt was made for me to devour."

Grinding against the heel of my palm, she moves her hips in time to the pump of my finger working in and out of her entrance. When I add a second digit, her moans reach a fever pitch.

Still buried inside her, I return my mouth to her clit, sucking the bud between my lips. The light graze of my teeth elicits the most enticing mewl of pleasure from her throat.

As much as I want to drive my cock deep into her cunt right now, this isn't about me. Harlow needs to know that she will always be my priority, regardless of anything else.

I live and die by the continued beat of her heart. The moment she takes her last breath, I'll cease to exist in this world, because I refuse to take a single step without Harlow by my side.

"I'm going to come," she whines.

I stop for a breath. "Spread those juices all over my face, baby. I want to be dripping in your come."

Driving my fingers into her in a relentless beat, I coax her to the edge then flick her clit one last time. It's enough to throw her into the darkness of ecstasy. Quivers overtake every limb.

Her hips still as she falls apart, crying my name so loud, I doubt the others will neglect to hear it downstairs. Her sweetness rushes across my tongue and stains my mouth.

Still kneeling at her mercy, I look up at her haze-filled gaze and make sure she's watching as I lick the fluid from my lips. Harlow's breath hitches, her blue eyes locked on me.

There's something primal and satisfying about knowing I'm swallowing her essence. She can never escape my orbit if I own a precious piece of her and keep it locked up, safe in the cradle of my inner self.

Rising to my full height, I slide a finger underneath her chin and seize her lips in a possessive kiss. Our teeth clash and tongues tangle, the salty burst of her come being exchanged between us.

"Enzo," she gasps into my mouth. "I need you to know that no matter what happens, I love you."

I rest our foreheads together. "I love you, Harlow, and I'll always keep you safe, even if I have to let the entire world burn to do that."

"And what happens if the only way to beat Michael is to give him what he wants?" She hesitates, uncertain. "My … death?"

Fingers digging deep into her skin, I ensure she's hanging on to my every word. "Then I'll stand back and watch him slaughter to his heart's content. I don't give a fuck about anyone but you."

"No." Harlow looks horrified. "I'm not worth all of this. I know you love me, but we have a job to do. You can't protect me at the expense of everyone else."

"Like hell I can't."

"Enz—"

"End of discussion."

"No, it's not. We're not going back to our old patterns."

Harlow turns off the shower and sneaks past me to escape. Sighing hard, I step out and grab the towel before she can, wrapping it around her body. She really is infuriating in all the best ways.

"That's not what I'm trying to do," I reason.

"Yes, it is. I can look after myself. I'm not going to spend the rest of my life living in fear to satisfy your need to wrap me in cotton wool. We're past that now. Catch up or move on."

Tucking a towel around my hips, I hug her from behind, stopping her from running away into the bedroom.

"I've lost everyone I ever cared about. My sister. My parents. Alyssa. Friends, co-workers. The lot. All dead and gone."

Spinning her around in my arms, I pin her against my bare chest, ensuring she can see the fire simmering inside of me.

"I refuse to add your name to that list. And I'm sorry, but I don't give a fuck if that makes you feel guilty. I'm in love with you, and I won't apologise for prioritising you above all else."

She shakes her head in annoyance. "Didn't I warn you months back about being possessive now that you officially have the *boyfriend* title?"

"You did, and I paid absolutely zero attention. Just imagine how possessive I'll be when I have the *husband* title."

Harlow halts, her mouth open. "Huh?"

"You don't think I'll marry you one day?" I cock an eyebrow. "Like I'd let any other bastard call you his wife and not me. You're mine. Get used to it."

Her anger melts into a shy, timid smile that reminds me of the broken girl I found in that hospital bed last year. She's still in there, however deep her damaged soul has been buried.

"You'd marry me? How would that even work?"

Unlocking the bathroom door, I follow her into the bedroom. "We'll see when Brooklyn marries those five oafs, I guess. If they can make it work, anyone can."

Harlow drops her towel then crawls into the unmade bed, completely naked. A lump sticks in my throat. Not even a fucking t-shirt. Now sleep is the last thing on my mind.

"She's asked me to be her bridesmaid," Harlow mumbles beneath the sheets. "I have no idea what I'm supposed to do. What if I let her down?"

Following her example, I leave my clothes off and climb into the bed. Her tiny frame immediately snuggles up to me, and her limbs curl against my side like garden vines.

"You could never let her down. All you have to do is turn up and look absolutely fucking beautiful. That shouldn't be hard at all for you."

Harlow scoffs. "Flirt."

"Complaining?"

"Not in the slightest."

She's out like a light and falls asleep with her ear resting above my heartbeat. In the darkness of the room, I let my terror escape its man-made prison. I finally have her, safe and sound.

We've survived so much.

If we were to lose her now, after a year of fighting tooth and nail for any scrap of hope, I can safely say that it would fucking devastate us. Irreparably so. My family would be done for.

I will do anything to prevent that from happening—even bloody my hands and risk becoming the monster myself. She's worth that risk.

The first name on my list?

Michael fucking Abaddon.

CHAPTER 5

Harlow

1x1 – Bring Me The Horizon (Ft. Nova Twins)

With the back patio doors open, balmy summer air leaks into the house. It still smells a little musty after being sealed for two long months, though I've been airing it out every day since we returned.

Spread out all around me, paint samples litter the worn floorboards. I'm trying to decide which colour to paint the accent wall that runs along the whole side of the house, joining the living room and kitchen together.

"Harlow Michaels has yet to make a single public statement," a voice emanates from the TV. "When will she speak up?"

The news is playing in the background with a hum of impassioned voices. I'm only half-heartedly listening. They've been playing the awful clips from the beach in Costa Rica non-stop.

Their speculation has yet to dissipate. I'm the focus of a whole bloodthirsty industry, and the pressure is starting to take its toll. I've found myself flicking on the news more and more often.

I want to know what they're saying. The whole world has an image of me that couldn't be further from the truth. Part of me is willing to disregard everyone's advice just to set that record straight.

"Tea or coffee?" Leighton breaks my thoughts.

Frowning at a paint sample, I hold it up against the wall. "Tea, please. Do you think this orange is too dark?"

"I'm not sure Hunter would approve of an orange wall, princess. So I think you should paint the whole damn house orange instead."

Snorting under my breath, I swap out the sample for a different strip. It's more of a burnt, homey orange colour, reminiscent of baked clay rather than a lurid neon.

Galloping in from chasing her ball outside, Lucky wraps her huge body around my legs, almost knocking me over. Her tongue laps at my right hand, demanding ear scratches.

"We're not leaving again," I whisper to her. "Don't worry, girl. I know you missed us."

Burying my fingers in her velvet fur that's coloured the lightest shade of golden blonde, she yaps happily. Ever since Hudson and Kade brought her home, she's been glued to my side.

Returning with two steaming mugs, Leighton boosts himself up to sit on the dining table. He takes one look at the TV screen then reaches for the remote to switch it off.

"Wait!" I exclaim. "I'm listening to that."

"They're just saying the same shit over and over again," he objects. "Why are you even watching this nonsense?"

"Because I want to know what they're saying about me. I refuse to bury my head in the sand any longer. It isn't healthy."

"Goldilocks, as proud as I am for you facing this head-on, listening to their constant stream of bullshit isn't helping anyone."

"Just leave it on. Please."

Deflated, he hits the mute button but leaves the TV on for my benefit. We return to studying the array of paint samples spread out all around us, denoting a million different shades of orange and grey.

"This one," he decides, tapping an orange square. "It's warm enough to make the room more inviting, but it's not too intense. It will work well with that light grey we already chose."

"You're right. It also matches the wood finishings in the kitchen, right? Nice and rustic."

"Rustic," Leighton echoes, smirking to himself. "Look at you, Little Miss Homemaker."

I smack a hand against his bicep. "You'll be the one painting, not me."

"I hate painting. Besides, I'm supposed to be clearing out the basement today to install the home gym later this week."

"Please? I can't do this alone."

He sighs dramatically. "Fine. You better make it worth my time."

"You know I will."

Dancing away from his grabby hands, I retrieve the furniture catalogue to show him the new rug and light fittings that I've narrowed down.

Hunter left us with his credit card and strict instructions to make this house a home. While we brought furniture with us, everything feels disjointed and out of place right now.

"I've picked out the other bits we need."

Leighton steals the catalogue to look at. "Nice cabinets. I like these new doorknobs too."

"Those ugly brass ones have got to go."

"We can take a trip out this afternoon." He drops the catalogue on the table. "We have to fix this place up before Mum comes over. She'll take one look and run away screaming otherwise."

"If you guys had let me call her, she could've fixed it up for us. Who chooses their own furniture when their mum is a literal interior designer?"

He pins me with a knowing look. "Because we don't want her input. This is your home, Goldilocks. You have to decorate it exactly how you want it. We all agreed on that."

I duck my gaze, feeling myself flush pink. I'm not quite sure when things shifted. Maybe it was the moment we were reunited among blood and death in that abandoned house.

The guys have treated me differently since then, not like I'm a china doll on the verge of shattering as I'd been dreading. Enzo's overbearing protective instincts aside, I feel like they see me as an equal now. A rightful member of their team.

I've finally earned their unconditional trust, and all it took was breaking the flimsy facsimile of what we kidded ourselves was enough before.

"Okay, then." I grin at him. "But if it looks terrible, I'm totally blaming you."

He playfully bops my nose. "I'll take it. I'm used to Hunter kicking my ass."

"There's no doubt about that."

The doorbell rings before the front door swings open. Theo has ordered a brand new, state-of-the-art security system, but it's yet to arrive. Until then, we're remaining armed and vigilant.

Leighton hops down from the table, and his easy smile vanishes. He starts to reach underneath the dining table where Hunter strapped a gun into place before a voice stops him.

"Only me!"

His shoulders slump. "Brooke."

The loud thump of her Doc Martens clatters down the wood-lined hallway. Platinum-blonde hair pulled up in a ponytail, her grey eyes sweep over the room then land on us.

"Hey, guys. Room for one more?"

Tall and muscled, her wiry limbs are wrapped in a pair of ripped black jeans and a faded band tee tucked in at the waist. She looks the same as always. Edgy. Dangerous. Aloof.

Ditching the samples, I race over to bundle her into a tight, breath-stealing hug. Brooklyn quickly reciprocates.

"I missed you." I squeeze her tight. "You're looking good."

"Hot as always, I know," she teases. "Costa Rica clearly agreed with you. Look at these fucking tits! Where did they come from?"

The tips of my ears burn hot at her compliment. I can hear Leighton chuckling to himself. My time abroad and a lot of calories have given me a newfound lease of confidence.

Releasing me, Brooklyn scans me up and down with a broad grin. "You look amazing."

"Stop it," I mutter. "I look the same."

"Fuck off! I'm so jealous of this tan you've got going on."

Ducking past me to ruffle Leighton's scruffy hair, she peels off her leather jacket then flops on the nearby sofa. I study her out of the corner of my eye while Leighton brews another cup of tea.

She's looking a little peaky. Although her skin is naturally fair, she's paler than usual, and her eyes are lined with dark circles. Even her frame appears slimmer than it was two months ago.

"What have we missed?" I ask pointedly.

Her eyes dart away. "Nothing really."

Warning bells sound in my head. We've been gone for a long time. Whenever we've spoken over the phone, Brooklyn couldn't wait for me to come home again. Now she can barely look at me.

"How's the last-minute wedding prep?"

"We're all on track." She shrugs, still not looking up. "Hudson and Kade have been pretty busy at HQ, so I've done most of it myself. Oh, Phoenix got the shit beaten out of him."

"So we heard." Leighton reappears and hands her a mug. "He should know better than to mess with Hudson's precious baby."

Brooklyn stares into her mug. "Eli still hasn't forgiven Hudson for almost breaking Phoenix's jaw in the fight. It was messy. Jude had to intervene to get them to speak to each other again."

"They better make up fast." I take a sip of hot tea. "You're getting married in six weeks."

She's still not looking at us. While I may not be the most socially experienced human, I can spot Brooklyn's red flags well enough.

The first thing to go is her eye contact. She's pathologically incapable of looking you in the eye when there's something eating away at her. It's like she doesn't trust us not to read it on her face.

"Leigh, do you want to go grab that paint?" I narrow my eyes on him. "We can get a head start before the guys get home from work."

"Now?" he asks in surprise.

"Yeah. We will get the woodwork all taped up."

"I'm not supposed to leave you home alone."

"Brooklyn's here now. I'm well-protected."

He seems to catch on when I raise my brows in a pointed look. His eyes dart over to Brooklyn and back to me, reading my silent order. Even he can sense that she's off.

"Alright, then. Don't burn the house down while I'm gone."

Brooklyn doesn't even acknowledge his bad joke, her attention fixed on the dark brown liquid in her mug. With a mouthed command to call if I need him, Leighton grabs the paint samples and ducks out.

When the front door closes, I take a seat on the sofa next to Brooklyn. She stares at the place where my fingers grasp her forearm in an attempt to drag her back to the present.

"What's going on, Brooke?"

"I'm fine," she rasps.

"How many times have you called bullshit on me? I'm about to do the same to you."

Shaking her head again, she worries her bottom lip with her teeth. I'm surprised to see that tears are pooling in her eyes, the shining trails streaking down her cheeks in threads of silver.

"What is it? Did one of the guys upset you?"

"No, no." She scrubs the tears from her face. "It's nothing. Leave it."

"The wedding? Did something go wrong?"

"Please, Harlow. I really don't want to talk about this."

But she does, otherwise, she wouldn't be here in the middle of the day. Her trust issues just don't allow her to blurt it out. I'll have to tease the truth free in order to get what I want from her pursed lips.

Tugging her hand into mine, I clasp her fingers. "I'm sorry that I haven't been around."

"You don't need to apologise to me. I understand why you guys left."

"Well, I am apologising. We packed up and left without properly explaining ourselves. I think we all needed some time away to repair what was broken, you know?"

Brooklyn exhales. "Yeah, I know."

"But I'm here now. Please talk to me. What's going on?"

Tears flowing faster than she can mop them up, Brooklyn finally looks up at me. I'm almost stunned to silence by the look of palpable fear wrapped around her silver irises.

"I think… I m-may be pregnant."

Mouth hanging open, I have no clue how to respond. Not a single word comes to mind. She takes one look at my speechless expression and bursts into even louder fits of tears.

"I don't understand." I pull her into a hug. "How? When?"

"My period is three weeks late," she hiccups. "I came off birth control last year when I started having side effects. We've been so careful since… but we had a drunken night last month."

"With whom?"

"All of them."

Ah, hell. I did not need the mental image of the six of them having an orgy in my head right now. Despite the part of me that's burning with curiosity at the sheer logistics of managing such an … um, endeavour.

"Did you do a test?" I ask next.

She shakes her head. "I'm too scared."

"Of what? The guys all love the shit out of you. They'd never leave you."

"It's not that." Her eyes clench shut. "I don't want kids. My parents fucked me up, and I can't risk doing that to another kid."

I cup her wet cheek. "You're not like your parents, Brooke."

"Aren't I?" she scoffs. "You know my condition can be hereditary. My whole family is dead because of the sickness in our blood."

Hesitantly, I stroke her tears aside with my thumb. I know that she was diagnosed with Schizophrenia as a teenager, earning herself a one-way ticket to the institute where she met the guys.

These days, she's medicated, and her condition is well-managed, aside from the odd slip-up. I can't think of a single person stronger than Brooklyn West.

She's been to hell and back, but she's lived to tell the tale. I'm not sure I could've pulled through the last year without her unwavering friendship and support.

"If you didn't have this diagnosis, would you want children?"

Eyes fluttering open, she shrugs. "I … don't know. How could I be a good parent? I'm barely capable of looking after myself. I'd be a disaster—"

"Now that's blatantly untrue," I interrupt. "You have survived shit that most people wouldn't dream of in their worst nightmares. You look after five idiots like a pro, and you're an amazing friend to us all."

"Harlow. Come on."

"No, I won't hear it." I grab her hand again. "I am in awe of your strength, and I don't know how I would've survived the past year without you. Give yourself some credit."

She laughs under her breath. "You're starting to sound like your damn therapist."

"Maybe you should listen to me, then. You can get from me what you'd pay Richards a hundred quid an hour to hear."

When her laughing subsides, she's sobbing again. I snuggle up to her side and hold her head against my chest. The tears flow until she has nothing left to offer and settles for a pained hiccup.

"I don't even know if the guys want kids," she admits. "It just never came up. We didn't exactly plan any of this. What if I want to … you know, get rid of it? And they don't?"

"Then you talk to them. How can you know what they're thinking if you haven't told them what's happening?"

She barks a bitter laugh. "Is this coming from you? The person who spent the last year bottling everything up and refusing everyone's help?"

I pinch her leg through her ripped jeans. "I'm gonna let that slide because you're a hot mess right now, otherwise, I'd be chewing your ear off. I've learned from my mistakes. You should too."

"You're right." Brooklyn sighs. "I'm sorry, that was mean."

"I'll let you off. We need to go buy some pregnancy tests."

Her head snaps up. "No."

"I won't let you do this alone. We're going to buy the tests and do them together. No matter the result, I'll support you and whatever you want to do. Deal?"

Bottom lip trembling, she summons a shaky nod. I stand up then pull her to her feet, but screaming red letters on the muted TV catch the corner of my eye.

Brooklyn freezes at my side as I grab the remote to unmute it. The same headlines they've been running for days have vanished, replaced by one far worse than I could've imagined.

"Local media discovered Harlow Michaels and her security team in rural Costa Rica. It is now believed they have re-entered the country, and for the first time in months, the suspect has resurfaced."

A blanket of ice slams into me, painful and petrifying. Brooklyn snatches my hand and holds on for dear life, ensuring I don't fall over with the weight of terror awash inside of me.

A helicopter shot shows an aerial view of a familiar beach. The feed is sweeping over the scene, crawling with flashing blue lights and authorities rushing to hide the awful sight from cameras.

"We warn our viewers, the following images are disturbing."

Emotion drains from my body, an unrelenting geyser draining me of all sense and care. I must be trapped in another lifelike dream. This cannot be real life.

"Fucking Christ," Brooklyn curses.

Vomit sears the back of my throat. The beach that features in my rare, happy dreams, usually walking hand-in-hand with the grandmother I'll never be reunited with, is painted across the screen.

But that isn't all.

There are bodies.

Countless dead bodies.

CHAPTER 6

Hunter

Living in Colour – Tropic Gold

My usually empty office is packed to the rafters with agents and various panic-stricken faces watching on in disbelief. The TV on the back wall holds everyone's attention, and the report is dubbed with subtitles.

You don't have to see the uncensored version to understand this message. The unmistakable shape of lifeless bodies has been arranged in meticulous detail.

Their limbs are positioned to spell a single word, ensuring the message meets its target without a crack of doubt.

REPENT.

I can't even count how many there are. One after another, the sand stained crimson-red. There must be at least ten to form the letters in sufficient detail. All lined up and left like a damn Christmas present.

Even if I can't hear the hum of voices all around me, the sharp snap of jaws moving and lips screaming out silent questions are enough to understand the hell that's just been unleashed.

At the back of the office, Theo is surrounded by his team, all ghostly white and a little green at the gills. Fox looks ready to hurl his guts up, and Rayna is clutching his arm tight.

Hudson and Kade are both flanking Enzo, the three exchanging what looks like urgent orders. I step between them to halt their conversation.

"We need boots on the ground. Forensics, security, the lot. We're going to have every reporter in Europe on that beach by tonight."

"*Need … go,*" Enzo signs back.

"Wheels up in half an hour. Call Lucas to start damage control. I want both security teams on the next helicopter out of here."

Kade asks Enzo a question, gesturing towards me. He translates his words in rapid, jerky sign language that I have to decipher.

"*Move … body?*"

Abaddon can't have pulled this off alone. The sheer strength it would have taken to lift and position so many corpses is unimaginable, let alone in a public place.

This must have been completed overnight. We know that he has supporters—the timely appearance of an accomplice allowed him to escape our clutches two months ago.

It's plausible that he had help this time around to pull off this stunt. If that's the case, then we're facing an even graver threat than before.

"He wasn't alone," I say grimly.

Pressing his phone to his ear, Hudson backs out of the room to make some calls. We've left Harlow at home with Leighton and a healthy fund to redecorate.

If she's seen the news, she'll be racing over here. That's the last thing we need right now. I tap Enzo's arm to regain his attention.

"Tell Harlow to stay away."

He signs a response. *"Bad idea."*

"This isn't about us sheltering her. It's for our benefit. We need to move fast and secure the scene. I can't afford to lose agents to keep her safe from the cameras right now."

With a terse nod, he follows in Hudson's footsteps to make a phone call. Theo leaves his team to get packed up and ready to move, coming to stop at my side instead.

His gaze is hard behind glasses framing fearful blue eyes. I'm sure the same apprehension is reflected in mine. He pulls his phone from his pocket to tap a text message to me so we can speak in full sentences.

If he managed to pull this off, there's no telling what he'll do next. Things are going to escalate.

"Yeah," I respond flatly. "That's exactly what I'm afraid of."

✝

The coastal breeze is chilly, despite the August sun beating down on us. Silent waves spread across the shoreline where one hundred of our finest men and women are battling against the elements.

Behind a yellow-taped cordon, local police have joined our best efforts to hold back a swarm of cameras, reporters, angry residents and fascinated onlookers.

With the collar of my light jacket turned up, I stand at the foot of a sloping sand bank. Metres in front of me, the first body is being sealed in a bag by our suit-covered forensics team.

Enzo is caught in an animated conversation with our head pathologist, Doctor Wheelan, discussing the thirteen bodies that were left for us to find when the sun rose.

The word *REPENT* is disappearing with each victim that's removed. You don't need a degree in forensic pathology to determine what happened here.

Every last deep, violent slash carved into each victims' wrists tells a harrowing tale. They all died still holding their bloodstained blades.

Thirteen identical suicides.

This is their repentance.

Back when I was in school as a kid, history was one of my favourite subjects. I always loved the stark, black-and-white certainty of facts that can't be changed by the present moment.

History is already bagged and buried. Controllable. Set. Even now, I remember writing a paper on Charles Manson for a module we'd taken on religious cults.

Everyone thought it was awesome, learning about that sick fuck. They were fascinated by the power he wielded, enough to turn his supporters into murderers, all in the name of some bullshit religious fanaticism.

Part of me wonders what those now-adult classmates are thinking while watching this unfold with the news playing on repeat. Bet they don't think it's so cool when there are thirteen corpses laying dead with slashed wrists.

My phone vibrates with another text message. I know it's her before I even look. She's been freaking out in the four hours it's taken for us to board an urgent flight to Devon to set up a cordon.

Harlow: What's happening? Did he kill them?

My protective instincts are screaming for attention right now, but I won't make the same mistakes that tore us apart already. She isn't a child. We're all in this together as equals.

Hunter: Looks like a mass suicide to me. We'll check for DNA.

Harlow: It has to be him. He brainwashed them into doing it.

Hunter: I think so too.

Harlow: He used to say that when the time came, the holy ones would have to prove themselves to earn passage to heaven.

Hunter: Earn passage?

Harlow: A payment. This is their sacrifice.

I tuck my phone away, feeling sick to my stomach. If he's working underground to inspire mass hysteria before his so-called rapture arrives, we're looking at a nationwide bloodbath coming straight for us.

Enzo dismisses the pathologists to continue their examination then walks over to me, his expression grim. I turn my back on the growing frenzy of onlookers to shield our private conversation.

"Well? What did they say?"

He scrubs a hand over his face. "*Suicide.*"

"You reckon he orchestrated it?"

Pulling his phone out as Theo did to communicate, he passes it over to me so I can read the message.

I think they walked down here, took their places and slit their own wrists on his command. Bled out within minutes. He arranged their bodies then left.

I've been thinking the same thing since we arrived, but if that's true, we're up against an even more formidable foe than we thought. That's a lot of power to wield over a whole group of people.

"We need IDs on all these people." I gesture to the bodies. "There has to be a connection between them. If we can find out where they came from, it could lead us back to Abaddon."

Enzo nods. "*Time.*"

"We don't have fucking time."

He pins me with an exasperated look.

"Enz, I want this son of a bitch rotting in a prison cell before anyone else gets hurt. He won't stop until he has an army of people like this, and then we won't be able to stop him."

Enzo glances back over at the madness threatening to overpower our barricade. The case has grown far beyond what we ever imagined. The whole world is watching us now.

He taps a reply into his phone and shows me.

What if we can't beat him?

"That isn't an option. We made a promise the day we met Harlow, and I'll die before I break it. She deserves to live in peace, and we won't rest until we get that for her."

Becket waves Enzo over, shouting something I can't discern. Letting him sidle away, I catch sight of a familiar face wading through the nearby crowd.

The agent holding Lucas back stands down when I shout his name. Appearing frazzled, Lucas straightens his shirt and meets me at the edge of the crime scene.

He begins talking, distracted by the scene, before he realises I can't hear a word coming out of his mouth.

"Sorry," he mouths.

I wave him off. "It's fine. What's the latest?"

He holds up a finger and fishes his phone from his pocket. Humiliation burns in my gut as he's forced to tap out an update in the notes app on his phone. This is fucking ridiculous.

No one would ever admit it, but I see the way they all look at me now. Equal parts pity and confusion as to why the hell I'm even here. Enzo's running the show in their minds.

Lucas sticks his phone under my nose. I'm getting really sick of having to communicate through text messages and hastily written notes.

We need to hold a press conference and release an official statement. I want to get Harlow in front of a camera.

"What? No."

He quickly types out a response.

A direct plea to the suspect and his supporters for their surrender will appease the media. If anyone can convince him to stop, it's her. She can appeal to them all for the violence to end.

I slap his phone against his chest. "Not happening. I won't say it again."

Lucas tries to stop me from storming off, but I brush straight past him and head for the shoreline. Being deaf has some benefits. Amidst all this chaos, I'm calm and collected in my silent bubble.

Starting out at the murky waters, lit by the beam of weak sunshine, I close my eyes. The tang of salt dances across my tongue, intermingled with the smell of death.

We have to catch this motherfucker.

I won't play his games again.

We've faced some monsters in our time. Real top-level, evil scumbags, the worst that humanity has to offer. I thought we'd peaked the day we saw Blackwood Institute lock its wrought-iron gates.

Then came this case.

It's taken everything from us. None of us have emerged unscathed, and we still have nothing to show for it. More bodies. Victims. Broken-hearted families. Exhaustion. Despair. A reputation in tatters.

What's worse is I wouldn't go back and stop myself from taking the case even if I could. This disastrous case has brought us the one thing that's given me the strength to keep fighting.

Our Harlow.

That's why we will see this through to the bitter end. Even if it bankrupts our firm and leaves us with nothing to return to when all is said and done. I couldn't give a fuck. I'll watch my legacy burn.

All for her.

And our future.

I'm not sure how long I stand there in total silence and darkness. My eyes don't reopen until someone taps my arm. Theo looks pensive as he gesticulates with his hands, spelling out a plea.

"Listen. Harlow … camera."

"Not you as well. This is a terrible idea."

His brows knit together, signalling his disagreement.

"You know full well this sicko can't be reasoned with."

"Try," he signs.

Pinching the bridge of my nose, I grapple with the tell-tale twinges of an oncoming migraine. I can't even blame the healing head injury for this one. Coming back to England was a shitty idea.

It's not about protecting Harlow. She isn't the timid, damaged wreck we found curled up in a hospital bed. The past year has allowed her to grow into a strong woman who's capable of handling herself.

But fighting this out in the public sphere won't be a clean battle. Centuries of torrid investigations into serial killers have proven that much. Public appeals are powerful, but monsters cannot be bargained with.

The last time I made decisions on her behalf, Harlow bypassed my authority and took matters into her own hands. I know she'd do it again in a heartbeat if there were even the smallest chance it would stop the violence.

She will have to decide.

This is her risk to take.

"This has to be her choice," I submit. "Harlow gets the final say."
Theo nods in agreement.
"Fine. Then let's make it happen."

SCENE DU
J.ROSE
ve spring

CHAPTER 7

Harlow

The Day That I Ruined Your Life – Boston Manor

I never thought I'd be back in the bowels of HQ witnessing another post-mortem take place. A stupid, optimistic part of me believed that I was ending this saga the day I ran from this very building.

On the other side of the tinted glass, the pathologists are picking over two bodies. After testing for any DNA evidence, they've snapped photographs of the gaping wrists and noted down their findings.

"Harlow?"

A hand lands on my shoulder, startling me. Theo's dressed in a green flannel shirt and faded blue jeans, looking even scruffier than usual after sleeping in his office the past few days.

"Hey."

"You okay?" He frowns.

"Are you?" I gesture towards the sliced open corpses. "This is the third post-mortem today. How are we back here?"

"I don't know, beautiful." Theo scrubs his weary face with the hem of his shirt. "I've never seen anything like this in all my time at Sabre."

"These people ... they were innocent. It's not their fault that Michael manipulated them into taking their own lives. They deserve better than this."

He rests a hand on my shoulder. "We're doing the best we can for them. It takes time to identify so many bodies."

"What about the connection between them?"

"So far, we've identified three individuals belonging to the same church parish. We're sending the Anaconda team to investigate."

My skin is itching with nervous energy. I want to grab handfuls of my loose hair and rip it clean out. It's not just this press conference... I feel like we're sitting on a ticking time bomb. This wasn't a parting gift—it's a warning shot.

Michael is ready to come out to play, and when he does, the streets will run red with blood. He has no qualms about butchering innocent people to achieve his goals. In his mind, God is on his side.

"We can still call the press conference off," Theo offers, taking the elastic from his wrist and giving it to me. "You're upset, and I don't want to make this any harder for you."

"No. I need to do this."

After quickly tying my hair up in a smooth ponytail, I try to scrub the nervous sweat from my palms. Even my breathing is shallow.

"Sure?" he double-checks.

"I'm not going to sit at home and wait for the next pile of bodies to turn up. The world needs to know what we're up against."

Snatching my wrist, he drags me into a tight hug that steals my breath away. "You're doing the right thing."

"I'm doing the bare minimum, that's all," I force out. "Listen, have you seen Brooklyn? Or heard from her?"

"Uh, no." He takes a step back. "Why?"

Shit. I can't betray her trust, even if she is avoiding my phone calls and text messages.

"Never mind. Let's go."

Taking Theo's hand, I let him guide me from the basement, then we ride the elevator to the ground floor. Tucked behind the reception, Sabre has a dedicated room for live conferences.

People are out there right now, being exploited and manipulated by my sadistic uncle. I know firsthand the sheer strength of psychological power he can wield.

Those victims were exactly that. Victims. He might as well have slit their wrists for them. That's why I have to do something before another drop of blood is spilled. Too many lives have been lost.

The hum of raised voices escapes the conference room, and I freeze in the middle of the foyer amidst a crowd of people. A wave of terror nearly knocks me off my feet.

"Shit," I curse.

Theo halts in front of me, inching a finger beneath my chin to tilt my eyes up to meet his. The certainty staring back at me leaves no room for the panic threatening to take over.

"You don't have to do this."

I blow out a nervous breath. "Yeah, I do."

"Seriously, Harlow. If it's too much, just say, and we'll call the whole thing off. I don't want you to be triggered by this."

"I can handle it."

His gaze softens. "I'm proud of you, beautiful."

"You are?"

"Of course, I am. This takes guts, and I'm going to be right there for every step of the way. You're not facing the world alone."

Tiny, electrified butterflies explode in my belly. I grab his shirt collar and yank him close, locking our lips together, despite Sabre's staff humming all around us.

Theo isn't like the others.

His care and affection aren't so freely given, but they're always there, however invisible they may seem to the outside world. He shows love through the pages of second-hand books and quiet gestures, not mere words alone.

Kissing me back with fervour, he forgoes the doubtful uncertainty that kept him from touching me for months on end. Now his true colours are unfurling, and his hunger sets me on fire.

Someone clears their throat. "Harlow?"

Breaking apart, we're both embarrassed to realise several members of the staff are giving us the side-eye. Standing close by, a spotlessly dressed stranger waits for us to separate.

No, he's not a stranger.

I almost didn't recognise him.

With his dirty blonde hair trimmed and gelled back, a pressed white shirt covering his filled-out frame and tucked into smart work trousers, my father looks like a brand new person.

"Oh," I squeak.

He chuckles under his breath. "Only me."

Theo releases me. "Oliver."

The guys told me a few weeks back that they intended to hire my father after he successfully helped me escape from Sabre's custody.

Who knew that my reckless self-destruction would be a successful job interview for his skills? Either way, I'm glad he was recruited and can now rebuild his life.

"Dad. What are you doing here?"

"Mandatory training," he answers with an easy smile. "I started my new job last week. Enzo's got me doing drills all afternoon."

"Are you settling in okay?"

"Well enough. It's been a long time since I had a proper job."

Dad still manages to look awkward, unable to close the distance between us. The last time I saw him, I was violently bruised, battered and broken after our shared close encounter with death.

He promised me that he'd do whatever it took to rebuild our relationship when I was ready to come home again. I wasn't able to answer him then, but staring at him now, my heart is set to burst.

"Can I … hug you?" I blurt.

His crystalline blue eyes widen. "Of course, love."

Stepping closer, I slowly wind my arms around him. It's like embracing a statue at first, frozen solid into stone, until the shock wears off and he bundles me into the tightest hug I've ever received.

With his face buried in my hair, we stand there for a moment, neither of us needing to say a word. The chatter of impatient journalists isn't enough to hurry this reunion.

"Did your break help?" he murmurs.

I blink back tears. "Yeah, it helped. I needed some time."

"I know. You're looking good."

"Thanks, Dad. You too."

Reluctantly releasing me, his eyes scan me up and down. While my injuries have healed into even more scars that mark my mottled skin, he still looks pleased to see me doing well.

"I missed you, kid."

My throat constricts. "I wanted to call you, but I didn't know what to say after everything that happened."

He shakes his head. "You don't need to apologise for taking the time you needed to get better. I'm here when you're ready."

Theo's voice interrupts us. "I'm sorry, but we should get in there before Enzo throws the lot of them out by their hair. You know how impatient he is."

That prompts a laugh from my father. It's low and barked,

sounding foreign to me, but at the same time, I recognise the sound. It causes happiness to surge through my veins.

"I have to say, I wasn't sure what to expect when I accepted your job offer." He shakes his head. "Having my daughter's boyfriend take such pleasure in beating the hell out of me wasn't my first thought."

"I'll tell him to lay off." I look over him again, searching for bruises. "Enzo's got a reputation for being hard on new recruits, from what I've heard."

"No need. The challenge is good for me." Dad hesitates, his brows drawn together. "I want more time with you, Harlow."

"More … time?"

"To get to know each other again," he clarifies. "I'm renting an apartment just outside of the city, now that I can afford it. Perhaps we could have dinner there one night?"

Dinner. It sounds so unassuming, but I haven't eaten a meal with my father in well over a decade. My ever-present anxiety dissipates into a strangely welcome sense of … excitement.

"I'd like that."

His smile broadens. "You would?"

"You have my number, right?"

"I do." His hand brushes my arm. "Thank you. I know you don't have to give me a second chance. I've done nothing to deserve it."

I have to blink aside tears to stop them from spilling over. "Everyone deserves a second chance."

"I want to be a real father to you. We lost so much time, and I refuse to waste another second. I hope you're okay with that."

Feet backtracking towards the hum of awaiting reporters, I summon a small, hopeful smile. "I am. I have to go."

"Good luck in there. Stick to your guns, and don't take any crap."

"Thanks, Dad."

Accepting Theo's hand again, I leave my father's grin to face the music. His words still ring in my head, warming the empty space in my heart left by every second of parental love I've missed out on.

Perhaps I can forgive him.

Perhaps I can forgive myself too.

The closer we get to the conference room, the louder the ruckus of conversing voices becomes. I take deep, even breaths, keeping the blank mask I perfected in the bathroom mirror in place.

"Got your statement ready?" Theo asks.

I pat the folded papers in my pocket. "It's here."

"Remember, they're going to throw all sorts of questions at you. We'll intervene if there's anything you shouldn't be answering that could compromise the investigation."

"You'll be there the whole time?"

"Of course. If you need me to get you out of there, just give me a nod." Theo tucks loose hair behind my ear. "I'll be watching."

Nodding, I pause on the threshold of the room for a final breath before stepping inside. Immediately, the chatter dies down into anticipatory silence.

The conference room is packed to the rafters with people. On a brightly lit, raised platform at the front of the room, a polished black table with built-in microphones faces the sea of faces and flashing cameras.

Sitting behind a name plate, Enzo's amber eyes lock on to me. He's already grimacing and looks on the verge of smashing the room to pieces just to get some peace and quiet.

"Smile," I mouth at him.

His glower deepens.

Well, I tried.

Kade and Becket sit on his right, both representing their teams and wearing equally grim expressions. I know it was a tough call, but Enzo decided it would be best for Hunter to sit this one out.

Giving my hand one last encouraging squeeze, Theo surrenders me. I walk alone up to my spot on Enzo's left side. Low murmurings follow every step I take.

Enzo pulls the chair out for me then settles a meaty paw on my shoulder as I sit down. His lips touch my ear to whisper low enough that the mic won't pick up his words.

"You've got this, little one."

"Thanks," I whisper back.

Pulling the handwritten statement from my pocket, I chance a look up at my audience. There must be at least fifty reporters in here, all poised and ready to tear my story to shreds.

The dead eyes of their cameras follow me. Even with a room full of strangers, I can feel his presence at the edges of my mind. Michael Abaddon. Pastor Michaels. Father. Uncle.

His many names are irrelevant. I won't let fear rule my life anymore. Clearing my throat, I tug the microphone closer.

"My name is Harlow Michaels. The world once knew me as Leticia Kensington, before I was kidnapped by the man this country has come to fear as much as I do."

Snap. Scribble. Mutter. Cough. The weight of countless eyes bore into me, broken by snippets of sounds, threatening to break my concentration. I clutch my statement a little tighter.

"I spent thirteen years in captivity, being beaten and tortured by someone who called himself my father. I have witnessed first-hand the atrocities that he has committed."

Memories threaten to overwhelm me. I pause, taking a sip from the glass of water next to my microphone.

"But I'm not here today to rehash what you already know. This week's discovery has proven that this monster is far from done with us yet."

Theo's anxious eyes connect with mine from his perch in the doorway. He nods in encouragement, his lips pursed into a flat line.

"I'm here to speak directly to Michael Abaddon." I flatten the paper clutched in my shaking hands. "I am begging for you to stop the bloodshed. You don't have to hurt anyone else."

A hand touches my leg beneath the table, squeezing my thigh. The warmth of Enzo's furnace-like skin is of little reassurance as the pace of snapped photographs picks up.

"You're killing in the name of God. He preaches mercy and love, not violence and hate," I continue unsteadily. "You can still stop this before it's too late. No one else has to die."

"You're the one who let them die!" a voice heckles.

My throat seizes up, the invisible hand of grief clamping down on the flow of air fuelling my words. One of the reporters—a young, scowling man—has risen from his chair.

"Take a seat, or you will be escorted from the premises," Enzo threatens. "That's your first and final warning."

When the cocky reporter refuses to back down, two of the silent, black-clad agents circling the perimeter of the room march towards him. I swallow down the nausea silencing my response.

"No, wait!" I shout.

Both agents halt.

"None of you know what happened to me during those years." I meet the reporter's gaze. "I've never spoken publicly before, and I know many have equated my silence to guilt."

"Harlow, why are you the only one who survived?" someone else interrupts.

"I didn't survive," I answer honestly. "I went into a cage as a scared, eight-year-old child, and I came out as a different person, thirteen years later."

"You're alive," she rebuffs. "Unlike others."

"That wasn't survival. There are parts of me that I can never rebuild. I'm not looking for sympathy, but I need the world to know that I tried my best to save the women held captive with me."

"No one else escaped the killer's clutches," an older female reporter speaks up. "What makes you so special compared to the other lives that were taken?"

"She isn't."

The harsh snap of Kade's voice startles me. His usual matter-of-fact demeanour and calm control aren't present today. A red blush of anger is creeping up his throat as he faces the room.

"Harlow is one of countless victims. If you all spent more time worrying about what Michael Abaddon is planning next rather than picking faults in our investigation, you'd know that."

"Kade," Enzo mutters. "Enough."

Sitting back in his chair, Kade ducks his gaze. Becket has rested a warning hand on his shoulder, cutting off another rant. The reporter sinks back in her chair, appearing chastised.

"He's right," I add with a shrug. "There is nothing special about me. I spent years watching the brutality of Michael Abaddon's warped ideology. I don't want to see anyone else get hurt."

Enzo leans forward towards his mic. "There are people out there who know where he is. Our suspect is being aided and abetted by a group of loyal followers."

"We are appealing directly to them to reconsider," Becket chimes in. "You are in control of what happens next."

Lifting the black remote control next to his nameplate, Enzo clicks the button that illuminates the projector screen behind us. I don't look back, knowing the scores of faces I'll find there.

Every single victim who has died at Michael's hands is being splashed across the wall. Countless lives. Bright smiles. Hopeful expressions. Family photographs, graduation pictures, the lot.

Their lives are right there, indisputable and forever lost. The old me would've allowed the thought of their deaths to tear my will to live apart, but now… I know that self-destruction isn't the answer.

I don't have to die for them.

I *have* to live in their memory.

"Is this a man you want to protect?" Enzo addresses those not in the room. "Think about what you are doing by helping him. He will continue to slaughter innocent people because of you."

"Can you confirm if the recent crime scene has been linked to Michael Abaddon?" another reporter questions.

Enzo nods. "While we haven't found any DNA evidence, we are confident in our theory that Michael has begun a campaign of mass suicides using brainwashing techniques."

"Should the public be concerned?"

"We are urging the public to remain calm—"

Before Enzo can continue the perfectly phrased reply that Lucas has scripted for him, I jump in with God's honest truth.

"Yes," I cut him off. "They should be very concerned. No one is safe from Michael's violence. No one."

A bubble of hysteria sweeps over the room as all of the reporters begin to talk over each other, shouting questions and vying for my attention. Theo's face has paled as he stares at me.

"This is what he does," I shout over the noise. "Michael manipulates and abuses. He beats and he kills. Those helping him should be afraid too. Once their usefulness expires, they'll be next."

Grabbing my arm, Enzo yanks me back from the microphone to

silence me. I peel his fingers from my blazer and push him away.

"We will never stop hunting you, Uncle." I ignore the flash of cameras. "You're going to pay for every single person you've hurt."

"Harlow, stop," Enzo hisses in my ear.

"I won't stop until your judgement day comes." I ignore him. "You will repent and be punished for all the lives you've taken."

Letting my chair scrape back, I shove past Enzo and leave the platform. Kade and Becket watch me slip around the back of the table to reach the exit at the rear.

"Harlow! Harlow!"

An agent opens the door for me then follows me out. When the sheet of metal slams shut behind me, I slump against it, a burst of defiant rage draining from my extremities.

I've escaped into a quiet corridor, where more agents maintain a tight perimeter for security. A familiar figure is leaning against the wall, fiddling with the shorter length of his dark beard.

When an agent taps his shoulder, Hunter's head snaps up, his chocolate-brown eyes wide with worry. The moment he sees me, his shoulders slump with visible relief.

I step straight into his arms, needing to feel the thud of his heartbeat against my ear. His chin lands on top of my head.

"I've got you," he hums.

That might have been the stupidest thing I've ever done or the bravest moment of my life. Either way, we have fired the next shot.

I have no doubt that Michael will fire back, and that's exactly what I want. We're going to find him before his rapture burns us all to ash.

I'm the only one who can do it.

His capture will be my reward.

CHAPTER 8

Harlow

Half-Life – Essenger

Poking plain porridge around my bowl, I ditch my spoon and opt for a swig of tea instead. Next to me on the table, my phone rests. It's still open on my text message conversation with Brooklyn.

Harlow: I'm worried about you.

Harlow: Have you told them about the baby?
What's happening?

Harlow: You don't have to do this alone.

She hasn't responded since we did those pregnancy tests together. The guys were at an urgent briefing with the Cobra team when all five pee sticks lit up with the same glaring answer. Positive.

Frustrated, I tap out another text message.

Harlow: I've been on house arrest since the press conference. Please come and break me out. Let's talk.

The sound of footsteps thudding down the staircase breaks my solitude, and I quickly lock my phone to hide the messages. No one else knows about Brooklyn's situation. I won't betray her trust in me.

Eyes half-open, Theo stumbles into the kitchen while slotting his black-framed glasses into place. His blonde curls are sticking up in a million directions. He looks far too cute for his own good.

"Morning."

He halts, yawning loudly. "You're up early."

"Couldn't sleep. What time did you get home last night?"

"More like this morning. I managed a few hours of sleep."

I frown at the pronounced circles beneath his half-open eyes. "You should go back to bed."

Stumbling towards the coffee machine, he locates a mug. "I have too much to do. The country is in meltdown after that press conference. We had over one hundred interview requests yesterday."

With his hot black coffee poured, Theo turns and spots the look on my face. I try to conceal my guilt, but seeing his frazzled state and knowing it's my fault is tough.

"I'm not blaming you," he explains.

"I blame myself, but I still don't regret it. I said what I had to. The world needed to know what he's capable of. Everyone should be worried, and lying to them won't help."

He sinks into the chair next to me. "I agree with you, but a head's up would have been good. Everyone wants to speak to you now."

"Enzo may regret telling me not to write that book."

Theo looks thoughtful, slurping on his drink. "For the record, I thought it was a great idea."

"You did?"

"People will always talk, whether you remain silent or not. The last year has proven that. I think you should seize the opportunity to take control of the narrative. Give them something real to talk about."

Staring up at him, I'm lost for words. "Huh."

"What?" He smirks at me. "It's your life, Harlow. You should live it however the fuck you want. Don't let Enzo or any of us stop you from doing that. We will support you, no matter what."

"I don't get it. Why?"

"Why? You're still asking us that?" Theo repeats, incredulous. "Fuck, Harlow. We all love the bones of you. That's why."

I feel my cheeks flush. "Maybe I just wanted to hear you say it."

He shakes his head. "You're such a fucking troublemaker."

Chest burning with emotion, the kitchen falls away until it's just Theo and his big blue eyes, staring at me like I'm his entire world. The months I spent waiting for him to admit that are insignificant.

He's mine.

In every damn sense of the word.

A wild energy takes over me, and I climb up on the table to knee-walk over to him. Pushing mugs, discarded newspapers and cutlery aside, I grab his plaid pyjama shirt and yank him towards me.

His eyes are wide with shock, but it doesn't stop his plump, inviting lips from slamming against mine. Positioned above him, I grip his shirt tightly and take control of our kiss.

The taste of coffee clings to his lips. When a groan rumbles from his throat, his mouth moves against mine, and I feel the brush of his tongue silently pleading for more.

That's the thing about Theo... He thrives on surrendering control to others. Our souls are so alike, and yet we still fit together in a perfect harmony, like night and day battling for control of dusk.

Scrambling off the table, I land on his lap then slip a leg on either side of his waist. Two hands grip my hips, balancing me as I writhe against the growing hardness pushing into my core.

"Harlow," he murmurs into my lips. "Should we..."

I moan in agreement while rocking against the firm press of his erection, now painfully stiff beneath me. Months of pressure are blurring my vision with an intense wave of need.

"Bedroom?"

"Right now," I agree.

Curling my arms around his neck, I cling to his body like a limpet as he rises to his bare feet. My lips suckle against the soft skin of his throat, covered in an almost invisible smattering of blonde hair.

He's lean and trim compared to the toned muscles of the others, but the ridges of carved iron beneath his skin are still well-honed. Theo lifts me and carries me up the staircase towards his bedroom.

Peppering kisses along his neck, jawline and lips, I begin to unfasten the buttons on his pyjamas. Theo pushes open his bedroom door and clicks it shut before setting me back on my feet.

"Harlow." He grabs my wrists, halting me. "We should talk before we do this. There's something you need to know about me."

"What is it?"

His eyes flick down, a frosting of pink dusting his cheeks. "I don't like the same things as the others … in the bedroom. That's why I've moved so slow with you."

Walking backwards, I settle at the foot of his double bed. "Then what do you like?"

Rubbing the back of his neck, he looks everywhere but at me. His room is still sparse and barely furnished, but there are wobbling stacks of books scattered across the floorboards, waiting to be organised.

A cluster of wires and computer equipment crowds the plain pine desk tucked into the corner of the room, and his curtains are a dark navy blue, blotting out the rising sun.

"I like to be dominated," he admits.

My breathing halts. "Dominated?"

"You know … controlled. I'm submissive."

The internet is a wonderful thing. I've trawled the depths of Google for answers about all the things I don't understand in the world. Before I lost my virginity, I even did research.

"Do you go to clubs and stuff?" I rack my brain for what I've read online. "Do … people tie you up and things like that? I've read a few books that had BDSM in them."

"Wait, you read dirty books?"

I quirk an eyebrow. "Sometimes. You told me to buy a Kindle."

"Hey, you burned through my whole paperback collection in less than a year. I had no choice."

"It's your fault for getting me hooked on books."

Stretching out my hand, I curl my fingers to beckon him closer. Theo steps between my splayed-out legs and runs a hand over my hair. I love the way his undivided attention makes me feel.

"Why didn't you tell me sooner?"

He bites his bottom lip. "I thought it might freak you out and ruin everything. Most men aren't submissive. I figured you wouldn't want me once you knew what I like."

"I would never judge you, Theo. And I sure as hell wouldn't walk away because you like something different from the others."

"It doesn't weird you out?" he worries.

"Of course not."

My heart is hammering hard with intrigue. I have no idea how to be what he needs, but I'm nothing if not resilient. I can figure it out for him. It may even be hot.

"You're going to have to talk me through this, though."

"It's fine," he rushes out. "You don't have to do this for me."

"But I want to."

He's studying me with such intensity, it's like he's pulling out the fleshy depths of my brain to inspect the neurons under a microscope.

"I could take you…" Theo finally says. "To a club."

My pulse skips a beat. "You'd do that?"

"We wouldn't have to participate or anything; we could just watch. It may help you to understand. But only if you want to."

Grabbing his wrist, I drag him closer until he collapses next to me on the mattress. Theo quickly pivots so that I can position myself above him, a hand on either side of his head.

"I'd love to."

"You would?" he laughs.

"I want to be a part of your world, Theo. If you'll have me."

He grabs my chin, clasping tight. "Just seeing you pinned beneath Leighton in Costa Rica had me hard. I wanted to fuck you there and then."

Treacle-like warmth pulses through my veins. Hearing the low rasp of Theo's usually soft voice is doing things to me. I'm convinced there's a dirty-mouthed devil in there somewhere.

"So why didn't you?" I purr back.

"Believe me, I wanted to. The sharing doesn't scare me, but I wanted to talk to you about this first."

"You are the sweetest person I know."

Straddling him, our mouths find each other again. This time, I push my tongue past his lips, demanding more of the fascinating gentleness that suffuses everything about him.

Clasping my hips, he rocks into me, the tantalising press of his hardness throbbing between my thighs. I now know what he needs. Submission. Control. All of the things I give to the others.

For Theo, I have to be someone else. The one in control of his desires and needs. Even thinking about it gives me a thrill I wasn't expecting to feel. He trusted me with this secret.

"I want you to take me to this club and introduce me to your world," I demand, our lips entangled. "Show me what you need."

"Fuck, Harlow." He peppers open-mouthed kisses down to the slope of my throat. "You never cease to amaze me."

Just as I'm about to tear the pyjamas from his body, the sound of the front door slamming downstairs, followed by loud shouting, causes us to jump apart.

"What was that?" I freeze.

Theo curses, lunging for his phone next to the bed. "Everyone else is still asleep. No alert on the security system."

"Brooklyn!" someone yells. "Are you here?"

I slump, clutching my chest. "That sounds like Jude."

We leave the bedroom and find Enzo racing downstairs ahead of us. He's the world's lightest sleeper, unlike Leighton who wouldn't wake up even if a nuclear bomb dropped.

We chase him down the staircase and emerge in the kitchen where two disgruntled men are searching the room like they're possessed.

Jude and Hudson work in tandem, checking every last corner. They both look equally rumpled, wearing sweats and T-shirts with matching bird's nest hair.

"What the fuck?" Enzo shouts at them. "Why are you shouting your heads off in my goddamn house? That key is for emergencies."

"This is an emergency," Hudson yells back. "Brooklyn didn't come home last night."

"What?"

"She's turned her phone off so we can't track her location either." Jude's gaze is lit with frenzy. "Have any of you seen her?"

"Not since our daily debrief yesterday morning." Enzo pushes rumpled hair from his eyes. "What happened?"

"We assumed she was in with Phoenix and Eli when we all got

home late from work, but she wasn't there this morning."

Terror wraps around my heart, its razor-sharp nails digging deep into my ventricles and cutting off the flow of blood. She's missing. I knew something didn't feel right.

"Did you guys have a fight?" Theo quizzes.

Hudson fists his hair. "No! She's been quiet, but we just assumed it's the case and stuff. We're all stressed as fuck right now."

"If you hadn't beaten the crap out of Phoenix, she wouldn't be upset with us," Jude snarls at him. "This is all your fault."

"My fault?" Hudson snaps. "Fuck you."

"Don't like the truth, Hud?"

"Get off my fucking back!"

"Guys." Enzo steps between them. "Blame each other later once we've found Brooklyn and made sure she's alright."

They take a step away from each other, though Hudson still looks ready to cave Jude's head in. Enzo stands firm in the middle.

Grabbing my phone from the dining table, I check the slew of unanswered text messages again. Nothing. She could be in trouble.

"Guys." I interrupt their scowling match. "We have to find her. She's ... well, I don't know... she needs you. More than ever."

"What are you talking about?" Jude glances at me. "Do you know something that we don't?"

Not even Leighton, semi-asleep and stumbling into the kitchen, breaks the pressure mounting on my shoulders. They clearly don't know what's going on.

"Harlow?" Enzo urges. "What is it?"

"I promised her that I wouldn't tell," I whisper dejectedly.

"Tell us what?" Hudson demands.

Wringing my hands together, I crack under the weight of their terrified eyes. I've never seen Jude look so scared. He's usually the solid pillar at the heart of their family, alongside Kade.

"The thing is, Brooklyn found out that she's pregnant a few days ago." I wince, feeling awful. "The tests we did were all positive."

Hudson's mouth hangs open while Jude blinks several times, as if he's expecting himself to wake up from one of those scarily realistic dreams. I shuffle my feet, feeling like the worst friend in the world.

"Pregnant," Hudson deadpans.

I manage a terse nod.

"With … our baby," Jude finishes.

They look like they've just witnessed Santa Claus leaving presents under their fucking Christmas tree. That would probably be less shocking than hearing this news.

"That's typically how it works," Enzo mutters. "Did you two skip sex ed in school or something?"

Baring his teeth, Jude rests a hand against the wall to hold himself upright. "We're having a baby. An actual … child."

"She's really pregnant?" Hudson repeats.

"Yeah. One hundred percent."

"Fuck," he curses. "Fuck! We're gonna be fathers."

Jude's mouth flaps open. "Holy shit."

When the shock wears off, the pair throw themselves at each other to kiss and embrace. Tears well up in my eyes just watching them.

Enzo's grinning from ear-to-ear, and Leighton's managed to wake up enough to join the bear hug with a cheer. Even Theo's cracked a grin.

"We still need to find her," I point out.

All sobering up, their joy is short-lived. Hudson and Jude look even more worried than before, their arms still wrapped around each other for support.

"Where would she go to hide?" Theo wonders.

"More importantly, why the hell is she hiding?" Hudson retrieves his phone and glowers at it. "She should've just told us."

"Brooklyn was scared of how you'd react," I answer his question. "She doesn't know if you even want kids, and she's worried about passing on her diagnosis. I've been trying to help her through it."

"Why the fuck didn't you tell us, then?" he barks.

"Hey," Jude interrupts. "Back off, Hud."

"We deserved to know!"

"Harlow's trying to help. It isn't her fault that Brooklyn didn't feel able to come to us. That's on us and us alone. We need to make this right."

Hands trembling, Hudson turns his back to collect himself. "Sorry, Harlow. I didn't mean to take it out on you."

"It's okay. I'm sorry that it's come to this."

Wrapping his arm around my shoulders, Enzo pins me to his side. I don't think he even realises that he's doing it, his attention captured by the phone in his hand. I can hardly move.

"Enz," I whisper under my breath. "I'm right here. Safe. It's Brooklyn we should be worried about."

"I just need to hold you for a second." His grip on me tightens painfully. "I can't fucking lose her too. Why didn't she call me?"

"I don't think she's thinking straight right now. We should all split up and start searching for her."

Enzo exhales deeply and releases me from his arms. "Go and wake Hunter up. I have a few ideas."

SCENE DU
J.ROSE

CHAPTER 9

Theo

Bad Decisions – Bad Omens

Arched slabs of moss-covered limestone topped with turrets mark the entrance to the City of London Cemetery. The air is heavy with thick humidity and the beginning wisps of a thunderstorm.

I haven't set foot through these gates in a very long time. For the first few months after we lost Alyssa, I'd visit her on a weekly basis, bringing flowers and an endless supply of tears.

Then I stopped.

It became too hard to live with the constant reminder of her absence. The hours I'd spend at her graveside were the darkest, loneliest moments of my life, and I had no choice but to stop visiting.

"She isn't going to be here," Hunter mumbles.

He's behind the wheel, driving us to the half-empty car park that precedes the thousands of graves. His grip on the wheel has tightened with every metre we've inched closer to Alyssa's final resting place.

We've split up into groups of two, scouring a list of spots across London where Brooklyn could be hiding. From her favourite restaurants and bars all the way back to our dark, shared past.

"She could have travelled up north to visit her mum's grave."

"*Scotland?*" I sign.

He watches me from the corner of his eye. "She can handle herself. I think she's hiding out somewhere. We'll find her."

I wonder if he has to believe that. We've lost friends and loved ones along the way, more than most people will experience in their lives. If we lost Brooklyn too, none of us would know what to do.

With the engine turned off, we both hop out of the car. The sun has disappeared, obscured by bubbling clouds. We're a minute away from being drenched in rain.

Checking that my weapon is secured, we take off down the stone pathway. Neither of us wants to be here right now. Hunter never even visited Alyssa's grave. Not once. He couldn't bear it.

Only a small handful of mourners are braving the volatile weather, ducking beneath willow trees and overgrown ferns to reach their lost relatives. It's a short minute walk to the top corner of the graveyard.

"Come on," I say to myself. "Please be here."

Banking right, I creep past dirt-streaked stones and overgrown tufts of parched grass. There's an ominous rumble above us, but the swelling clouds don't release their moisture yet.

Jude chose the position of the grave, tucked beneath a cherry blossom tree that blooms with beautiful pink flowers in the spring. Her gravestone is clean, unlike the others, and adorned with old flowers.

Hunter stops beside me. "She's not here. Let's go."

I hold up a hand to halt him.

"I'm not going any closer," he insists.

"*Why?*" I spell out with my hands.

"For the same reason you stopped visiting her years ago. Come on, we still have other places to check off our list."

With a huff, I leave him behind and creep closer. I know Brooklyn and Jude visit here together. While Alyssa was her best friend, Jude lost his sister. He can't stop acknowledging the fact that she existed like we did.

After checking that the coast is clear, I crouch down in front of the letters that are still scored on my heart. I can admit that I love Harlow now, but part of me will always belong to Alyssa.

I know Harlow understands that. It's part of the reason I love her so much. She has enough space in her heart to accept our flaws and imperfections without letting them change her feelings for us.

I miss Alyssa, but the moments when I'm with Harlow are the closest I've felt to feeling alive in years. She's defibrillated my long dead heart and given me a second chance at life.

That's worth risking everything for.

Even at the risk of heartbreak.

"Hey, Lys." I stare at the clusters of decomposing roses. "It's been a while since I last came and saw you."

It isn't enough. She's laid here all alone, abandoned by the people who swore to keep her safe. I owe Alyssa's ghost more than that.

"I'm sorry I left you all alone. It was too much."

The silent stone grave doesn't answer me. We have other places to be, but the carved letters of Alyssa's name demand the truth.

"I met someone," I admit. "You'd like her. She's sweet but fiery when she wants to be. In many ways, she's the total opposite of you. Her vulnerability is her strength, and she isn't afraid to use it."

The crunch of footsteps approaches. Hunter settles by my side, his lips pursed together. When the first drops of rain begin to fall, neither of us moves. We sit side by side, united in our grief.

"Do you think she'd be happy for us?" Hunter asks thickly. "For finding Harlow?"

After a beat, I nod back.

"Yeah. I think she would too."

We sit for several silent minutes, the rain slowly picking up speed and drenching us in warmth. When Hunter stands, he offers me a hand up. I accept with a sigh and meet his reddened eyes.

"I'm sorry," he blurts.

I frown at him in confusion.

"I spent years punishing you for what happened to Alyssa. Sabre took over, and I left you to struggle alone. I hate myself for it. I'm so sorry."

Pulling him into a hug, I slap him on the back and gulp down a rush of emotion. I never thought I'd hear him say those words, and I didn't know I even needed them until now.

Somehow, somewhere, I hope that Alyssa is content while watching down on us, knowing that we made it.

Holding him at arm's length, I pray he can read my lips. "You kept … us safe. Let us … help you … now."

His smile droops. "I don't need your help."

"You don't have to do this alone."

He frowns at my mouth, and I know my words have gotten lost in translation. I sign them out instead, watching Hunter sigh as he pieces the sentence together.

"I don't recognise my own life right now." He looks back at Alyssa's gravestone. "I haven't felt this lost since she died."

"*Help*," I sign back. "*Your … family.*"

"You can't fix this, Theo. No one can. I need to figure out how to live with this on my own."

I can almost feel Alyssa's sharp-eyed glare cutting into the side of my head, like she's sat atop her own grave and watching me fail to punch through Hunter's shields.

Nearby rustling drags me back to the rising storm around us. I blink through the rain to find a soaked figure traipsing between the gravestones. *Fuck!* It's her.

"Brooklyn!" I shout.

Hunter follows my line of sight. She doesn't respond to our shouts of her name, wandering up and down the lines of graves without stopping to look at any of them.

Racing through the grass, we catch up to Brooklyn, and Hunter seizes her hand. She's wrenched to a halt, but her glazed-over eyes remain fixed on the clouds.

"Brooke." I cup her wet cheek. "It's me. Theodore."

Two shiny, silver-grey eyes slide down to me. "I can't find him."

"Find who?"

She shakes her head, like she's blowing the cobwebs free. "Logan. He told me to meet him here. I can't find him."

"Logan?" Hunter reads her lips. "Did she just say Logan?"

I wave him off. "Brooke, we need to get out of this rain. Come and get dry in the car for a moment."

"No," she protests. "I need to find Logan. He's expecting me."

Jerking my head, I gesture for Hunter to grab her other arm. We capture her between us, towing her rain-soaked body through the graveyard.

Her protests are feeble at best, another blaring warning sign. Brooklyn doesn't do anything against her will. She should be punching us in the dicks and threatening death if we don't let her go.

"You're okay." I stroke a hand over her goose-pimpled skin. "The car's just over here. A few more steps."

Resting Brooklyn against the bonnet, we check her for injuries. Her clothes are dirty and soaking wet, but she's unscathed.

We can't fit three people in the convertible. Hunter's texting fast, updating the others and sending the nearest team our location.

"They're coming."

I approach Brooklyn with caution. Her hands are clasped over her flat belly as if she's envisaging the life growing deep inside of her.

"Brooke? You with me?"

"Logan," she murmurs. "He'd know what to do. Is he here yet? Did you see him?"

Right now, I'm glad Hunter can't hear Brooklyn begging to see her brother. He's been dead for over two decades. God knows what she's seeing that we can't.

"Where did you see him?" I ask gently.

Tears slick down her pale cheeks. "Last night. He told me to meet him here. I need him to tell me what to do."

My heart splinters in my chest. I hold her close and rub circles on her back. She shudders from the rain coupled with her rising sobs, and every stuttered breath pains me to hear.

"I can't have a baby," she hiccups.

"Shh. It's going to be okay."

"No, it's not. I can't be a mum. I'm going to fuck this kid up like I've fucked up everything else in my life."

Tightening my grip on her, I watch Hunter begin to pace up and down the car park, his agitation growing. Every glance he takes in Brooklyn's direction increases his restlessness.

While he may not always show it, he's the reason Brooklyn and her men are still alive. Hunter gave them all a chance when no one else would, and he loves each of them to death.

"What's going on?" he snaps.

Tucking Brooklyn's head under my chin, I free up my hands to fingerspell. "*Logan.*"

"Goddammit. She hasn't had an episode in years."

Keeping her trapped against me where she can't run off, we wait for backup to arrive. It doesn't take long for the throaty purr of Hudson's Mustang to break through the torrential rain.

With a squeal of tyres, it comes screeching around the corner, breaking several speed restrictions. Brooklyn snuggles closer to me, subconsciously seeking reassurance.

"Is it Logan?"

I stroke a hand over her hair. "No, Brooke. We're all here with you, though. You don't need to be scared."

The car lurches to a halt next to the convertible, then three pairs of legs climb out. Hudson, Phoenix and Eli are all frantic, their clothes creased from hours spent driving around.

"Brooke," Eli yells louder than I've ever heard him speak before. "You found her."

He and Phoenix approach together to ease her from my arms. She collapses in the middle of them, and her cries echo throughout the rain-slick car park.

"Firecracker." Phoenix runs his hands all over her, needing assurance that she's intact. "You scared the living fuck out of me."

"Nix," she breathes. "You're here."

Pressing himself into her spine, Eli buries his face in Brooklyn's drenched, blonde hair. He's shaking like a leaf with nerves.

"You promised to never run away from us," he accuses. "We deal with things together, not apart."

That's when she breaks, and all of the terror spills out. Brooklyn sobs into Phoenix's t-shirt, and the pair of them have to hold her upright.

"Where was she?" Hudson walks over to us, each step laden with exhaustion. "We've been driving around the city for hours."

"She was just walking around the graveyard." I gesture towards the gravestones behind us. "Not far from Alyssa."

"The others are on their way. Has she said anything to you?"

"She's been asking for Logan."

"Logan? You're sure?" he repeats.

"She's seeing him again."

With a curt nod, Hudson approaches Brooklyn to embrace her. Eli and Phoenix surrender her to him, both hanging within touching distance for their own sanity.

"Blackbird." Hudson tugs her into his arms. "I'm gonna scream at you later for doing this. Just let me hold you first."

I watch the four of them cling to each other like the storm will tear them apart. Relief crashes over me in tumultuous waves. Our fucked up family isn't intact without them in it.

"Thank God." Hunter stops at my side. "That was a close call."

"I'm going to take her home," Hudson announces. "We need to deal with this together. Can you ask Richards to make a home visit?"

I nod back. "I'll give him a call."

"Thanks, Theo."

Letting them bundle Brooklyn into the Mustang to get warmed up, Hudson hands Phoenix his car keys so that he can drive them home. He climbs in the back with Brooklyn instead.

We're in serious shit if Phoenix can't even crack a smile at being given the privilege of driving the Mustang. He still looks shaken up, even with Eli holding his hand tight.

Pulling out my phone, I hit Richards's name on speed dial. He answers within seconds, his rich baritone laced with worry.

"Theo? Do you have an update?"

"We've got her. Who called you?"

"Enzo." He sighs in relief. "He put me on standby hours ago. I returned to Clearview in case she somehow found her way there."

"Graveyard," I rush to explain. "They're heading home now, and you're needed. She's had a relapse. A bad one."

Richards doesn't often swear, but his muttered curse is all too appropriate in this situation.

"Tell them I'll be there in an hour."

"Thanks, doc."

He disconnects the call without a goodbye as the low growl of another engine joins us in the car park. Enzo's beast of an SUV tears into the space next to us in record time.

"Theo! Hunter!"

Harlow flies out of the back door, almost tripping and faceplanting in her haste to get to us. She's been distraught all morning.

"What happened? Is Brooklyn alright?"

"It's okay, beautiful. She's fine."

Enzo climbs out of the car, his expression steely. "I thought we'd find her at that weird record shop she likes. Good work, guys."

Still flustered, Harlow slips her hand into Hunter's and sags into his side. I know she feels shitty about spilling Brooklyn's secret. I can see the guilt overpowering her relief.

"Should we go over to theirs?" she suggests.

"They want to be alone."

Her shoulders slump. "This is all my fault. I should have raised the alert when Brooklyn stopped replying to me days ago."

"You couldn't have known," Enzo comforts. "She's an adult. All we can do is our best to look out for each other when things get bad."

His eyes flit over to Hunter, standing slightly back from the group and locked in his own world. I watch Enzo swallow hard.

Harlow shakes her head. "I'm worried about how the guys will react. Brooklyn may need someone there to have her back."

"They love her to death," Enzo disagrees. "None of them would ever leave her, even if she killed a fucking puppy."

"I guess you're right."

"Come on." He tugs her hand into his. "Leighton's waiting at home for us. You can choose what takeout we order tonight."

"A high honour indeed," she snorts. "Leighton may have something to say about that. You know how weird he is about food."

"And I'm tired of eating pizza like it's going out of fashion. Let's get out of this place. We have work to do."

After untangling herself from Enzo's possessive hold, Harlow approaches me and drops a kiss on my cheek. Her lips tease the shell of my ear so she can whisper without being overheard.

"So… about this morning."

I wind an arm around her waist. "What about it?"

"Can we pick up where we left off?"

Letting the other two climb back into their cars, I back her up against the polished metal before pecking her lips. She feels so fucking good clasped in my arms.

I have no idea how I survived so long without touching her, but that time is long gone. After this morning, I want to finish what we started. We've wasted enough time.

"Date night this weekend?" I suggest in a low voice. "I'll take you to a club in London."

"Really?" she asks excitedly.

"If that's what you want. I have somewhere in mind."

"Then it's a date."

SCÈNE DU N
J.ROSE

CHAPTER 10

Harlow

Who Do You Want – Ex Habit

Checking my reflection for the fifth time, I anxiously smooth the loose, glossy brown curls that hang over my shoulders. I spent an hour applying my makeup, something I've never bothered to do before.

I'm wearing full war paint tonight—thick, glamorous lashes and deep-red lipstick that highlight my blue eyes. Brooklyn even gifted me one of her little black dresses for good luck, sending it over with Hudson while she remains at home recuperating.

The short, flowing chiffon fabric teases my upper thighs, covering my matching pink lace bra and panties. I've shaved every inch of myself in preparation for my first date with Theo tonight.

"Princess?"

Bedroom door creaking open, Leighton's headful of hair pokes inside. He looks me up and down with a low whistle of appreciation.

"Shit. I am so jealous of that four-eyed fucker right now."

I slip my ID and phone into my handbag. "Thanks, Leigh."

"Seriously, you look incredible." He bites his bottom lip. "Sure I can't convince you to stay at home with me instead?"

"I'm sure you'll survive one night without me."

After striding into the room, he steals my handbag and throws it on my unmade bed. I'm scooped into his arms, my breasts straining against the square neckline of the dress as he smashes me into his chest.

"You know where he's taking you, right?" he murmurs.

"I do."

"Enzo's furious. I think he's ready to lock Theo in his car boot instead of letting him take you to some kinky sex club for a first date."

I click my tongue. "You make it sound so seedy."

Leighton chuckles. "Oh boy. You're really in for a shock tonight. Do you have any idea what happens in these kinds of places?"

"Well, no. But I'm going in with an open mind."

Sliding a chunk of hair behind my ear, his lips tease mine. "Just the idea of him fucking you in front of an audience makes me stabby."

"An audience?" I choke out.

A grin lights up his face. "Precisely my point. Just take it slow. Things can get crazy in these clubs, and you need to be careful."

Pecking his lips, I try to sound more confident than I feel. Leighton doesn't need to know how nervous I am about this date.

"I'm not going to be doing anything in front of anybody. Stop worrying. You know Theo will look after me, no matter what."

"True." His lips trail along my jawline, planting soft kisses. "Watch yourself, and call me if you need us to come rescue you, alright?"

"Deal."

His hands sneak beneath the hemline of my dress, and he groans as his fingertips stroke the edges of my panties. My stomach somersaults at his light touch.

"You better leave before I bend you over this bed, and trust me, Theo won't be able to tear you away from me if that happens."

Placed back on my feet, I kiss him again, slower and with all of my appreciation. If it wasn't for Leighton, I doubt I'd even have the confidence to consider going to a place like this.

He was the first one to build me up and give me power over my own life. While the others thrive on protecting me, all Leighton wants is to cherish every inch of my soul, and I love him for it.

After grabbing my handbag and heels, I tangle my fingers with Leighton's and follow him downstairs. The hum of the TV playing accompanies pots and pans being loudly bashed together.

In the kitchen, Hunter is knee-deep in ingredients and cooking some complicated dinner. Enzo sits at the breakfast bar, a pile of folders and paperwork spread out in front of him with a beer.

He swivels on his barstool, his mouth falling open. Following Enzo's line of sight, Hunter freezes mid-chopping with a knife in hand.

"Fuck," Enzo curses. "I'm gonna murder that bastard."

"I called dibs." Leighton skips to the fridge to retrieve a beer. "Form an orderly queue behind me for your turn."

With an eye roll, I walk into Hunter's arms, careful of the knife still clasped in his hand. His chin lands on top of my head.

"You look beautiful, sweetheart," he rasps. "I know I still owe you a date. I should be the one taking you out tonight."

I look up into his espresso eyes and mouth, "I love you."

I'm rewarded with the thing I wanted most: his smile. They're few and far between still, so I've made it my personal mission to score one every single day.

"Becket and Tara will meet you both there." His eyebrows knit together. "They'll give you some privacy, but don't go anywhere without them."

I know better than to argue with Hunter. This was their one condition for letting us go into the city despite the investigation and current risks. Two of Sabre's best agents are going to be tailing us the whole time.

He squeezes me tight then plants a kiss where his brother's lips claimed mine. I'm handed off to Enzo, his paperwork forgotten.

"I don't like this." Enzo picks me up in a hug. "Keep your phone on you at all times. The tracker is activated. Watch your back too."

"This is supposed to be a bit of fun. You're making it sound like we're heading into a war zone."

"You are," he growls. "The entire country is freaking out over those suicides and the press conference. If anyone recognises you, Becket and Tara are under strict instructions to haul ass."

"We'll be fine, Enz."

Gripping my chin, his eyes scour my face. "Promise me you'll be careful, little one. Don't make me regret approving this date."

I doubt he gives a shit how controlling that sounds, but the reality is, we're all beholden to Enzo's approval these days. Nothing is safe.

"I promise," I assure him.

He ducks down to whisper in my ear. "I'm fighting the urge to rip off this stupid little dress and fuck you right here on the breakfast bar for both of them to see."

"Hands off the goods. This dress isn't mine."

"You think I give a rat's ass whose it is?"

Teeth sinking into my earlobe, the violent growl of his voice causes warmth to flood between my thighs. The worst part is, I wouldn't even complain.

The staircase creaks as Theo heads down to join us, and Enzo begrudgingly puts me down with a scowl. My heartbeat stops the moment my date arrives.

"Oh," I squeak.

Who the hell is this guy?

His timid, unassuming disguise thrown to the flames, the Theodore I know has been replaced by a smouldering stranger. Any coherent thought flies straight out of my head.

From the tight black dress shirt highlighting his wiry lines of usually concealed muscle to the fitted seam of his trousers and open leather jacket, Theo has abandoned his chrysalis.

Even his black-framed glasses have been replaced by contacts. His blonde ringlets are slicked back, showing off his sharp angles, cut-glass cheekbones and a freshly shaven face.

"Here, let me get that for you."

I feel Enzo's finger beneath my chin as he clicks my mouth shut. I'm surprised there isn't a puddle of drool gathering at my feet.

"Why doesn't she react like that when I walk into a room?" Leighton pouts.

I expected perhaps a fresh flannel shirt, maybe a pair of jeans without holes in them. Not this sexy Greek god who wouldn't look amiss on the pages of a glossy magazine.

"You ready?" Theo asks awkwardly.

"I'm gonna need a minute."

His cheeks darken. "Isn't that my line? You look phenomenal."

"Alright," Enzo mutters. "That's enough flirting for my ears. Get the fuck out of here before I lock the pair of you up."

Theo grabs my coat then opens his arms for me to step into it. I let him assist me, my belly awash with those damned nervous butterflies again.

He kisses my temple and intertwines his fingers with mine. All three sets of jealous eyes in the room are narrowed on us both.

"Head's up."

Hunter tosses a pair of car keys through the air, leaving Theo to catch them. I recognise the Costa Rican keyring I bought him as a joke—a bright pink tortoise.

"*Sure?*" Theo signs.

Resuming his methodical chopping, Hunter nods. "Crash it and there'll be hell to pay."

"Alright, then." Theo tucks the convertible's keys into his pocket. "Ready to go, beautiful?"

"As I'll ever be."

†

The moment I slide out of the cherry-red convertible, leaving my handbag safely stowed inside, I'm hit by a column of heat. London feels boiling hot tonight.

Shadows drape the quiet street, and the hum of music emanates from behind locked doors. We've parked in a tight space that's surrounded by expensive sports cars.

"Just how exclusive is this place?"

Theo clicks the car door shut. "Members only. I haven't been here in a long time, but it's the best around and costs a small fortune."

"And you can afford somewhere like this?"

"I own a portfolio of stocks that outweighs Sabre's entire net worth. Who do you think bought the house?"

I gape at him. "Um, Hunter?"

Theo shakes his head.

"Wait, it was you?"

"I covered it," he reveals shyly. "Sabre isn't my only source of income. I just don't like to flaunt it like other people."

His eyes stray over to Becket and Tara, both dressed down in matching black outfits, idling in their car down the street.

"Let's go inside."

Clinging to his arm, I follow him towards the sound of music. There's a discreet door in the red-brick building, tucked beneath an overhang and marked by roped barriers.

After ringing the buzzer, the door swings open to unveil a heavily-built security guard. Theo pulls out his wallet then hands over a gold card that has an engraving in the matte material.

TARTARUS.

"Mr Young," the man booms. "It's been a long time."

"It has," Theo says stiffly.

"Donatella will be glad to see you."

His hand clenches mine tighter. "I'm paying for discretion, Kaleb. Remember that."

"Right you are." He clears his throat. "She's hosting a private show in the Indigo room. I'd avoid going there tonight."

With a terse nod, Theo steers me inside, and I'm engulfed in darkness. Thick, blood-red carpets swallow the click of my heels while black and gold brocade wallpaper muffles all sound from outside.

The throaty purr of violins and a crooning voice beckons us farther into the low-lit shadows. My nails dig into Theo's hand.

"Who is Donatella?"

"Someone best left in the past," he answers.

"Could've warned me that we'd be bumping into your ex-girlfriend."

"She never made it that far." He holds open a lacquered black door for me. "I'm here with you, Harlow. No one else."

With a breath for courage, I step into the unknown. Music meets my ears, soft and sensual, breaking the silence of the welcoming bar.

Velvet chairs surround flickering candles, offering intimacy to the darkness. Behind the well-stocked bar, a gilded mirror gives a snapshot of the luxury on all sides.

The handful of guests wear smart business attire and dresses, sipping on their crystal glasses of liquor. No one looks up at our arrival, all content to mind their own business.

"Drink?" Theo asks.

"Sure. It's quiet here."

"For now. It's still early."

Escorting me to the bar, Theo orders two glasses of wine, sliding a stack of cash from his wallet. I bite my lip, curiously studying him as the barman pops the cork and locates two glasses.

"I can feel you looking at me." Theo accepts the wine. "Look, I didn't know she'd still be here."

"It's not that. I don't care about her. She's in the past, right?"

"Right."

"Then she isn't my problem."

He clinks our glasses together. "What is it, then?"

I hesitate. "You're different here."

Placing a hand on the small of my back, he guides me into an empty corner where a loveseat is quietly tucked away from sight. I slide in, taking a sip of wine.

"Is that a bad thing?" he asks nervously.

"No." I rest a palm on his leg. "I just haven't seen you … well, comfortable in your own skin."

Theo inclines his body, blocking out the rest of the bar. His hand scrapes through his gelled curls and messes them up. I lean closer so our thighs brush under the table.

"How did you end up coming to clubs like this?"

He shrugs. "I grew up in foster care. You see some sick stuff in those places. A friend introduced me to the scene when I was sixteen, and it offered me an escape."

"What happened to your parents?"

"Your guess is as good as mine. I have no memory of them. My records said I was abandoned before I even spoke my first words."

Pain lances across my chest. "I had no idea."

"It's fine," he consoles. "I don't like to talk about them. Family didn't matter to me until I met Hunter and Enzo."

I take another small sip. "So you came to places like this to get away from it all?"

"I thought I had no control over my life. When I watched someone be dominated for the first time, I realised that control is meant to be surrendered. That's where power lies."

His hand runs up and down my arm in a slow, agonising rhythm, following the melody of violins in the background. If it wasn't for the music, I'd forget we're still inhabiting the real world at all.

I can't see beyond his quirked lips and the oceanic shimmer of his eyes. He's observing every last tell, reading my mind for any signs of judgement.

"You're waiting for me to run," I guess.

"Do you want to?"

I place my hand on top of his, covering my thigh. "Nope. I want you to tell me what you like. Show me your world."

"Sure that's what you want?"

Pushing his hand higher, I spread my legs, forcing him to feel the damp lace covering my pussy beneath my dress. His eyes blow wide.

"Show me, Theo."

His nail skates over my covered clit, sending pulses straight to my core. He barely has to touch me, and I'm already panting with need.

"Follow me. Remember, we can leave at any time."

After letting him pull me to my feet, I tug the hem of my dress down to hide my state of arousal. We knock back our wine then link hands again, winding through the darkened bar.

Bearing left, there's another door leading deeper into the club. We have to pass a second security guard, the flame-haired woman checking Theo's card again.

"Only certain membership tiers are allowed beyond this point," he explains under his breath.

Tucked into his side, the thump of the doors closing behind us sets my pulse skittering. A pair of curtains is drawn back to admit us into the next level of the club, and the entire scene changes.

"This is Tartarus," Theo explains.

The huge room is split into sections: observing and participating. On curved, raised stages, satin-covered beds are dotted about. Perfectly aligned rows of chairs offer seating to the audience.

Half of the beds are full, occupied by onlookers. To my right, a plump woman in emerald

is bent over a bed, her bright-red ass cheeks being swatted with a paddle.

Each time the bare-chested man at her rear strikes her, the crowd seems to lean closer, drawn into the punishment. The crack of the leather paddle smacking her flesh elicits loud moaning.

"Come on." Theo's arm circles my waist. "I want to show you something."

We merge into the buzz of people, their eyes too distracted by debauchery to clock our identities. Another stage holds a couple—the man restrained with leather cuffs and pinned to the bed.

I gulp as his back arches, exposing his asshole to the lube spread over it. The naked woman held above him flourishes a long, black-coloured instrument, trailing it down his spine.

I've googled enough to know what a dildo is. Brooklyn even

suggested I should buy one a few months back during one of our embarrassing conversations.

"Is she going to put that inside him?" I ask in a hush.

"She's going to wear it," Theo whispers back.

That's when I notice the belt attached to the base of the dildo. It's pulled around the woman's waist and fastened, positioning the shaft over her crotch.

I can't tear my eyes from the show. Her fingers are buried in her partner's ass, stretching him wide to receive the dildo's swell. He strains against the cuffs when she eases inside his rear.

"Oh my God," I breathe.

Theo stands behind me, his body pressing into my back. I can't help grinding against his hardening dick while watching the pair beginning to fuck for everyone to see.

"He seems to be enjoying it. I didn't know women could do that."

His breath is hot on my neck. "You'd be surprised. It's a pretty common fantasy, but no one talks about it for some reason."

"Have you ever done it?"

His silence answers me. Holy shit. I really don't know my blue-eyed book geek at all. That only increases my determination to understand the real Theo.

Thighs pressing together to ease the ache, I undulate against his cock rocking into my butt. The man is grunting loudly on stage, the cuffs keeping him pinned as he's fucked from behind.

A distant part of me wonders if I should be triggered by this, but the consenting agreement of these two adults is nothing like the depravity I watched. I can separate the two.

"Does watching them fuck turn you on?"

"Yes," I admit. "Am I ... supposed to do that to you?"

Theo's laugh is warm like molten caramel, oozing over my

heightened senses.

"Easy, angel. Let's learn to walk before we run."

Tugging on my hand, Theo makes me tear my gaze from the show. They've amassed quite the crowd. I want to watch what happens next, but the adjacent stage catches my eye.

Instead of a bed, there's a single chair placed in the middle. Ankles and wrists bound with thick ties, a brown-haired man is tightly restrained. It's the ball between his lips that shocks me.

"What is that?"

"A gag," Theo supplies.

"Doesn't it hurt?"

"No. It's a little uncomfortable."

He's being circled by a seasoned predator, inching ever closer to her kill. The woman's angelic, blonde hair brushes her lower back in a tumbling wave. It offers the only coverage for her naked body.

But it's the confident sway of her hips that fascinates me. She's lording herself over him, her gagged partner unable to utter a single word, though I doubt he'd protest.

When she unveils a silk tie, I watch her wind it around his head. He's tied, gagged and blindfolded. There is no greater state of surrender than the trust he's placing in her.

"You okay?" Theo checks.

I absently nod back. All I can think about is how much power she has right now. This man's life is held in the palm of her hand. I can see every ounce of confidence that power is imbuing her with.

"We can sit down if you want," he offers.

I'm steered over towards the nearest chair. Theo takes a seat then tugs me onto his lap. The welcome pressure of his cock returns.

"She's so stunning," I whisper in awe.

He sweeps hair over my shoulder. "Not a scratch on you, though."

We both watch as the woman kneels in front of her captive and takes his length deep into her mouth. She sucks his dick, bobbing up and down until it's glistening with saliva.

"How does she know if he's enjoying it?"

"There are rules." His arms squeeze my waist. "He can tap out at any time if it gets too much. There's an agreed upon signal."

Gorgeous curves rising, the woman spreads her legs on either side of his waist, holding her entrance above his erection. Her hand clenches around his throat before she sinks down on him.

"I know it looks scary, but this is what he needs. Total submission. And she needs that potent sense of power just as much."

Riding her partner's cock with bouncing strokes, her head is thrown back, and hair tumbles down her back in a glistening curtain.

She looks like one of God's precious angels, twirling in the devil's arms with a smile on her face. Liberation is her reward for embracing that sin.

"I want to be that formidable." I shift, relishing the thickening shaft beneath me. "No one could ever hurt someone as powerful as her."

Theo tugs my dress strap aside to kiss my shoulder. "I want to give you that power, beautiful. All of it and more."

His hand sneaks beneath my dress to cup my mound. I moan under my breath, glancing from side to side to check that no one is looking at us. We're all caught under the same spell.

Theo squeezes, his thumb circling my clit through the wet lace. I grind on his hardness, wanting a relief to all the excruciating tension that's built between us.

Pushing my panties slightly to the side, his finger eases between my folds to find my entrance. I have to bite my tongue to hold in a moan as he drives a digit deep inside my pussy.

"That's it, angel," he encourages. "Ride my fingers. No one is watching us, trust me."

I should be finding a quiet corner to die of embarrassment in, but the feeling never comes. All I want is to emanate the beauty in front of me, taking the pleasure she wants with zero apologies.

She's her own god.

I want to steal her confidence for myself and let it burrow beneath my skin. It's all there for the taking—power, control, confidence. There are no bars holding me captive now.

Lifting my hips, I gasp as Theo pushes a second finger into my slit. I'm so wet and wildly turned on, I can almost feel my pulse thrumming against the shell of my skin.

Every time his fingers thrust back into me, I move on his lap, deepening the intrusion. It feels so forbidden to be chasing an orgasm in front of strangers, but their eyes don't touch us.

Just as the woman I'm copying halts and screams out her own release, an orgasm barrels into me, hard and fast. The wave overwhelms me without warning.

I sink down on Theo's fingers and slap a hand over my mouth to silence the moan begging to escape. My entire body is tingling, but still, I want even more from him.

"Fuck, Harlow. You are the most stunning creature I've ever seen," he purrs underneath me. "Did my angel come?"

"Yes." I sigh happily.

"You're not done, are you?"

He slides his fingers out from beneath my dress then lifts them to his mouth before greedily sucking them clean. Holy hell.

"I've dreamed of tasting your juices for months," he rasps. "You're as sweet as promised."

"Theo," I pant. "Do we have a room or something?"

"I've booked one for the night."

"Take me there right now."

Standing on trembling legs, I lean heavily on him as we leave the show behind. The flashes of bare skin and a cacophony of moaning melt into insignificance. His hand in mine is all I can feel.

Through another set of doors, a long, carpet-lined corridor offers reprieve from the people. Door after door stretches down the hallway, all numbered.

Struck by desire so intense it blurs my vision, I seize a handful of Theo's shirt and slam him into the wall. My mouth attacks his with such violence, I hardly recognise myself.

Tongue breaking past his lips, I steal the breath from his lungs with each crazed second. Something has been ignited deep within me, kindling flames that promise to devour us both.

Hitching my dress up to my waist, Theo grabs my ass and lifts me up. I wrap my legs around his waist and let him carry me down the corridor, too busy sucking on his bottom lip.

Room twelve.

The snick of the lock turning cuts through my hunger, and I offer him a second to breathe. We're in our own private room, where another satin-covered bed fills the space.

On the panelled walls, two racks of equipment await my perusal. Everything is available—cuffs, ties, gags, whips ... too many toys to count. I don't recognise half of it.

"Woah."

"Everything is cleaned by the staff." Theo places me back on my feet. "It's part of the membership, so it's safe to use."

On him, my inner-demon finishes.

Seizing hold of that tiny voice that's vying for ownership, I let its darkness shroud me. There's no one watching now. I can risk dipping a toe into Theo's world.

Walking to the first rack, I drag my fingers over a red leather riding crop. "How many women have you brought here?"

He doesn't immediately answer.

Stroking a long purple dildo, I round on him. "Answer the question, Theodore, or this is going to end very quickly."

"Just Alyssa," he submits.

"And how many times have you visited here alone?"

"I used to come once a week before I met Alyssa. But never since her death."

Lifting a pair of thick leather cuffs from the wall, I test the weight in my hands. "You should have told me about this long ago."

He swallows hard. "Yes."

"So why didn't you?"

His eyes follow me over to the bed, the light blue depths almost entirely covered by the expanded black expanse of his pupils. I drop the cuffs on the bed and return to the rack.

"Theodore," I prompt.

"I … was afraid of losing you. Before we'd even met, I felt like I knew you." He hesitates, his voice cracking. "The day I handed you Laura's bone, I realised I loved you too."

And there it is.

The thing I've been waiting for.

Heart squeezing with emotion, I fight the urge to wrap myself around him. I've died a thousand deaths while waiting for those words to leave his mouth.

I didn't think a human heart could hold so much love until I met the guys and realised I could love four people equally, with enough left over to learn to love myself as well.

"Harlow?" he asks uncertainly. "Everything alright?"

"Yeah. Good."

Too curious for my own good, I select a ball gag next. It's smaller than the one the woman was using and a little less intimidating. It gets thrown on the bed.

I turn back to him. "Take your clothes off."

Theo obliges without hesitation, unbuttoning his shirt then sliding it off his sinewy shoulders. His trousers go next with his shoes, revealing the tented material of his black boxer shorts, where he stops.

"Didn't you hear me?" I snap, loving the thrill of being so demanding. "Everything off."

His mouth quirks with a smile. "Sorry."

Stepping out of his boxers, Theo stands completely naked. His cock is generous, smaller than Enzo and Hunter's terrifying lengths, but still a real handful.

Sliding the dress straps off my shoulders, I drag the flowy fabric down, exposing my lace underwear. He hums in appreciation but remains frozen in place.

"Lay on the bed," I instruct.

Theo's head dips in a nod. "Yes."

Positioning himself on the satin sheet, his eyes eat me up, noting every last angle on display. Attempting to embrace my newfound courage, I saunter over to him.

"How does this work? What do I do?"

"Whatever you want," he explains.

"The consent is implied?"

"If I need you to stop, I'll shake my head from side to side three times. Happy with that?"

My chest warms. "I'm happy."

Climbing onto the bed, I knee-walk to him, unclasping my bra in the process. My breasts fall free, and Theo licks his bottom lip.

"You're fucking perfect, Harlow."

Picking up the gag, I climb onto his lap to straddle him. "Quiet. I'm the only one allowed to talk now."

It feels foreign in my hands, but Theo's mouth opens, and he accepts the ball between his lips. I fasten the buckle at the back of his head then quickly mess up his hair.

"I hate this gel," I complain. "You look so handsome, but I prefer your curls all messy and wild."

He blinks in response.

Stroking a hand down his chiselled abdominals, I palm his cock then gently squeeze. His Adam's apple bobs tellingly.

"Do you want me to suck it?"

He blinks again.

"I can't hear you, so I guess it's my choice."

I swear, Theo smiles around the gag.

Pushing his shoulder, I lay him down then kneel between his legs. Uncertainty threatens to break my veneer of self-assuredness, but I quickly crush the feeling.

Tonight, I'm not Harlow Michaels.

I'm just … Harlow.

Whoever the fuck I want that to be.

His velvet shaft pushes past my lips to nudge the back of my throat. I suck my way down to his balls and cup the softness in one hand. Theo's hips buck upwards.

"No." I halt, licking my wet lips. "Still."

When he's stopped moving, I return to his length, taking it even deeper into my mouth. It's heady, the sense of empowerment I get from him obeying my commands.

Mouth popping off his dick, I pump his shaft and spread the stickiness of my salvia. All I can think about is finally feeling his cock filling me up, ending months of waiting.

"You made me wait." I sigh dramatically. "It's only fair that I do the same to you, don't you think?"

I have no idea what his blinking means this time, but I'm pretty sure he's acquiescing. Standing up, I hook my fingers into my panties then slowly drag them over my hips.

"Touch yourself, Theodore."

His hand dips between his legs to fist his cock. I watch him work his shaft for a moment. Tiny tremors quake across my skin at the sight.

When I bring my fingers to my pussy, I find slick warmth waiting. I'm still humming from the orgasm he teased out of me, and I easily slide two digits inside my entrance.

Theo's eyes are trained on me, watching every flick of my bud, thrust of my fingers and moan tearing free from my mouth.

The weight of his gaze is so sensual, I don't even need to feel his skin on mine. We're connected at this moment. The air between us is charged with our mutual longing.

Moving back to the bed, I pick up the leather cuffs, inspecting the supple material. They're thick and strong. Unbreakable. A lump gathers in my throat, but I swallow it down.

No fear.

I'm in control.

As I kneel next to him, Theo doesn't have to be told what to do. He offers me his wrists, holding them out to me like a peace offering. It feels eerie to be cuffing him.

I have to pause for a second, struggling with the brush of anxiety that brings. Theo touches my arm, his thumb circling in a silent soothe. He can read my hesitation from a mile off.

"I'm in control," I say aloud, needing the certainty to quash the memories. "I'm in control."

His stroking continues, reiterating my words. With the nerves dissipating, I tug his wrists into the cuffs then lift his arms above his head to the bed's metal railings.

After attaching the cuffs to the bed, I inspect my work. He's fully restrained, every line of supple, hair-dusted muscle exposed. Not a single word can escape his mouth.

"You pushed me away for so long," I scold. "All I wanted was to be yours, Theodore. In any way that you'd have me."

His legs spread as I settle above him to straddle his waist. I drag my nails down his torso, tracing the tantalising 'V' marking my target.

"I fell in love with you long before I allowed myself to admit it. The distance between us didn't matter to me."

Guiding the head of his cock to my entrance, I circle the tight slit, almost groaning at the exquisite torture. The relief is so close.

"It didn't matter because I love you too." I meet his gaze. "I'm tired of taking this slow. You complete me."

Taking his full length inside my cunt, I watch his eyes roll back in his head with pleasure. Fireworks explode inside me, revelling in the moment of pure satisfaction.

He's mine.

And I am his.

Lifting my hips, I push down on him, stealing every proud inch of his length. He stretches my walls, filling me to the brim with the perfect amount of pressure.

Cupping my breast, I tweak my nipple, loving the bite of pain. My hips rise and fall, finding a steady pace that strokes the wild, untamed animal inside of me that's beginning to find her voice.

I wish I could hear him, but the intensity reaches a boiling point without that line of communication. All I have are his upward thrusts, sliding deep into my pussy.

This is his surrender. His torn-out heart is being offered to me on a platter. He doesn't care what I do with it as long as I keep his trust safe, tucked safely inside where it can't be broken.

"I need more," I whine.

Riding him a little faster, each pump chases that elusive dose of ecstasy I can feel at the edges of my mind. It's on the cusp.

The increased pace intensifies the sense of fullness, his length surging into me at a bruising pace. More. More. There's no space left for doubt or hesitation in our relationship.

It's just us.

Forever.

Not even God can change that now.

With my climax nearing, Theo grants me control of every step closer to the edge we're both longing to dive off. I set the pace, the speed, the battering of our bodies.

All while his eyes stare up at me, filled with longing and the inevitability of his soul tangling with mine. I'm being worshipped and claimed in the same fell swoop.

Grabbing the gag's buckle, I quickly unfasten it then throw the ball aside. Trails of saliva spill from Theo's lips, but his ragged breaths don't last long before my lips seal on his.

Our mouths clash—silent, deadly, determined to paint the other in promises only our souls can keep. There's no taking this mutual branding back now.

"Are you close?" he growls into my mouth.

"Yes," I moan back. "I want you to fill me up."

Rutting into me, Theo steals the tiniest bit of power back and delivers the final, punishing blow. My orgasm hits me again, stronger this time, like a bulldozer demolishing any remaining lucidity.

I cry out his name, stilling to feel the rush of warmth that follows his seed spilling into me. He jerks beneath me, grunting through gritted teeth as his climax follows mine.

When my body feels too heavy to hold up, I slump onto his chest, my face hiding in the crook of his neck. Even without clothes on, his scent is still the same, like the pages of books are baked into him.

"Harlow," Theo heaves. "Fuck, angel."

Body humming with an incandescent sense of bliss, all I can do is groan a wordless response. I've gone boneless on top of him.

"Why didn't we do this six months ago?" he laughs.

Managing to lift my head, I grin back at him. "No idea. We wasted a hell of a lot of time reading books and trading theories."

"When we could have been fucking between the chapters?"

"Something like that."

Lifting myself off his chest, I unfasten the cuffs to release his wrists. Theo winces as he brings his arms down, working the blood back into his limbs.

"Are you okay?"

"I'm perfect." He cups my cheek, running a thumb over my bottom lip. "You're perfect. That was perfect."

And just like that, I'm a blushing fool all over again. I can't quite hold the strong, sexy persona in place, but she's still there. Biding her time beneath the surface.

"What I said earlier... I meant it. No more hiding. I love you, Harlow. And I'm all in. No matter what."

I'm not sure my body can hold the doubling of my heart. It's fit to burst with so much happiness, and I don't know what to do with it.

"I love you," I murmur back.

"Swear on it?"

Curling up on his chest, I kiss the throbbing vein at his neck, evidencing the organ that now beats solely for me.

"Yes. I fucking swear on it."

SCENE DU NOISE
I ROSE

CHAPTER 11

Harlow

HeartLESS – You Me At Six

Doctor Richards's attention is glued to the heavily laden pages of the notebook I surrendered to him almost an hour ago. He's barely come up for air, allowing his cup of tea to go cold.

"Harlow, this is really excellent stuff." He glances up. "When did you write all this?"

I fiddle with a loose thread in my cardigan. "After we found those bodies on the beach a couple of weeks ago. I didn't know how to deal with it, so I started writing instead."

"I'm glad that you found a healthy way to cope with how it made you feel. It must have brought up a lot of emotions."

"Yes, it did, but it also helped to get it all out."

"This is written as if to an audience. I wonder if you've given our last conversation some more thought?"

I anxiously twist my fingers together. "I'm not sure when I stopped writing for myself and started writing for someone else."

Richards nods. "Tell me why you wrote these words."

"I want the world to know that I'm not him," I say slowly. "We share the same blood, but we couldn't be more different."

"For a long time, you couldn't see that difference." He smiles broadly. "How does it feel to acknowledge it now? To release guilt that doesn't belong to you?"

"It feels … free."

He runs a finger over the indents in the paper where my handwriting grew manic. I wrote until my hand screamed in pain.

It's like this elemental energy took over, and all I could think about was spilling my guts on the page. With every word, I was chasing that freedom, determined to keep it in sight.

"So what now?"

"Enzo's warned me off publishing anything." I shrug, trying not to let my disappointment show. "Especially after that press conference."

"Is that so?"

"He thinks it's the wrong time, and it'll cause more harm than good."

"Enzo is allowed to have his opinions," Richards dismisses. "But he isn't my patient. I want to know what you think."

"I think I want to do it. The whole world is against us. How could telling my truth make things any worse than they already are?"

Placing the notebook down, Richards crosses his ankles. "Have you heard of the Chinese proverb that says break the kettles and sink the boats?"

"Uh, I don't think so."

"Soldiers going into battle burned all their supplies and escape routes, leaving no choice but to advance into enemy territory. In doing so, they won the war."

I retake the notebook and hug it to my chest. "I'm not sure I understand."

"Sometimes, we need risk in order to succeed. You're standing at that same crossroads right now. To burn or not to burn."

His words give me pause. Enzo suggested the exact same thing. The power of destruction is within my grasp if I want it.

"Set the world on fire," I whisper to myself. "That's what he said my story would do. You think I should do it anyway?"

Richards chuckles. "I'm your therapist, Harlow."

"So?"

"I can't tell you what to do, but I think you have the power to change the world with your words. You get to decide what to do with that power."

This risk could backfire and destroy what remains of our life here. People don't always want the truth—especially not if it's ugly. But if I don't tell it, I know I'll always live with regret.

To burn or not to burn.

The choice is mine.

A sharp rap on the door to our meeting room interrupts the session. The door slams open, and Brooklyn walks into the room. She stops still when she sees me.

"Oh, crap."

"Brooke!"

Throwing myself at her, it takes her a moment to break free from her automatic urge to recoil and finally hug me back.

"Hi."

"I've been calling and texting all week."

She releases me, her smile contrite. "I needed some time to get my head screwed back on after what happened."

"Are you feeling better?" I ask, searching her face.

"A little bit. I'm still off work for now."

Clearing his throat, Richards rises from his chair. "You're early,

Brooke. I never thought I'd see that day come."

"Sorry, doc. I didn't mean to interrupt."

"No bother. Shall I give you two a moment?"

I nod, prompting him to slip outside. With the door clicked shut, tears fill her silvery eyes and quickly spill over.

"I'm so sorry, Harlow. I didn't mean to scare you. When I have a relapse, I don't know that what I'm seeing and hearing isn't real."

"It's okay. We were just worried about you. I'm so sorry for breaking your trust. I didn't mean—"

"Hey," she cuts me off. "You're a good friend. I needed help, but I wasn't ready to admit that. I'm glad you guys tracked me down."

I'm so relieved, I hug her again. She laughs it off and lets me deposit her in my vacated chair. I crouch down next to her then rest a hand on her leg.

"What happened?"

"I told the guys everything," she explains. "We talked it through together as a family. With the wedding in three weeks, I guess everything got to me."

I swipe the moisture from her cheek. "Did you figure out what you're going to do?"

"I think so." A tentative smile blooms despite her tears. "We want to keep the baby."

Unable to stop myself, I squeal in excitement. I promised myself that I'd keep a straight face and support her no matter what, but it just slips out.

Brooklyn looks terrified still, but her smile is so darn wide. She seems like herself for the first time since we returned to England.

"You're going to be a mum." My own eyes burn with tears. "Oh my God. I'm going to be an auntie!"

"Hell yeah, you are. I'm not doing this shit without you."

"I can't believe it."

We embrace again, both choking on happy tears. Among all the pain and anguish, this is a glimmer of hope that our family needs.

"I have no idea what the fuck I'm doing."

"We'll figure it out." I squeeze her leg reassuringly. "Parenting can't be that hard, right? I'm sure there are books and crap on it."

"Trust me, Kade's already ordered them all. We've had boxes full of stuff arriving for days."

"You're kidding me?" I scoff.

"I wish. Kade was already a controlling asshole, but now he's monitoring my vitamin levels and meal planning."

I'm not even surprised. If she gets to the end of her pregnancy without murdering all of them, I'll take that as proof God does indeed grant miracles.

"Eli was the hardest to convince." She rubs her temples. "He's freaking the fuck out about being a parent. Neither of us had good examples to follow, more so than the others."

"Is he okay?"

"Not really, but we're working on it." Her hands move to cup her flat midsection. "We have to make this work, for the baby's sake."

A twinge of pain cuts across my chest. The whispered voice of a ghost sneaks in before I can halt its progress, like Richards has trained me to do.

I want my baby to live.

But not in this place.

I won't let him win.

Excitement wasn't a word I ever had cause to use in the basement, but watching Adelaide's belly grow with each passing day inspired hope in my soul for the first time in years.

That twisted hope only grew when she bled to death. When she died, I was given a glimpse of a way out from all the bloodshed.

It was the first time Michael had the doors of heaven slam shut in his face, no matter how loudly he screamed and begged for her baby to live so he could steal it for himself.

"Are you okay?" Brooklyn prods.

Snapping out of it, I force a smile. "Yeah. I should leave you to your session. I'm sure you have a lot to get your head around."

"Wait. You don't need to plaster a smile on for my sake, Harlow. Finding those bodies was seriously fucked up."

"Yeah," I deadpan.

"You want to talk about it?"

"I think I'm done talking." My grip on the notebook tightens. "It's time for me to do something about this. People need hope."

She rests a hand on top of mine. "I'm proud of you. I wish I was bringing my kid into a better world. You actually have the chance to make that difference."

"I think you're all overestimating me."

Brooklyn rolls her eyes. "Trust me, I don't overestimate anyone. People let you down less that way. You survived something truly harrowing. The world needs to know that hope is out there."

Patting her leg, I stand up before tucking my notebook back into my handbag. Richards waits outside the meeting room, but his back is turned to me.

"She's ready for you."

He doesn't respond, too busy staring down at the phone clasped in his hands. His shoulders are carved with tension.

I stop next to him. "Same time next week?"

Fear spikes through me at the pale pallor of his skin. It's like the life has been drained from his veins and overcome by shock instead.

"Is everything okay?"

My voice seems to startle him from his daze, and he slams the phone against his chest to hide the screen from me.

"Doctor Richards? What is it?"

"Harlow." His voice is a panicked wheeze, eyes darting from side to side. "I … uh. *Ahem.* Same time, that's fine."

"What were you looking at?"

"I … well, nothing."

The lie is painted all over his face.

"What is it?" I push him. "Is someone hurt?'

"It's just…"

With his mouth hanging open on another excuse, I snatch the phone from his hands. I can hear Brooklyn joining us, but I can't see beyond the live newsfeed in front of me.

"Harlow," Richards warns. "Don't look at that."

"What is this?" I whisper in terror.

The news is playing a video that's been sent to them. It's almost black, but the weak light of an underground room illuminates the haggard, bearded face staring back at me.

Even through a screen, his sick smile drips with evil. Michael looks thinner than the last time I found myself bloodied at his hand.

His grey hair is unwashed and limp, but his usual robes appear to be clean. There's something different about him, though.

"Hey." Brooklyn tries to grab the phone from me. "Come on, give me the phone. Let me check it first."

"No. It's him."

The malevolence behind Michael's smile isn't laced with his usual unholy intent. He looks smug. Confident, even. His eyes are gleaming bright, full of familiar, maniacal fire.

"Did she fool you all with her little act?" he cackles. "Poor, innocent Harlow, playing the victim for the whole world to see."

The video crackles, overtaken by a grey-scale clip of my now-infamous press conference, superimposed over his face. My voice is tinny over his laughter, the clips intermingling.

I won't stop until your judgement day comes.

You will repent and be punished.

"Will I?" Michael mocks. "I wonder, darling niece, what the world would think about your sob story if they knew the real truth."

I fight the urge to smash Richards's phone against the wall, over and over until that voice disappears from my consciousness. Worse still, I know this is being broadcast around the world.

Michael has broken cover.

We're being fed to the wolves.

"Sabre has been keeping a secret from you all," he continues gleefully. "I am not the one you should be worried about. They're protecting a cold-blooded killer."

"Okay, enough," Richards interrupts. "I think you should stop watching. He's trying to get in your head—"

"No," I interrupt.

"She has branded me a monster for enacting the Lord's mercy." Michael tuts under his breath. "The only killer here is you, Harlow. You're the only one with blood on your hands."

I feel like the floor falls out from beneath my feet, leaving me to plummet to my death. Richards's hand grabs my forearm to stop me from slumping. I'm unable to tear my eyes from the screen.

He's gone.

Another video plays.

Even from the strange angle, offering a bird's eye view of the basement, I recognise the cage where I spent so many years of my life. Shadows stretch across the walls and floor, but two figures are clear.

"No," I moan. "No, no, no."

Laura lies still in an expanding puddle of blood while a thinner, dirtier version of myself strains to reach between the rusted iron bars to strangle the life from her lungs.

Wringing.

Twisting.

Squeezing.

I choked her until her jerking limbs stilled. On the phone screen, I watch myself flinch away from my friend's corpse, curling into a tight, sobbing ball on the floor.

The phone falls from my hands, hitting the thick carpet with a thud. That moment is permanently charred on my mind, haunting every breath I've taken since I murdered Laura.

"We all know who the killer is here." His voice echoes from the dropped phone. "Behold, the real Harlow Michaels."

The worst part is he's right. This is the real me. The bare, stripped-back, animalistic version of myself he made me into.

"Is this a person you want to protect?" Michael taunts. "Will you believe the lies she tells about me? She is a cold-blooded killer."

"Where the hell did he get that video?" Brooklyn snarls.

I swallow the acid searing my vocal cords. "He must've been filming in the basement. I had no clue."

"You wanted to fight me," the voice continues. "I will bring a war to your doorstep. Nothing will stop me from completing my mission. You've been warned."

The buzz of reporters reacting to the footage melts into the background. I'm trembling with rage. I won't accept his guilt. Never again. He's the evil one here.

"Harlow." Brooklyn strokes a hand down my arm. "You need to stay calm. We can fix this."

I brush her aside. "I am calm."

Richards eyes me apprehensively. "You are?"

Ignoring both of their stares, I pick up the fallen phone and offer it to Richards. He gingerly takes it, preoccupied by studying me.

"If Michael wants a war, then that's exactly what he'll get. I refuse to spend another moment of my life feeling guilty for his crimes."

Richards tucks the phone into his pocket. "What are you going to do?"

"Give the people what they want." I tap the notebook tucked in my handbag. "He will have no supporters left by the time I'm done telling the truth. This is a fight I'm going to win."

Darkness fills Brooklyn's gaze. "He's going to come for us all. This won't be a pretty fight. Are you ready for that?"

Courage steels my spine.

"Bring it on."

CHAPTER 12

Leighton

Pirate Song – Mehro

My punch connects with Harlow's ribcage, and she hisses out in pain. Drawing back, I dance around her on light feet. Her hands are curled into fists and waiting for an opening to clock me.

"Again!" Enzo shouts.

"I'm trying!" she yells back. "He's too fast."

Ducking low, I snake an arm around her waist and use it to flip her over. She smacks into the workout mat, and the air is knocked from her lungs with a grunt.

"Or you're just too slow." I loom over her. "You're not concentrating, Goldilocks. Focus your mind."

"I am fucking focused."

"No. You're still thinking about that video. Focus!"

Straying too close while lecturing her, I'm late to dodge her hand that snaps out to catch my ankle. She wrenches me off balance, using her weight to send us both tumbling across the mat.

"Focus *your* mind," Harlow growls back. "I'm concentrating just fine."

Manoeuvring herself on top of me, her fist draws back for the perfect strike. She halts the killer punch at the last second, and her knuckles scrape my nose.

"You can't pull your punches in real life."

"Do you want me to break your nose?" she smarts. "And ruin such a pretty view?"

"Aw. You think I'm pretty?"

Pacing the edges of the room, Enzo glowers at us both. "Stop fucking flirting, and beat his ass. I'm not training you to have morals."

With a grin lighting her lips, Harlow draws back her fist then clips me in the face. It's a tamer blow than the one she pulled, but it still makes my teeth rattle together.

"Better." Enzo crouches down to eye us both. "Again."

After scrambling to our feet, we resume our dangerous dance, circling one another like predators on the hunt. She's been training with Enzo for months, and his hard work has paid off.

Our little Harlow isn't a timid, broken wallflower anymore. She's managed to hold her own for forty-five minutes of fighting, and I haven't gone easy on her.

"Getting tired, Goldilocks?" I taunt her.

She wipes sweat from her forehead. "Hell no."

Lashing out, my kick connects with her torso. She grunts in pain, folding over to cushion the blow. Enzo threatened death if I wasted his time, so I've got to at least act like I want to hit her.

Although I can't lie … the look on her face when she punched me so hard I spat blood turned me on so fucking much.

"Come on. You gonna wimp out on me? I expected better."

"Fuck you, Leigh," she hisses.

"Not until you finish the job, princess."

Harlow lunges towards me and moves so fast, I can't stop her from jabbing her fist into my throat. She rises to her full height then pulls her fists back up to go again.

"Good! Advance," Enzo orders.

There's no time to retreat before she's on me—strike after strike, her knee smashing into my stomach, an elbow in my ribs. I collide with the weight bench and almost trip over it.

Her teeth are bared in a grimace, but her attack doesn't let up. She leaps on top of me, her legs trapping my waist in a vice. When her knuckles crack into my cheek, I spit more blood on the floor.

"Do you relent?" she gasps.

Grasping her ponytail, I yank hard and force her head to tilt up to me. She grits her teeth against the pain, letting me capture her lips in a furious kiss before I release her hair.

"Do you?" I mimic.

"Never."

With a huff, I heave her from my lap and flip us around so her back meets the smooth leather of the weight bench.

"So be it."

Settling between her splayed legs, my hips rock into hers, mere millimetres of sweaty fabric keeping me from fucking her senseless while Enzo watches the show.

I'm not particularly shy, and if it pisses him off, then even better. I'll fill his precious girl with my come and make him watch as she swallows a mouthful of my cock.

"Surrender. I win."

"You son of a bitch," she spits.

Each shift of her gorgeous curves hardens my dick. I'm pressed right up against her heat, desperate to slide into her wet cunt. Cheeks coloured pink, she looks sexy as hell right now.

"This wasn't part of the training," Enzo complains from across the room. "Take your hands off *my* woman before I remove them with a blunt knife."

"Why don't you go find that knife while I make Harlow come a few times?" I retort. "Then you can do whatever you want."

"Do I not get a say in this?" Harlow sighs.

With an eyebrow quirked, I grab the mound of her hot, soaked pussy through her leggings. She can't help but react and digs her nails into my biceps.

"You don't want me to bend you over this bench and slide my cock inside your tight little pussy?" I sneer in her face.

"No," she whines.

"I don't believe you."

Something tells me I could make her come just by whispering filth in her ear. I will die without a single complaint as long as I'm buried between her thighs, making her body sing.

Enzo crouches down on Harlow's other side, scraping his eyes over her tight clothing and the obvious pebbling of her nipples that poke through her pink sports bra.

"She looks fucking good, doesn't she?" he muses.

Still cupping her cunt, I squeeze gently. "She'd look even better without these stupid clothes on. You got a preference, Enz? Front or back?"

"I've wanted to fuck her tight backside for months." Enzo runs a fingertip over her chest, circling both nipples. "What do you think, little one?"

"I-I've never d-done that," she stammers.

"We can help you," I purr, shifting my crotch against her core. "It takes some preparation, but I can just imagine your perfect tits bouncing while we fuck both of your holes."

"Amen to that," Enzo agrees.

Grabbing her leggings, I tug them down her legs then toss them over my shoulder. She's wearing a scrap of drenched cotton, the fabric white against her slim, tanned legs.

"Were you this wet when you fucked Theo?" I wonder.

"Leigh!" she exclaims. "I am not answering that."

"I want to hear all the details. What did you do to him, huh? Was it some freaky shit?"

"We are not discussing this!"

Enzo takes over to slide her panties down. With the scrap of fabric bunched in his fist, he brings it to his nose and inhales deeply.

"I can smell just how much you want it," he comments with a smirk. "A few dirty words and you're soaked for us."

Harlow blushes red. "I can't help it. I'm sorry."

I deliver a sharp slap to her now bare cunt. Her back arches as her mouth falls open on a gasp.

"Never apologise for that," I berate.

Enzo nods in agreement. "Not unless you want us to punish you."

"P-Punish me?" she gasps.

A dark smile in place, Enzo looks up at me. "Shall we?"

"Be my guest, man."

While I haven't shared with Enzo before, I'm not going to turn down the opportunity. Even if it entails seeing his bare backside and dick. It's nothing I didn't see in prison. I can deal.

Gripping her sports bra, Enzo yanks it over Harlow's head, allowing her tits to spill out. He kisses across her chest, sucking a nipple between his teeth.

"Enz," she moans. "Fuck."

Enzo traces her lip, pushing his thumb into her mouth. "I want to push your boundaries, little one. Mind if I play a little rough?"

"Please do."

I step back to give him some room. Enzo studies the wall of supplies in our basement gym, and when he pulls the long, rubber length of a skipping rope from a hook, my interest piques.

Harlow looks equal parts fascinated and nervous, but she doesn't freak out. Not even when he tugs her to stand up from her splayed-out position on the bench, her entire frame bare.

"Do you trust us?" Enzo demands. "I'm not doing this if there's even a crack of doubt, so tell me straight."

She licks her lip. "I trust you both with my life."

"Give me your wrists, then."

Surrendering to him, Enzo loops the skipping rope around her wrists in a perfect sliding knot. He drops a kiss on her shoulder before holding her hips to boost her up into the air.

The rest of the rope is wound around the high, metal frame of the workout equipment. Tied in another knot, Harlow is left suspended, her arms above her head and tiptoes brushing the floor.

Enzo steps back to admire his handiwork. "That's a hell of a sight. What do you think, Leigh?"

"Fucking perfect."

"She's all ours."

"You want to go first?" he invites.

"Go ahead. I want to see her writhe while you fuck her senseless."

Enzo snickers. "That can be arranged."

Harlow hangs helplessly while we talk, barely able to hold herself up. The entire length of her scar-laden body is exposed to us both. She can't even attempt to cover herself.

The old slashes that carve the Holy Trinity into her torso are more faded than her newer scars, including the bright-pink, taut lines where that asshole Abaddon started to carve her up.

Even covered in more scar tissue than skin, she's the single most beautiful sight in the whole goddamn world. Every mark is evidence of her sheer resilience and determination to survive.

Harlow Michaels is a lioness.

Our fucking lioness.

"Guys," Theo shouts from upstairs, his voice breaking the moment. "You need to come and see this."

"We'll be right there," Enzo calls back.

But he doesn't move. He's far too busy circling Harlow's prone form, devouring every part of her with his eyes. When he smacks her ass, she vaults in the air.

"Oh God!"

"You can't hide from us like this," he teases. "We can do whatever we want to you now. This is your punishment."

"More," she pleads.

"You want me to spank you again, baby girl?"

Harlow nods, biting her lip in earnest. "Yes."

"What did I tell you before?"

"Yes, sir," she recites.

Fuck. Me.

That's so hot.

She cries out again when he slaps her ass. My cock twitches with need at the sight.

"Good girls get spanked when they ask nicely," Enzo taunts. "But if you want me to let you come, you'll have to beg."

"Please," she immediately begs.

"Not yet, baby. Be patient."

His hand strikes her left breast, and blood rushes to the area, leaving a mark on her skin. She whimpers, the sound sending heat rushing straight to my painfully hard cock.

"I want you to ride my face."

"What?" Harlow breathes.

Growling to himself, he lifts her legs then encourages them to wrap around his neck. She's suspended at the best height for his mouth to access the folds of her cunt.

Gripping her ass cheeks, Enzo buries his face between her thighs. I slip a hand inside my shorts to find my shaft. This is hot as fuck to watch. Even if he's the one eating her sweet pussy instead of me.

"Didn't you hear him?" I recapture her attention. "Ride his face, princess. Move your hips, and let his tongue fuck your hole."

Fingers curling around the rope at her wrists, Harlow lifts herself, using her legs around his neck for balance. She pushes her pussy into him and slowly begins to gyrate.

Her eyes find mine. "Like … this?"

"Perfect," I praise.

Enzo laps at her centre, his mouth attacking her heat like he's a starving man gifted his first meal in months. I can hear how turned on she is by the wet smack of his lips devouring her.

"Enzo," she cries out.

He pauses for a breath. "Come on, beautiful girl. I want you to squirt your juices all over my face."

Diving back into his meal, he attacks her with the kind of ravenous need that only Harlow can inspire. Everything about her innocent, untouchable demeanour makes her irresistible.

She's gorgeous without even realising it, and there is nothing more attractive than that. I've been with my fair share of women, and none of them compared to the goddess caught between us four idiots.

Still grinding herself against his mouth, Harlow finds her rhythm. Her hips move faster, and Enzo can't get enough, holding her ass tight as he sucks on her clit.

I fist my cock and stroke, base to tip, imagining Harlow's pert pink lips wrapped around me instead. I'll wait for my turn. The sight of her riding Enzo's face is worth my patience.

Pushing a thick finger inside her slit, Enzo works her cunt into a drenched furnace. Every time he circles her nub, she throws her head back, and a guttural noise erupts from her mouth.

"I'm almost there."

"Good girl," Enzo approves.

I have no doubt that Theo can hear her falling apart as he works in the kitchen above us. Let him listen. This incredible creature is ours to toy with as we please.

Shuddering through the waves of her climax, Harlow's legs tighten around his neck. She guides herself to a peak and screams out his name.

When she's still, Enzo lifts his head and gulps down air. There's moisture scored across his mouth and cheeks, evidencing her orgasm. He dives in for a lip-smacking kiss so she can taste herself.

Harlow doesn't bat an eye, stealing her own come back with each stroke of their tongues colliding. She kisses over his lips and cheeks, her tongue flicking out to cleanse him.

"That's my perfect girl." Enzo nuzzles her neck. "You did good."

I love watching Harlow when she's feeling embarrassed. It's hilarious. The way she wraps herself in innocence to disguise the curious demon rearing its head within her is so hot.

"Guys!" Theo yells again. "This is urgent. You can screw each other later. Get up here."

Still fisting my dick, I consider putting a bullet between Theo's eyes. As we discovered in Costa Rica, the little shit has an uncanny ability to act as a cockblock at the worst possible moments.

"Move," I snap.

Pushing past Enzo, I'm still pumping my shaft. Harlow's widened blue eyes watch me approach, and she wiggles in the air when I stop in front of her.

"Leigh," she whispers.

"I know, Goldilocks. I want to fuck you right now, but Captain Cockblock calls, so we're gonna have to pick this up another time."

Seizing her hip, I shove my face in the swell of her tits. Her high-pitched groan when I bite down on her rosy bud finishes me off. I can't hold it in for a second longer.

Squeezing my length, I explode all over her belly and legs. Harlow holds steady, letting me paint her in my seed.

"Oh my God."

Stifling a laugh, I hold her up to relieve the pressure on her wrists. "Sorry. I couldn't stop myself."

Running my finger over the slope of her stomach, I collect a sample of come then lift it to her lips. She doesn't even fucking hesitate before accepting the gift and licking my finger clean.

This girl.

This motherfucking *queen*.

Pulling off my T-shirt, I use it to wipe the stickiness from her body then loosen the rope from her wrists. Harlow slumps in my arms, her body still trembling as I place her on her feet.

"You good, baby?"

"Uh-huh," she hums back.

Her eyes flick over to Enzo. Even I can see the strain against his black workout shorts. He's struggling to contain himself.

"Go on." I push her towards him. "I'll go upstairs and keep Theo occupied until you're done. Make it quick, though."

"I can do quick," Enzo affirms.

Harlow nods. "Me too."

Leaving my ruined T-shirt on the floor, I swipe the hair from my face and head for the stairs. A glance over my shoulder reveals Harlow bent over the workout bench as Enzo settles at her rear.

I can't resist watching for a few seconds—my cock is getting hard again already. Harlow slaps a hand over her mouth to remain quiet as Enzo pushes into her slit from behind.

"Hold on," he warns.

Pinning her against the bench, his huge hands cup her breasts while spearing her cunt. He's like a fucking wild animal. That bench is going to break in half if he moves any faster.

Jesus Christ.

What I wouldn't give to pin her sexy body in a sandwich between us. I wouldn't mind rubbing dicks with Enzo if it means I can fill every available hole she has to offer.

Repositioning my dick, I emerge upstairs. In the kitchen, Theo and Hunter are sitting at the dining table. I can hardly see them through the stacks of case files.

They're working on the connection between each of the thirteen suicides. Four are from the same church parish, while the others were based in nearby cities and towns.

"Only me. They're just finishing up."

Theo snorts. "So I can hear."

"You were listening?"

"Kinda hard not to."

Grabbing a bottle of water from the fridge, I take a second to admire Harlow's hard work in the past few weeks. This place looks brand new.

The whole open-plan kitchen and living room has been refreshed, courtesy of several long days spent decorating. Her clean white lines, black accents and burnt orange paint really did the trick.

"Leigh," Theo calls. "Come look at this."

"What is it?"

"I've got something."

"You managed to trace the origin of that video?" I guess.

"He was sloppy this time," he confirms. "I've decrypted the metadata and triangulated a location for the source. It correlates with four of the connected suicide victims."

Blood roaring in my ears, I race over to the table to look over his shoulder. Hunter's sitting to his left, his eyes racing over the laptop screen.

Even Lucky has perked up from her snoozing under the table. She's still attached to us at every available opportunity and demanding cuddles whenever we have a spare second.

"We've got him this time," Hunter declares.

"*Maybe*," Theo replies with sign language. "*Fake?*"

He shrugs. "Only one way to find out if it's authentic."

The intricate, black-and-white map on Theo's laptop is reminiscent of something from a movie. Major cities, busy motorways and the red spots of surveillance feeds are laid out.

Theo highlights the coordinates he's located, magnifying the location embedded in the data behind the video. By retaliating to Harlow's threat, Abaddon has shown his hand.

"Tregaron?" I read off the screen. "That can't be right."

Theo rubs his eyes behind his glasses. "It's a quiet market town. Perfect place to hide. That video looked like it was shot in a basement or crypt."

Finger tapping the search area, Hunter narrows his eyes. "There. Is that a church?"

Nodding, Theo is preoccupied by pulling up the government's

curated list of church parishes. If this piece of shit is hiding anywhere, it'll be there. The rural location is a great disguise.

"We need to dispatch a team immediately." Hunter pulls his phone out to fire off text messages. "Who knows how long he's planning to remain there?"

I grab his wrist to still him and mouth, "Already gone?"

"Thong?"

"*GONE*," I enunciate.

"What if Michael is already gone?"

I nod in confirmation.

"Well, then at least we can pick up his tail easier," he muses. "This is still a solid lead."

How he still has the strength to be so damn optimistic, I'll never know. I can't stand to think about how long we've wasted on Michael Abaddon and this endless wild goose chase.

In less than five minutes, Theo pulls together a bare bones profile on Tregaron's church. Registered clergy, public finances, affiliated members, the works.

"Jesus, Theo. You should do this for a living."

"Hilarious," he says dryly.

"How do you dig this information up?"

"I could tell you the colour of the royal family's underpants if I had enough time. This is a piece of cake."

"People would pay good money for that information."

"Huh. Maybe a career change is in order."

"You hate the royal family."

He snorts. "People can't afford to put clothes on their kids' backs. We don't need a throne made of gold."

Theodore Young—closeted anarchist and the voice of reason in this backwards fucking country. We really must be in the end times if he's talking politics.

Harlow's red-tinged face appears from the gym first, walking with an ever so slight limp. Her ponytail has fallen out, spilling curling hair over her shoulders, the flyaways stuck to her forehead.

"What is this, the walk of shame?" Hunter chuckles.

Closing the door to the basement, Enzo pins him with a glare. It only makes him laugh even harder. They couldn't be more obvious.

Harlow glows an even brighter shade of violent-red. "Can we move on? Theo, what have you found?"

"We've got a possible location."

Theo tilts the laptop screen so she can study the small search radius. Hunter's poised to intervene if she shows even a crack of panic.

None of us expect her to be eerily calm and devoid of emotion when she looks up from the laptop and finally responds.

"Let's go get this son of a bitch."

SCÈNE DU ROSE
192

CHAPTER 13

Harlow

HOPE – NF

T he hum of the helicopter drowns out the sound of my erratic heartbeat. Even with headphones in place to protect my ears, I can feel each frantic flap of the rotors taking us over the Welsh border.

In the seat next to me, Hunter's cocoa eyes are lit with anticipation. He's clinging to the edge of his seat, his palpable excitement held back by nothing but his belt.

I tap his shoulder then sign, *"Are you okay?"*

His mouth stretches in a smile. "I can feel it."

"What?"

"The helicopter." He rests a palm against the door. "I can feel the rotors beating. It's almost like I can hear again."

I'd forgotten how handsome he is when smiling from ear-to- ear. I love every version of Hunter, but this is the person who stole my heart. Pieces of him are coming back to life.

Dressed in a pressed, white shirt, his favourite leather holster and a suit jacket rolled up to show off his tattooed forearms, Hunter looks every inch the heartless businessman who found me in the hospital.

But this time he wears a bulletproof vest on top. Enzo threatened extreme violence if Hunter refused to wear it. He's taking no more risks with his best friend's safety.

"It's like I can taste it," he says in wonderment. "The vibrations are running through me, but I can't hear the sound. My other senses are piecing it together."

He can hear it then.

Only in his own, unique way.

I lean close and speak slowly so he can read my lips. "Sounds like?"

The look he offers me is pure magic.

"The best fucking thing I've ever heard."

An invisible hand clenched around my throat, I grab his shoulder and slant my mouth against his. I want to swallow his happiness and lock it in a strong box, where he can't dismiss it again.

This is living.

He's still capable of it.

After lifting the case at his feet, Hunter scans his thumbprint on the concealed pad and clicks it open. Inside, nestled in black foam, is a compact handgun that's far fancier than the one I've trained with.

"For you," he says simply.

I frown at him.

"You've been training hard for months." Hunter lifts the gun. "This is your graduation present."

"*Really?*" I sign.

"Just don't shoot me. I'm full of holes as it is."

Fingers spasming with excitement, I eagerly accept the gun. It feels perfect in my hands—not too heavy, the grip melded to my palm.

I check the magazine to ensure the safety is clicked on before aiming it at the helicopter's metal wall, finding the perfect aim that's been drilled into me.

"You look good with it," he compliments.

I kiss him deeply, despite the pilot sitting metres in front of us. We're minutes from touchdown to meet the others, but I don't care. Every second with Hunter is precious after almost losing him.

Tapping my fingers to my chin, I push them forward, signing *thank you*. His lips curve in another heart-stopping smile, all lit up for me.

"You're welcome," he whispers back.

The pilot's voice buzzes through my headset, warning of impending touchdown. I settle in my seat and let Hunter strap a sleek leather leg holster to my cargo-covered thigh.

"You're all set, sweetheart."

Slotting the gun into place, he drops a kiss at my temple. I'm kitted out just like one of them, mirroring Enzo in my all-black ensemble and matching bulletproof vest.

"Nervous?" Hunter murmurs.

I shake my head.

"It's okay if you are. This is your first active operation. I was shit scared during my first raid."

Holding his hand in mine, I draw circles on his palm, realising just how calm I feel. After so much torment, it's like my mind has finally decided that enough is enough.

Descending through the cover of night, the darkness of Wales's rolling hills greets us. We cruise above shadowed farmland and countryside, all concealed by the lack of city lights.

From our research, we know the picture-perfect town of Tregaron is nestled amongst steep hills and white-painted cottages. It's a quiet market town, unassuming and quaint.

The perfect hideout.

This better be it.

"There." Hunter leans over my shoulder to point. "Church."

The two glossy black helicopters embossed with Sabre's logo descend ahead of us, circling the arched turrets of an old, medium-sized church. The structure is lit by flashing blue lights.

Theo used his terrifyingly fast computer skills to locate the council's clerk and contact him, granting us permission to land in a farmer's field at the edge of the village.

The town's local police force is awaiting our arrival. A cordon has already been established, ensuring that no one enters or escapes. If there are people inside that church, they're trapped.

After touching down, we step out into the swaying crops to join the others. Becket and Enzo disembark from the left helicopter, leaving Hudson, Kade and two other agents to jump from the last.

"Harlow."

Hunter taps my shoulder, his palm outstretched. I take the tiny, nude-coloured earpiece then slot it into place. He checks it before pulling my ponytail over my shoulder.

"You're my ears tonight."

"No pressure," I mutter to myself.

"Hmm? I didn't catch that."

Plastering a weak smile into place, I nod instead. "I said *okay*."

"No, you didn't. Don't lie." Leighton's disembodied voice speaks into my ear. "You read me, princess?"

"Copy that. We've arrived safely."

Another familiar voice joins him and whispers straight into my brain. It's like I'm carrying them around with me.

"Be careful," Theo cautions. "We're keeping surveillance from above. No heat signatures or signs of life."

"Michael isn't here?"

"He could still be underground."

The hum of a drone passing above us marks his words. Theo's eyes and ears are everywhere, even from his office two hundred miles away. He doesn't need to be here to be deadly.

"I see you," he offers.

I wave up at the drone. "Hi."

"You look good, beautiful. Nice holster."

Playfully wiggling my leg for the drone to spot, I blow him a kiss. "Thanks. Little graduation present."

"Suits you."

Enzo races to my side, searching over me with a tension that only I can read on his schooled expression. He notes the gun strapped to my thigh and nods to assure himself.

"You like it?"

I tap the holster. "Love it."

"We chose it especially for you. There's a sensor in the grip. It's coded to scan your fingerprints, so only you can fire it."

"Seriously? That's awesome."

"You're welcome," Theo speaks into my ear. "I designed the tech myself. Consider it a precaution."

"Thanks, Theo. Very thoughtful."

"Fuck roses and chocolates, right?" he chuckles. "Women want martial arts lessons and guns to shoot us idiots with."

"You're right there."

"Police have a cordon up, the place is surrounded," Leighton cuts in. "No way in or out. If Abaddon's in there, he's ours."

I study the flash of blue lights, with numerous urgent voices wafting through the night from the crime scene up ahead. Judgement day has arrived for my uncle.

The prospect of coming face-to-face with Michael again should put the fear of God in me. Instead, I'm almost salivating with the need to see him cuffed and humiliated.

Before I can take off, Enzo snatches my arm. "Not so fast. The only reason you're not grounded with Brooklyn is the fact that I've trained you myself. Watch your six, and be careful."

"Brooklyn's pregnant," I lash back. "You trained her yourself too."

"Want me to stick a fucking baby in you? I'll do it right here. At least then I'll have a reason to lock your ass down, safe at home."

"So romantic."

"It could be," he combats.

"We can hear everything you're saying," Theo hisses into our earpieces. "Threaten to impregnate Harlow again and I'll be forced to crash a ten-thousand-pound drone into your head."

"And be thankful my brother is deaf, or you wouldn't live long enough to put a bullet in our target," Leighton adds cheerfully.

"No impregnations today, then," I surmise.

Shrugging off Enzo's grip, I shake the hand that Becket offers to me. He claps my shoulder, also noting the weapon on my thigh with a pleased grin.

"You're looking well, Harlow."

"Thank you. Where are Ethan and the others?"

He slots his earpiece into place. "Mexico. We're running a sting on a human trafficking ring with connections to big players in London and the States."

"Mexico?" I whistle. "That's far out."

"Ethan's boyfriend introduced us to a victim living in a town not far from here called Briar Valley. She's helping our investigation bring down the assholes trafficking kids on our fucking doorstep."

"Sounds like a hell of a woman."

"She really is." He smiles. "You'd like her. I'll introduce you guys sometime."

"Alright," Enzo barks. "Let's move out."

After clambering through the stalks of corn, we emerge on the nearby road, moving across in a tight formation. Several police cars are parked outside the church with flashlights marking the perimeter.

Enzo walks ahead to shake the nearest outstretched hand. Dressed in an ill-fitting suit that barely contains his potbelly, the grey-haired man who greets him scans over us all.

"Mr Montpellier, I presume?"

"Detective," Enzo answers. "Any trouble?"

"Not a peep. We spoke to Father Yule. Evening prayers finished at six o'clock, and he left an hour after. Door's unlocked."

"Is the scene secure?"

"No one's entered or left."

When Enzo moves to walk past him, the detective shoots out an arm, preventing him from passing.

"We've seen that video circulating in the news." His eyes stray over to me. "Seems to me like the person you should be investigating is standing right there."

"We don't have time for this." Enzo scowls at him. "Unless you'd like to explain to the Prime Minister himself why you allowed our suspect to escape, I suggest you step aside."

"You can't barge into my jurisdiction and—"

With a snarl, Hunter flashes past us both and seizes the detective by his shirt. He hauls him so close their noses brush, and the frosty bite of his voice sets my teeth on edge.

"This is our crime scene," he hisses. "Step aside before I do something I won't regret in front of all your men."

"Just who do you think you are?"

Hunter's very limited patience snaps, despite not being able to hear the asshole's remark. Enzo yells at him to stop just as he clocks the detective in the face.

"Motherfucker!" the detective howls.

"I did warn you," Hunter drones. "We're in charge now."

Taking my hand into his, he yanks me past the stunned faces of several police officers. I've seen Hunter in action before, but he's well and truly done with bullshit now.

God help us all.

"What happened?" Leighton asks urgently.

"Your brother punched a detective."

"Jesus Christ. Keep an eye on him."

"Copy that."

With agents flanking us on both sides, we duck beneath the cordon and approach the church. Enzo and Hunter both have their guns raised, leaving Hudson and Kade to watch their backs.

Keeping my weapon in place, I straighten my spine and lead the group. With the sheer weight of highly-trained muscle behind me, I can put one foot in front of the other without fear.

"Careful, Harlow." Enzo checks the entrance before gesturing for me to go ahead. "Stay sharp. Don't forget your training."

"Do you want to go first?"

"No. You've got this."

Fuck, if that doesn't feel good to hear. The lazy smile he offers me seals the deal. I need a repeat of our sexy gym session after this.

Breath held, I twist the ornate knob to creak open the church's arched door. Pitch-black darkness and the dampness of stone floors awaits, laden with the scent of burned candles.

"Flashlights," Enzo instructs.

Bright beams of light cut through the suffocating darkness. Stepping into the devil's lair, I glance around. It's a fairly small church, with a few dozen carved pews presided over by an altar.

The air is deathly still. Too still. No signs of life break the shadows draped over the furniture and gleaming crucifixes. Fanning out, the guys scour the place in less than a minute.

"Clear," Hudson shouts.

"Nothing here," I relay into my earpiece. "You guys see anything?"

"Negative," Theo replies. "Check the crypt. You'll lose us underground, but we're keeping watch from above."

"Be careful," Leighton adds.

"We will, Leigh."

"You fucking better, Goldilocks."

Enzo points to the iron gate holding the stairs leading beneath the church. With a nod, Hunter ducks in front of him to lead. The gate creaks as it's wrenched open, unveiling our next stop.

Most churches have crypts beneath them, especially the old ones. The basement where I spent my childhood was thankfully empty of gravestones or ancient corpses. Only fresh ones graced its halls.

I snatch Hunter's arm to stop him. "Wait."

He glances at my mouth, confused.

"I hear something."

His brows furrow. "You what?"

Stopping beside us, Enzo's head is cocked. "I hear it as well."

There's a tinny sound echoing up the steps leading into the inky-black depths. I quickly sign a warning to Hunter. He cocks his gun, nodding and taking a tentative step into the unknown.

Step.

Step.

Step.

We inch farther into the belly of the beast. The sound morphs from a distant whisper to the scratching melody of a gospel song being played. Terror inches up my spine.

Those awful songs were the soundtrack to many clean-up sessions. Mrs Michaels loved a soundtrack to accompany her work. It was the only time I ever saw a phone.

"He's playing music."

Enzo's big hand lands on my shoulder. "I'm right behind you, baby. He won't get a chance to hurt you again."

"Swear it?" I ask, feeling insecure.

"On my damn life. You won't let him."

His implicit trust in my new skill set propels my feet forward. I can confront the devil with Enzo propping me up every step of the way. He won't let me fall, but if I do, I know he'll follow me.

With flashlights illuminating the thick dust of the crypt, the bodies behind us fan out, ready to fire off a shot at any moment. My heart leaps into my throat when light sweeps over the back corner.

The phone is resting on top of a large, rusted, blue barrel, surrounded by several others. Voices intermingle, reaching a harmony and ending the song on a high note.

The Lord has heard my plea.

The Lord accepts my prayer.

Humble yourselves under the mighty hand of God.

In my mind, the unknown voices meld into one that's deep and booming. I can hear him in my head, his sadistic laugh echoing on a loop. He has to be here. We can't have lost him again.

"Fan out," Enzo orders.

In less than a minute, the crypt is declared clear. No trace of our demon. But when the song crackles, its symphony interrupted by the lash of laughter, my hackles raise.

"Did you really think it would be that easy?" Michael cackles through the speaker. "I'm disappointed. I thought taking down the almighty Sabre Security would at least be hard."

"Hiding again, Uncle?" I shout back.

"Not at all, dearest niece."

"Come and face me yourself, then."

"I'm too busy for your childish attempts to derail the Lord's plans for us all. There's work to be done before judgement day comes."

"So what? Where does it all end?"

"With a world purged of all its evil sins," he says simply, like it's the most logical thing in the world. "I'll consecrate this new earth with the blood of those who must die first."

"Killing more innocent people isn't the answer," I try to reason. "Tell me what you really want. Why did you release that video?"

"Because you needed a reminder," he sneers back. "I am the one in control, Niece. I gave you the chance to rule with me. You refused."

"You won't stop me from showing the world who you really are. Video or not. Your downfall is coming."

"My downfall?" He laughs hysterically. "Oh, precious, little Letty. You were supposed to rule by my side. I didn't want it to end like this."

"Guys," Hudson murmurs.

He gingerly inches closer to pick up the phone. We're connected to a live voice call, but the phone is plugged into something else.

"Hud?" Kade prompts.

"Hang on."

He traces the wire from the phone's port to a small, black fuse box tucked between the barrels. A single red light blinks on the dashboard.

"Is that…?" Hunter's voice catches.

"For everyone will be salted with fire," Michael taunts. "Do you remember your scripture? You've heard that one before."

All pairs of uncertain eyes lock on me. I gulp down the bubble of nausea threatening to choke my words.

"Mark, 9:49."

"Very good," he compliments. "You could have ruled by my side. The kingdom of God was right there for the taking, and instead, you chose a life of sin."

Kade joins his brother then, and with difficulty, they manage to crack open the lid of one barrel. The eye-watering scent of fuel infiltrates the crypt.

"Your rapture has come early," Michael declares through the phone. "I won't allow you to interfere with my work any longer."

"It's a fucking bomb." Kade drags his brother backwards. "The phone… That's the detonator. We need to get out of here!"

Michael's voice almost sounds sad. "I will finish the work we started alone. Goodbye, Harlow."

"Wait!" I scream.

"Ten, nine, eight…"

"Move!" Enzo roars, almost yanking me off my feet. "Everyone outside!"

My vision flashes in and out, the seconds slowing into an agonising crawl. It feels like God himself has hit slow motion on his remote and sits back, enjoying the show from the comfort of his crumbling throne.

Enzo half-drags me back upstairs, and I have enough sense to grab Hunter's hand to pull him along with us. I will not lose them. Not like this.

We emerge back in the church, all stumbling and racing at full speed to clear the blast zone. Theo and Leighton's voices return, both shouting for an update.

"Bomb!" I yell back.

Several police officers startle and shout as we burst outside, screaming our heads off. None of them move at first, too confused to understand us.

I've barely set foot on the cobblestone path snaking through the graveyard when there's an ungodly rumble behind us. The sound obliterates everything, blotting out the rest of the world.

The gates of hell open underneath us, rumbling and shaking the very earth that supports our feet. Searing heat sets my back alight before the blanket of night is ripped wide open by fire.

"Harlow!" someone screeches.

We're all propelled forward, tumbling through nothingness with the force of the explosion at our backs. Stained glass shatters, voices wail in pain, and God laughs at our stupidity.

Foolish fucking humans, being swiped away with a flick of his thumb. Perhaps Michael was right... His God doesn't care after all.

Colliding with something hard and jagged, my head explodes in a riot of blistering pain. I peer through the layer of hot, gushing blood that soaks into my face.

But I can't see anything apart from smoke and flames. Gloom has ravaged the night and obliterated any specks of light that previously guided our steps. Smoke burns my eyeballs and poisons my throat.

"Goldilocks!"

I'm dreaming.

Someone's speaking.

"Fuck, please talk to me!"

Who is that?

"Please, baby. Answer me. I'm begging you. Please be alive."

It takes a moment for reality to sink in, my mind wading through the waves threatening to drown it. The earpiece is still intact in my ear. Leighton's begging for a response.

Coughing so hard I retch, it takes several panicked seconds of chest clutching and moaning in pain before I manage to draw a breath.

"Harlow! Stay with us."

Clutching my throbbing forehead, my hand comes away slick with blood. I have no idea how I'm still conscious, but the acrid stench of fumes pierces my grogginess.

"I'm bleeding," I wheeze out.

"Harlow!" Leighton shouts in my ear. "Jesus Christ. You're alive! Help is on its way. I need you to hold on."

Hunter. Enzo.

Kade. Hudson.

It's impossible to see even an inch in front of my face. The air is choked with ash and thick black smoke, making breathing almost impossible.

I wipe blood from my eyes again, battling another wave of dizziness. It's taking all of my willpower to remain conscious.

"F-Find … them…"

"No!" Theo shouts frantically. "Don't move."

"Find … H-Hunter and Enzo. F-Find th-them."

Ignoring their disembodied protests in my ear, I grab handfuls of dirt as I try to pull myself upright. The whole world is tilted on its axis, a breath away from falling into an abyss.

With bloodstained hands cupped around my mouth, I scream at the top of my lungs.

"Enzo!"

Nothing.

No answer.

Vision clearing, I can see smoke rising from the smouldering, semi-destroyed ruins of the church on the left of me. Flames climb so high, they seem to lick the black night sky.

"Enzo!"

The muffled groans of someone responding guide my steps. I fall to my knees and have to drag myself back up several times, feeling the hot wash of blood leaking down my neck.

My feet connect with a boulder, spreadeagled on the dirt. Fuck. It's him. Letting my legs collapse, I fall on top of Enzo's body. He's coated in a layer of ash, streaked with blood and dirt.

"Enzo," I whimper, shaking his arm. "Please wake up."

After several desperate shakes, a tiny moan escapes his lips. Pain-filled amber eyes slowly open and land on me through the haze.

"H-H-H…"

"Shh." I check him for injuries, finding blood everywhere. "Don't talk. Help is coming."

"H-Hunter," he gasps.

Holding back a sob, I pull my earpiece out then slot it into his ear, shouting at the others to keep him awake. Enzo's hand is limp as I drop it back at his side.

Sheer desperation drives me forward, tripping over rubble and debris. Destruction surrounds me on all sides. We've been abandoned, left to die out here in fire and brimstone.

Even though he can't hear me, I scream Hunter's name until my dying voice shrivels up. The sound of shouting is intensifying, and the falling ash eases enough to reveal the flash of emergency lights.

Please, I beg the silent observer to our agony. I'll die right here, right now, as long as Hunter and Enzo can walk free. My life is worthless without them.

On the verge of passing out, my foot catches on something. I stumble to the ground, warmth smacking into me as a tangle of broken limbs breaks my fall.

Sobbing frantically, I search for a face with the last wisps of my strength. They're twisted at all the wrong angles, shards of bone slashed through skin and drenched in crimson.

My fingers connect with an arm, searching higher to find the torso. I want to throw up when I realise that it isn't attached to the nearby body, the limb torn clean-off by the explosion.

With the bellows of help growing louder, I drag myself closer to the dead body, a heartbroken plea on my lips. Pieces of bone and disconnected flesh are scattered all around me.

Please, Lord.

Don't punish them for my sins.

Let them live.

But this Lord is not the merciful, benevolent God who graces the pages of Bibles replicated millions of times across the globe.

If people would only dig a little deeper, they'd find God's far darker truth in those pages.

Nobody is spared his wrath. Not even the good ones who don't deserve it. We're all victims at the whim of an indifferent being. The trick is to realise that no amount of faith can prevent the inevitable punishment.

"Please don't be dead."

But it's too late.

Becket's eyes are empty.

Lifeless. Gone.

SCENE DU RIS
J.ROSE
spring
player's getting
played chant
Witt Major Ross
argue Paul Shirley
NOT
RK

CHAPTER 14

Propped up by Leighton's arm curled around my chest, he guides me over to the nearby sofa with tentative steps. Each movement causes the stitched wound on my side to burn.

"Almost there," he grunts. "Fuck me. You're heavy."

"Didn't ask for your help."

"We almost lost you. Let me do this." Leighton carefully guides me onto the sofa, his usual smirk nowhere in sight. "Do you need anything?"

"My gun," I growl back. "So I can put a fucking bullet in that sick son of a bitch's brain once and for all."

He rolls his eyes humourlessly. "Painkillers and a cup of tea it is."

"I'm not Hunter. Make that a whiskey instead."

Leighton offers me a salute then heads into the kitchen where Theo's on the phone with the superintendent, getting his ear chewed off. His forehead rests on the breakfast bar.

I didn't bother to offer to take the call. I'd tell her to fuck her own ignorant asshole with a goddamn breadknife right about now.

"With all due respect—"

He's interrupted again.

"Yes, ma'am. I understand that."

His ability to remain calm and rational is exactly why Theo is handling the avalanche of shit raining down on us and not me. Though he has kept a keen eye on me since I walked in, as if he thinks I'll vanish at any moment.

We had a close call.

It's shaken us all.

The explosion sent shrapnel tearing through my abdomen, narrowly missing my left kidney. After undergoing minor surgery and being held overnight, I discharged myself from the hospital.

"Harlow!" Hunter calls out.

Limping into the room, she ignores him attempting to tow her back to bed. He escaped the blast relatively unscathed, with only bad bruising and a few deep scratches.

"Enzo," she gasps. "You're home."

Harlow limps over as quickly as her bruised body will allow, throwing her arms around my neck and showering me in tearful, relieved kisses.

"I was so worried about you."

"I'm here," I reassure. "Nothing a few stitches couldn't fix."

"You were in surgery when they discharged me. I've been waiting all night to hear from you."

"I'm sorry, little one. Doctor said I'll have a nice grisly scar, though."

"Sexy," she jokes.

"Now we're even."

"Not quite. I'm still winning in the scar department."

Curling up next to me on the sofa, her legs pull up to her chest for comfort. Lucky immediately appears and jumps up to stretch across our laps. She licks my hand for attention.

I stroke her golden ears. "It's okay, girl. I'm here."

"She's been like this since we got home." Harlow rubs her underbelly. "I think she can sense when someone's hurt. I haven't been able to shake her all day."

"Dogs are intelligent. She's worried about us."

"About *you*," Harlow corrects.

My heart fucking twinges, barely held together by imaginary scraps of bandages and duct tape. While I laid there, choking on ash and blood, all I could think about was Harlow.

Losing her.

Losing our future together.

And what I'll sacrifice to stop that from happening.

"Are you in pain?"

"No," she whispers. "They gave me some painkillers. It looks a lot worse than it is. Mild concussion and seven stitches."

The nasty gash is on her forehead, stapled and bandaged to hide the flash of bone. She'll have a hell of a scar to boast about her survival.

"Did you discharge yourself?" Harlow asks.

"Yeah. Pointless place."

"You had to have surgery." Her eyes narrow on me. "Leaving the hospital against medical advice is stupid."

"They fished the shrapnel out and stitched me back together. I'm fine."

We're lucky that no one else was seriously injured, including Hudson and Kade. But we still sustained one casualty. That's one too many.

"I can't believe he's dead." I cover my face with my hands. "Becket was a good agent. Loyal to the bone."

She takes my hand and squeezes. "I'm so sorry, Enz. Did you train him yourself?"

"I trained the whole Anaconda team." With a sigh, I look into her tearful eyes. "He'd been with us for almost a decade."

"Christ. How's the team?"

"Ethan's broken the news to Tara and Warner. The whole team is fucking devastated. They're going to fly home tonight."

The two brothers reappear with drinks in tow. I'm handed a crystal tumbler of whiskey while Harlow accepts an herbal tea from Leighton.

"Thanks."

"You're due to take some more painkillers."

"I'm good, Leigh."

"Nuh-uh." He waggles a finger in her face. "Enzo's out of action, so I'm on overbearing asshole duty. I'll get your meds."

I flip him the bird, and he blows a mocking kiss at me. Even in the midst of a full-scale crisis, we can still count on Leighton to be a jackass, though I can see the strain behind his smile.

"How's he coping?" I whisper.

Harlow winces as she swallows a mouthful of tea. "As well as we can expect. Both him and Theo were shaken up when we got home."

"What about Hunter?"

"Not a word. He's in shock."

"Shit."

Sitting cross-legged on the floor with his usual steaming cup of tea in hand, Hunter is paying us no attention as he stares at the violent red letters blasting us on the TV's news channel.

Prolific killer strikes again.

Huge blast destroys local village church.

Sabre Security confirms one casualty.

"I've kept an eye on him," Harlow adds. "The doctors ran some tests on him at the hospital before we were declared fit to leave."

"And?" I wince.

"He should count his lucky stars that the blast didn't worsen his condition."

Lucky. That word doesn't really feel applicable at the moment.

"Did you hear from your aunt?" Harlow sighs tiredly.

"She's been calling all day. I can't face her yet."

Hayley's protective as hell, and her fussing isn't needed right now. All I want is to take a machine gun to the streets and kill every last sympathiser that Abaddon has out there.

"Oh my God," Harlow curses.

Following her line of sight, I look up at the TV again. There's a live shot of Sabre HQ in the background, but it's surrounded by swarms of furious people waving placards.

Countless enraged faces scream at the top of their lungs, hurling abuse at our security team, who are attempting to hold them back from crossing the strict perimeter.

"Is that blood?" Leighton reappears with a pill bottle. "Holy shit."

Someone in the mob has thrown a water bottle of gloopy, red liquid through the air. It hits one of our agents, Franklin, square in the face, leaving him covered in what I hope is fake blood.

"Please tell me this isn't live." Harlow covers her mouth. "Is that a photo of me?"

Sure enough, some asshole has pasted a snippet of that godforsaken video on their placard. Harlow's naked, emaciated body strangling Laura to death is being touted for everyone to see.

"Enough. Leigh, turn it off."

Before he can oblige, the video shifts back to the studio where

BREAKING NEWS is flashing across the screen. I watch Hunter's face darken as Sally Moore takes over the coverage.

"We can confirm that responsibility for the blast has been claimed by none other than serial killer, Michael Abaddon. The following message was anonymously published online minutes ago."

Rather than Michael's familiar, ugly mug swimming into sight, three hooded figures wear masks that cover their faces. Painted in bright-red on the black material of each is a Holy Trinity.

"The blast was just the beginning," an eerie voice warns. "A season of violence has commenced. Now is the time to rise up and join the Lord's holy army."

A person steps into the forefront, their shoulders hunched. "Together, we will cleanse the world of all its sinners."

"The rapture is almost upon us," the other adds. "We have much work left to do. Take to the streets, and reclaim this world in God's name."

A third figure raises their hands in a call to prayer. "We are the Angels of the Abyss. This will be your only warning."

Leighton turns off the TV, his face paler than fresh snow. "Fucking hell."

Stepping into the room with his laptop in hand, Theo rests against the wall. "I've got the intelligence department working on tracing that video. It isn't looking good, though."

"Angels of the Abyss?" I repeat.

"We did some research a couple months ago." Theo checks the case file on his laptop. "Michael's surname is actually interesting. The definition of the word *Abaddon* is a bottomless pit in the depths of hell."

"What does that have to do with these people?"

"In mythology, Abaddon is an Angel of the Abyss and servant

to chaos. It seems he's formalising his following into an official cult."

"Even his fucking name is evil?" Leighton scoffs. "What is with this guy?"

"It's what he was born to do," Harlow replies flatly. "The devil marked his soul from the moment he was born. He's pure evil, walking in human skin."

Slumping next to Hunter on the floor, Theo drops his head into his hands. I'm shocked when Hunter slides an arm around Theo's shoulders and tries to offer some comfort.

Huh. That's new.

"What's going on?" Hunter asks.

Theo types an answer on his phone as he speaks. "The blast has been designated an act of terrorism. The superintendent has handed the investigation over to the Counter Terrorism Division."

"What?" I demand. "It was Abaddon and his supporters. That's our case."

"Apparently, the decision has been made."

"Well, tell her to fucking unmake it!"

"You think I didn't try that?" Theo hisses at me. "Go and call her yourself if you think you can do any better."

I back down, gutted by the image of Becket's broken corpse sprawled across the ground. I woke up long enough to see him.

"Clearly, I can't do any better." I ignore their gazes. "Becket was a good man and an even better agent. His death is on me."

"Enz—" Harlow begins.

"No. I was running that operation, and now I have to call his family to tell them he why he isn't home. He had a wife and three kids."

Letting my head fall against the sofa cushions, I stare up at the freshly painted ceiling. We've arranged our fair share of funerals over the years. It doesn't get any easier.

I feel sick to my stomach that I'm still alive to feel relieved and sitting in this room, a little broken but unbeaten. So many lives have been lost on my watch. Yet I still live.

"We can't let him win," Harlow declares. "Terrorising people to get their compliance is what Michael does. If we let this beat us, he'll strike again, and harder."

Draining his tea, Hunter runs a hand over the shaved expanse of his head before interjecting. "We need to send a team to go door-to-door in Tregaron."

"*Why?*" Leighton signs.

"He knew exactly when to strike, and four of those suicide victims were from the same region. His followers are there. They will know where he's going next."

Dread slips into my veins and metastasises until it feels like the blood has frozen inside of me. We were so stupid, too eager to end this case to consider the risk.

The attack was orchestrated, planned to perfection. He baited us with the video, drew us in then went for the jugular. It's sheer chance and a dose of luck that we escaped with our lives.

"We can't send the Cobra team back there." Theo pins me with a glare. "You should have seen Brooklyn at the hospital with them."

"How bad was it?" I sigh.

"She was a nervous wreck."

"That reminds me… I'm tripling the security at the wedding next weekend." I knock back a mouthful of liquor. "That bastard won't get another chance to hurt the people I care about."

"You think she'll go ahead with it, given all the crap going on right now?" Leighton wonders. "Is it too late to cancel?"

"There's no chance I'm letting her cancel." I shift into a comfier position. "That bastard doesn't get to take anything else from us."

Theo's phone chirps again to demand his attention. He answers with a lacklustre grunt that betrays his exhaustion.

"Hey, Rayna. What is it?"

A second later, he sits ramrod straight.

"She's on the line now?"

His eyes have lasered in on Harlow at my side, nursing her herbal tea. She lifts her head, limbs stiffening at his facial expression.

"What is it?" Harlow asks.

He holds a hand over the phone. "Incoming call to the Sabre line from Bronzefield Prison. It's your mother. She's asking for you."

Harlow almost drops the cup of tea until I snatch it from her, narrowly avoiding the slosh of boiling hot liquid.

"Why is she calling me now? After all this time?"

Theo grimaces. "Sounds like she heard about the explosion on the news. She's asking to speak to you."

"Not a chance," I cut in. "You don't owe that evil bitch a second more of your time. Let her sit and fester."

Harlow shakes her head. "Theo, hand me the phone. I'm not afraid of her."

He lifts his hand from the mic. "Rayna, patch us through. Keep the call monitored in case we need it for court evidence."

"Harlow," I mutter under my breath. "You don't need to do this. She's only reaching out to try to stop you from testifying against her."

"I know that," she whispers back. "But I'm not going to live my life in the shadow of her crimes. I've wasted enough time feeling scared."

She takes the phone from Theo, pausing for a deep inhale before hitting speakerphone. We all lean a little closer.

"Harlow?" Giana's voice is a tearful whine. "Are you there?"

"I'm here," she responds coolly.

"Oh, thank God. I saw a news report about the explosion, but they wouldn't let me call until this afternoon."

"Why did you call?"

She sniffles. "I didn't know if you were alive. The news said there was a casualty. I've been sick with worry, thinking it was you."

Elbows braced on her knees, Harlow's eyes screw shut. "I'm fine. Minor injuries. Goodbye, Giana."

"No, wait—"

"We have nothing further to discuss."

"Harlow, please," Giana begs. "I've left you alone since that night, but we need to talk. I've added you to my visitation list."

She scoffs. "I'm not coming to see you."

"There's still so much that you don't know. I've done some terrible things, but I'm trying to put it right. Let me explain."

In the corner, Theo is transcribing all of Giana's words into a text message on Hunter's phone for him to read so he isn't left hanging. We're all silent, allowing Harlow to make the final decision.

"I spent so long wondering what I did to deserve all the pain your brother put me through," Harlow says thickly. "But it wasn't my fault, was it?"

"No, darling," Giana concedes, sounding unlike herself. "It was entirely my fault, and I know that now. Please hear me out."

Hesitating, Harlow looks around the room, meeting each of our eyes. Hunter and Theo both shake their heads, but Leighton nods, encouraging her to do it.

She looks at me last. I have to cage my protective instincts in an unbreakable prison in the furthermost corner of my mind.

Sliding my thumb along her jaw, I gently stroke her cheek. "It's your call. I'll support you, no matter what."

Harlow nods tightly. "Fine."

"You'll come?" Giana gushes.

"If this is an attempt to stop me from testifying at your trial, then don't bother."

"I know," she submits. "It's not about that. I have information about Michael that I think you should know."

This manipulative shit-stain has been dodging the authorities' questions for months. I've kept up with her case over its slow progress.

She's facing serious charges for the false imprisonment and torture of Candace Bernard alone. This trial is for those charges, and Harlow will be called as a witness.

If she decides to proceed with prosecuting her mother for the kidnapping, Giana could be facing another messy legal battle and a life sentence.

"Was there something else?" Harlow sighs.

"Just... please be careful." Giana chokes up again. "You know what he's capable of."

"I'm well-protected."

"Not from him. Nobody is. I know you don't want to hear it, but I love you. I've lost Ulrich, and I can't lose you too."

That's when the tears break free from Harlow's eyes, slipping down her cheeks in a sparkling waterfall that boils my blood.

"That's the thing, Mum. You already lost me."

She hangs up the call, unclenching her white-knuckled fist and handing it back to Theo. Before any of us can say a word, Harlow swoops from the room, and we're left gaping after her.

"Shit," Leighton curses. "Should we have intervened?"

I finish the rest of my whiskey. "She needed to do that herself. We can't fight her battles for her anymore. That time has passed."

"Harlow was already devastated about that damn video leak before the explosion," he highlights. "I'm worried about her."

"She's stronger than you think."

"Speaking of," Theo intervenes. "Harlow asked me to find some publishing houses that would be interested in her memoir. We've got floods of offers coming in already, especially after the video."

"Theo! You know this is a bad idea."

"Do I?" he snaps back. "Abaddon is making a mockery of us with these taunts. This is an opportunity to regain the public's confidence."

"By sacrificing Harlow to their judgement?"

"Yes," Hunter speaks up, his eyes on our mouths. "Until she knows the world forgives her for what she did to Laura, she can't let go of her guilt. This is how she heals."

"We have to support that," Leighton agrees.

"And if they don't forgive her?" I challenge. "You saw those placards. What happens when this backfires? This could destroy the progress she's made."

"Then we're here to catch her," Theo answers. "Fuck everyone else. But she will never get that closure if she doesn't try."

I can't argue when all three of them gang up on me. I want Harlow to heal and move on more than anything, but the thought of her getting hurt because of this stupid book is unbearable.

"Fine." I struggle to my feet, intending to refill my glass. "You better get her a good deal. She deserves to be paid a small fortune for this memoir."

Theo offers me a crooked grin. "Like I'd settle for anything less for our girl."

"Too fucking right," I growl.

Returning to the kitchen to pour another glass of whiskey, I flinch when a pounding fist almost smashes through the glass of the front door. The cavalry has arrived.

"Leigh!" I bark. "Your parents are here."

"Let them in, then."

Grumbling to myself, I disable the brand-new security system then unlock the door, only to be barrelled over by all five feet of a dishevelled Della in designer sweats.

"Enzo Montpellier!" she yells at me. "Your aunt has been trying to get hold of you all day. Answer your bloody phone!"

"Della," I wheeze, concealing the pain her tight hug brings. "I'm not long home from the hospital."

"Then you should have called in the car on the way home," she scolds. "She raised you better than that, young man."

Letting her ball of frantic energy pass me, I accept the firm handshake that Ben, Hunter and Leighton's father, gifts me.

His smile is nonexistent, replaced with a worried frown beneath his ice-cold, brown eyes and quiff of styled silver hair.

"What the hell have you got yourselves into?" he hisses quietly. "I've heard from my contacts in the force that the blast has been labelled a terror attack."

"It was him." I clap his shoulder. "Targeted attack, not terror. It's a ploy to remove our jurisdiction. We've pissed off some powerful people."

"I taught you to know when to cut your losses. This is a zero-sum game. Maybe it's time to relinquish control."

"With all due respect, Ben, you didn't teach either of us to quit in the face of evil. If we don't win this war, no one ever will."

His intelligent eyes soften. "You're living for all the people you've lost, son. Remember that. Don't waste what God's given you."

Letting Ben pass me, I ignore the sound of emotional reunions in the living room and drain my second glass of whiskey. It boils in the pit of my belly.

My entire family may be dead, but that doesn't mean I can't risk my life doing whatever the fuck I love. If I die fighting evil, then I can be proud of the work I've done.

Snaking back into the living room, I watch Della fuss over her oldest son. She's more overbearing than ever, smothering Hunter in kisses and attempting to speak in bungled sign language.

Ben is more reserved. He's a good man, no doubt about that. But the approach he's taken to his son's deafness would infuriate most.

It's prompted him to retreat, and I know Hunter sees that as shame, even if it's just Ben's emotionally-stunted way of dealing with trauma. He hates being powerless to help his son.

"What about Harlow?" Della traps Leighton in a hug. "Was she hurt?"

"Pretty bad head injury, but thankfully, no permanent damage," Theo replies. "We got lucky."

"Becket didn't," I interject.

All eyes in the room turn on me. Recoiling, I start to back away on instinct. I don't need their half-assed platitudes. It was my call to send Becket in on active duty.

Mine.

And mine alone.

Fleeing upstairs, I check each room in turn until I arrive at my own bedroom. A lump beneath the sheets, Harlow has slipped one of my loose, oversized hoodies on.

She lies curled up, her hand working overtime as she writes furiously in her newest journal—I've lost count of which number this is. She burns through so many.

"Little one?"

Her head doesn't lift.

"All he does is kill. Kill, kill and kill some more." Harlow sniffs, her tears flowing. "That's why I have to write this book, Enz."

"I know, baby." I slip into the room then click the door shut. "You aren't him."

"But does everyone else see that? The entire world has probably watched that video. They've all seen me kill Laura."

"Fear brings out the worst in people. You survived when no one else did. That makes you an easy scapegoat."

"I want nothing to do with him." She scrubs the tears on her cheeks. "The moment anyone hears my name, they think of him."

Thumping over to the bed, I move slowly to avoid pulling my wound and climb in next to her. Harlow snuggles into my chest, her tears staining my loose, black t-shirt.

"What if you changed it?" I suggest.

"What do you mean?"

"Your name. It's a simple legal process; our lawyers could take care of it overnight."

"I don't understand."

"You could remove all traces of Leticia Kensington and Harlow Michaels. Become someone entirely new if that's what you want."

Eyebrows screwed together, she looks torn. "But… I am Harlow. She's the person I became to survive, and I'm proud of that."

"Well, what about getting rid of the Michaels part that Abaddon gave you? It isn't really your name. You don't need to keep it."

That makes her pause.

"Whose surname would I take?"

"You've got three available for the taking," I point out with a grin. "Harlow Montpellier has a nice ring to it."

Her breath catches. "Is this… are you proposing to me?"

"No! That's not what this is."

The disappointment that infiltrates her blue eyes makes me feel like the stupidest bastard on the planet. I cup her cheeks.

"I didn't mean it like that. You know how I feel about you. When I do propose, I want it to be special. This is more of a solution."

"It's not exactly romantic," she murmurs.

"Just think about it. If doing this will give you some peace, I know any one of us would happily give you our surname to use instead."

She leans into my touch, wearing a tiny grin. "Thanks, Enz. I'll think it over. You don't need to do this for me, though."

"You think it'll be a hardship? Seeing my name after yours, marking your gorgeous little ass for the whole world to see?"

"Well, maybe."

I drop a kiss on her nose. "Think again. I'd tattoo it on your forehead if I could. Don't tempt me."

"You have some serious control issues."

"Stating the obvious, huh?"

She buries her face in my neck. "Can we just hide here forever? I don't want to face the world anymore. I'm tired of everything."

Clamping my arms around her, I hold her so tight, I can feel the expansion of her lungs with each breath. I came so close to losing her all over again.

Each time we face death, I wonder if this will be the final crushing blow that finishes us off. I'm not a God-fearing man, but part of me wonders how we've survived so much, if not for divine intervention.

"Harlow," I whisper brokenly. "I love you too fucking much to lose you. Promise me that you'll walk away if things go south."

"Walk away? From whom?"

"From us. We have no choice but to fix the mess we've made of this investigation, but I won't put you in danger again."

She looks up, her eyes burning with indignation. "Fuck you. I won't let you fight this war alone."

"Harlow, please."

"No!" She shoves my chest to move away from me. "We're a family. That means we live and die together, no matter what."

"Our family means fuck all if we're dead."

"Then I'll follow your infuriating, over-controlling, possessive fucking backside to the afterlife and haunt you there instead."

"Now you're sounding like one of us." I wrap a strand of hair around my finger then gently tug. "I love you to death, Harlow."

"You once told me that's exactly what it would take to tear us apart." Her smile slices my chest open and takes my heart into her bare hands. "But not even that could keep me from loving you."

Our lips seal the promise—meeting, parting, exchanging a lifelong vow in the whispers of our stolen breaths. From the moment I saw her in that hospital bed, I knew she would be my salvation.

All we have to do is beat the devil.

Then perhaps we'll get our happy ending.

SCENE DU
J. ROSE

CHAPTER 15

Harlow

FOXGLOVE – Boston Manor

"**A**lright." Brooklyn claps her hands together. "Listen up, dickheads. The wedding is in less than twenty-four hours, and we have a lot to get done."

Spread throughout their kitchen, our entire family is sipping on extra-strong doses of coffee and attempting to keep up with her pacing the length of the room.

"Phoenix! Wake up!"

Startled out of his semi-awake daze on their sofa, Phoenix offers her a contrite smile in apology. Eli's head is pooled on his lap, the pair lazily curled together like sleeping cats.

"Sorry, firecracker."

"Your grandma is arriving in two hours." She glowers at him. "I'm trusting you to keep her the fuck away from Kade's sister and her boyfriend."

"Still can't believe she's coming," Phoenix mutters.

Kade glowers at him. "None of us can."

I lean closer to Jude. "What's the deal?"

"Phoenix's nana used to be … well, I guess you could say she was a gang leader. She retired a few years back, but before then, she supplied half the drug trade in London."

"My sister's been dating Ajax for six years," Kade adds, his still-bruised face drawn into a grimace. "He was the best friend of Pearl's old runner, Zeke. He died of an overdose years ago."

"She killed him?" I gasp.

"Her drugs killed him. Though she tried to murder his fiancée before that. Real pleasant woman."

"You're the one who told me to invite her!" Phoenix objects.

"Yeah, because I didn't think she'd actually come."

"Hey!" Brooklyn snaps at them. "Didn't I say shut up and listen?"

"Yes," Kade submits.

Phoenix hangs his head. "Sorry."

"We have guests to pick up and keep from killing each other. The flower lady has the flu. Teegan's car has broken down, and I'm pregnant, so my dress doesn't fit! I don't need you two fighting as well."

"But your tits look amazing," Hudson hoots.

"You assholes knocked me up three months before my wedding. Be glad we're still getting married at all, bigger boobs or not."

Moving stiffly, Enzo intervenes. "Alright. Sit your pregnant backside down, wildfire. I need to run through security measures."

I pat the empty barstool next to me. "Come finish your coffee, Brooke."

"Is it decaf?" Kade's head lifts. "No caffeine allowed during pregnancy. I bought more of that lactose free milk too."

"Kade motherfucking Knight," Brooklyn seethes. "You won't live to make it down the aisle if you lecture me about my diet one more time. Sit down, and shut up."

He spreads his hands and backs off. Brooklyn cuts him a final stern look before retaking her seat at my side to finish her coffee.

"We're all driving to the venue in convoys of three." Enzo folds his arms and scowls. "No one moves a fucking muscle without an armed escort. Keep your security trackers on you at all times."

"Isn't this overkill?" Phoenix sighs.

Enzo rounds on him. "If you get killed by some cult-worshipping fuckhead, you can dig your own grave and pay for the funeral too."

"That won't be necessary." Eli burrows closer into Phoenix. "He'll be on his best behaviour. Won't you, Nix?"

"Always am," he replies cheekily.

"Was the pair of you fucking in my office with the door open being on your best behaviour?" Jude drawls. "You messed up my filing system."

"Like you haven't done that with Hudson," Phoenix combats. "You shouldn't have left it unlocked if you didn't want us to use it."

"Enough," Enzo bellows. "Jesus H. Christ. Pay attention, or there isn't gonna be a wedding tomorrow."

Brooklyn wasn't kidding when she said they were all antsy and getting rowdier the closer the wedding has gotten.

"There are going to be fifty agents guarding the ceremony and reception," Enzo continues. "Everyone needs to follow protocol and be prepared for anything."

Leaning back, I feel a column of warmth against my spine. Hunter is standing behind me, gazing out of the window at the rain clouds while nursing his cup of tea.

I tap his shoulder.

"Hmm?" he startles.

"Okay?" I mouth.

Hunter nods. "Looks like it's going to rain."

Leaning over me to look at the rain clouds, Brooklyn grumbles under her breath. "It wouldn't dare."

After running through the safety measures—four times, to be precise—Enzo reluctantly dismisses the group with a final barked command to remain armed at all times.

Three cars are heading to the train station to collect guests while Kade is off to pick up his sister and mother from the airport. Both are flying in from the States.

The only ones without family attending are Eli and Jude. Neither has any family left, and even though Hudson is also an orphan, he still has his adoptive family to support him.

"Harlow, are you well enough to pick up our dresses?" Brooklyn shoves her hair up into a ponytail. "I need to sort out this flower disaster."

"Of course." I instinctively touch the dressing smoothed across my forehead. "I'm feeling fine. Leighton and Hunter are coming into the city with me."

Enzo opens his mouth to complain, and I wave him off.

"We will have security with us."

"Take the SUV," he orders. "It's armoured."

Hunter's chin lands on my shoulder. "Is he fretting?"

I lift my fist to mime a knocking motion, spelling out *yes* in sign language.

"I'm more than capable of taking care of them, Enz," Hunter smarts. "I don't need my hearing to kneecap anyone who threatens Harlow's safety."

Enzo backs off, signing a quick apology. After the explosion, he's been hanging over us both like a fucking rash. It's only worsened as the daily protests outside HQ and beyond have continued.

Everyone grabs suitcases and strewn-about luggage, piling out of the house in formation. There are seven cars in total, and we'll all congregate again tonight at the hotel near the venue in outer London.

"Ready?" Leighton kisses my temple.

"Let's go. Can I drive?"

"If you're feeling up to it? Did you take any painkillers today? I don't want you falling asleep at the wheel."

"For the last time, I am fine. My head doesn't even hurt anymore. I've got a job to do, so let's go."

He chucks me the keys. "I'll put the learner plates on. Hyland and Ethan will follow a few cars back."

"The Anaconda team's back at work?"

Theo appears in the doorway from his silent perch at the back of the room. "They insisted. The funeral isn't until next week."

"Which straw did you draw?" I step into his arms.

"I'm giving Brooklyn's maid of honour a ride. You haven't met Teegan yet, have you?"

"Not yet. Is she nice?"

"She's quirky as hell, but you'll like her."

An insecure part of me wants to feel threatened by Brooklyn's best friend coming to town, but I'm happy she's going to have all of her loved ones there. No one deserves this more than her.

The company SUV is parked behind Hudson's Mustang, overflowing with boxes of liquor to be transported. We throw our luggage into the boot.

"You remember that lesson I gave you a couple of weeks ago?" Leighton asks. "This isn't a cheap dirt bike."

"I think so."

"Try not to get us killed on the road." He winks at me. "I've got a hot date tomorrow with a sexy bridesmaid."

"Oh? Who would that be?"

"Not sure yet. I'll have to use my charm and magical pickup abilities to score. Any thoughts on how I should wear my hair?"

"How about stuck down a fucking toilet?" Hudson shouts from the Mustang.

Leighton shoots him the bird. "Shut it, Romeo. You want a black eye at your wedding?"

"I'd like to see you try, Leigh. It's been a while since I broke anyone's legs."

"Guys," I moan. "Literally drowning in testosterone here. Get in the bloody car, and give it a rest before I get a migraine."

After piling into the SUV, Hunter takes the seat directly behind me and drops a kiss on my head. Leighton attaches the learner plates then climbs into the passenger seat.

"Okay then, like we practised. It's an automatic, so just ease down on the accelerator. Don't do what you did last time."

"You didn't warn me it would shoot off the tarmac," I complain.

"I'm supportive of you being a petrol head." Leighton cranks the volume on the radio. "Just pass your driver's test first, alright?"

I start the engine, slot it into gear and gently press down on the pedal to back out of the drive. Enzo watches me reverse before he gives me a thumb's up and disappears.

With the blare of Leighton's music in the background, I pull a stolen pair of Hunter's aviators on and merge into traffic. Ethan follows closely behind in another blacked-out SUV.

Driving an automatic is a hell of a lot easier than navigating a temperamental dirt bike. Learning to drive was on my list of things to do, along with the school classes I'm still taking.

"The dress shop is in Shoreditch." Hunter leans between the seats. "Keep an eye out for idiot drivers. London is full of them."

"Ladies and gentlemen, my brother." Leighton scoffs. "The king of the idiot drivers in his stupid red convertible."

I indicate left and turn. "You love that thing."

"Only because I don't have a car of my own."

"I wondered about that. You never wanted to buy one?"

Leighton's jaw clenches. "When we met, I was fresh out of prison. The past year has been for me to acclimatise to the world again too."

Reaching over the console, I rest a hand on his thigh. "I'm sorry, Leigh. I didn't mean it like that."

"No, it's fine. It's just…" his eyes dart to the mirror to check that Hunter isn't watching. "I've taken handouts from everyone since I was a kid. I want to stand on my own two feet now."

The traffic begins to pick up, so I stick to the left-hand lane, following the navigation deeper into the East End.

"What do you want to do?"

He shrugs. "I'd like to start my own marketing agency. I just don't want to accept family money to do it. If I can find an investor, then great."

"Leigh… I had no idea. Why haven't you talked to us about this? I think you'd be great at that."

"For the same reason I don't want Hunter to know," he answers easily. "I don't want to be helped. I fucked up my life, and I'm going to get it back on track."

My heart swells for him. Leighton is the most underestimated member of our family. But when shit hit the fan, he was the first one to step up and take control of Sabre.

"I know that whatever you decide to do, you'll be amazing at it. I'm so proud of you, Leigh."

He turns his megawatt smile on me. "Thanks, Goldilocks."

"When you figure it all out, let me know. I'll be the first one there to cut the ribbon and pop the champagne."

"You hate champagne."

I stifle a laugh. "Yeah, I do."

The glare of red lights alerts us to halting traffic. I carefully brake and draw us to a stop, craning my neck to figure out what the holdup is. Everyone's jammed into a tight, winding London street.

"What is it now?" Leighton grunts. "Fucking traffic."

"Is it an accident?"

"Let me hop out and look."

Boosting himself up in the open door, he peers over the lines of parked cars. Hunter slides a hand between the seats, and it reappears holding … a bloody gun.

"Hunt!" I wave my hands in his face.

He checks the chamber and shrugs. "You can never be too careful. I don't trust London anymore, and neither should you."

Leighton hops back down and shuts the door. "We need to get out of here. Right now."

"What is it?"

"Some kind of demonstration."

"Protest?" Hunter checks.

Leighton shakes his head.

Before I can fire off another question, the buzz of coalescing voices breaks through the blaring car horns. It's an odd humming sound, raising high then dipping low in a haunting harmony.

"Is that … praying?" I ask in disbelief.

Slamming the car door, Leighton hits the locks. "It's chanting. They're coming. Let's move."

"I can't! We're boxed in."

Cars have gathered behind us, sandwiching us between impatient drivers and the belch of their exhausts. Ethan and Hyland are trapped several cars behind us.

"Thank God for tinted windows," he mutters. "Keep your fucking head down, and stay away from the window."

Heads bob through the crowd of cars, and that's when I begin to panic. Hands are raised high into the sky, palms up to receive the Lord's light with each lament.

The crowd of people are crying out in prayer, filtering between parked cars and causing havoc. Glinting crucifixes circle their throats, blessing them in holiness.

But it's their faces that are truly terrifying. All have mirrored the lunatics that appeared on our TV screen—scrawling Holy Trinities across their cheeks in bright-red ink.

"The team found nothing when they went door-to-door in Tregaron." I watch the flow of people. "Not even the priest knew what was in his crypt. Where did all these people come from?"

"I think it's safe to assume Abaddon has supporters across the country," Leighton says grimly. "They're coming out of the woodwork for his sick cult."

Hidden behind the tinted glass, we sink lower in our seats and watch the parade filter past. My heart is bruising itself against my ribcage with fear that we'll be spotted.

"I think I prefer the protests over this," I whisper from my ducked position. "Why are they doing this in public? Everyone thinks Michael is a terrorist."

"Hasn't stopped his message from spreading like wildfire," Leighton replies. "These nutbags still support him."

"Support what? Butchering people?"

The crack of a window rolling down startles us both. Hunter has inched his open enough for their prayers to float inside the car.

"What are they saying?" he asks.

Lord above, hear our prayers. We cleanse ourselves before you. Grant the Angels of the Abyss your mercy. We are your faithful servants on this earth.

"This is fucking twisted," Leighton hushes.

I fingerspell the word *prayer* to Hunter, and he quickly rolls the window back up. Floods of people are passing us now. There must be dozens of them joining the show.

In front of us, a car door slams, emitting a tall, middle-aged man in a slick business suit. He begins screaming at the people, jabbing his finger towards the blocked road.

"Ah, hell. This is going to get messy."

I glance behind us. "We're still stuck."

"Should we make a run for the dress shop?"

"We can't just leave the car here."

"Screw the fucking car!" Leighton exclaims.

Shouting erupts, then a man from the praying masses steps forward to placate the angry motorist. Their noses almost touching, they scream at each other, a breath apart.

When the first punch flies, the man with the Holy Trinity painted on his face lunges aside to duck the blow. This only infuriates his opponent more, and the pair begin to grapple.

"We need to run." Hunter tucks his gun into the waistband of his fitted black jeans. "This is about to escalate."

Sure enough, the shouting reaches a fever pitch. Prayers turn into furious barbs. More drivers exit their cars and begin screaming, their collective aggression spiralling.

"You crazy psychopaths!" someone screams at the praying herd. "Get out of the road, and go see a doctor!"

"Sinner!" another shouts back. "You will burn in the Lord's almighty fire. Now is the time for repentance."

The glint of a small knife being pulled catches my eye. It slashes through the air, warning the motorist off his furious attack.

When the pair collide, the knife caught between them, they fall backwards and hit my window. The car shudders from the impact, but Enzo's bulletproof glass holds strong.

Michael's indoctrinated drone looks like a demon brought to life, his eyes swirling with divine rage as he lashes out with the knife. It catches his opponent in the arm, and blood sprays across our car.

"That's it!" Hunter yells. "Let's move."

He leaps out, and we follow suit. Hunter rushes to grab me before I get lost in the tangle of people and half-throws me over the bonnet where I land in Leighton's strong arms.

"Gotcha," he huffs.

Fighting echoes all around us. With a glance back, I catch the next strike of the blade. Nursing an arm injury, the poor guy has slumped to his knees, the knife cutting a jagged slash into his face.

"Repent!" the fanatic bellows.

Blood sprays through the air, intensifying the bubble of panic and rage. Hunter takes a running jump and glides across the car's bonnet on his ass, landing on the other side with us.

"There!" He points towards a side street leading away from the road. "Ethan and Hyland will find us on the GPS."

Leighton snags my hand and drags me along. I can't move fast, my head spinning with vertigo from each jolt causing spikes of pain to tear through my healing head injury.

"Leigh," I puff. "Slow … down."

When my legs are swept out from underneath me, I slump against Hunter's chest. He's scooped me up in a fireman's carry after catching up to my stunted running.

I snake my arms around his neck and take the gun from his

waistband. Violence is breaking out all around us as tensions boil over. I can't run, but I can shoot anyone who chases us.

We almost run headfirst into a gaggle of Michael's newest fans, standing slightly back and watching the others with stunned faces. None look ready to partake in the fighting.

"Go!" I shout at them. "You don't have to be a part of this."

The blare of approaching police sirens causes them to scramble, bailing before the handcuffs are pulled out. I curl closer to Hunter to conceal the gun from the authorities as we run.

"Here!" Leighton shouts, pointing to get his brother's attention. "Inside."

We're across the street and close to escaping when two bodies step into our path. Their faces are stained with the painted marks, separating them from the melee of drivers swarming in a panic.

Leighton skids to a halt. "Get out of our way."

The taller woman, her silvery-black hair pulled back in a severe bun, sneers at him. She looks like she's just discovered the holy grail.

"You know who she is?"

"More importantly, do you know who we are?" Leighton lashes back. "Move before I make you."

"No can do." Her friend steps forward. "I can't believe my eyes. Harlow Michaels, in the flesh."

"Sweetheart," Hunter whispers, barely audible. "Take the gun back out, and point it at them. We're too exposed here."

I gape at him.

"Do it," he demands. "I don't give a shit what the law says."

Before I can raise the gun, Leighton launches himself at the pair. His fists blur, smashing into their unwitting faces and drawing blood.

I've never seen Leighton move so fast, stepping out of his skin and becoming a person we haven't seen before. A deeper, darker version of himself, left behind bars.

"I warned you." He boots the man in the ribs. "Feel free to pass the message along to your friends. We won't be intimidated."

With a terse nod, he gestures for us to walk past the groaning pair. Neither say a word, too busy moaning in pain.

We run past them and down the street, bursting into a tiny antique bookshop. It's deserted, but I can hear the whimpering of someone hiding behind their counter.

Taking shelter behind a stack of books, Hunter crouches down but still holds me in his lap. His gaze is fixed out of the window at the flash of bright-blue lights arriving.

Leighton struggles to catch his breath. "What kind of prayer circle carries knives? Like, what the hell?"

"This is what Michael wants," I wheeze. "Mass slaughter of those he deems unworthy."

"Those assholes recognised you straight away. I don't like this. It feels like a witch hunt."

"I can see Ethan," Hunter rumbles beneath me. "I think he's bleeding. They're coming this way."

Remaining crouched behind the book stacks, we all flinch when the door to the shop is thrown open. Hyland's shoulders brush against the frame before he ducks inside, followed by Ethan.

"You alright?" Hyland approaches us.

Leighton waves him off. "We're fine."

Seeming slightly unsteady, Ethan slumps against the closed door. Blood is trickling from the corner of his mouth and nostrils. Someone's given him a damn good punching.

"This crazy son of a bitch clocked me when I told him to move," he struggles out. "Some of them were even armed."

"It isn't a demonstration," I supply. "This is an armed mob."

And something tells me this is just the first of many. Fear is a formidable contagion, and there's no quarantining this sickness.

He promised, after all.

Our world will burn.

SCENE DU NO
J.ROSE

CHAPTER 16

Harlow

'␣ve never attended a wedding before. The only marriage I had to observe as a child was the sham perpetuated by Pastor and Mrs Michaels. A partnership forged in darkness.

My parents' marriage was equally flawed and toxic. Part of me is glad that I suppressed those memories and portions of that time are still fragmented, never to be pieced back together.

Sliding into the deep-purple silk slip that we managed to rescue from the dress shop after our ordeal yesterday, I slide the spaghetti straps up my shoulders to hold it in place.

"Okay," I reassure myself. "We're all in."

The silky material is butter-soft and whispers over my scarred skin, covering the worst of the marks while leaving my clavicles and a sensual hint of cleavage on display.

It's a beautiful, gothic shade, reminiscent of amethyst but dipped in a stunning hue of darkness. Brooklyn wanted me to be comfortable and checked that I liked the cut beforehand.

I'm wearing my long hair loose in lightly tousled waves to conceal the bandage still on my forehead. The stitches are due to be removed next week, so coverage was a last resort.

I turned down the offer of professional makeup. The thought of a stranger breathing all over me wasn't appealing. I've kept it simple—thick lashes, glossed lips and light eyeliner.

"Harlow?" Theo knocks on my door.

"Come in."

Stepping into my hotel room, his appearance takes my breath away. Theo cleans up seriously well. His blonde curls are slicked back while his contact lenses are in place, and his blue eyes shine with excitement.

The suit he wears is perfectly fitted and highlights every single lean inch of muscle that builds his frame, topped off with a dark-purple bowtie that matches my dress.

"Holy shit," he curses.

"That bad?"

He takes my hand, spinning me in a circle so he can inspect me. "Of course not. You look phenomenal."

My neck burns with a blush. "Thank you, Theodore. You don't look so bad yourself. Nice bowtie."

"Brooklyn insisted."

"Of that I have no doubt."

Planting a heavy kiss on my lips, he lingers for a moment, his tongue stroking mine in a seductive beat that scatters my thoughts.

Even his kisses taste like home—warm, familiar, comforting. Like stepping into a room with a roaring fire while it's raining outside and curling up with your favourite book.

His hands slip down the curve of my body to cup my ass through the dress's clingy material. I gasp into his lips, rocking against his crotch and the hardening press of steel.

"I have bridesmaid duty to do."

"Screw the wedding," he purrs. "Let's hide up here together instead."

With great self-control, I push him back. "No can do, I'm afraid. You don't want to see what happens when Pregnant Brooke meets Bridezilla Brooke. It's not pretty."

Theo groans. "I really don't want to see that."

Grabbing my clutch bag and phone, I kiss his freshly-shaven cheek then escape before we miss the wedding entirely. We're staying in a nice hotel that's a couple of streets behind the venue.

"I need to go check on Brooklyn." My short high heels sink into the hotel's carpet. "Who's our ride to the venue?"

"Enzo. He refused to let anyone else do it."

"Figures. See you down the aisle?"

Theo's smile lights up his face. "I'll keep an eye out for you, beautiful girl. You're going to smash it."

"I'm going to trip up and embarrass myself."

"But you'll look gorgeous doing it," he jokes. "Go on. I've got to give Kade's sister and boyfriend a ride."

After blowing him a kiss, I slip down the corridor to Brooklyn's room and knock on the door. It opens to reveal a stranger grinning at the sight of me.

"Harlow?" she guesses.

"Um, hi."

I'm bundled into a patchouli-scented hug. The girl's a few inches taller than me, her short, styled, black pixie cut revealing rows of ear piercings that contrast her pale, rice-powdered skin.

She's a quintessential goth, decked out in layers of silver jewellery, dark tattoos and raccoon eyeliner, but her smile is wide and genuine.

"Teegan, I'm guessing?" I laugh.

"Tee!" Brooklyn's voice calls. "Let her breathe."

"Oh God, I'm sorry." She lets me go. "Yep, I'm Teegan. I promise, I'm not a total weirdo. Brooklyn's just told me a lot about you."

"It's nice to finally meet you."

"Likewise."

She's dressed in a matching dress to mine, the purple silk showing off the ink on her arms and chest. I love her already. Warmth exudes from her in a way I wasn't expecting from an old friend of Brooklyn.

Led inside the bedroom, there's another woman inside. She's pushing sixty but wears her age with refined elegance. Her silvery hair is twisted in a classy up-do, contrasting her light blue dress and heels.

"This is Janet," Teegan introduces. "Kade's mum."

I tentatively accept her handshake. "Hello."

She beams, stretching deep smile lines. "Oh, Harlow. I hope my boys have made you feel welcome in London."

"Your Hudson's adoptive mother, right?"

"Yes. My daughter and I have been looking forward to meeting you. Cece is a defence lawyer in New York. She's kept an eye on your case."

"Thanks. That means a lot."

"Harlow! Get your ass over here."

Sitting at the dressing table in the corner of the bridal suite, the sight of Brooklyn causes me to freeze. She's kept her dress choice a closely-guarded secret until this moment.

"Oh, Brooke," I gush.

She looks over her shoulder. "Too much?"

"It's perfect."

Her flawless, ash-blonde curls lay in stark comparison to her stunning midnight black dress. She stands, lifting the full, A-line chiffon skirt to fan out in a cloud of inky blackness.

The fitted bodice is peppered with tiny sapphires, setting sparkles off against her skin. A thin thigh split offers a flash of her long, toned leg.

"Teegan said I look like the Corpse Bride."

"Hey," she protests. "That was a compliment. The guys are going to fucking lap it up."

"You are getting married in an abandoned church," I point out. "It doesn't even have a roof."

"Like I'd ever step foot in a real one. It was this or a graveyard. I had to make an executive decision."

Lifting the split in her dress, she pulls a black lace garter higher up her thigh. Tucked inside, the flash of a small blade catches my eye.

"Is that a penknife?"

Brooklyn strokes a finger over the blade. "It belongs to Eli. Personal joke."

Fussing over her, Janet smooths the back of Brooklyn's dress and straightens the black-diamond crusted piece in her hair. She declares the job done with a nod.

"Darling, before we leave… I have something for you."

Janet opens her purse then slips out a tiny silver coin. Eyes shining with tears, Brooklyn covers her mouth.

"Something old." She winks. "It's good luck to put a sixpence in your shoe. Call me old-fashioned."

"I think I like old-fashioned. Thank you, Janet."

"How many times have I told you? It's Mum."

Even I'm choking up. I accept the arm Teegan wraps around me for moral support. Watching them together is so beautiful.

"Mum," Brooklyn echoes shyly. "Thank you for being here on my wedding day. It… It means a lot that I'm not alone."

Her eyes move over to us. We crowd them both until the four of us are hugging and laughing through our tears.

"You've got all of us," Teegan reassures.

"Forever," I add.

Janet breaks the hug to rest a hand on Brooklyn's still-flat belly. She's smiling like her whole life has culminated in this single moment.

"Let's get you married, then. My sons are waiting with those other three handsome men. You're going to give them all heart attacks."

Brooklyn blows out a breath. "That's the plan."

†

London is full of quirky surprises. This one may be even better than Theo's abandoned underground carriage, tucked out of sight in a bustling neighbourhood.

On the outskirts of the city, the destroyed ruins of a mid-eighteenth-century church have been left undisturbed. Crumbled limestone slabs and smashed stained glass litter the grounds.

With the sun hanging low in the sky, the state of desolation is lit with tiny glowing lights strung to every piece of rubble and the beams exposed by the collapsed roof. The effect is mesmerising.

It's a carcass, dressed in light.

I've never seen such imperfect beauty.

Enzo pulls up outside the venue then kills the car's engine. He's quiet today, his posture carved with obvious emotion. This is a big day for him too. His little sister is getting married.

"Can you guys give us a sec?" he asks thickly.

"Of course." I step out, holding the door for Janet and Teegan. "We'll be here when you're ready."

Remaining inside the car, I watch Enzo turn to speak to Brooklyn. His words for her are private. She laughs and has to wipe even more tears aside. The pair hug tight before joining us.

"I think I've cried all my makeup off." Brooklyn smooths a hand over her dress. "I'm not sure I can do this."

I tuck a loose curl behind her ear. "We're going to be with you every single step of the way. Your boys are waiting in there for you."

She takes an uneven breath. "I'm about to be a wife … and a mum soon too. I never thought I'd see either of those things happen."

"You deserve this, B," Teegan says. "The girl I met in Blackwood didn't want to mean anything to anyone. But look at this beautiful family you have instead."

"I'm damn lucky, aren't I?"

Enzo joins us on the pavement. "You sure as fuck are."

He looks good enough to eat in black trousers and a matching pressed shirt, gaping open at the neck with no tie in sight. His amber eyes are almost glowing, and his smile is incandescent.

Janet snaps a quick photo on her phone before tucking it away. "I am so proud of you, Brooke. I'll see you inside."

Letting her head inside to join the other guests, Enzo checks in with security, who maintain a water-tight perimeter. After our close call in Shoreditch, he arranged an additional twenty agents for security.

Satisfied that we're secure, he takes his place at Brooklyn's side, though his apprehension is still clear. The police arrested dozens of people last night, but many fled too fast.

"Ready?"

She nods. "I am. Please don't let me fall over."

"I wouldn't dare, wildfire."

The roar of guitars and thumping rock music invites us inside. Teegan stands next to me, linking our arms before handing me a black-rose bouquet to carry.

"Is that *Bring Me The Horizon?*" she laughs.

Brooklyn accepts Enzo's arm to hold. "Like I'd walk down the aisle to anything else. Eli chose the song, though."

"Of course, he did."

Stepping inside the ruins, the flicker of hundreds of red-wicked candles on the stone floor light the early evening shadows. I hold on to Teegan as we walk to the heavy beat of music.

There aren't many guests, only family and friends. I spot the guys first, their heads all straining to catch sight of me. Leighton and Hunter stand shoulder-to-shoulder with Theo behind.

But nothing compares to the five stunned faces at the head of the church, their mouths all hanging open as they spot their bride for the first time.

Brooklyn's men are dressed in matching, all-black suits and dark-red bowties. They've all cleaned up—even Phoenix has styled his currently lime-green hair into a semi-tidy state.

When he thinks no one is looking, Jude brushes a stray tear from his cheek. Kade notices and punches him in the arm as Hudson kisses him, fighting his own smile.

After completing our walk, we hug each of the guys then take our places on the left-hand side.

"Thank you," Jude says to us. "You both look amazing."

"Purple suits you both," Hudson agrees.

Teegan sticks her tongue out at him. "Eyes on the prize, Hud."

He looks back at the incoming spectacle, his mouth slack. Brooklyn and Enzo walk down the aisle with all eyes trained on them. I've never seen Enzo look so bloody proud before.

Brooklyn's fighting another wave of tears as he kisses her cheeks and hugs her so tight, it must creak her bones, before handing her off to Kade. Theo makes room for Enzo next to him.

The guys take turns greeting their bride, exchanging kisses and secret whispers. Watching them together is mesmerising. For all their sharp barbs, their love is incomparable.

Kade turns to face everyone. "Thanks for coming, everyone. This isn't a normal wedding. Nor is it a legal one. We wanted to do this our way with all of our loved ones here to watch."

Standing opposite them, Brooklyn lets Kade take her hands first. He ducks to kiss her knuckles and gives her a boyish smile.

"The day we met, I thought you were the most beautiful thing I'd ever seen. Even when you shut me down. I'm so glad I didn't take no for an answer."

She sniffles. "Me too. You saved my life, Kade."

"I'll spend the rest of our lives keeping the promise I made to you all those years ago." He looks down at her midsection. "I love you and our baby. Thank you for being mine."

Teegan steps forward to hand Brooklyn the white-gold ring, engraved with a secret message inside that none of us have seen. She shakily slides it onto Kade's finger then kisses him.

"I love you."

"Ditto, love."

After another kiss, Kade steps back to let his brother move forward. In typical Hudson style, he sweeps Brooklyn backwards until she's bent over in his arms to accept the smack of his lips.

"Words have never been my strong suit," he says with a short laugh. "I'm not sure I ever deserved your love or forgiveness, but I will never take either for granted. You're my whole fucking world."

Stepping forward, I pull the next ring from my dress's built-in pocket and hand it over. Brooklyn slots it into place on his finger.

"Can't get rid of me now," Hudson smarts.

"Looks like it. We're stuck together for life."

"I've wanted that since we were sixteen years old." He smiles down at the wedding ring. "Always and forever, blackbird."

Sealing the deal with a kiss, he's reluctant to release her so Phoenix and Eli can step forward together. Like they'd ever dare to do anything apart. These two are a package deal.

They take one of Brooklyn's hands each, their bodies so in tune, they move like shadows of each other. Phoenix keeps one arm wrapped around Eli's waist, but he lets him go first.

"Baby girl," Eli rasps just loud enough for us to hear. "I wanted to thank you for giving me a voice again. For making me strong and for showing me what it means to be loved."

Teegan hands Brooklyn the next ring, and she hesitates, lifting her dress to reveal the penknife stuck inside the black lace garter.

"Donec mors nos separaverit," Brooklyn murmurs. "Until death do us part, Elijah. Nothing will ever change that."

With the sweetest smile bringing out the emerald green of his eyes, Eli accepts his ring then captures her in a whirlwind kiss that communicates all they don't want to say aloud.

"I'm still terrified of being a dad, though," Eli admits with a tiny laugh. "Like, petrified."

"If this baby has half of the beautiful soul inside you, we're on to a winner," she says into his lips. "Trust me."

"Always," he echoes.

Phoenix steps into the mix and kisses Eli first, burying a hand in his dark crop of curls. Brooklyn's mouth surrenders to him next, tying the three of them together.

"What he said," Phoenix jokes. "I'm not sure how any of us ever survived without you in our lives. Good thing we'll never have to find out."

"Don't speak too soon." Brooklyn accepts the next ring from me.

"I may trade you in for a younger model yet, Nix."

"Good luck getting rid of me. I'm notoriously difficult to remove once I've latched on."

"Don't we know it," Eli comments.

Brooklyn wiggles the ring onto Phoenix's finger, then the three of them crash together, kissing and hugging. I swear, I catch the shimmer of a tear running down Eli's cheek.

His smile is the biggest I've seen so far. He's always carried his sadness around with him, even in his happiest moments. But right now, joy is flowing off him in waves.

When they eventually part, there's just one person remaining. Most of the occupants of the abandoned church are in tears—including Kade's mum and his sister, Cece, in the front row with her boyfriend, Ajax.

None of us knew what to expect for this ceremony beyond the unconventional. There's no scripture or bullshit, semi-sexist vows in sight. Just love, respect and honesty in their purest forms.

Sat a few seats behind them, Leighton has an arm slung around his brother's shoulders. Theo's doing his best to relay their vows in rapid sign language with Hunter's smile showing his appreciation.

"Jude," Brooklyn calls. "Come here."

Lingering at the edge of the group, Jude appears the most nervous of them all, at total odds with his usual veneer of self-assuredness. Flashes of his tortured alter ego still filter through at times.

Teegan hands the last ring over to be slotted into place, and Brooklyn takes his right hand instead. The smooth stump of his missing left hand is tucked into his pocket.

"Saving the best until last?" Jude laughs.

Her lips crinkle in a smile. "I knew you'd be the most nervous. I just wanted to make you wait."

"Sadistic much?"

"Only for you, Sev."

Holding his hand tight, she gently slides the ring into place. "You kept me alive when nothing else in the world could've convinced me to take another breath."

Jude nods, not trusting himself to speak.

"I vow to spend the rest of my life repaying you for holding my hand through the darkest of times."

Stepping back into the mix, Hudson pulls a ring box from the pocket of his suit jacket. He offers it to Jude. Nestled amongst blood-red velvet is the most stunning ring I've ever seen.

The gold band is embedded with tiny, dark green emeralds, perfectly contrasting the black-diamond of Brooklyn's engagement ring. It's totally unique and one of a kind.

"We chose it together," Kade reveals.

Taking the ring from the box, Jude carefully slides it onto her finger. "Will you take us to be your fucked up, over-controlling, somewhat mentally unstable husbands?"

She throws her arms around his neck. "I fucking do."

The ruins of the church erupt in raucous applause. Everyone is on their feet, clapping and shouting in celebration. It's a deafening roar that bounces off the crumbling structure.

Brooklyn kisses each of her men again, then they all turn to face the crowd as a united front, their hands linked together. I can barely see through my streaming tears.

"Let's go party!" Phoenix yells.

The applause intensifies, and they lead the way through the broken church to the courtyard outside that's lit with more clusters of red candles. I hang back.

Theo is the first one to catch up to me. "You did well, beautiful."

I hide my face in his neck, letting people slip past us to enjoy the last glimmers of sunshine. The warmth of bodies presses around me as the others join us for a group hug.

With all of their hands touching my body, hope swells deep inside the coldest pits of my heart. If Brooklyn and her men can make it work against the odds, so can we.

"Drinks?" Leighton suggests hopefully.

I swipe beneath my eyes to clean the trails of mascara. "Make mine a double."

CHAPTER 17

Hunter

Homemade Dynamite – Lorde

Sitting at our corner table, the flicker of hundreds of candles lights the night air. Tiny lanterns are strung between willow trees and huge branches, adding to the romantic glow.

I wish I could hear the music everyone sways to on the paved area that's turned into a makeshift dance floor. Instead, all I have is my own silent breathing.

It's enough.

Nothing can ruin this moment for me. Not even the gaping loneliness that's been clawing at my chest for months. We don't get much cause to celebrate in our lives.

But tonight?

We're fucking *alive*.

Knocking back my glass of red wine, I stand to head for the dance floor. My parents are locked in a waltz, having arrived a little late but keen to celebrate the family's day.

Behind them, Brooklyn is caught in a gentle sway between

Phoenix and Eli, looking so goddamn content it hurts my soul. Not everyone we rescue makes it, but she has.

We can be proud of that.

Searching through the dancing throng, I spot Harlow's shimmering, purple dress in the back corner. She's drinking wine with Kade and his sister, the three of them laughing about something.

As if she can sense my attention, her eyes search through the crowd then land on me. The smile that tugs at her lips is breathtaking.

I crook a finger, beckoning her over. Making a swift exit, she finishes her drink and ditches it to approach me. I extend a hand, silently inviting her to dance.

I don't need to hear the stupid music. The sheen of happiness glowing in her eyes will be my melody. It speaks loudly enough.

Her lips move on a word. "France?"

I frown at her.

She shakes her head with another laugh. "Dance?"

"Oh." I take her hand and draw her close. "I happen to be an excellent dancer. But only for special occasions."

Harlow's hand moves to cup the back of my neck, then she presses against my chest, flashing delectable cleavage that beckons my eyes down. I think my heart stopped the moment I saw her earlier.

My lips touch her ear. "Have I told you how beautiful you look tonight?"

With a smile, her mouth trails up my throat, planting feverish kisses until her lips meet mine. She replies with touch alone. It speaks far better than words now.

I twirl her around, moving in a slow, languid rhythm to the chasm of utter silence. She steers our turns, guiding me by the sounds I can no longer recognise.

In my head, I can remember all the sound fragments I cherish more than anything. The high, timid tinkle of her voice when we first met. The hammering of her heartbeat. Her contagious laugh.

The sounds are still there.

Locked up safe.

That doesn't stop grief from strangling my throat like spikes of barbed wire, though. I would give anything in the entire fucking world to hear her laugh one more time. Anything. Even my life.

She was the one strobe of light in my dreary, black-and-white world after Alyssa's death. Everything and nothing have changed since then. Harlow is still my compass, guiding me through the night.

With one hand, she points to me and draws an invisible circle in the air to sign her question. It's easier now to piece the words together in sign language.

"*Are you okay?*"

I swallow the burning lump in my throat. "I really wish you'd stop asking me that."

Her gaze doesn't waver, still seeking an answer.

"Fine. I want to experience this like everyone else is."

Sadness invades her blue eyes.

"No," I blurt. "I don't need you to feel sorry for me, sweetheart. I'm having a good time. It's just … not all there."

Gaze hardening with conviction, she takes my hand and steers me past dancing guests. At the front of the courtyard, a DJ is playing songs behind a professional setup of decks.

There's a full-sized speaker blasting music to the wedding party, almost as tall as me. Harlow guides me over to it then stops.

"*Listen,*" she signs.

I stifle a laugh. "I can't fucking hear, remember?"

With an eye roll, she lifts my hand and places it on top of the hole-spotted casing of the speaker. Immediately, all of my other senses are drowned out by the sensation.

Vibrations pulse through my palm, exploding across my skin until I'm tingling all over. Each time the bass in the track plays, it thumps through the speaker and my hand.

I can feel it.

Hear it.

Breathe it.

Ignoring the fact that I must look like a lunatic, I wrap an arm around the speaker and press my ear to it. The effect is so intense, I could cry from the sheer sense of relief.

The vibrations are rattling through my bones. Head to toe. Beat after beat. The hum of the music slips beneath my skin and surges its way up my spinal cord to be composed by my mind.

Harlow's fingers move in a semi-circle. "*Music.*"

I'm glad the only light comes from the lanterns and candles. No one can see the tears I have to blink away. Months of numbness are forgotten in a single moment of bliss.

Grabbing Harlow's waist, I hold her close, and we sway to the music. She's listening with her ears while I listen with my soul. Together, the soundtrack is complete.

The need to show her how much this means to me is so strong, I have to fight the urge to tear the silk from her body and bend her over in front of the entire crowd.

She's like a drug to me—potent and life-destroying in all its addictive power. I'd tear down civilisations and slaughter whole armies to get my next fix.

"Sweetheart," I growl.

Harlow glances up at me. Her features are softened by alcohol, the oceanic depths of her eyes glassy with slight inebriation. I can feel the wine humming in my veins too.

Her lips move on a word I can recognise. "Yes?"

"I'm done dancing."

Clutching the lapels of my shirt, she searches around, her gaze landing on Enzo. He's talking to Phoenix's grandma, Pearl, and avoiding the cigarette smoke she blows in his face.

Harlow jerks her head. "Okay."

Letting her tow me this time, we stop at Enzo's table. He's resolutely refused to drink, preferring to check in with our agents at their posts every half hour instead to ease his paranoia.

I watch Harlow take a seat in his lap and plant a kiss on his stubble-covered cheek. Pearl laughs behind her large serving of whiskey and offers me a nod. She knows I'm far from her biggest fan.

Enzo quickly ditches her then casts one last look around the remaining guests. At his post, Ethan nods to him, confirming he'll keep an eye on things so we can bail.

"*Hotel?*" Enzo signs to me.

I nod, accepting Harlow back into my arms. It's taking all of my self-control not to grab the pert, rounded cheeks of her ass that her silk dress is accentuating in all the right places.

Making a hasty exit, we leave Leighton and Theo to their increasingly messy drinking game with Hudson and Jude. I'm too busy pressing Harlow between us in our haste to escape.

Locating Enzo's SUV, I take the passenger seat, yanking Harlow's arm so she falls onto my lap. Her dress pools at her waist, legs planting on either side of my thighs.

"You look so gorgeous today." I grab a handful of her hair and pull to seize her lips. "My cock has been hard for hours."

Her mouth falls victim to my savagery, teeth and tongue bruising and nipping. The alcohol fuels our collision until she's kissing me back just as hard to stake her own claim on me.

Enzo climbs behind the wheel and floors it, clearly desperate to join our gasping tangle. I slide my hands beneath her dress and groan. She's literally torturing me.

"Where are your bloody panties?"

Harlow shrugs, wearing an innocent smile.

"If I'd known your pussy was bare beneath this dress all day, I would've fucked you in front of the whole church hours ago."

Her mouth returns to mine, fierce and demanding. I sneak a hand between her thighs to find the heat at her core. With a mere few touches, she's wetter than a nun with her damn crucifix.

"Fuck, sweetheart. This pretty little cunt of yours is so wet."

Thumb circling her clit, I have to grab her hip as the car swerves to prevent her from falling off my lap. Enzo's driving at breakneck speed to pass the two streets between the church and our hotel.

Her mouth falls open on a silent moan as I push two fingers into her slit, curling them slightly to hit that inner sweet spot that I know she loves. Harlow lifts from my lap then moves to ride my fingers.

"That's it, baby," I praise. "Enz, hurry up, or I'm going to fuck her in this car for the world to see."

I'm not able to decipher the movement of his lips, but he's probably cussing me out. I won't get her to myself tonight, but that's okay.

The car judders to a halt, and he shoots out, the slam of his door rocking the structure. Harlow's still grinding on my lap, greedily taking the slow thrust of my fingers into her cunt.

When the door is ripped open to reveal Enzo, wild-eyed and baring his teeth, I realise we're in for a rough night. I pull my hand from between her legs and let him take her.

The security guard on the reception desk gives us a very strange look as we race past—Harlow tossed over Enzo's shoulder with her silk-covered rear being spanked by him.

When the elevator seals us in privacy, the hunt is back on. Enzo lowers Harlow from his shoulder then slams her spine into my chest. By some miracle, I'm able to string together the words his lips spell out.

"Fuck you ... raw ... tonight."

Grabbing Harlow's wrists, I pin them to her sides so Enzo can do what he pleases to her. She's imprisoned at my mercy, a tiny slip in comparison to his intimidating height above her.

Harlow's head tips back to release a moan as he skates his teeth down her neck, one hand cupping the generous mound threatening to spill from her neckline. I can see her hard nipples from here.

He releases her when the doors open, and Harlow lets me escort her to our bedroom, my steely grip on her wrists not easing. Once Enzo's unlocked the door, all bets are off.

He lifts her body and holds her against his waist to walk over to one of the two double beds. I follow, stripping off my suit one layer at a time, fumbling over the buttons in my haste.

Harlow is tossed on the bed in a flustered heap. Ripping the shirt over his head, Enzo quickly steps out of his suit trousers. His boxers go flying next. He's wasting no time.

Plunging my hand into my tight boxer shorts, I push them down then fist my shaft. Enzo lazily prowls towards Harlow's splayed-out body. He grabs her dress, pulling it off to reveal her scarred frame.

With the scrap of silk discarded on the floor, Enzo kisses his way up her legs to reach between her thighs. She's fisting the bedsheets already. Our angel is so sensitive to touch. It's hot as hell.

Moving closer, I pump my cock, standing off to the side so I have a perfect view of Enzo lifting Harlow's legs and pushing them open to dive into her sweet cunt.

Ducking down, I seize Harlow's lips and swallow her moans.

She's writhing on the bed, her thighs clamped around Enzo's head as he eats her out with the enthusiasm of a fucking food critic.

"I'm going to fuck that pretty mouth of yours while Enzo eats your cunt." I spread her lips with my thumb. "Open wide, sweetheart."

Kneeling on the bed next to her, I turn Harlow's head then feed the length of my dick into her mouth. The minute her pink lips wrap around the head, I'm done for.

"Christ, Harlow."

She greedily takes my length deep into the prison of her throat, lips cinching around the shaft to create the most delicious sense of pressure. I pump my hips and roughly fuck her mouth.

I know the minute Enzo pushes his thick fingers inside of her. Harlow's mouth tightens even more and almost finishes me off. I'm cutting her moans off with my cock.

Stopping for a breath, Enzo drops a mouthful of spit directly on the quivering lips of her cunt. I watch with interest as he slathers it across her clit and entrance before lining himself up.

His lips carve out a readable sentence. "Going to … split … gorgeous pussy … in half."

Harlow's teeth graze against my length when he surges inside in one smooth, brutal pump. It takes all of my self-control not to shoot my load down her throat.

Every time he thrusts inside of her, she milks my cock even harder, fighting to remain attached. Enzo's fucking her as roughly as promised, and it's one hell of an amazing view.

On the verge of losing it, I grab her chin and pull myself out. Trails of saliva and pre-come are leaking from her lips, and I can't stop myself from dragging my tongue over the seam of her mouth to clean it up.

"My turn," I purr. "Enzo needs to learn how to share. Let's teach him a lesson."

Holding up a hand to halt his thrusts, I crawl behind Harlow on the bed and pull her upright. Following my pointed finger, Enzo takes her place, lying down opposite us on the mattress.

She kneels on her hands and knees, curving her spine at the perfect angle as I move her into a doggy position. Harlow takes a handful of Enzo's cock then accepts it into her mouth instead.

Settling behind her, I have a perfect, undisturbed view of her dripping folds and tight asshole. Harlow holds Enzo by the hips and lets him abuse her mouth as brutally as he pleases.

But I still have control.

They're both my victims tonight.

Dragging two fingers through the slick juices of her cunt, I spread the moisture upwards to cover her back entrance. Harlow's entire frame shudders. This hole is still unexplored.

"You have such a tight little asshole." I run my thumb over the ring of muscle. "It's just begging for my cock to fill it up."

God, I'd love to hear her whines right now. Her attention is still fixed on the grunting lump beneath her as she sucks his dick.

Finger drenched in her come, I gently push against her hole, easing it inside the vice-like warmth.

"We need to start getting this hole ready to be fucked. I want to watch you fall apart with both of us buried inside of you."

The tiny earthquakes wracking her body betray how much she's enjoying being caged between us. I can see how wet her pussy is from the glistening moisture covering it.

With Enzo fucking her throat and my finger pushing in and out of her ass, her senses must be on overdrive. Spreading moisture over another finger, I push her further and slide it into her cunt.

With a digit in each hole, I begin to thoroughly fuck my girl in time with the upwards thrust of Enzo's hips. We're filling every available inch of her right now.

When Harlow's walls tighten around my finger, I know an orgasm is sweeping over her. Enzo takes advantage and increases his strokes until the widened 'O' of his lips communicates his own climax.

Harlow swallows every last drop, even as her release holds her captive. Head hitting the mattress, Enzo pants for air, allowing her to look up and lick the drops of escaping come from her lips.

I don't give her even a second to recover. I've waited long enough. Holding her hips, I position myself against the curve of her ass then spear her cunt in one fell swoop.

God-fucking-dammit.

Without my hearing, every other sense is dialled to ten. I can feel every single curvature of her sweet pussy, clenching tight around my cock and daring me to fill it up.

I move hard and fast, making eye contact with Enzo as he catches his breath beneath Harlow. He can deny it all he likes—voyeurism is as much his kink as it is mine.

When I push a finger into her backside, Harlow's head throws back. I can imagine her overwhelmed howling. That sweet, innocent-as-fuck voice contorted with agonising pleasure.

All those painful months we wasted will always prey on my mind. Our lives aren't guaranteed. I've learned that we can lose everything we ever held dear in a single fucking heartbeat.

There's no time to live safely. We have to walk on our tiptoes along the edge of a cliff and pray the wind doesn't knock us off our feet into the clutches of an early death.

That's the exhilaration. Living every single moment like it could be our last and not taking a single breath for granted. Harlow is my reason for living now. She's my redemption.

Cracking a hand against her ass, I savour the pink print that tarnishes her skin. I'm close to exploding. She's hugging my cock in all the right places.

With a final pump, I bellow and spill my seed deep into her. I can feel her orgasming again. Her pussy is clenched tight around me, and every limb trembles with the aftershocks.

Enzo grabs a handful of Harlow's hair and kisses her to silence the screams I cannot hear. Slumping behind her, my lungs are on fire. The haze of alcohol has dissipated after our frenzied fucking.

She doesn't protest as I find the willpower to scoop her up, loving the shine of my come streaming down her thighs. Where it fucking should be.

"Let's get you cleaned up."

In the attached en suite to the hotel room, I turn on the walk-in shower then set her down beneath the hot spray. Harlow moves to make space for me to join her.

It takes a couple of minutes for Enzo to catch up. The shower is big enough to fit all three of us with multiple shower heads exuding steam-laced heat. We all huddle together.

Lathering her hands in hotel shower gel, Harlow begins to massage it into my chest, taking the care to clean each ridge. I tip her head up so our eyes meet.

"Thank you."

Her eyebrows crease.

"For never giving up on me."

"Never," she mouths. "Love… you."

"Even when I drive you crazy?"

Harlow laughs and nods back.

"Well, same. Even when you drive me crazy too."

I thought I had unconditional love before. I'm not so sure now.

I loved Alyssa… but the way I feel about Harlow defies such easy categorisation. She's everything.

The air in my lungs.

The pump of my heart.

My world begins and ends with her.

I stroke my thumb over her cheekbone. "One day… that's going to be us up there."

Her head tilts in a question.

"Branding our names on your fucking soul for the rest of eternity." I look up at Enzo's grin to include him in the sentiment. "I want forever with you."

Enzo leans close to kiss her wet shoulder, the curve of his lips reiterating my vow. We've talked about our intentions. I know he feels the same way.

I'd marry her tomorrow if I didn't think the idea would scare her. But one day… that dream will be a reality. I won't let life tear the chance of happiness away from my family again.

I'll keep fighting for that.

For her.

For the rest of our lives.

SCÈNE DU MÉ...

CHAPTER 18

Harlow

Misery Business – Paramore

Adjusting my ponytail for the millionth time, I stare into the window in the corner of my laptop at the shiny pink scar on my forehead. It's relatively neat now that the switches have been removed.

Who thought it was a good idea to add that distraction to online video calls? I'm freaking out with every second I have to stare at my own reflection while waiting.

This meeting has been scheduled for the last couple of weeks, and I've grown even more apprehensive as it has drawn closer. I wouldn't even be here if Theo didn't sort everything for me.

With Brooklyn on the third week of her six-week honeymoon and Sabre fighting fires on all sides, I've kept busy with preparing for exams this week, marking the end of my online classes.

"Just breathe," Theo advises.

"Easy for you to say."

"Everything's going to be okay. I'm here with you."

We're hidden in the quiet sanctuary of his office in HQ. I opted to tag along with the others into London, needing moral support for this call.

"What if they don't want to publish my book?" I bite my lip. "I know nothing about writing. It's just a bunch of messy journals."

Theo reaches across the desk to take my hand. "It's far more than that, and you know it. Just hear what they have to offer."

"What did their email say?"

"Not much," he reveals. "We got a lot of interest in the proposal I put together for you. This publishing house was the most reputable."

"What if they laugh at me? This could be some sick prank. The entire world hates my guts for what I did in that video."

Theo squeezes my fingers. "Have a little faith, beautiful. There are people out there who still want the truth. They're just being drowned out by fear and suspicion."

Taking another measured breath, I smooth my plain white blouse and watch the clock tick down to the hour. Faith is in short supply around here, especially with the mob still protesting outside.

There's a beep before the meeting starts, and Theo sits up a little straighter next to me. I refused to do this meeting without him.

"Hello, Harlow."

On the screen, a brown-haired woman with friendly almond eyes and an easy smile appears in her smart business wear. I give her a little wave.

"Hi. Thank you for meeting with me."

"Good morning," Theo chimes in.

"My name is Abigail. I'm the executive editor here at Hawkstone Publishing. One of my agents passed your information along to me."

"We were expecting to meet with William." Theo stacks the sheaths of paperwork in his hands. "I've been communicating with him regarding Harlow's submission to your press."

"Of course," Abigail begins. "But given the pseudo-celebrity status of Harlow and Sabre Security, I thought it best to handle this myself."

Anxiety floods my system. This woman is the top dog. This could go one of two ways, and I'm terrified of the potential rejection.

"There is a lot of interest in your story, Harlow." She smiles kindly. "I'm sure you are apprehensive about publishing your story."

"It's a little nerve-racking," I admit. "But I think I could do a lot of good with this memoir. I want to help other people like me."

Abigail spins her fountain pen in hand. "And that is exactly what I wanted to hear. Tell me more about your motives."

"I'm not sure she—"

I rest a hand on Theo's leg beneath the desk. "No, it's fine. I know many people think I'm doing this for fortune or fame. My intentions relate to neither of those things."

She nods enthusiastically. "So what do you want?"

"To show the world that it's possible to survive and rebuild your life. I lived without hope for so long. I want to give the world what I needed as a scared child who thought she'd never escape."

Scribbling notes, Abigail's eyes are lit with a gleam of excitement that punches through my overwhelming fear.

"This is a very competitive market that you're breaking into," she advises. "But something tells me your book will be in very high demand. I'd be honoured to publish it."

"You … would?"

Abigail's smile softens. "I think it's time the world heard from the girl who lived, rather than the monster who silenced her. I want to give you that voice, Harlow."

A confusing concoction of relief and appreciation causes my eyes to sear with tears. That was the one thing I lived without for thirteen years of my life: a voice.

That's what this whole journey has been about. Rediscovering my own strength and using it to build a life beyond my trauma. This feels like the end of a very long and tumultuous road.

"I'm sure you're fighting off our rivals' attention, so I'd like to make you an offer. We're anticipating a great deal of demand for this memoir, and I hope you'll find the terms favourable."

Theo's phone pings with an incoming email. He quickly opens it and scans over the lines of text in the attached documents. I watch his mouth fall open on a silent curse.

"That's … reasonable," he rasps.

"I'm glad you think so," Abigail chuckles. "I wouldn't want to lose this opportunity to our competition. Feel free to consult your legal counsel, and let me know as soon as possible."

I can't fully read the blur of numbers over his shoulder, but the rows of zeros scrawl across his phone screen.

"Harlow?"

My eyes snap back to the laptop. "Yes?"

"I wanted to say that I think what you're doing is incredibly brave," Abigail offers. "Not many people would have the conviction to share their demons with the world."

I gulp down the lump in my throat. "Thank you."

"We want to honour you and your story in the most authentic way possible. I hope that you'll think about my offer."

"I will."

"Good. Well, then. I'll await your call." She flashes teeth in a bright smile. "Thanks for your time."

Theo signs off the call for me then shuts the laptop. "That was interesting."

"What the hell just happened?"

"You got yourself a publishing deal." He kisses my cheek. "And half a million pounds in advance."

My heart stops. "Half... What?"

"You fucking did it!"

Theo crushes me to his chest so tight, I struggle to breathe. My head is spinning from the last ten minutes. None of this feels real.

When he releases me, Theo's grinning from ear to ear. I cup his jaw and drag him into a heart-pounding kiss that brings me back to reality.

"None of this would've happened without you," I murmur into his lips. "I didn't do this. You did."

"Not a chance. Don't do yourself a disservice. They want to publish your book because of *you*, angel. No one else."

A tentative knock on his office door forces us apart. Theo calls for them to come in, then my father appears in the doorway, his dirty blonde hair matted with sweat from another training session.

"And?" he asks excitedly.

"I ... got offered a deal."

"Oh my God! That's amazing!"

He rushes into the room and nearly yanks me off my feet with the strength of his bear hug. With my dad's arms around me, the tears finally break free.

"I'm so proud of you," he whispers into my hair. "I know this can't be easy, but you're doing something incredible."

"Thanks, Dad."

"He isn't going to win, love. This is your fight, and we're all here to support you every step of the way."

My heart explodes with love as he kisses my temple. I had no idea what having my father around would be like, but I want him in my life. Regardless of the past.

"I need to get washed up." Dad releases me. "Shall we celebrate tonight?"

"I'd like that. Want to come over to ours?"

"Sure. I'll bring the food."

"Leighton eats for three," Theo chips in. "He suffers from hollow bone syndrome, apparently. That was his latest excuse."

Dad snorts. "Got it. Lots of food, then."

He disappears, leaving us to pour over the complicated contracts and legal jargon attached to the publisher's email. Theo forwards it to Sabre's legal team, seeming satisfied with the content.

"What happens now?"

"Once we get the all-clear from legal, we'll contact Abigail and take it from there. They will handle everything."

"This is really happening, isn't it?"

Theo runs a hand down my arm. "It sure is. Your dad's right. This is an amazing achievement. You should be proud of yourself."

Before I can respond, his ringing phone cuts me off. Theo quickly answers then listens to the roar of Enzo's voice down the line.

"Woah. Slow down, Enz."

As he listens, his eyes widen in a look I've become sickeningly acquainted with. Horror. It's never far from our lives of late.

"We're coming up."

Ending the call, Theo glances up at me with pupils split wide open. Darkness and death stare back at me in familiar shades.

"Reports of bodies are coming in from local police. The team's waiting upstairs for us to do an emergency debrief."

"Bodies?" I repeat. "Plural?"

All he can offer is a terse nod.

Leaning heavily on him for support, we race upstairs to Hunter's office. Theo fumbles the code several times in his nervousness. The door wrenches open before we can unlock it.

Leighton's face is pale as he spots us. "Quick. Come in."

Entering the evidence-lined walls of Hunter's office, the remaining members of the Anaconda team sit at the long conference table opposite Enzo and Hunter.

All eyes are focused on the TV screen relaying a live feed from a body cam. No one dares to speak a word. Not even a greeting as we hastily take our seats.

"What's happening?" Theo asks.

Ethan spares us a glance. "Reports started coming in half an hour ago. One location at first. Then two others were confirmed in different cities by local departments."

"Is it him?"

"The markings are all there."

I reach for Leighton and curl my arm around his, needing a tether. Since the violence that broke out before the wedding, tensions have been escalating daily, but Michael has remained silent.

It's almost like he doesn't need to speak anymore. This country is a tinderbox sitting next to a raging inferno. The spark he lit was enough to achieve his aim. Widespread terror.

"Three l-locations?" I stammer.

"That's three separate murders at the same time in totally different corners of the country," Enzo confirms grimly. "Copycat kills."

"So it wasn't Michael?"

"He could have coordinated the attacks with help." Leighton blows out a breath. "Unless this is some asshole looking for a cheap thrill."

"Local police just sent us this footage," Enzo adds.

On the screen, we're guided into the depths of a sunlit forest. The trees are all burnished in autumnal colours as October arrives. Each crunch of the police officer's footsteps strikes me in the chest.

But the awaiting sight defies expectations. I know the depths of my uncle's depravity. This senseless violence is branded with his trademark.

Swinging in the trees, three bodies drip with congealed trails of blood. Their flayed skin is on display, bare without clothing. It exposes the vicious slashes of the Holy Trinity disfiguring their chests.

Roughly tied nooses hold the victims by their necks, faces blue and skin waxy as they gently sway. Slashed and displayed like hung meat.

"Fuck me," Hunter mutters.

The remaining members of the Anaconda team—Tara, Warner and Ethan—sit together in horrified silence.

"Three deceased," the officer reports. "All marked and hung from nooses. No signs of life. They've been here for a few hours, at least."

"I need you on the ground immediately." Enzo points at Ethan and Tara. "I don't want this leaking to the press until we have the scene secured."

He nods solemnly. "We'll take the helicopter to Grantham."

"There are reports of another crime scene fifty miles east in Wisbech." He turns to Warner. "Establish a perimeter and report back. Take Hyland with you."

Following a round of agreement, all three of them disappear. Enzo slumps and bangs his head on the table as soon as they've gone.

"Fucking copycats. This can't be real."

"It was inevitable," Theo consoles. "I'm surprised this didn't happen sooner. Abaddon may not even be involved."

"It's worse if he isn't. We don't need more psychotic killers terrorising the country when we can't even catch the first one."

Still silent, Hunter is watching the recorded police feed, his lips pressed into a tight line. Officers are roping the scene off with blue tape and going about their formalities.

I wish I didn't recognise the look on his face. Hell, I wish I wasn't feeling the exact same thing. Defeat. We've barely come up for air, and another wave is crashing down on us.

"Michael has formed a whole underground network," I croak. "This has gone beyond a few crazed supporters."

"He's escalating," Enzo agrees. "Abaddon organised those suicides. Hid undetected in Tregaron. Blew up the church. Now this."

Theo nods thoughtfully. "No one causes all this chaos alone. We aren't fighting him anymore. We're fighting a whole fucking army."

"So how do we beat them?"

No one jumps to answer my question. With hysteria crawling up my throat, the brief sense of empowerment I felt coming out of that meeting is blown to pieces. I can never win.

Not while he's still out there.

Hunting and killing.

"Giana," I blurt. "She claimed to have new information about Michael. I've delayed visiting her for weeks now."

"No," Leighton says flatly. "She's bluffing."

"Probably."

"Then don't waste another moment of your time on that woman. We all know she doesn't have shit on Abaddon. She's just desperate."

I don't need to say aloud what we're all thinking—*so are we.* Michael has driven us to the point of desperation and beyond.

"What other leads do we have?" I point out. "The suicide victims have turned up nothing but a flimsy connection. Tregaron was a dead end. Any evidence in that crypt died with Becket."

"We're about to have a morgue full of bodies," Theo supplies. "If

Abaddon's training copycats, they'll be sloppy. We may have a lead."

"Can we wait that long? What if he goes out tomorrow and orders the deaths of a dozen more people? What then?"

Enzo slams a hand down on the table. "It won't get that far. Go and see Giana. Get any information you can."

I nod, deflating.

He looks to Theo. "Call the superintendent, and set a meeting. I want every fucking police officer in the country on the streets going door-to-door. It's time to kick things up a notch."

Relaying his words to Hunter in sign language, Theo looks solemn. Even among the clouds at the top of Sabre's skyscraper, the screaming and shouting on the street below us filters through.

Violence has become widespread, with more and more public demonstrations breaking out into scuffles between those driven hysterical by Michaels's warning and everyone remaining sane.

"We need to request some kind of nationwide curfew. The entire country is on fire. Abaddon is using that chaos to his advantage."

"Once you make that call, we can't take it back," Theo argues. "We'll be playing into public fear by locking people down."

"I don't give a flying fuck," Enzo spits back. "We're going to flush this bastard out by force. Someone knows where his base is."

With the decision made, Theo drops a kiss on the top of my head then disappears to make the call. If anyone can convince the superintendent to launch such a huge operation, it's him.

Standing up to follow in his wake, I fish my phone out of the pocket of my parka.

"I'll request visitation with Giana in Bronzefield. She's already added me to her list. I can go after my exam finishes tomorrow."

"I'll take you there." Leighton sighs. "You're going to need backup. It'll be like a trip down memory lane."

"You were in Bronzefield?"

"The one and only."

Hunter pauses the video and opens another email, a new file attached. "I need to review these before we make any official statements."

"*Lucas?*" Enzo fingerspells to him.

"Make the call. It won't be long before the vampires are hammering on our front door. He needs to handle the fallout."

Hesitating on his way out of the room, Enzo turns to face me. "Fuck, Harlow. I forgot about your meeting."

"Oh. It doesn't matter now."

His brows pinch together. "Like hell it doesn't. What happened?"

All three of them are waiting for my answer. Flushing under the spotlight, I wrestle with my guilt for still feeling excited, despite the fresh wave of violence.

"I've been offered a contract and … *ahem*, half a million pounds in advance. They're going to publish my book."

Shooting out of his seat, Leighton rugby-tackles me in a hug that almost knocks me off my feet.

"Jesus fucking Christ, princess!"

Spun in a circle, he sets me down on my feet again, only for Enzo to swoop in next. He flattens me against his chest, and his lips bruise mine in a celebratory kiss.

"I am so proud of you."

"I haven't done anything," I laugh into his mouth.

"This is all you. Own it, angel."

When he kisses me again, all of the anguish dissipates. The blood. The bodies. The threats and violence. In Enzo's arms, he is my single point of existence.

I never would've survived the past year if I didn't have them by my side, but Enzo was the one who tossed all reservations aside, putting his love and devotion into a total stranger.

He gave me a life.

A future.

A brand-new family.

This moment isn't mine. I don't own even a fraction of it. All that I am is a result of their faith in the broken, damaged girl they rescued from that hospital.

When Enzo finally sets me back down, there's one more set of eyes burning a path across my skin. Hunter has abandoned his urgent emails in favour of joining us.

"You got it?" he asks.

I nod back.

"I knew you had it in you." He shakes his head in mirth. "Come here, sweetheart."

Stepping into his arms is easier than drawing in one breath after another. My body recognises his on an instinctual level, our souls imprinted with the same lifelong brand.

"When we first met, I knew that you were something special," he whispers into my hair. "It has been an absolute fucking honour watching you blossom into the person I always knew you were."

My tears soak into the pressed fabric of his dress shirt, revealing the dark swirls of ink underneath. That is Hunter's power—the ability to make me feel like I'm the only person in his entire world.

Fuck the investigation. Fuck Michael Abaddon. Fuck everything and everyone but us. Our family. None of this means anything if I don't have them … forever.

Even if our love is relegated to the afterlife. For the first time, I can see the end in sight. It's coming up on the horizon. But we won't reach it without a final sacrifice.

They've done enough.

I won't let the devil take them too.

SCENE DU NOIR
J. ROSE

CHAPTER 19

Harlow

Lost In The Moment – NF & Andreas Moss

Bouncing on the balls of his feet beside me, Leighton is palpably nervous. Enough that he didn't crack a single joke during the two-hour car ride it took to reach the prison.

We both stare up at the imposing, barbed wire topped gates of Bronzefield Prison. It's a dreary, grey-scale structure, uniform and utterly devoid of any personality.

Pain and sadness seem to ooze from the cinder blocks, baked in between layers of cement and security alarms. This place is high security and notorious for its violent offenders.

"Never thought I'd be back here."

I glance up at Leighton's grimace. "Only this time, you're not entering as the same person you were all those years ago. Don't forget that, Leigh."

"You have too much faith in me," he mutters.

"Someone has to."

"And I love you for it, Goldilocks. Let's get this over and done with. We're needed back at HQ for a debrief in three hours, and we still need to celebrate you passing those exams."

"I'm really not in the mood to celebrate."

He locks Hunter's red convertible. "I'm not having any of that. You've been working towards this for months. We're celebrating."

"We'll see."

Taking his hand, Leighton leads me up the long, paved walkway towards the prison. Each step causes my anxiety to spiral.

There are tall guard towers on both sides, boasting the beady eyes of surveillance cameras and posted prison guards. No one gets in or out of this place without it being monitored.

The closer we get to the unscalable, high walls of this utilitarian nightmare, the tighter Leighton's white-knuckled grip on my hand becomes. I'm almost holding him upright.

We're stopped in the entrance and accosted by a circle of security officers, preventing us from travelling any farther. After checking their paperwork, I'm led to the side and have to surrender my handbag to be searched.

"Christ alive," an officer exclaims. "Rodriguez."

Leighton removes his belt and drops it in a tray to be scanned. "Dean. Bet you didn't expect to see my face here again, did you?"

Dressed in a neat uniform, Dean chuckles. "To be honest, we placed bets on how long you'd survive the outside world. I lost a hundred quid because of you."

"You bet against me? Seriously?"

"Sorry, kid. Thought it was a safe bet."

With another grumble, Leighton lifts his arms to be scanned over with a wand, searching for any contraband. We're both declared clear and given back our valuables.

"Who are you here for?" a female officer drones behind Perspex glass.

"Giana Kensington. She's expecting us."

Peering at her computer screen, she pops a dramatic bubble of gum. "She's been on suicide watch for the past month. No visitors allowed."

"Wait, what? Suicide watch?" I exclaim.

"We booked an appointment with the warden." Leighton pulls his wallet out then slides a professional-looking ID badge across. "Sabre Security."

Dean whistles under his breath. "Fuck me sideways. You're working for big bro now?"

Leighton resolutely ignores him and waits for his ID to be slid back. Our female officer disappears to make a quick call, clearly annoyed that we've forced her to get off her ass.

When she returns, a pot-bellied man in a blue suit follows her. His eyes are sharp and unimpressed, landing on us both with a look of disgruntlement.

"You're here for Giana Kensington?"

I straighten my spine. "We are."

"We don't normally allow visitation for high-risk inmates, but I've been instructed to make an allowance." His voice is dripping with displeasure. "I don't take kindly to being told what to do with my damn inmates."

"Look," Leighton cuts in. "We're here on official business with clearance from well above your pay grade. Giana is being questioned as part of an official investigation."

"I'm quite aware of her charges. We don't usually take inmates pre-trial. She's an exception to that rule."

"Then this isn't a normal visitation request, is it?"

The warden's shoulders slump. "I suppose not."

"So take us to the inmate, and stay out of our way, or I'll happily make a call to your superior and inform them of this delay to our investigation."

Knowing he's beaten, the warden waves for us to follow him into the depths of the prison. We're sandwiched between Dean and another security officer, giving me a second to grab Leighton's arm.

"Where did you get that ID badge from?" I whisper.

"Like it?" He smirks at me. "Perks of taking over while Hunter was laid up. Pretty sure I'm the first recruit Enzo hasn't had the pleasure of torturing for weeks on end."

We fall silent as the layers of air-locked security doors and barred grates are unlocked in turn, each with a loud screech. My head is thumping with a headache already.

Our escorts guide us past ajar office doors and the odd inmate being supervised while carrying out chores. The signs take us down three flights of stairs, into the lower levels of the prison.

"You remember this floor?" Dean goads. "I enjoyed slinging your ass in solitary confinement enough times for getting into the stupidest of fights."

Leighton winces, avoiding my eyes. "I remember."

"Who would've thought you'd be on the other side of these doors, huh?"

"Look," I snap at him. "We didn't come to reminisce. Leighton is here in an official capacity as my security detail. You're not permitted to speak to him."

Chastised, his mouth flops open comically before he wrenches it shut. The dumbfounded look on his face is priceless, but Leighton's grateful smile is even better.

At the front of the solitary wing, its wiped-clean floors dripping with the scent of industrial bleach, a tiny interview room sits behind the guard's station. We're directed inside.

"You have fifteen minutes," the warden informs us curtly. "Make it count."

"We'll take as long as we need," Leighton drones. "Now go."

His face slowly turning purple, the warden makes a hasty exit. We take our seats in the two metal-framed chairs on one side of a rickety table, then I curl my hands into fists underneath it.

"You're sounding more and more like your brother with every day that passes," I mutter.

Leighton snorts. "That's a terrifying thought. How are you holding up?"

"I … really don't know. I thought I'd be more nervous, but now I'm sitting here, all I feel is anger."

"Talk to me," he entreats.

"It's just that it didn't have to be this way."

"I know, princess. But Giana made her choice."

He's right. She chose this. But that doesn't change the fact that in the hazy state of relief that followed Michael's escape, I was able to say that one word aloud.

Mum.

But she isn't my mother. Giana hasn't earned the privilege of that title. She knew what her half-brother did to me, and still, she led me straight back into his clutches.

"We'll find out what we need to know then split," Leighton decides. "I have zero interest in staying in this hellhole for a second longer than we have to."

I look around the plain, mouldy room. "How many times were you put in solitary for fighting?"

He shrugs. "Lost count."

"I can't imagine you being that … angry."

"Trust me, I can be angry when I need to be. You don't survive prison without demanding other people's respect. That's earned in blood, not happy sentiments."

I study his hands, clasped together on top of the table. The thick layers of scar tissue that mar his knuckles told me of the violence he'd seen the moment we met.

Yet still, I can't fathom how my Leighton—sweet, affectionate and caring—could hurt someone enough to earn himself a ticket to this circle of hell. He doesn't have a bad bone in his body.

"Sometimes I catch myself missing this place," he admits.

"Why?"

"It's hard to explain. I didn't have to live up to anyone else's expectations here, only my own. I was free to be as violent and self-destructive as I wanted to be."

My heart twinges. "Leigh."

"I know. It wasn't healthy, and I don't really miss it. But sometimes my brain does subconsciously."

"I'm glad you're not still in here," I say quietly. "We never would've met otherwise, and I couldn't have survived the last year without you."

Leighton's eyes soften, his smile blossoming. "Me too, Goldilocks. You saved me in more ways than I can explain."

I grasp his hand. "We saved each other."

"And we always will."

"Always," I echo.

The slap of footsteps approaching interrupts our conversation, and we both smooth on blank expressions. When the door swings open again, a stranger is emitted into the room.

Hair lank with grease and sallow cheeks framing haze-filled eyes, Giana Kensington is far from the put together housewife that offered me tea and biscuits at her dinner table.

She's cuffed at the wrists and ankles, the pointy bones of her slimmed-down body concealed in a baggy, grey jumpsuit. The moment she sees me, her lips part on a relieved whine.

"Harlow."

She remembers my name now, at least.

"Giana," I say stiffly. "Sit down."

Shoved into the chair opposite by the unknown guard escorting her, Giana winces slightly at the rough treatment. He retreats to the corner of the room to keep a wary eye on her.

"You came," she breathes out. "I'd given up hope when you didn't show after our phone call."

"Some things came up."

She cuts her escort a wary glance. "I'm not given much access to the outside world. They stopped giving me updates on the case when I was put in solitary confinement."

"The warden said that you're on suicide watch," Leighton chips in. "Didn't fancy making it to your own trial, huh?"

Her head sinks. "It's not like that."

"You deserve your day in court for all the deaths you've enabled by protecting that sick son of a bitch. Killing yourself won't stop justice from finding you."

"Leigh," I interject. "Enough."

He sinks back in his chair, starts the voice recorder on his phone and places it on the table. Giana's tears are falling in silent trails down her cheeks.

"I never meant for things to turn out like this," she says in a distraught voice. "I'm sorry for so many things, Harlow. But I'm not sorry for bringing you into this world. I'm proud of the woman you've become."

Looking away from her, I strangle my own emotions to keep them at bay. I can't be fooled by her again.

"I'm not here to talk about us, Giana. Tell me about Michael."

She looks crestfallen but nods in defeat. "I had no idea what I was getting myself into when I first met Michael."

"We know about your mother. Did you meet him after she died?"

Giana nods. "I tried to build a relationship with Michael, but I didn't know the truth. He was living with his wife a couple of hours away under a false identity at the time."

"What happened between you?"

"He came to visit me. You were very young at the time, and … there was something about him. This strange, dark power that clung to him like a shadow."

"Seriously?" Leighton scoffs.

"He was very manipulative," she hits back. "You didn't know that you were under his spell until it was too late. I was lost, and … and … I hated my life."

"You had me and Dad."

She wipes her eyes with her cuffed wrist. "Your father is no saint, Harlow. He had demons of his own. I couldn't cope with being a parent alone. Things were hard for us."

"So what did Michael have on you that made you so blind to the truth?" I lean forward in my seat. "We've spoken to witnesses from his past, and we know he abused Rosetta."

"She was his victim too," Giana agrees. "I didn't see it until it was too late. He told me that the baby was fine… I didn't know that she'd lost it."

My breathing halts. "What baby?"

"Their baby. Rosetta was pregnant when I met Michael. She lost the baby a few months before … he took you."

"Who told you this?" Leighton snaps.

"Rosetta did." Giana sniffles. "She tried to warn me about him, but I was so blinded by the crap he stuffed my head full of. I couldn't see past the madness he sparked inside me."

"You met her?" I ask next.

"Only once. She came on his last visit to our house. Michael convinced me that if I didn't surrender you to him, my soul would be damned. I was so afraid of him."

The thought of Rosetta trying to warn Giana off her plan to sacrifice me, concocted in the manic state of insanity she fell into, sparks a feeling deep in my chest.

Rosetta had been under his almighty control for years by then—beaten, brutalised, her mind broken and moulded into an inhuman mockery of her former self. But she still tried to stop him.

How did that final spark of light get snuffed out, birthing the hateful, bitter woman I later came to know? The Mrs Michaels who spent a decade torturing me was not the same person Giana met.

"How did she lose the baby?" Leighton's question drags me back.

"I don't know. She wouldn't say, but it was obvious that he was beating her. She was black and blue. I think he brought her there as a warning to stop me from backing out of the plan."

"A warning," I repeat. "Because you didn't have even a crack of doubt about sacrificing your only child to the devil himself, right?"

"Please, Harlow," she begs. "It wasn't that simple. He spent months terrorising me. I was already a wreck, and he used that to his advantage to break me down."

I want to throw up on the scratched metal surface of the table. I'd almost forgotten how flimsy her excuses are when spoken out loud.

"That's why he wanted me, isn't it?" I slam my hands on the table. "Rosetta lost his child, and he wanted a replacement. I was his newest pet project."

Giana breaks down. "Yes. I believe so."

With the floodgates open, every last repulsive detail makes sense. He spent months torturing and assaulting the women he brought down into the basement. It was a vicious cycle.

Only when he grew bored of their screams would he enact the final stages of the ritual and take their lives. After they'd proven themselves worthless … by failing to produce him another child.

Holy shit.

"That's why he hurt all those women," I rush out. "He chose sex workers like his mother … and tried to impregnate them to recreate his own childhood. To rewrite his own history."

"This is sick," Leighton curses. "That's his mission? To kill off all the unworthy in his stupid fucking rapture and repopulate the earth with his rape babies instead? Seriously?"

I can't answer him. All I can see in my mind's eye is the look of unadulterated rage on Michael's face as Adelaide bled out—stealing yet another potential life from his grasp.

She survived far longer than any of the other girls, even as he continued to inflict his twisted desires on her. All because of the miracle she carried.

"I need your help." Giana's voice is high with desperation.

"My help?" I laugh.

"Please. You know he won't stop until he completes this godforsaken mission. I need you to keep Ulrich safe for me, Harlow. Don't let Michael hurt him too."

"That's why you called me? To bribe me into protecting the kid you replaced me with?"

"No," she blurts. "Of course not. I needed to see you and make you understand. I'd do anything to take back what I did to you, but I can't. I'm paying the price for my sins now."

Leighton clenches my hand, encouraging me to end the conversation. I let go of him and push his touch aside.

"I could press charges against you for my kidnapping and have you sentenced to life inside this prison. Give me one good reason why I shouldn't do exactly that."

"I can't give you that," Giana admits. "I deserve to die in this place. I've made my peace with that fact. But I'm begging you… Don't let Michael punish my son. He's innocent in all of this—"

"Ulrich is safe," Leighton interrupts. "I know Enzo has had someone checking on him ever since you were arrested. Call your damn husband, and speak to him instead."

"Foster has been refusing my calls for months." She chokes back another sob. "He won't even let me speak to Ulrich. I know Michael will come for him to punish me."

If Enzo has Ulrich under surveillance, then he's safe as can be. I know that Enzo wouldn't let anything happen to an innocent child.

"You promised me information," I snarl impatiently. "Tell me what you dragged us here for, and I'll see what I can do about your family. No promises."

"You'll protect him? Ulrich?"

"I'll speak to Foster and tell him to return your calls. The rest isn't up to me."

Her nod is jerky. "I'll take anything. I just need to hear my son's voice."

"Then give us your information. Last chance."

I watch the defeat settle over her in an invisible cloud of volcanic ash. It saps the last of her strength, and she folds, barely able to lift her head.

"There's another one of us."

"What do you mean? Another what?"

Her tears drip into her lap. "Another sibling. Our mother had a third child. If anyone knows where Michael is right now … it's Daphne."

SCENE DU RK
POSE
300

CHAPTER 20

Theo

Overgrown – Mountains Of The Moon

Spread across the living room floor, old cartons of last night's Chinese food and empty beer bottles litter the space between our stacks of files. *The Office* is on in the background, courtesy of Harlow and Leighton.

It's almost dusk on our second day of research. We've been scouring the depths of the internet and public records for information about our target in an attempt to build a profile.

Daphne Portcastle.

She's the twist in this tale that none of us anticipated. Giana kept the existence of her half-sister secret for all these years. She hasn't even seen or heard from her in well over a decade.

"My eyes feel like they're on fire." Leighton lays spreadeagled on the floor amidst the leftover food. "Is there more coffee?"

"Just brewed a fresh pot," Enzo rumbles from behind a stack of printed sheets. "What was the name of Daphne's husband again?"

"Christopher Lang," I recite tiredly.

"I've tracked down a marriage certificate," he confirms. "Christopher was declared dead seven years ago, and Daphne sold their house two years after that."

"Where?"

Enzo peers down at the records. "Fuck me. Fifteen miles outside of Newcastle."

Shooting upright from her position in the corner of the room, Harlow startles Lucky's sleeping form spread across her legs.

"Did you just say Newcastle?"

Checking the paperwork again, Enzo nods. "Affirmative."

"And what years were Abaddon and Rosetta living in Newcastle? Before Kiera's death?"

I scour through the case files on my laptop, tracing a messy, winding path through the last fourteen years. It's all here. The final puzzle pieces that need to come together to catch our killer.

"Lee and Natasha Heston, aka Abaddon and Rosetta, moved away from Newcastle after Kiera's body was discovered." I scan the complex timeline. "They were in the area at the same time."

"Son of a bitch," Enzo curses.

Leighton reappears in the room with a steaming mug of coffee. "Michael was hiding out near Daphne's hometown after he kidnapped Harlow. That can't be a coincidence."

"And when Kiera's body rocked up, Michael and Rosetta ran to escape suspicion," Enzo adds. "Assuming brand-new identities elsewhere in the country."

"At the same time Daphne's husband miraculously dies and leaves her an expensive home to sell," I finish for them. "This all fucking stinks, doesn't it?"

"We need to track her down." Harlow strokes a hand over Lucky's golden fur. "She has to know something."

Compiling all the information into a secure message to the intelligence team, I send it off, marked as an urgent action. We've got all of Sabre's might driving this investigation to its close.

Now that we've successfully tracked down Daphne's identity, we can begin running my facial recognition software. The moment she surfaces, we'll have a location to follow up.

With much persuasion, the superintendent obliged our request to order a nationwide crackdown. Every police force in the country is out on the streets, breaking up the hysteria and scouring for intel.

We'll rain down the power of the whole fucking country and its rage on Daphne's head, if that's what it takes for her to give up Michael.

"Any update on those post-mortems?" Enzo checks.

"Nine bodies across three different crime scenes have been transported to HQ for processing. All adults, most middle-aged, found carved up and hanging from nooses."

Leighton slurps his coffee. "Suicides?"

"The nooses were tied all wrong. They were hung by someone. Almost like—"

"Rosetta's body," Harlow finishes.

I close my laptop. "Exactly."

"He's taunting us. Michael wants us to know that he's behind these copycat kills, even from afar."

"We need profiles on all of them." Enzo glances over to me. "See if there's any correlation with the previous victims from the beach."

"Already got Rayna on it. She's working overtime with her new intern, so we should have some more information soon."

"That intern's gonna run away screaming from the company after this fiasco." Leighton chuckles. "Way to scare them off."

"We're running a company here," Enzo complains. "If they don't like it, they can go work in a bloody tea room instead."

"That's great for staff retention, Enz."

"I really don't give a shit."

The creak of Hunter moving around upstairs abruptly silences them. He's been unresponsive since taking a large dose of migraine medication.

"How long was he out?" Harlow sighs.

"Only a couple of hours." Enzo scrubs a hand over his face. "I've told him to talk to his specialist about these headaches at his checkup next month."

"Like he'd do that willingly," I comment.

"Maybe they can offer something else that will help." He turns to Harlow. "Will you go with him? He's refusing to let me come."

"Enz…" she begins.

"You know Hunter won't ask for our help, even when he needs it. He should have someone there with him for moral support."

"What makes you think he'll listen to me?"

Leighton waggles his eyebrows. "You could always persuade him."

"Classy. I'm not going to sleep with your brother to blackmail him into taking me to his appointment."

"Who said anything about blackmail?" Leighton snickers. "That asshole will do anything for you, and you know it. Don't underestimate the power you have over him."

"He's right," Enzo agrees. "Talk to him."

"Alright, alright. I'll give it a shot."

Clambering to her feet, Harlow dislodges Lucky then disappears upstairs to track Hunter down. I hope she'll be able to talk some sense into him. The rest of us don't have any hope.

He's had several regular checkups since his accident and has forbidden any of us from attending outside of driving him there.

Hunter the control freak is out in full swing.

"He won't do it." I take a swig of long-cold coffee. "You know how terrified of weakness he is."

"Leaning on his family's support isn't a weakness," Enzo argues. "We're supposed to look out for each other."

"I'm not disagreeing with you. But he doesn't see it that way, no matter what we do. This is a road he wants to walk alone."

"Like everything else," Leighton mutters. "How the hell did we end up here? Mum calls me fishing for information on Hunter. Me!"

"Regardless of the shit going on with Hunter, you should be proud of how far you've come." Enzo looks at him meaningfully. "He's lucky to have you as his brother."

Gaze ducking, Leighton smothers his grin with another sip of coffee. "I guess so."

"Sorry to break the moment," I interrupt. "But what are we going to do about Giana? We've got eyes on her husband and son. They're both secure."

"Is she still on suicide watch?" Enzo studies another sheet of paper.

"It sounds like that'll be the case until her trial begins." I stretch my arms above my head. "The warden told me what happened. Giana made some threats to the prison counsellor and was found cutting herself."

I wish I didn't feel any empathy for that batshit crazy woman, but part of me empathises with her. In Giana's own way, she was also a victim of Abaddon and his depravity.

That doesn't negate her own crimes, though. She still made the choice to support a murderer and lie to us all. For that alone, she can never be forgiven in my mind.

"What exactly does she want Harlow to do?"

"Giana wants her to meet the husband and convince him to allow visitation for the kid," Leighton answers. "He hasn't taken any of Giana's calls for months and cut off all contact."

Enzo scoffs. "They're better off without her."

Two pairs of footsteps thump down the stairs. Bare-chested and wearing low slung pyjama bottoms, Hunter pads into the room, escorted by Harlow.

"Look who's up," she says cheerfully. "Make some room."

Sweeping paperwork and several manilla files off the sofa, Enzo clears space for Hunter to sit down. He looks barely awake and a little disorientated.

I point to my forehead then tap.

He collapses on the sofa. "Still pounding."

Leighton disappears, returning with a glass of water to wash down the handful of brightly coloured pills in his palm. For once, Hunter doesn't protest and accepts the medication.

"What's the latest?" he grumbles.

Passing over the marriage certificate for him to inspect, Enzo quickly fills him in on our findings. No one drops off the radar entirely. Not even Abaddon managed to do that. We might have picked up his trail through our newest suspect.

The strange sound of scuffling from outside the front window causes Enzo to freeze, hands raised mid-sentence. "Is the pizza here?"

Leighton bounces on the spot. "He's probably lost again. I'll get it."

Stealing Enzo's wallet full of cash, he sprints for the front door to fetch our food. I'm convinced he has a tapeworm. He eats like he's been starved his entire life.

"Little shit," Enzo curses. "Can't he use his own money?"

"He prefers yours," I joke.

Hunter studies the marriage certificate. "We need to pull on the superintendent's resources and have the police looking for Daphne too."

Enzo shakes his head. "If we spook her, she'll run."

"Or it may do the opposite and flush her out," I argue.

"She may not even be in the country. Harlow doesn't remember her. It's possible she's got nothing to do with this case at all."

"Guys," Hunter snaps. "Still here. I asked the fucking question in the first place."

I apologise in sign language then quickly translate our conversation. If Daphne's been aiding Abaddon from the shadows all along, she may be our smoking gun.

"There's no one here!" Leighton calls through the house.

BANG.

A sudden explosion of shattering glass drowns out the sound of his voice. The front window explodes, sending sharpened shards tearing through the curtains.

Shouting follows the blast. Several bricks crash through the remaining broken windowpanes, adding to the confusion and noise as the security alarm blares.

Enzo bolts upright and slides a hand beneath the coffee table. It reappears wrapped around a compact, black handgun.

"Get down!"

That's when the first flames appear. Clinging to the curtains, the fire catches at the bottom then begins to spread fast. A burning bottle hurtles through the window.

It's a Molotov cocktail.

They're flying through the gap in the destroyed window, spreading the potent stench of fuel across the room. Roaring flames reply in turn.

"Fire!" Harlow screeches.

Launching across the wooden floor, I tackle her, and we hit the teal-coloured rug with a thump, my body absorbing the impact and bite of glass.

When another bottle is launched through the now-destroyed window, it almost sails straight into us until Hunter bats it aside.

"Move!" he roars.

Harlow yanks me up. "Where is Lucky?"

Faintly, we can hear her panicked yipping from the dog bed in the kitchen. We bolt from the burning room then chase after Enzo to find safety from the fire.

Enzo's biceps bulge against his T-shirt as he lifts Lucky's huge, muscled body into his arms. We break outside together, the growing flames illuminating the scene.

"Leighton!" Harlow screams.

Through the smoke pouring from our house, we can see the cause of all the commotion. Figures dart between the parked cars in the driveway to join the group gathered in front of the garage.

Curled into himself to absorb the blows raining down, Leighton's trapped between four of the dark-clothed men. All of them are kicking and punching, giving him no time to fight back.

"One more move and I'll blow your goddamn brains out." Enzo trains the gun on their group. "Step back. All of you."

Three of them reluctantly raise their hands, but one of the guys boots his foot straight into Leighton's face. It causes Hunter to break out in a run, spurring on the others to do the same.

"Someone stop Hunter!" Enzo shouts.

He's already thrown himself into the melee to protect his brother. Fighting breaks out as the group of attackers swells in size, even with the gun aimed at them.

I have to grab hold of Harlow to stop her from chasing after Enzo. He's determined to balance the scales. We're outnumbered, and the house is exploding into ravenous flames behind us.

"Let go of me. Theo!"

Pinning her back against my chest, I hold her in a vice. "I'm sorry. I have to protect you."

"No! I need to help them!"

All we can do is watch as Enzo tucks the gun into his jeans then unleashes hell, his fists moving in a ruthless blur to cut down the sheer muscle and numbers stacked against him.

Hunter strikes one of the attackers in the stomach and breaks his nose with a punch to the face. He moves to trip up the guy's friend, knocking him unconscious with a brutal blow.

Moving in a blur, Lucky launches herself at the closest figure and takes him down with all of her weight. She begins to tear into the skin on show through his dark clothing—biting, grinding and ripping him to shreds.

"Lucky!" Harlow calls.

"She's fine," I try to soothe. "Enzo trained her well."

"I don't want her to get hurt!"

But Lucky moves just as she's been trained to, zipping between Enzo and Hunter, tearing at any available body parts.

They cut down the group with deadly ease, overpowering the hotheads and betraying their lack of preparation. Enzo halts before getting the last standing asshole in a headlock.

"Enough. Who are you?"

With his backup now bleeding and collapsed across our driveway, the man lifts his head to reveal his identity. A lead weight settles in the pit of my stomach.

"Fuck you, Enzo," he spits.

"Matthew? Seriously?"

I ease my grip on Harlow. "Becket's brother."

She breaks free from my hold and races over to Leighton. He's conscious but grunting in pain from being challenged four-to-one.

With Hunter's help, the pair of them get Leighton sitting upright, his face already swollen with multiple bruises and a split lip. Enzo strangles Matthew a little harder for good measure.

"Why are you here?" he demands. "This location is classified information. How'd you find us?"

"From the person you got killed." Matthew coughs out -bloodstained spit. "Becket is dead, and there's no accountability."

"He was on active duty," Enzo snarls. "Burning my fucking house down isn't going to bring your brother back!"

"We had to bury him in pieces!"

"Becket knew exactly what he was getting into when he joined Sabre." He drags Matthew to his feet. "You're going to pay for this. I don't care whose brother you are."

"You didn't even attend his damn funeral!" Matthew yells back.

If Becket wasn't already dead and buried, Enzo would kill him for spilling classified information to his brother. He's hospitalised ex-employees for less. Our safe location is now burnt.

"Are you okay?" Harlow fusses over Leighton.

"Fucking peachy," he replies nasally.

"You're bleeding!"

"It's alright. Bit more concerned about our house."

Her attention turns to Matthew, pinned and unable to run away with his thugs. Harlow crouches down in front of him, her features obscured by thick plumes of smoke.

"Be thankful I understand what losing someone you love feels like, otherwise, I'd be letting Enzo snap your neck for hurting one of our own."

Stretching to her full height, she turns to return to Leighton's side, but a sneer from Matthew halts her steps.

"My brother is dead because of you."

"Watch your mouth." Enzo tightens his headlock. "Or this won't end well for you."

"I've seen the video." Matthew coughs through the smoke. "You're a murderous little whore, aren't you?"

The nerve in Harlow's jaw tics. She's halted on the pavement, the reflection of flames flickering deep within her eyes.

"My brother died protecting you! And from what? You're no better than that sick monster."

"One more word and I'll end you myself," Enzo threatens. "No one talks to her like that."

The scream of an approaching police siren and multiple fire engines punctuates his words. Behind us, glass explodes and smoke billows out of our house. The flames are only getting bigger.

Our lives are burning to ashes, and there's nothing we can do about it. Case files. Clothing. Framed photographs. We're well versed in loss, but this still fucking hurts.

"Don't get me started on him," Matthew spits at Hunter. "Am I supposed to feel sorry for him? He's the worst of them all. That bullet should've killed him."

Spinning on her heel, Harlow marches right up to him and gets in his face. She's almost unrecognisable beneath the growing cloud of fury that's consuming the person I know.

"Your brother was a good man," she hisses. "He died doing what he loved. That's his legacy."

"Is that what you tell yourself so you can sleep at night?"

"It's what I know."

Before Enzo can choke him to unconsciousness, Matthew hacks another mouthful of spit and launches it straight into Harlow's face. The bright-red mixture of saliva trickles down her cheek.

"I hope the killer finds you and finishes what he started. We've leaked this address to the media. Good luck hiding now."

Right on cue, the hum of an approaching helicopter slices through the sound of our home burning. He wasn't lying. The cameras will be flashing very soon.

Her anger replaced by cold calculation, Harlow looks up into the narrowed slits of Enzo's eyes. He lifts a brow, silently seeking her permission to dole out a punishment.

"He hurt him," she states in a cold, calm voice. "Nobody hurts *my* Leigh."

The tiny nod of approval she gives him makes me so hard, I'd let her fuck me in the splattered blood stains covering our driveway.

"What the lady wants, the lady gets." Enzo smirks with pleasure. "See you in court, motherfucker."

His scarred fist smacks into Matthew's face so hard, I can hear the crack of his bones breaking. He's forced to spit out a bloodied tooth at Enzo's feet, but he refuses to back down.

"If my brother could see you now..."

"He'd be the one breaking your spine for being fucking stupid instead of me," Enzo returns.

Punching him over and over until his face resembles a swollen, meaty pulp, Harlow watches the whole thing. She doesn't flinch once, even as blood splatters across the driveway.

When Enzo grabs his arm and pulls at such a sharp angle that it elicits a disgusting *crack* of bones shattering, Matthew finally screams.

The sound causes my stomach to roll.

This isn't us.

We don't hurt innocent people.

I approach Harlow and rest a hand on her shoulder. "Enough. He's an idiot, but he isn't our enemy."

"Look at Leighton," she replies emotionlessly. "They started this."

"And we have to end it. But not like this."

Thwack. Thwack. Thwack.

The blows rain down. All of Matthew's remaining conscious friends have taken several steps back from Enzo in preparation to run away. His face is dripping in splattered blood.

"Stop," Harlow commands.

Enzo freezes with his fist drawn back, a second from delivering another killer punch. He glances back at his commander.

"Let the police have what's left of him," she instructs.

"Sure I can't just kill him?"

Harlow looks around at the now-terrified onlookers. "They've got the message."

With a curse, Enzo cracks Matthew's skull against the pavement. Blood streams down his beaten face as he falls unconscious, though he's still breathing, which is a miracle in itself.

Harlow glowers at the slumped, bleeding body at her feet. The darkness that crept over her is receding like waves washing back out to sea, bringing her back to herself.

"Thanks," she mumbles.

Enzo flashes his teeth. "Don't mention it."

"Our location is blown."

With Leighton's arm slung around his neck to carry him, Hunter helps his brother hobble despite his pained wincing.

"We need to go," Hunter declares. "Let the police haul these assholes away."

Enzo nods, the flash of blue lights illuminating his grimace. "If the world knows where we are, then Abaddon and his psychopaths do too."

SCENE DU
J.ROSE

CHAPTER 21

Harlow

Devil in Her Eyes – Bryce Savage

Being smuggled into HQ like a fugitive is a new experience. Even in the dead of night, it hums with activity and teams still immersed in their workday. The company never sleeps.

Hunter leads the charge, taking us through an empty service floor that has access to the emergency staircase. We wind higher through the building—limping, ash-streaked and exhausted.

"Where are we going?"

Theo adjusts Leighton's weight leaning on him. "Remember those apartments we told you about? They're kept for emergencies. We need somewhere to lay low."

I clutch the dog lead in my hand. "We should've stayed and faced the cameras. Those people attacked us."

"You really think the world will have much sympathy?" he says bitterly. "They'd pour more fuel on the flames if given the opportunity."

Down a thickly carpeted corridor, we reach the apartments. It's quieter up here with just the hum of the building accompanying our hurried footsteps. Hunter uses his swipe card to unlock the door.

Inside the welcoming darkness, he begins to flick on light switches. It reveals a huge, luxurious apartment with polished floors and full-length, tinted windows offering a panoramic view of London.

I unclip Lucky's lead. "In you go, girl."

She chases after Hunter, her ears still pricked up and muscles tensed. For a dog, she's remarkably in-tune with our emotions. I think she'll bite the heads off the next people to fuck us over.

The kitchen and living room are all open-plan, lit by a chandelier hanging from the ceiling that stretches up into the heavens. All the furniture is made from glass, polished steel and butter-soft leather.

Lingering by the door, Enzo's unable to take another step. He's still covered in dried blood, despite cleaning up in the frantic, high-speed car ride over here to escape the media.

I stop in front of him. "What are you thinking?"

His raw amber orbs peer down at me. "They attacked us in our own fucking home."

"I know, Enz."

"If I can't keep my family safe there, where can I?"

"This isn't your fault. You can't blame yourself."

With a roar, his fist crashes into the wall. Plaster cracks in rapidly spreading spider webs, and he barely bats an eye. Not even when blood trickles across his busted knuckles.

"Please, Enz," I beg. "Talk to me."

"I'm tired of this life," he snaps. "We've spent our careers fighting for justice for people who can't do it themselves, and it means nothing. Nobody has our backs."

"You've helped so many people. Don't let this convince you otherwise. What happened to Becket isn't on you."

"Yeah, it is," he deadpans. "I'm done."

"What does that mean?"

"It means that I'm done fighting. We built this business, and we can tear it all down just as easily."

I try to catch his arm, but he pulls it free then stalks off down the corridor towards the elevator. It takes all of my self-control not to follow him and attempt to patch all his mental wounds.

"Harlow!" Theo calls. "Come inside. He'll be fine."

I reluctantly close the door. "I'm worried about him."

"Let him beat the shit out of some punching bags for a few hours, and he'll come back."

A feral part of me is itching to join him. The overwhelming anger I experienced in that moment was more intense than anything I've ever felt before.

I couldn't handle the sight of Leighton on the ground. Gone is the girl who could watch the people she loves get hurt without doing something about it. Now I have the freedom to *be* fucking angry.

"Goldilocks," Leighton croaks. "Come here."

My feet are rooted to the spot.

Hunter checks the freezer and wraps a handful of ice cubes up to give to his brother. Accepting it, Leighton's demanding stare doesn't stray from me, even as Lucky yips for his attention.

"Now," he adds.

"Is Becket's brother going to be okay?"

Theo fishes out his phone. "I'll check in with the police department to get an update. The fire should be out by now."

Stepping through the balcony doors that lead outside, he leaves me with the two brothers and all of our pent-up emotions.

Hunter scavenges the minibar tucked into the corner of the room and settles on the sofa, clicking his tongue for Lucky to join him. He checks her paws for any injuries then rubs her belly.

"You did good, girl," he coos.

She licks his face, happily snuggling up for a celebratory cuddle. Hunter tucks into a bottle of rum and leaves me to face Leighton.

"Come on, Harlow. You're safe now."

"Safe?" I scoff. "I'm not worried about my safety. I told Enzo to beat the shit out of Matthew back there. Me. I'm the reason he feels like crap."

Leighton moves the ice to his other cheek. "The son of a bitch deserved it."

"That doesn't excuse my behaviour. I don't hurt people. That isn't me." I wince as blood dribbles down his chin. "But I couldn't just let him get away with hurting you."

Leighton ditches the handful of ice and throws his arms open. "I can't move, so you're gonna have to come to me to hug this out."

"Hug it out? We're not kids."

"And that wasn't a fucking invitation. Get over here."

Reluctantly crossing the room, I step between his open legs and bury my face in the stained material of his shirt. He smells like blood and smoke, but he's still my Leigh beneath the acrid scents.

"You're exactly who you are meant to be." He strokes a hand over my ashy hair. "Never doubt that. I love you for who you are."

"Even when I scare myself?"

"Especially then."

With a sigh, I take his hand in mine. "Let's get you cleaned up. Do we have a first aid kit? You've got some nasty cuts."

"We should check the bathroom."

Leaving Hunter to nurse his bottle of rum, we inch through the darkened apartment. Three bedrooms branch off from the hallway, the beds unmade and air thick with dust.

"People don't stay here much?"

"Don't think so." Leighton hisses in pain. "How the fuck did we end up here? Running for our lives? We're supposed to be the ones in control."

"I don't have a good enough answer for you."

"Well, someone owes me a bloody good answer for trashing my pretty face. I'm going to look like a bruised piece of fruit by morning."

Despite everything, I choke on a laugh. "You're still beautiful to me, Princess Leigh. Bruised fruit and all."

"Better be," he snarks.

In the bathroom, I sit him down on the closed toilet lid then peel his stained t-shirt off, leaving his sweats still in place. There's a first aid kit tucked underneath the sink with some other toiletries.

Soaking a washcloth in warm water, I tilt his chin up then begin gently wiping the blood away. The swelling is pretty bad, but he's a tough cookie and doesn't complain as I poke the mottled skin.

"What's the verdict?"

I narrow my eyes on him. "No more fighting for you."

"Can't cage a wild animal, Goldilocks."

"Watch me. I don't give a shit if it hurts your ego. Next time a group of people come for you, run in the other direction."

"I thought I could take them all."

"Maybe we need to check you for a brain injury too. You were outnumbered and didn't stand a chance."

"Ouch. You're mean."

"No. I'm just done watching the people I love get hurt."

After cleansing the cuts across his forehead and lip, I declare the job done. He doesn't need stitches, just more ice and a damn good talking to for picking a fight with an army of fully grown men.

With my task complete, the darkness crawling across my mind comes rushing back. I busy myself, cleaning up the first aid kit so

Leighton can't see how badly my hands are shaking.

I'm still angry.

Fucking furious.

No matter how hard we try, the world is constantly pushing us ten steps back for every inch we claw ourselves forward. God is laughing in our faces and destroying everything with a swooped hand.

"Harlow? Want to come and choose a bedroom?"

"I … need a minute. You go."

"But—"

"Go, Leigh!" I shout.

In too much pain to argue, Leighton slips from the bathroom. I'm left with my hands braced on the sink as I stare deep into the pits of my black pupils. I don't recognise who stares back at me.

Giana. Michael. All the women living in the shell of my heart, forcing me to put one foot in front of the other for them.

I've spent months trying to figure out exactly who the real Harlow is, beyond the people who have dictated my life for so many years. But the idea of that angry, violent person being me is horrifying.

Before I realise what I'm doing, my hand lifts to tangle in my long mane of smoky hair. I twirl a strand around my finger then halt on the verge of tearing it clean out.

"No," I whisper to myself.

But the voice is still there—rising from the depths and making its presence known. I doubt it ever left. More like it hibernated.

Flicking the walk-in shower on, I'm about to strip off and step inside when it hits me again. Begging. Pleading. Demanding pain and control in the only way my broken self knows.

I'm not sure what drives me to call Theo's name. It tears from my throat without being told. I hold myself on the verge of relapsing as his hurried footsteps approach from the other room.

"Harlow? Where are you?"

"Bathroom!"

The door crashes open, and when Theo spots me, the tears threatening to spill down my cheeks and a hand tangled in my hair, he blanches.

"What's going on?"

Eyes closing, I feel the tears escape. "I'm so fucking scared of being the person the world thinks I am."

"Oh, beautiful."

It has to be him. Theo knows me better than I know myself, even the corners of my soul that will never see the light of day. He conquered them long before I even knew his name.

"You're in shock," he murmurs, his arms wrapping around my waist. "Can you let go of your hair and talk to me, please?"

My grip on the strands tightens. "We're spiralling out of control. Even Enzo is ready to walk away. The case has beaten us all."

"Bullshit. I promised you that we'd end this, and that's exactly what we're going to do. You have a book to publish when we're on the other side of this fight."

"And who will I be on the other side?" I throw back. "Am I battling to see this through just to lose myself all over again?"

Clasping my hips, he flips me around then shoves my back into the ceramic sink. Theo doesn't peel my hand from my hair. Instead, his mouth slams onto mine with the strength of a fatal collision.

His ferocity steals my breath and locks it in a bomb-proof box in the deepest, darkest pits of his heart where I can't take it back.

"You listen to me," he whispers fiercely. "I don't care who you are on the other side of this because I know the woman I love."

"What if she isn't me?"

"Then I'll love whatever version of you remains when all is said and done. There's nothing you can do to stop me from wanting to spend every single moment of my life by your side."

"Theo," I sob into his lips.

"I won't hear it. You need control?" He releases my mouth and grabs my wrist. "I'll give it to you with pleasure."

Theo moves my hand to clasp his throat, encouraging my nails to slice deep into his skin. I can feel the pounding of his heartbeat beneath my fingertips.

"I wouldn't give myself to you if I didn't trust the person I know you are," he says throatily. "And believe me, angel, you own every inch of my mind, body and soul."

When he kisses me again, it's softer, coaxing, whispering to me in dulcet tones. He's torn his heart out and now offers it to me, blood-slick and still beating, on a platter.

I want it.

I want him.

I want *us*.

Pushing his chest, I shove him backwards into the still-running shower. We meet beneath the hot spray, the water soaking into our clothing and melding us together.

I don't care. All I want is for him to pick up the shattered shards of my heart and glue them back together. I can't do it myself right now.

Theo's mouth devours mine, submitting to the beat of my tongue lashing his. He grabs the hem of my t-shirt then pauses to yank it over my head, exposing my bare breasts.

Still wearing blackened pyjama bottoms, I shove them over my hips then kick them out of the shower. "Strip."

"Yes, angel."

Peeling off his soaking-wet flannel shirt, jeans and boxers, he throws them out to join my pyjamas. With all his bare, chiselled body on display, I let myself return to the confidence I found in Tartarus.

I remove his glasses and yank sharply on his curly hair, encouraging him to sink to his knees in the shower. Theo obliges without a single ounce of protest.

"Take my panties off," I order.

His thumbs hook into my panties to pull them down, exposing my pussy to his awaiting mouth. He plants kisses on my pubic bone, skating down until his tongue flicks across my clit.

I fist his hair tighter. "More, Theo."

His tongue slides between my folds and licks up the length of my slit. When his finger circles my bundle of nerves before pushing inside me, I have to brace a hand on the tiled wall.

"My beautiful girl has such a pretty cunt," he purrs against my pussy lips. "Tell me what you want me to do."

Head thrown back, I savour the thrust of his finger gliding into me. My legs are already trembling from the slow tease.

"I want you to make me come with your tongue."

Sucking my clit between his teeth, he chuckles against my folds. "You're the boss, beautiful."

Pushing a second finger into my core, his mouth attacks me in a frenzy of licking and sucking, mirroring the stroke of his digits entering me.

With my emotions still running haywire, it doesn't take long for the pressure to begin to build. Each time he slides back inside, his thumb circles my clit.

"So sweet. You're perfect."

I can hardly see him through the steam billowing inside the shower. His grip on my hips and the torture of his tongue against my folds cuts through the temporary blindness.

When my lower belly tightens, I feel my walls clench around his fingers. A loud moan escapes my lips as my release quickly overwhelms me. I come all over Theo's face buried between my thighs.

Still quaking with aftershocks, I don't need a second to breathe. The darkness will only come flooding back. I yank Theo to his feet then wrap a hand around his proud length.

"I want you to fuck me until I can't think of anything but your cock worshipping me," I command. "You got that?"

He parts the steam to kiss my lips. "Anything for you."

Following my instincts, I keep a firm grip on his shaft and tug him along. He follows me out of the shower, letting me gently pull him as we return to the bedroom.

Pushing aside pillows, I flop onto the bed, spreading my legs wide open. Theo's eyes eagerly eat me up, his hand stroking over his length.

Movement over his shoulder causes me to sit up. Leighton has tracked us down and saunters into the room, still managing to look like a prowling tiger beneath his mottled, purple bruises.

"You kicked me out to replace me with Theo, huh?"

I gulp hard. "It wasn't like that."

Stopping behind Theo, he rests a hand on his bare shoulder. "You're hogging all of my girl's attention, Theodore."

His throat works up and down. "You want me to apologise or something?"

"Actions speak louder than words. I want to join this sexy little game of yours. Think I've earned myself an invitation."

"I'm not in charge, man."

Leighton winks at me. "Harlow?"

I wave him forward. "You can join us."

Dropping his hand, he pushes Theo forward until he's crawling across the unmade bed on his knees. Leighton stands over us both in a position of supreme power.

Settling himself between my thighs, Theo peppers kisses across my breasts, taking a hardened nipple between his lips. I can feel his length nudging my leg close to where I want it.

"Please," I mewl.

"Did you hear her?" Leighton growls. "She needs you to fill her up. Look at that perfect, pink cunt just begging to be touched."

Spurred on, Theo lines himself up. "That I can do."

With a slick thrust, he slides deep inside of me. Seeing his wide blue eyes above me as he groans in pleasure feels strange after the intensity of our first time.

He may be on top, but with Leighton dictating our movements, Theo's still surrendering. His hips draw back, then he pushes back into me as Leighton watches on.

"You can do better than that," he goads. "I thought you liked following orders, Theodore? I told you to fuck her. Hard."

With a secret smile that only I can see, Theo picks up the pace until he's hammering into me. With both of their eyes watching my every move, I feel like I'm under a spotlight.

"Better," Leighton praises.

Sneaking around the bed, he runs his fingers through Theo's wet curls before stroking a hand across the sheets. My heart seizes when he kneels on my right side, pushing his sweats and boxers down.

"While Theo's doing such a good job of pummelling your sweet pussy, I want to ride that gorgeous mouth of yours."

I tilt my head to the side, my lips parting to greedily accept his length. Leighton pushes his cock into my mouth until I'm filled with both of them and trapped in torturous submission.

With Theo still thrusting into me, determined to steal another climax, Leighton begins to fuck my mouth as roughly as promised.

I'm overwhelmed by the sense of fullness.

"Doesn't she look good being fucked by us both?"

"Too right," Theo hums back.

Tongue sliding against Leighton's shaft, he nudges the back of my throat with each pump of his hips. Moisture sears the corners of my eyes, but I don't care. I love his playful roughness.

Between them both, I'm a gasping, shaking mess in minutes. There's no escaping the onslaught, but rather than being triggered by the vulnerability, I'm revelling in it.

"Stop," Leighton orders.

Leighton pulls out of my mouth before he can finish, his breathing ragged. He forces Theo to halt with another barked command.

"On the bed. I want her on top of you now."

I cry out when Theo follows his orders and pulls out, leaving me on the cusp of another orgasm. He lies down on the mattress next to me and lets me climb on top of him.

"I want you to ride Theo's cock like the good little princess you are," Leighton instructs smugly. "Then we'll let you come."

Biting my lip, I line up his dick then eagerly sink down on it. From this position, it reaches an even deeper angle, setting off tiny fireworks beneath my skin.

When I feel Leighton's weight dipping on the bed behind me, I lift my hips and begin to find the rhythm that worked for me before. Knowing he's watching the show only makes me more eager to please.

"Is our girl doing a good job?" Leighton asks.

Beneath me, Theo's nails cut into my hips. "Fuck yes, she is."

"Perhaps I should reward her with another cock, then. What do you think, Goldilocks?"

His fingers skate down the length of my spine, curving around my ass before delivering a hard spank. I can't help yelling a curse, the burst of pain heightening my state of arousal.

Leighton finds the ring of my asshole then glides a moistened finger over it. I cry out again when he eases it inside, the intrusion feeling almost normal after the last few times he's experimented.

"You need to be nice and relaxed for what I have planned," he whispers behind me. "So that means I need you to come again."

With Theo rutting up into me to meet my strokes, I can feel the crest of my release approaching. Between both of them, it's impossible not to feel spoiled, drowning in their love and attention.

Leighton spanks me again, harder this time, jolting Theo's length still buried inside my core. With his finger pumping in and out of my back entrance, I can't hold it in any longer.

"Oh God!" I scream out.

His mouth falling open, Theo finishes at the same second, his length jolting from deep within me. I can feel the rush of warmth as his seed fills me up, our releases feeding each other.

He slumps on the bed, still clasping my hips and staring up at me with those bottomless, light-blue eyes that are filled with lazy satisfaction.

Leighton's chin drops on my shoulder. "Good show, guys. But I have an even better one planned."

Lifting my ass so that Theo slips out of me, Leighton's hand dips between my legs. My face feels like a furnace when I realise what he's doing with the warmth leaking out of me.

"Jesus, Leigh," Theo curses.

"You had your turn. Now it's mine."

He's spreading Theo's hot come all over his own length, lubricating it up without an ounce of shame for swapping fluids like they're neighbours borrowing baking powder.

I feel his fingers back at my aching core, soaking them in my come to move to my asshole. I'm a dripping, sticky mess, but that doesn't slow Leighton down.

"You still trust me?" he asks gruffly.

Hands splayed on Theo's chest for balance, I wrestle with my nerves. "I do, but I'm not sure about this."

"I'll look after you, princess. I'm not going to hurt you. If you want me to stop, I'll stop. Okay?"

"Okay."

"Keep your eyes on Theodore. I want him to see just how much you love my cock in your asshole."

Beneath me, Theo tightens his grip on my hips. "I've got you, angel."

I'm not sure I can blush any harder. There's no room to hide. I haven't got a single ounce of privacy as Leighton blows past the limits of my experience in the bedroom.

Pushing his finger back into my ring of muscle, he spreads the lubrication farther to moisten everything up. I'm as relaxed as possible after being awarded two orgasms already.

"I'm going to go nice and slow," he murmurs.

Then I feel the tip of his length pressing at my rear. He holds it there for a moment, gently nudging against me and letting me get used to the strange sensation.

"Easy, baby."

"It's okay," I moan.

"Reckon you can take some more?"

"Yes… More."

Theo chuckles beneath me. He has a front-row seat to Leighton's performance, trapped by the weight of my body. But I don't see him even attempting to escape.

Moving slowly, Leighton ever so gently pushes another inch

inside. I gasp loudly, too overwhelmed to know how to feel.

The sense of pressure is greater than when he's fucked me with his fingers back there, and while it's uncomfortable at first, the pleasure quickly follows as my body adjusts.

"Fuck, Harlow," he grunts in my ear. "I've wanted to do this since I fucked you in that hotel. Now I own all of your firsts."

"Don't get too cocky," I groan back.

"Try and stop me. I want everyone to know that fact. You were mine before any of these idiots even had a chance."

Theo's hands move to cup my breasts, massaging them and tweaking my stiff nipples. The extra stimulation makes me dizzy with the tides of ecstasy threatening to consume me.

Drawing back out, Leighton pushes into me again, still moving slow so I can adjust to the burning sensation of his cock stretching me. The initial spikes of pain melt into mind-numbing pleasure.

"Does it feel good, baby?"

"Y-Yes."

"Do you like it when I fuck your tight asshole?"

He pushes deeper inside me, stretching me even further. My eyes scrunch shut as another mountainous wave of bliss crashes over me.

"Oh, fuck. Yes. I like it."

"I always knew you were a dirty girl," he teases, hitting my ass cheek again. "Look at your precious angel now, Theodore."

"She looks damn good to me," he returns.

Leighton keeps inching in, testing the boundaries of my sanity and shattering them beyond comprehension. The idea of doing this scared me before, but I trust him with my life.

The waves of strange, paralysing pleasure are too strong to contain. My limbs are shaking as moans fall from my lips.

There's a throat clear from elsewhere in the room that has us all freezing up. I wrench my eyes open to look over my shoulder.

Kill me now.

Enzo and Hunter are watching our tangle of sweaty limbs with matching surprised expressions. Neither looks like they expected to walk into this particular scenario.

"Well..." Hunter leans against the wall. "Don't stop on our account."

"We'll just patiently wait our turn," Enzo adds, his bare chest slick with sweat from the workout he's returned from.

"Our turn?" I squeak.

Leighton spanks me again, jolting his dick inside of me. "Focus, princess. I said eyes on Theo. Not them."

When I don't immediately look back down, his hand dips around my waist to find my bundle of nerves. He flicks it before slapping his hand directly on my cunt.

"Fuck!" I cry out.

"I said *focus.*"

With Theo still fondling my breasts and Leighton beginning to move at a gentle pace, I can hardly hold myself upright.

The weight of four pairs of eyes is searing my flesh and melting it down to the bone. Every single inch of me is theirs to peruse.

Leighton grabs a handful of my hair then tugs to pull my head back. His teeth graze my earlobe before biting down.

"Want two of us inside you at once?"

"What?" I manage to gasp.

Chuckling, he releases my hair. "Mind shifting up a bit, Theodore? I want to see how my girl handles two of us fucking her."

Theo wiggles out from underneath me, using the space Leighton creates by lifting my hips without exiting me. I can't see who he waves over, but the pad of footsteps joins us.

Standing behind Hunter, Enzo nudges him forward, giving him first dibs. Both of them can't tear their eyes from me.

"Now this I want to see," Enzo says with a filthy grin. "You're caught in a Rodriguez sandwich, little one."

Taking Theo's place on the bed, Hunter's already stripped off his ash-stained clothing. Leighton lowers me back down onto him, his cock still sliding in and out of my rear with increasing strokes.

Sandwiched between both brothers, all I can do is hold on for dear life as Hunter sheaths himself inside my pussy. He drives into me slowly, letting me release a strangled, inhuman sound.

"Jesus Christ," he swears, sliding out and back in again even deeper. "Fuck, sweetheart."

I feel like I've been dipped in fuel and set alight. They're both inside me, breezing past every mental barrier and setting up shop. My body is no longer my own.

It belongs to them.

I think it always has.

My mind is being bulldozed and scattered in ashes by the rhythm of them both fucking me. I don't even have enough mental strength to question the ethics of their cocks rubbing up inside me.

"Shit," Leighton hisses over my shoulder. "I'm going to come. You're too tight. I can't hold it."

"Come, Leigh," I mewl.

When he roars behind me, I feel his release mix with the stickiness of Theo still covering me. The silent man in question is sitting at the head of the bed, watching everything with fascination.

Leighton slumps on my back, holding his weight off me as he catches his breath. He's slipped out of me, and his come is spilling down the backs of my thighs.

I hold on to Hunter's shoulder for balance when he clambers off the bed. Leighton stumbles and lands next to Theo, still panting. The pair are sitting there like cinemagoers. All that's missing is the popcorn.

"Harlow," Hunter growls. "Look at me, baby. Not them. Let me see those beautiful eyes."

Refocusing on him, I let his hand sneak up my body and wrap around my throat to ensure I can't look away again. Without sound, he's reliant on sight alone to experience this moment.

"I've come close to losing you too many times," he says darkly. "I fucking hate that you're not safe with us."

Resting my hand on top of his, I encourage him to squeeze my throat harder, giving him the sense of total control he needs. None of us are okay right now, or we wouldn't be doing this.

Hunter's hand forms a tightening necklace that cinches around my neck, restricting the flow of air. But there's no panic. No fear. I'm safe in his hands, and that's exactly what he needs to see.

"Yours," I mouth clearly.

His brown gaze is almost pitch-black. "Mine."

Hips bucking at a brutal pace, far faster than the others and their tentative efforts to ease me in, he sprints towards the finish line.

My chest begins to burn from the restriction of air, but it only makes things more intense. Each feeling is tripled, increased by my mind grasping for anything to hold on to.

When Hunter dives off the edge into his own climax, he finally finishes. The timing is excruciating. Air races down my windpipe to inflate my lungs, on the verge of screaming for relief.

Gasping, I slump onto his chest, feeling his release mingle with the mess that's staining every inch of me. All of them mix and become one deep inside of me.

Kneeling on the bed beside me, Enzo grasps my jaw and tilts my lips to meet his. He smells sweaty from whatever he disappeared to beat to take care of his aggression.

"You tired, baby?"

"Hmm," I hum unintelligibly.

His lips tease mine. "I think you're done."

Eyes flinging open, I grab his wrist before he can retreat. "No, I'm not done. I want you too."

Enzo chuckles. "I'll carry you to the shower. How about that?"

I narrow my eyes. "Don't you want to fuck me, Enz? The rest of your family has."

Challenged levied, I watch his pupils expand, devouring the floating embers that light his amber eyes. I haven't come this far to leave him unsatisfied now.

With the others still watching, Enzo lifts me from Hunter's lap. He disregards the slick mess we've created for ourselves and positions me on his waist, like I weigh little more than air.

"You're so fucking bad," he says under his breath. "I was going to be all gentle and shit, but not when you tease me like that."

"I never asked for you to be gentle."

Sneaking a hand between us, I nudge down the waistband of his grey sweatpants. Those tight things should be illegal anyway.

"Greedy tonight, aren't you?"

My hand sneaks inside his boxers to find the promise of his hard length. "Just enjoying what's rightfully mine."

"All at once, huh?"

I look over at Leighton's pleased grin. "Leigh interrupted. I take no responsibility for this mess."

"Aren't you sore after all three of them?"

"A bit," I admit, feeling the ache between my thighs. "But I still want you."

"I'll try to be gentle, baby girl, but I need you so fucking bad."

Pinning my back against the bedroom wall, Enzo shoves his sweatpants and boxers down low enough to free his cock. His hips pin me in place before his hands return to my ass cheeks.

"I don't need you to be gentle with me," I goad.

His grin widens. "Well, it's their turn to watch you take my cock. You just saved the best until last."

When he surges into me, I hold on to his neck to take the rough thrust of his hips. I have a perfect view of the other three lounging on the bed like purring lions, full of their latest meal.

"Are they watching?" Enzo asks.

"Yes," I moan.

"Yes, what?"

He stills, holding back his next thrust.

"Yes, sir."

"Good girl. They may have had you first, but I'll be the one finishing the job."

When he slams back into me, I scream out his name for all of them to hear. Enzo's intensity is on a whole different level.

Battering his seal of possession into the very fabric of my being, he adopts the quickest pace of them all. His gentleness never arrives, and I'm so thankful for that. I want him to be rough with me.

I feel tiny in his arms, caught between the hard wall and his rippling, mountainous muscles. He ducks his head to bury it in between the rise and fall of my breasts.

His teeth nip each swell, sucking my skin into his mouth to leave a dark trail of bruises for the world to see. None of us would be here, together right now, in this room, if it wasn't for him.

He spent months keeping us all together as life tried to rip us apart at the seams. For that, I owe Enzo. My life. My soul. My vulnerability. Everything I have left to give.

Taking every beat of his cock slamming into me, he reignites my core through the fog of exhaustion. I didn't think I could possibly orgasm again, but the pangs are already starting.

"Come," he coaxes, slamming home each word with a thrust. "I know my perfect little whore has another one in her."

"You are the only man on this planet I'd allow to call me that," I pant. "Be honoured."

"You bet I am."

With my eyes locked on Hunter, Leighton and Theo, I relinquish my last scrap of control. It starts slow—building, expanding, taking over every last sense.

Enzo follows me into oblivion and surrenders at the same time, roaring through his own climax. We're both panting and tangled, our bodies slumped against the wall as we ride our releases.

I tuck my head into the crook of his neck, too tired to hold it up for a second longer. My entire body is quivering with the after-burn of another shattering orgasm.

"You okay?" Enzo huffs.

"I don't think I can walk right now."

His body vibrates with a laugh. "Good thing I've got you, then."

Tucking his arm underneath my legs, he pulls me into a cradle position so I'm tucked into his chest. My eyes fall shut, a warm hum of satisfaction pulsing through my veins.

Returning to the bathroom, Enzo yells at the others to get the bed made up then closes the door. He props me on the bathroom sink then turns to flick the shower on.

"Where did you go?" I ask sleepily.

His shoulders tense. "Downstairs to the gym. Needed to punch something."

"You didn't do enough of that tonight?"

"Clearly not." He finally turns to me, his gaze shadowed. "I meant what I said, Harlow. I don't know if I can do this job anymore."

Catching his hand, I tug him closer and press a kiss right above his sternum. "You don't have to. All I want is for you to be happy."

"If we don't do this, who will?"

"Anyone. I don't care, Enz. You're more than the people you save. After all you've been through, you deserve some peace too."

Eyes lowered, Adam's apple bobs. "I swore to you that I'd wipe out every last trace of Abaddon, and I intend to keep my word."

"And when the work is done?" I prompt.

"Then … I'll do what I should have done a long time ago and walk away. No one else is going to live my life for me. I have to do it."

Letting him lift me into the shower, I curl up against his body beneath the spray. "Where will you go?"

"Where will *we* go?" he corrects. "Our family is all that matters to me now. We can choose our next steps together."

"Sabre is Hunter's whole life. Do you think he'd walk away just like that?"

"I doubt he would have returned from Costa Rica if we didn't make him. Everyone has their limits, little one. We've reached ours."

Lifting onto my tiptoes, I strain to capture his lips. "Then we run. Together. I'll follow you four to the ends of the earth."

"Then it's a deal."

Lathering his hands in shower gel fished out from underneath the sink, I let Enzo wash every inch of me, cleansing all evidence of what just occurred in the bedroom.

He dips a hand between my legs to wash me, taking care to be gentle and checking that I'm comfortable, even after that sex-pile. His attention is still focused entirely on my needs.

"I'm so tired."

Stepping out, Enzo grabs a towel then wraps me in it. "You can rest now, baby. We're safe here for tonight."

"What about tomorrow?"

Tucking a towel around his hips, he lifts me back into his arms and carries me into the bedroom.

"That's tomorrow's problem."

Another bare mattress has mysteriously appeared on the carpeted floor next to the bed. Theo and Leighton are already collapsed on it, leaving space for us to join Hunter on the bed.

Enzo dries me off and passes me into Hunter's arms. I'm tucked beneath a sheet and spooned in the curvature of his frame. The bed dips with Enzo's solid weight joining us.

In the darkness of the room, I whisper that I love them. We may have lost everything we own tonight, but we still have each other.

Nothing can take that away.

Not now. Not ever.

SCENE DU
J.ROSE

CHAPTER 22

Harlow

Sad Day – FKA twigs

Holding Enzo's hand in a deathly tight grip, I stare past the layers of armed security at the madness swarming HQ's entrance. This is the biggest crowd that we've seen by far.

It's impossible to avoid the hysteria sweeping over the entire country now that we're holed up in the apartment above us. Anger has transformed into something far more worrying in the past week.

Madness.

Terror.

Sheer fucking delirium.

Gaggles of people form prayer circles, calling up to the heavens for protection when the approaching rapture arrives. Their hands are marked with symbols—identical Holy Trinities.

"How has Michael caused so much damage in such little time?"

Enzo shrugs in dismay. "Fear spreads far quicker than any disease. People genuinely believe the shit he's drilling into his followers."

"It feels like the world is ending."

"I suppose in their minds, it is."

It's clear that they all believe it too. Michael and his Angels of the Abyss have spread their insane message far and wide. Many people now believe that some kind of rapture is approaching.

"The sooner we get a hit on Theo's software for Daphne, the sooner we can end this." I blow out a breath. "I don't want to see where this is going."

"Me neither," he says grimly.

"Are Ethan and his team back from scouting out Grantham?"

"Arrived home last night. They're travelling to Wisbech tomorrow to investigate the other pool of victims and their families."

"And? Any leads?"

"The three victims all attended the same Bible study class," Enzo explains. "He interviewed the other attendees, but they didn't see anything out of the ordinary."

"How did Michael get his hands on them, then?"

His expression is haunted. "By speaking in whispers. That's why people are so afraid. Anyone could be next, and there's nothing they can do to keep themselves safe."

"This is ridiculous. He isn't the devil. Michael is just a man."

"Could just a man do all this?" Enzo gestures outside. "I'm not so sure anymore."

I want more than anything to be able to disagree with him. But after all the death and destruction I've seen my uncle inflict, I'm lying to myself by pretending like Lucifer himself doesn't dwell beneath his skin.

No mere mortal could commit so many atrocities and still have the strength to rain chaos on a whole nation. Still, it isn't enough. He wants more... More pain. More blood. More atonement.

Michael isn't human.

He's a spawn of Satan.

"When's your call with the publisher?"

I try to blink the grit from my eyes. Compiling my journals into something semi-resembling a manuscript has taken countless hours of painstaking work. Thankfully, I stored them in Theo's office and avoided losing them in the fire.

"This afternoon."

"You signed the contract?" he asks.

"Yesterday. I'm turning over my work, and then it'll go into editing. Abigail wants me to be involved every step of the way to make sure they don't lose my voice."

"That's good, little one. It sounds like they're looking out for you." He drops a kiss on top of my head. "I'm so fucking proud already."

"I haven't published anything yet."

"But you will. I'm glad you didn't listen to me." Enzo gestures outside. "This is exactly why you need to speak up for yourself."

"Well, I think it's safe to say I can't make the situation any worse."

"Unfortunately, that's true."

Hyland appears and waves at us from across the reception where a tall, dark-haired man wearing thick black glasses over his eyes awaits. Foster. He's arrived.

"Here we go," I mutter.

"Still don't think you should be doing this."

"A deal's a deal, Enz. I'm not a liar. Giana gave us the information we needed, so I need to keep my end of the bargain."

"You're far too much of a good person for this world."

"Says you."

"Me?" Enzo scoffs. "I've never been called a good person before. An angry, oversized wanker with a penchant for violence? Sure."

I squeeze his hand then release it. "Well, that too. Particularly the violence part, but we love you for it."

"Ha. Thanks, baby."

Forcing myself to ignore the shouts of frenzied prayers that still manage to leak through Sabre's tinted glass entrance, we approach Foster together. That's when I spot him.

I've only ever seen my half-brother once, the day I stalked his school, hunting Giana down after I ran from Sabre. He must be eight or nine years old. His cute face is rounded with youthful innocence beneath lightly curling hair that matches mine.

Foster's eyes connect with mine from across the room. His reluctance is clear. Neither of us wants to be doing this. Unfortunately, Giana has fucked us both over.

I let Enzo stretch out a hand for him to shake first. "Thanks for coming in. I hope the protests didn't make things too difficult."

"We were brought in through the loading bay," Foster returns in a deep voice. "Quite the scene you've got outside."

Enzo gently pushes me forward. I take Foster's hand with the same enthusiasm I'd have for hugging a venomous snake.

"Harlow," he says.

"Hello."

"It's been a while. Mind telling me what you invited us here for before we go any further?"

I anxiously wring my hands together. "I thought it was time we talked." My eyes stray to the boy at his side. "All of us."

Looking over me with interest, Ulrich's mousy brown hair lays on his head in an untidy pile. We don't look much alike, despite our half-shared DNA.

Foster clears his throat. "This is my son, Ulrich." He tugs on his hand. "Ulrich, this is Harlow. She's…"

He trails off, unable to finish.

"I'm a friend of your mum," I quickly add. "It's nice to meet you. I'm sorry about all the noise outside."

"It's okay," he replies softly.

"No school today?"

He looks up at his father. "Dad said we were visiting London. I want to go to the Natural History Museum to see the dinosaurs."

A lump sticking in my throat, I crouch down on one knee to reach his height. "Do you like dinosaurs?"

Ulrich watches me suspiciously. "Yes."

I can't explain the tangled ball of emotion tightening my chest. There are too many warring sides to categorise. I'm ashamed to admit that a broken, bitter part of me wants to hate this kid.

He got a life.

A childhood.

The family I never had.

But a greater part of me feels a strange, unexpected sense of kinship. We have the same coloured hair. Giana's DNA flows in both of us—and therefore, Michael's DNA too.

He's like me.

An anomaly.

Hope born from darkness.

"I wanted to have a chat with your dad for a bit." I smile apologetically. "Is that alright? If you're hungry, my friend here can take you to the canteen to get some food."

Enzo lifts an intimidating paw to wave. "It's burger day. We even have milkshakes to go with them."

"Can I go, Dad?"

Foster unlatches his clenched jaw. "I don't know."

"The building is secure," Enzo reassures. "No one's getting in or out. You can come find us when you're done talking."

Taking a moment to deliberate, Foster eventually nods. He makes Ulrich take Enzo's hand, despite his wariness of the giant boulder that stands several feet over him.

"Meeting room on the tenth floor is all yours."

"Look after him," I instruct.

Enzo flashes me a toothy grin. "I'll have made a Sabre agent out of him by the time you get back. Don't you worry."

At the look of horror on Foster's face, Enzo guides Ulrich away. I can't help but watch the kid go, and at the last moment, he glances over his shoulder to frown at me again.

"He seems pretty switched on."

Foster laughs weakly. "You could say that. He's smarter than me already. No idea how such a bright spark came from us."

Eyes meeting again, his smile quickly fades. I let Hyland take the lead to guide us to the elevator, falling back into an awkward silence that doesn't break until we reach the meeting room.

"I'll be just outside." Hyland holds the door open for us. "Shout if you need me."

"Thanks."

The look he flashes Foster must put the fear of God in him. I gesture for him to take a seat and sit down opposite.

"Sorry. He's being paid a small fortune to keep me safe. It makes him pretty standoffish at the best of times."

"I noticed." Foster braves a chuckle before growing serious. "Why am I here, Harlow?"

I take a breath. "I've been to see Giana in prison. She asked me to reach out to you in return for information on Michael Abaddon."

His face pales. "I've not answered her calls for a reason. You could've spared me the trip. I'm not discussing Giana."

"She's still your wife, and Ulrich's mother." I sigh tiredly. "She's still *my* mother. We at least need to talk about this."

"There's nothing to say. That woman spent our entire marriage lying to my face. As far as I'm concerned, Ulrich has one parent."

"As do I. See? We're on the same page."

"Then why are you delivering her damn messages?" he snaps, his patience fading. "Look what she did to you."

"Because I am nothing like her," I fire back. "Nor my uncle. I take promises very seriously. Talking to you was her price."

That knocks the fight out of him. He scrubs his face, appearing far older than his years. Giana has well and truly broken him.

"You're right. I'm sorry."

I shrug off his apology. "I get it. If I could pretend like she never even existed, my life would be a lot easier. But that's not how family works."

"I've tried to keep all of this from Ulrich, but he's far from stupid," he replies defeatedly. "Her face was splashed all over the news for weeks. I never answer his questions."

"If it makes you feel any better, I don't have the answers to my own questions. I'm just trying to survive this and live to tell the tale."

Nodding, Foster sits back in his chair. "Go on, then. What does she want from me?"

"Contact with Ulrich."

"That isn't going to happen."

"Then tell her that yourself," I reason. "She's on suicide watch until the trial. At least put her out of her misery."

"Doesn't she deserve to be miserable?"

Hesitating, I stare up at the ceiling. "Giana and Michael became who they are through hatred. If we live our lives in the same way, we're only continuing their legacy."

Foster remains silent.

"I refuse to breed more evil from my suffering," I finish with a half-smile. "All I want is to have a normal life."

"You don't want revenge? Not even a little bit?"

"All that would create is more heartache and pain."

"Christ, Harlow," he curses. "How can you sit there and say that after all they put you through? Aren't you angry?"

"I'm angrier than people realise. But I have four men hell-bent on destroying Michael. One of us has to be thinking about the future too."

"You deserve that," Foster says honestly. "A happy future. No one deserves that more than you do. And I really hope you get it."

Sharing a moment, we both take a pause to gather ourselves. He smooths his polo shirt then offers me a nod.

"I'll speak to Giana. I'm not promising anything more than that."

"Thank you."

"I've been asked to testify at her trial. Her defence lawyer wants me to fuck up the prosecution's entire case."

"What are you going to do?"

"Tell the truth, I guess. The person who traded you off to that monster isn't the woman I married. At least I didn't think she was."

When I don't immediately respond, he braces his elbow on his knees to lean closer to me.

"The prosecution is calling you as a witness?"

"Yeah," I say flatly. "I don't want to dig up the past and have my trauma picked apart by a jury. But I have no choice."

"Getting her prosecuted is the right thing to do. You're not the only person she hurt."

"I know… It's just going to be hard seeing her up there."

"You really care about her?" he asks.

"I wish I didn't care at all, but I know what Michael did to her.

She didn't stand a chance. Neither did his wife."

"I'm not sure I can ever forgive Giana for lying to me." His hands clench into fists. "But I can make this right for Ulrich's sake."

"Forgiveness isn't as black-and-white as people think." I spare him a sad smile. "You can hate someone with every fibre of your being and still forgive them for breaking you. The two can coexist."

"Do you forgive him? The killer?"

I don't answer at first.

"Shit," Foster swears. "I'm sorry, Harlow. You don't have to answer that. I have zero right to be digging around in your head."

"No, it's fine." I swallow to clear my suddenly dry throat. "I can't forgive him for what he did to my friends, but I can understand the reason his evil came to be."

"Is that enough?" He stares openly at me.

It takes a moment for the right answer to come.

"It's enough for me," I reply thickly. "I can't live my life otherwise, and honestly, all I want is to live. More than anything."

Looking into each other's eyes, I feel like we've found common ground for the first time. We've both been betrayed by the people we love. But that doesn't mean we can't choose to let go of that hurt.

"We should go and rescue Ulrich before Enzo gets him running drills with the new recruits."

"I promised him a trip to the museum for coming with me." He shakes his head. "That kid is obsessed with dinosaurs."

Holding the door open for him, I'm shocked to silence as he bundles me into a fast, tight hug that ends as quickly as it began.

"I know this means absolutely nothing to you, and I'm just some stranger, but I'm happy that you've found a home here."

"Thank you," I croak. "That actually means a lot. Even coming from you."

He flashes me a grin. "I guess I'll see you at the trial next. Save me a spot in the shitshow?"

"You bet."

We return downstairs then track down Enzo in the canteen. As promised, he's elbow deep in a tray stacked high with greasy cheeseburgers and loaded fries.

Ulrich is slurping on a strawberry milkshake and dipping his fries into the thick, pink liquid with enthusiasm. We join them in the quiet dining area where only a handful of others are eating.

"Hey, bud." Foster takes a seat next to his son. "What the heck are you doing to those fries?"

"Enzo taught me to dip them into my milkshake," he replies matter-of-factly. "I thought it was gross until I tried it."

Curious, Foster steals a fry and dips it in. His nose is scrunched up in distaste at first before he changes his tune.

"That's actually not bad."

I steal a bite of Enzo's burger. "Where did you learn that?"

"Leighton." He shrugs, his cheeks packed like a hamster. "He made us all try it out."

"Knew it. Only Leighton would think to do such a thing."

When Ulrich's done devouring his milkshake and fries, he shyly studies me from out of the corner of his eye. His dad stands and gestures for him to follow.

"We should get going." Foster glances at me. "I'll see you soon, Harlow. Keep in touch."

Enzo's eyebrows shoot up into his crop of wild black hair. It's amazing what sharing mutual trauma can do for a relationship.

"I will. Be safe."

Taking his father's hand, Ulrich politely thanks Enzo for the food, and the pair are escorted away by Hyland to leave the building.

But at the last second, Ulrich breaks away and comes running back.

"Um, Harlow?"

I stand up. "Yeah?"

"I heard Dad shouting on the phone when Mum got taken away by the police. Are you really my sister?"

Heart squeezing, I kneel on the floor to reach his height again. "We have different dads, but yes, I am your half-sister."

"I always wanted a sister to play with." He frowns to himself. "Mum bought me a dog instead."

"Ulrich!" Foster calls.

"You should go with your dad."

But he stays rooted to the spot.

"Can I see you again? I miss my mum. It's quiet at home without her. I… I'd like a friend."

It takes all of my strength to hold the rush of tears at bay. Unleashing a smile instead, I rest a hand on his shoulder.

"We can be friends if you want. I'd like that too. I've never had a brother before."

"If you want to come to the museum with us, you can. It has a Titanosaur that's twelve metres long."

"It's a bit hard for me to go outside right now," I let him down gently. "But next time we'll go to the museum together."

"You promise?" he challenges.

Drawing an invisible cross over my heart, I release his shoulder. "I promise, little man. Your dad has my number if you want to call and talk to me."

"Okay." Ulrich begins to backtrack. "Bye, then."

Watching them leave, bundled away by security to slip outside discreetly, I feel the first blooms of hope in a very long time. The roots unfurl around the broken mess of my heart and begin to bud.

That's exactly why I can't hold on to my anger and hatred. No matter the pain. No matter the damaged voices in my head, screaming for their own taste of vengeance.

We still have hope, and I won't ever let that be stolen away from me again. Even if Michael wins and this has all been for nothing.

"We have incoming," Enzo warns.

Looking up, I spot them before Brooklyn shrieks my name at the top of her lungs. She's flanked by Hudson and Kade.

"Brooke!"

The handful of staff in the canteen watches us rush across the room to throw ourselves at each other like a pair of lunatics. She cinches me into a lung-squeezing hug.

"Miss me?"

"You're back." I release her then gawp down at the swell of her belly. "And looking pregnant all of a sudden."

"I'm almost nineteen weeks."

Hudson and Kade bundle me into hugs next, the former messing up my hair with a playful snort. I shove him away then inspect their matching golden tans.

"How was Bali?"

"Hot," Kade complains.

"It was beautiful." Brooklyn swats his arm. "We got home last night."

His meal discarded, Enzo sweeps her off her feet in a bear hug. "I missed your annoying backside around here, wildfire."

"Same here." Her smile fades. "We heard there has been some trouble while we were gone. What the hell is going on outside?"

"Michael's new friends." I wave off her frown. "I want to hear all about your honeymoon before we talk about this crap."

"Kade has some great stories to share." Hudson laughs. "You want to tell them about your drunken antics, or should I?"

"You promised," he accuses. "What happened in Bali, stays in Bali. I was celebrating."

"I'll totally tell you everything later," Brooklyn whispers to me. "He was in a state after a few too many strong cocktails."

"Brooke," he whines.

"Sorry, sorry!"

Unable to stop myself, I yank her back into another hug. "I missed you guys so much."

SCENE DU NO
PROSE

CHAPTER 23

Enzo

Everything Once – Hotel Mira

Pacing up and down Hunter's office, the countless printed photographs covering every inch of the walls around me are a constant taunt. The list of victims has only grown.

We've added the nine bodies from last month's copycat killer to the melee of destruction. With no DNA evidence or witnesses, their fates still remain unknown.

"The news has broken about Harlow signing a publishing contract." Lucas's voice rattles through the speaker of my phone. "Surprisingly, the response hasn't been awful."

"Come again? Did you say *not* awful?"

"Sabre has its critics, but the public seems genuinely interested in hearing her story. They want to know what really happened to all those women."

Propping an arm against the floor-length window, I rest on it. "Well, that's an unexpected turn of events."

"We're working with the company's marketing team to ensure

that Sabre is represented in the best light. My team is handling it."

"This is her story. It isn't about us or the company. Harlow should be able to tell it however she wants."

"I'm just doing my job, Enz. There's not much else I can do to help these days. Let me keep what remains of your reputation intact."

I resist the urge to pull the trigger and give him free rein to destroy the remnants of the company we've built from scratch. Since talking to Harlow, all I can think about is leaving.

Running.

Hiding.

Fucking anything.

I just want out. The years of trauma and emotional exhaustion are finally catching up to me after being buried in the irretrievable pits of my psyche. We're all burnt out and at our wits' end.

"I have to go, Lucas. Got a briefing with the superintendent in half an hour, and I need to practise my nice face."

"You have one?" He snorts.

"Apparently not, hence the practising."

"Well, good luck with that. Tell Harlow to check her emails later. I need a few quotes to go in our press release about the book."

Ending the call, I toss my phone on Hunter's cluttered desk. He's at the hospital with Harlow, attending his monthly checkup.

The stack of paperwork that Sabre's legal team had delivered sits discarded next to my phone. I took the liberty of getting the necessary forms together for Harlow.

I wish I could say that it doesn't bother me whose surname she chooses. This isn't about us. It's her way of reclaiming her identity.

That doesn't stop me from itching with a caveman-like need to fill out the paperwork myself and stamp my surname on there, regardless of what anyone else thinks.

My phone vibrates with a text, and I snatch it back up.

Harlow: Arrived at the hospital safe. Just waiting to go in.

Enzo: Good. How is he?

Harlow: Nervous, I think. I'll keep you posted.

Enzo: Stay with Ethan, and be safe.

Harlow: Always x

The door to the office creaks open, emitting a bleary-eyed Theo back in his usual flannel shirt and tight grey jeans.

"You got a minute?"

I wave him in. "Sure."

He lumbers over to the conference table then perches on the edge. "Two of Matthew's friends have been released on bail."

"What the fuck?"

"They've been told to steer clear of us or risk being thrown back in prison if they violate the rules."

I bury my face in my hands. "Jesus fucking Christ. They burned down our goddamn house, and no one gives a shit?"

"They were charged, Enz. Matthew and the others couldn't afford the bond and are still locked up. That's something."

"What did the fire department say?"

"It's still a disaster zone," he confirms. "Massive structural damage caused by the fire. The property has been condemned."

"Awesome. That's just what I wanted to hear. So we're now homeless on top of being totally fucked, right?"

"I'd hardly call being forced to live in a multi-million-pound skyscraper homeless, but if you insist on being dramatic, sure."

"I really don't want to hear your optimism right now." I sigh.

Hopping off the table, Theo trails closer to rest a palm on my shoulder. "We made it out safely."

"This time. What about the next time our family is in danger? We never should've taken this case in the first place."

"But then we wouldn't have Harlow," he reasons.

And the thought of living a single goddamn moment without Harlow makes me want to jump off a fucking cliff.

Theo moves to the desk, picking up the stack of legal papers. "Harlow's going ahead with the name change, then?"

"She wants to get it sorted before things progress with the book. That bloody surname has haunted her for too long."

"Not sure one of ours is much better. The entire world knows and hates us all by now."

I look back out of the window at the early November mist clinging to London's skyline. It's a wet, dreary day as winter arrives, replacing golden leaves with rain and misery.

"Where would you go?"

"Hmm?" Theo hums distractedly.

"If you could leave the city. Hell, this whole country. Anywhere in the world to start a brand-new life, where no one knows our names."

Dropping the paperwork, he moves to my side. "Honestly? I have no clue. This life is all I've ever known."

"Maybe that's the problem. We've spent so long running from one fight to the next, we forgot to stop and actually live for ourselves."

"I'd be open to a change."

"You would?" I repeat in surprise.

Theo shrugs, his eyes on the gloomy sky. "Hacking began as a way for me to survive. I've been lucky to make a career out of it. That doesn't mean I want this forever."

"I don't think I've ever seen you without your laptop in hand." I gesture towards the device left on the table. "Who's this new Theodore Young?"

He fights off a laugh. "He grew up."

"Speaking of… You still haven't told Harlow that it was your birthday last week, have you?"

Ducking his head, he stares down at his Chucks, battered and mud-streaked from overuse.

"I don't celebrate. You know that."

"She'd kill us both if she knew."

"Which is exactly why I've kept it a secret," he retorts. "I've never celebrated my birthday, and I'm not starting now."

I clip him around the back of his head. "You're still a mystery to me, even after all these years."

"I'm going to take that as a compliment."

"Yeah, it really wasn't one."

Theo pushes his glasses up to rest in his blonde curls so he can scrub his face. "You know I grew up without a family. Birthdays just weren't a thing. It isn't a big deal."

"Do you ever think about finding your family?"

He spares me an uncertain look. "Where is all this coming from today? You're starting to freak me out a bit."

"Just thinking about stuff. That's all."

Replacing his glasses, he wipes a non-existent speck from the window. "I used to. Sometimes, I dream about them, but I can never see their faces."

"Maybe they had a good reason for leaving you in foster care all those years ago. You don't want to find out?"

"I don't fucking know, Enz." He sighs unhappily. "I have my family right here. That's all that matters to me now."

The blare of a screeching alarm emanating from his phone

interrupts us. Cursing, Theo grabs it and peers down at the screen.

"No way."

"What is it?" I ask urgently.

"We've had a hit on the facial recognition software we've been running on public CCTV feeds. Daphne's emerged."

"Fuck!"

Racing over to his laptop, Theo loads his complex, hand-coded surveillance program. It's taken years of perfection and first helped us when Harlow went missing in Croyde.

Fingers flying across the keyboard in a frantic blur, Theo locates the hit then loads the feed for us to check. It appears to be a camera outside a tiny village shop and petrol station.

I scan the grainy feed, unable to suck in a breath. Theo's frozen in place next to me, waiting for our target to come into sight.

"Please," he begs.

When a short, rounded woman walks into shot as she heads for the cash machine, I feel my heart explode. Her head tilts up, clocking the camera before quickly hiding her face and leaving with her cash.

I search through the stacks of files scattered across the table and locate the sparse profile we've gathered on Daphne. We managed to find an old driver's licence photo in government records.

"Is it her?" I hold the piece of paper next to his laptop screen. "She left as soon as she spotted that camera."

Theo rewinds the footage. "Maybe."

Setting it to slow motion, we both glance between the two images. It's all there. The sharpened hook of her nose, round chin and wide-set features beneath floss-like, silvery hair.

"Fuck," I repeat in awe. "Fuck! That's her."

He double-checks the location. "Holcombe. Christ, that's close to where those bodies were found on the beach."

"When was this?"

"Couple of hours ago. It takes time for the software to process through millions of CCTV feeds across the country."

I grip the edges of the table, taking a moment to focus myself. We've been waiting for this news ever since Giana spilled her guts about her secret half-sister. It's been agonising.

"Call Rayna. We need to speak to the owner of that petrol station and get a trace on the bank card she used to withdraw the cash."

Theo's already on the secure channel we use to communicate. His fingers quake with each movement across his keyboard.

"This is it," he says excitedly. "If she's helping Abaddon, she will lead us straight back to where he's been laying low."

I clap his shoulder. "Nice work, Theo. You just broke this case wide open."

"We still need to find the damn woman."

"Just take the compliment for once in your life."

He snorts. "Thanks."

"Alright, enough of that. Get an ID on that bank card, and see if she owns any property in Holcombe. I'll call the others."

"Leighton's at lunch with his parents," Theo replies. "He's going to pick Hunter, Harlow and Ethan up from the hospital."

Stepping out of the office, I try Leighton's phone first and get no answer. The same for Hunter and Harlow. Ethan picks up on the first ring with a barked greeting.

"Enzo."

"We've got something here. I need you to bring them straight back from the hospital when Hunter's done with his checkup."

"Got a bit of a situation here too. Hunter had a meltdown after his appointment. I think Harlow's with him now."

"What?" I snap. "You're there to keep them both safe, goddammit.

You need to find them right now."

"Copy that."

"Call me when it's done."

With the call disconnected, I look around the office again. The faces staring back at me suddenly feel alive—their eyes lit with defiance and demanding my attention.

I can't let this be my legacy. If we're going to leave Sabre to serve the next generation, we have to finish this. Our chance to bring Abaddon down has finally arrived.

"Fox is speaking to the owner now." Theo sits at the table, facing his laptop. "We'll hack into her banking records to get an address."

"Good. Ethan's tracking down Hunter and Harlow to bring them both back here. Sounds like the appointment didn't go well."

"Are they okay?"

"I don't know yet. He's going to check back in."

Firing off a text message to Hudson, I take a seat and wait. It doesn't take long for him, Brooklyn and Kade to bound into the room, leaving their late breakfast in the canteen behind.

"You found Daphne?" Kade exclaims.

"Almost." Theo pulls out the chair next to him. "I could use your help overriding these security protocols."

Kade takes a seat as Brooklyn nears to circle an arm around my neck. She's on light-duty after insisting on still working despite her pregnancy. None of the guys were happy about it.

"You okay?" she murmurs.

"I just need this to be it."

"I know, big guy." She moves a hand to her belly. "We're going to finish this together."

"There's no *we* in it. You're grounded. No exceptions this time."

"Hey!" she protests. "This is my case too. I want to see it through just as much as you do."

"That's final, Brooke. I'm not risking anyone else. We've lost too much already, and I won't fucking lose you too."

With a sour look, she reluctantly backs down. I don't give a shit if it hurts her precious feelings. Becket already paid the price for my decisions, and that won't happen ever again.

"Fox?" Theo picks up his ringing phone. "Tell me you have something."

He listens and curses under his breath. Kade hands him a piece of paper so he can write the information down that Fox is relaying.

"Good work." Hanging up, Theo looks around at us all. "We've got a name. She's been living under a false identity."

Springing into action, Kade takes the information and begins to input it into the laptop he brought with him.

"Do we really think she's spent the last decade helping this asshole without anyone knowing?" Hudson wonders.

"Why else would she leave her entire life behind and adopt a new identity?" Brooklyn replies. "She has to be with him."

"You said that Harlow has no memories of her," he reasons. "She can't have been there."

I crack my knuckles impatiently. "Harlow would also be the first to admit that her memory isn't the most reliable thing."

When Kade yells at his laptop, hazel eyes blown wide and darting between us, my anticipation peaks. I've never felt so nervous before.

Taking a look, Theo breaks out in a smile. "We've fucking got her."

SCENE DU CRIME
J ROSE

CHAPTER 24

Harlow

I Run To You – Missio

Sitting in the hospital waiting room, I watch Hunter's leg jiggle. He's wound tighter than a coiled spring and refuses to speak to me, despite allowing me to come along today.

Dropping a hand on his shaking leg, I squeeze to get his attention then lift an eyebrow in a silent question.

It's weird to see him dressed in a plain T-shirt and fitted, designer jeans, forgoing smart attire. He's wearing his hair shaved still, the scar across his skull shining in the light.

"I'm fine," he grumbles.

I don't need to use sign language for him to see my disbelief.

"It's just a checkup. You didn't need to come."

His lying is so obvious. I know Hunter better than he thinks. This stubborn, macho display only solidifies my belief that he's actually crying out for help.

The hair on the back of my neck stands on end. Breath held, I glance around the quiet waiting room. It's empty aside from two women sitting opposite and whispering to each other.

Nudging Hunter, I glance over at the women, indicating for him to look. His thick brows are drawn together as he studies them, his leg still shaking up and down to an anxious beat.

"Ignore them," he murmurs.

The scowl on the older woman's face deepens. Neither of them looks happy to be trapped opposite us, even in a hospital waiting room.

I'm surprised by how much it hurts to be hated by total strangers, but having Ethan standing on guard makes me feel better.

"Mr Rodriguez?" a voice calls.

Gently touching his arm, I point towards the audiologist peeking his head out of the office door. Hunter grabs my hand so fast, I almost jump out from my seat.

He squeezes my fingers in a death grip but refuses to move. I mouth a question, asking him what's wrong.

"Nothing," he blurts.

I raise a brow. I'm not blind.

"Just… I don't want to go in."

Offering him a hand, I mouth back. *"Here."*

Even if he thinks that he doesn't need me, I know he does. Trying to cope with this alone is killing him inside. I'll follow him until he's sick of the sight of me if that penetrates his shields.

He must read it on my face—the sheer desperation I feel to carry some of this burden for him. His expression breaks, offering a peek of the torment beneath his façade.

"Please don't leave me," he whispers, unable to hold it in for a second longer.

The last piece of my heart shatters.

"Never," I sign back.

Inside the doctor's office, we take seats opposite a paper-strewn desk. Doctor Vorderman took over from the intensive care team when Hunter was discharged and has monitored his recovery in the many months since then.

She accompanies her words with sign language. *"How are you?"*

"Fine," he grinds out.

I have to bite my tongue to prevent myself from answering for him. The stress of the investigation and being forced to flee our second home in less than six months is far from *fine*.

"I've looked over the results from your recent set of scans." She writes on a whiteboard to communicate the longer sentences. "You're seven months into your recovery."

"And?" Hunter prompts.

"There has been no improvement in your right eardrum's functioning. This is likely to be the final result now."

Hunter turns to look out of the window, offering a view across London's many glittering skyscrapers. He doesn't respond to her attempts to recapture his attention with waved hands.

We didn't expect his hearing to ever come back on its own. The other doctors confirmed that the accident permanently damaged the remaining functionality of Hunter's hearing.

But I think a part of him was still holding out hope, no matter how remote. We can't help but wish for the unattainable in life. Hope is simultaneously our biggest flaw and greatest asset.

"I'm sorry," I rush to apologise. "He's having a difficult time right now."

"Understandable," the doctor hums. "I'm sure this isn't the news he was wanting to hear after all these months of recovery."

"What are our options?"

"Now that we have a better understanding of his situation, we're willing to consider a surgically fitted cochlear implant."

"Surgery?"

"Yes," she confirms. "But I must stress, it isn't a guaranteed fix. Hunter has sustained severe damage to both of his eardrums, and there's no fix for that."

I turn to the frozen statue of tension next to me. Hunter has completely zoned out, his gaze unfocused and hands curled into white-knuckled fists. He's done engaging.

Poking his side, I make him look at me. "*Listen.*"

He dismisses me with a shrug.

I grab his shoulder. "*Surgery.*"

I want to smack him hard enough to knock some sense back into his stubborn backside. Avoiding reality isn't going to make this any easier.

"Here." Doctor Vorderman slides a brochure over. "This details the pros and cons. He needs to think over this carefully."

Hunter reluctantly accepts the paperwork and scans over it, his eyes slowly widening as he reads through the complex procedure.

"Will it work?" I ask.

"Not necessarily. There are risks involved with this operation. The implant bypasses the internal damage to stimulate the auditory nerve directly. It doesn't cure his deafness."

"So he still won't be able to hear?"

"At best, it will offer a representation of the environment that will allow Hunter to comprehend and piece together certain sounds."

"Like a puzzle."

"Precisely," she answers.

Hunter watches our exchange, his eyes tracing our lip movements and following the doctor's written communication on the whiteboard.

"How soon can we do it?" he demands.

She taps the list of potential complications and risks outlined in the brochure. Hunter ignores her completely, his mind already made up.

"I want to do it as soon as possible."

"*Think*," she signs.

"I don't need to think about it. I've made my decision. I want to do the surgery. You said that I'm ready, so let's do it."

He flinches when I try to take his hand in mine. I halt, my chest stinging from the rejection. His shields are slamming back down.

"I'm doing this. That's my choice."

Reluctantly, Doctor Vorderman nods. "*Okay.*"

With a throat clear, Hunter abruptly stands up and storms from the room, the brochure still clutched in his hands like a precious diamond. The office door slams shut behind him.

"I'm so sorry."

"Please don't apologise," she consoles. "Sudden loss of hearing is a deeply traumatic event."

"He's been struggling for a while now. His headaches are so debilitating. Is there anything we can do?"

"Unfortunately not. They may ease over time, but this is an aftereffect of his head injury that we anticipated."

I bite my lip, wrestling with the truth. "I'm worried about his mental health too. We thought returning to England would help, but he still won't let us in."

"Do you know if Hunter has been accessing any psychological support? Perhaps talking to a professional will be beneficial."

"We tried to convince him to speak to a therapist, but he refused. He isn't exactly the talking type."

"Of that, I'm convinced." She laughs. "I can recommend several local charities and services that work with the deaf community that may be useful. He should talk to someone."

Once she's scribbled down some websites and contact numbers, I accept the sheet of paper with a weary sigh.

"I'll talk to him."

"If he's going to do this surgery, he needs to be in the best frame of mind. It will be a long recovery, and Hunter will have to relearn how to communicate if the implant is successful."

I already know that none of us will be able to talk Hunter out of this, no matter the risks involved. He'd risk a deadly infection or making his condition worse if it meant he may hear again.

"There is support available for you as well," she adds meaningfully. "You're all adjusting to a new way of living, and that's tough."

"We have each other for that."

"It's something to bear in mind."

Muttering my thanks, I take the papers and stuff them into my handbag. "What happens now?"

"We will schedule an appointment with the surgical team to discuss the procedure and make the necessary arrangements."

"Good. We'll wait to hear from you."

"Thanks for coming in, Harlow."

Taking my handbag, I rush to leave and head back into the now-deserted waiting area. Hunter is nowhere to be seen, but Ethan is still propped up in the corner of the room.

"He went for some fresh air."

"Please can you bring the car around?" I sigh. "I'll track him down and meet you downstairs."

"Sure you don't need help?"

"No, I've got this."

Exiting into the adjacent concrete stairwell leading deeper into the hospital, I search around for Hunter's broad shoulders and shaved head. It doesn't take me long to track him down.

Knees pulled up to his chest and face hidden from sight, he's sitting on the top step, his shoulders shaking. It breaks my heart to see him so lost and alone.

"Hunt," I croak.

None of us can truly penetrate the lonely bubble that's suffocating him, using sign language or not. It's just a sticking plaster.

Sitting on the step next to him, I lean my head on his shoulder. His breaths are coming in sharp, pained inhales, and his head droops to rest against mine, too heavy to hold up.

"I can't live like this anymore," he says in a thick voice. "It's killing me inside. I've lost everything—my hearing, my work, my whole life."

Lifting my head, I slide a finger under his scruff-covered chin to bring his dark eyes back to mine. The espresso-coloured depths shine with angry tears.

"You haven't lost me," I enunciate slowly so he can read my lips.

He tries to shake his head, but I grip his chin tighter.

"You will never lose our family."

When he can't interpret what I'm saying, I repeat the words slower, signing out the words to accompany my lip movements.

"It's so fucking hard just to have a normal conversation," he rasps. "Look at us. I wish I could hear what you're saying to me."

Pecking the corner of his mouth, I kiss along his cheekbones, up to the socket of his left eye. Tears soak into my lips, allowing his grief to pierce deep into my heart.

"I've given you my heart, and I won't take it back, no matter how much you're breaking it by pushing me away."

"You want me to do what to you?"

Hunter is completely confused now and fighting to hold in a strangled laugh. Sometimes, even I forget he can't hear me.

"*Lip-read*," I spell out with my hands instead. "*Practice*."

"Or maybe I just hear what I want to now," he jokes, wiping his cheeks. "The world is more tolerable that way."

Sliding his hand into the mass of my hair, he tilts my head up to crash his lips into mine. I squeak in shock, caught in the hungry storm of his teeth and tongue.

His other hand roams down my body to squeeze the swell of my breast through my T-shirt. I don't have a bra on. With the madness of the past couple of weeks, we haven't done laundry yet.

Hunter's finger teases the hardening pebble of my nipple, sensitised by the cotton covering my chest. Fire sweeps over me until all I can think about is climbing inside his skin to meld us into one.

"Come on." He takes my hand. "I want to feel your pretty cunt hugging my cock, and I don't give a fuck who hears us."

Half-carrying me down the stairs, we burst onto the floor beneath the auditory clinic. It's a quiet treatment centre, but the reception desk is deserted, and there's no one in sight.

Two powerful arms latch around my waist, and I swallow a squeal as Hunter hoists me up. I'm pinned over his shoulder, and the hospital blurs around me.

He sneaks into an empty booth then drags the medical curtain across to hide us. When his palm cracks against my ass, I yelp in shock.

"Hunt—"

Dropping me to the linoleum, Hunter shoves me against the wall. His hips pin me with no space to flee, allowing his mouth to pepper kisses against my throat.

Teeth cutting into my skin, he sucks on my neck to leave a mark, his cock pushing into my core. This angry brand of hunger is new, but it turns me on far more than I'd ever expect.

Gripping the waistband of my jeans, Hunter shoves them over my hips and peels them off. I grab his shoulders as he lowers himself to the floor, kissing my quivering pussy through my panties.

"I want to taste your come on my tongue," he says darkly.

"We can't do this here."

But his eyes aren't watching for my response. He's preoccupied by yanking the panties down my thighs and securing his mouth to my bare mound. I arch my back, unable to hold in a groan.

Swiping his thumb over my clit, his tongue slips between my wet folds to lap at the heat gathering inside of me. When he spears my entrance with his tongue, my thighs close around his head.

With desire-flecked eyes flicking up to watch me, he sucks my clit into his mouth. The attention of his lips on my bundle of nerves sends bolts of sizzling electricity up my spine.

I don't care where we are anymore. All I can feel is him—kissing, sucking and licking every inch of me with so much enthusiasm, I'm on the verge of bursting already.

"That's it," he purrs. "Let me taste those sweet juices."

Hips bucking, my vision explodes when he pushes a finger deep inside my slit. He barely has to touch me. I'm already gone, the pent-up backlog of sensation washing over every inch of me.

"So soon?" he teases. "You're such a fucking good girl. Let me clean that up for you."

Hunter's tongue laps up the warmth trickling over my cunt, cleaning up the mess he's made for himself. I blink to clear my vision, my legs trembling from the powerful aftershocks.

Drawing to his full height, there's a wicked gleam in his eyes. Holding my hips, he quickly spins me around and steers me over to the unmade hospital bed in the corner.

"Bend over, sweetheart. Spread those legs for me."

Wrapping my fingers around the metal bars of the bed frame, I push backwards against his erection. Fuck, he feels so big and hard against my entrance, even through his jeans.

The clink of his belt causes my pulse to spike. I pant and writhe, bent over the bed until the softness of his tip is pushing up against my slit. He's an inch from heaven. I need him to fill me up right now.

Hunter's cock inches just inside of me. "You're so goddamn tight."

The bed rattles as he pushes deep in one thrust. I scream out, gripping the bars tighter. Stars explode behind my eyelids, and Hunter curses before pulling out to slam straight back in.

With only a scrap of curtain protecting us from anyone who may walk in, I'm so wildly turned on that I don't even care why Hunter's doing this. If he'd rather fuck than talk, then I'll take his rage.

Hand snaking around me, his fingertips crawl upwards to press against my lips. I accept the digits and swirl my tongue around them.

"Perfect, baby," he praises.

With his fingers soaked in my saliva, I have no idea what to expect until I feel them reappear between my spread ass cheeks. Moving higher, Hunter circles the tight ring of my back entrance.

"Being inside you with the others was so hot," he admits. "I've thought of nothing else since. I can't wait to share you again."

Head thrown back, I bite out another loud moan as his index finger pushes inside me.

He moves so slow; it's a torturous tease, feeling his finger easing into me while I'm still full of his huge length.

"My tight girl. Does that feel good?"

I find the sense to nod.

"Let me fuck both holes now, then."

Easing his finger out, his breath is hot against my ear as he pushes it back in at the same time his cock surges into my slit. His timing is perfect.

Swivelling his hips, a hand pushes against my tailbone to bend me even farther over. I'm splayed across the cheap hospital mattress, the cool plastic making my nipples sing.

With his length battering into me, thrust after thrust, the pressure inside my core grows again. The bed is rattling with each movement, but the echo of voices snaps me out of the haze.

"First appointment is in thirty minutes. Can we get the booths all prepped and ready?"

"Of course, Doctor Malik."

Startled, I push myself upright and grab Hunter's wrist to force him to stop. My nails bite into his skin, and his hips halt behind me. Looking over my shoulder, I mouth through my panic.

"People."

"Shit," Hunter curses.

Pulling out, he allows me to stand and turn around. Before he can pull his jeans back into place, I grab a handful of his white t-shirt.

"No," I enunciate.

"What do you want?"

Warmth is soaking into my thighs from my first release. He's transformed me into this needy, wanton animal, and I refuse to leave this booth without getting exactly what I want.

"You."

Brows raised in surprise, his hands seize my hips and lift me up. My legs automatically wrap around his waist until I'm clinging to the hard, chiselled lines of his chest.

"I want to come again," I mewl desperately.

He reads the plea on my lips. "Better be quiet then, if you don't want to get caught."

The hum of conversing voices picks up, adding weight to his words. I battle to hold in a strangled cry when he slides back into me, taking advantage of the position to seek an even deeper angle.

Kneading my ass to lift me with each pump, Hunter controls the frenzied tangle of our bodies like a merciless puppet master with no morals. All he wants is the promise of my release seeping into him.

"Check booth thirteen for swab packs, will you?"

"On my way," a voice acquiesces.

I smack his chest to mouth a warning. "*Coming!*"

With a wickedly devilish grin, he slaps a hand over my mouth and ducks behind the screen separating the two beds in the booth. We just fit behind it, our bodies barely covered by the plain fabric.

I scream into Hunter's hand when his cock surges back into me, despite the shadowed figure that draws back the booth's other curtain and enters to check the supply cupboard.

They're only a couple of metres away, but the voice counting supplies doesn't stop Hunter from trapping me against the wall and resuming his cruel, battering pace.

He leans close to whisper in my ear. "Come all over my cock, sweetheart."

Driving into me, he takes me to the edge of oblivion and gleefully shoves me off into the abyss. I throw my head back, my loud moan silenced by his palm.

The threat of getting caught adds power to the waves lapping at my insides. They're encroaching higher, forcing my release to rise into a threatening tsunami.

If he wasn't holding me up, I'd melt into a satisfied puddle at his feet. I'm nothing more than putty in his hands, being moulded into a shape of his choosing, and it feels so good to be owned.

"Fuck," he pants.

The nearby shadow suddenly halts. "Is someone there?"

Heart leaping into my throat, I slap my hand over Hunter's mouth.

We're both shuddering and fighting to breathe evenly, but the rush of panic only heightens my surging adrenaline.

Letting the silence drag for a moment, the footsteps eventually move away, leaving the booth. The need to giggle inappropriately rises up my windpipe, but I hold back.

This is not a position I want to be caught in by a complete stranger—butt naked with Hunter's come running down my legs.

Releasing my clamp on his mouth, I let his forehead connect with mine. We suck in each other's air for a moment, neither willing to move despite the people moving around us.

"I'm sorry," he blurts, his nose nudging mine. "I've pushed you all away. It doesn't mean that I don't want to be with you."

I stroke a hand over his neat beard, silently forgiving him.

"Thank you for sticking with me," he continues gruffly. "Not many people would. You've saved my whole family, Harlow."

I'd give anything in the world to be able to whisper how I feel and for this awful barrier keeping us apart to crumble. But there's nothing that would ever convince me to abandon this man.

He saved me once.

I'll happily spend the rest of my life, long or short, repaying that debt a thousand times over. If nothing else, I can die knowing that I have loved, and I am loved, so very deeply.

Sliding my arm around his chest, I use the tip of my finger to carefully trace a reply on his back. His eyes narrow as he attempts to decipher each imaginary letter drawn on his t-shirt.

I LOVE YOU.

His mouth crinkles in a satisfied smile. "Yeah. Ditto."

As we rush to replace our clothing and find a way to sneak out of the clinic without being spotted, I feel my phone vibrating in my jeans pocket.

"Shit," I curse to myself.

There are four missed calls from Ethan and a dozen more from Enzo. The additional text messages from Theo force my heart to leap into my throat.

> **Theo:** We've got a location for Daphne.
> This is it.

Hunter peers over my shoulder and blanches. "They've found her?"

I nod back.

His hand slides into mine. "You're not happy?"

Chest tight, I try to categorise what I'm feeling. The relief I was expecting never comes. Instead, I manage a shrug.

"I'm scared."

His eyes are fixed on my lips. "Scared?"

I nod in confirmation.

"Of what?"

Confused tears begin to roll down my cheeks. Hunter takes the time to kiss them away, one by one, his thumbs stroking my skin.

"The end," I mouth back.

It takes him a second to compute my words before he smiles in that toe-curling, forbidden way that first entranced me, despite how utterly petrified I was of him back when we first met.

"This isn't the end, sweetheart. It's the start of our forever."

CHAPTER 25

Harlow

Alone Made of Ice – Maldito

Crouched in the back of the insulation-lined van, I let Enzo adjust the straps on my bulletproof vest. He's been hard-faced and deep in concentration since we landed at the private airfield a few hours ago.

"Is that tight enough?" he asks.

"I can barely breathe."

He loosens one of the straps to release the pressure on my lungs. "Better?"

"Yeah, thanks."

Checking over my body armour one more time, he nods to himself. "You're ready to go."

I grab his hand before he can pull away. "Please talk to me."

Blowing out a breath, Enzo sits back on his haunches. He's had to crouch low to fit inside the support van that's accompanying our convoy of vehicles, carrying weapons, supplies and surveillance tech.

"You've already made up your mind about coming on this raid. I can't stop you."

"You trained me yourself," I remind him.

"That didn't stop us from getting blown to hell in Wales. We can handle this. I don't know why you're taking the risk."

"Because if Michael is in there, I want to be the one who puts an end to this. If you don't get why that's important to me, then I can't help you."

When I try to dodge past him to slip out of the van and join the others, Enzo bands an arm in front of the door to block me.

I'm trapped and pulled backwards until I fall onto his lap. Two terrified amber eyes peer down at me, shadowed by the scruff of his raven hair falling over his face.

"Little one," he rasps.

"Just let me go."

"No, listen. We haven't come this far for me to lose you now. I promised you his head on a platter, and I will deliver."

"I don't need you to deliver," I snark back. "This is my fight as much as it is yours. We do this together or not at all."

His chest vibrates with a sigh. "You're getting as stubborn as Brooklyn. Do you know that?"

I can't help but laugh. "Someone has to keep your ego in check. We're a team. Let's end this as a team."

Lips finding mine, he kisses me passionately, communicating all of the fears that we could spend hours arguing about.

We're both fucking scared, but that isn't going to stop me from doing this. I've earned the right to be on this team.

"I love you," Enzo murmurs into my lips. "Whatever happens to us when this case is over, I need you to remember that."

"And I need you to know that the only reason I've made it this far is knowing that after this, I get to keep all of you. Forever."

"Forever," he echoes.

Swinging the door open, he helps me climb out into the cool lash of winter air. The memory of Costa Rica's warm sandy beaches from the summer feels like a distant dream now.

"Can I start a petition for us to go back to our private villa afterwards?" I joke. "I've decided this country is too cold."

Enzo kisses my temple. "Works for me. I miss our daily dirt bike rides. We still need to get you a bike for this country."

"Let's add it to the after list."

"The after list?"

"I'm keeping one for when this is all over."

Linking hands, we head for the gathering of teams outside Theo's blacked-out surveillance van. We're set up in a remote field, surrounded by abandoned barns that our police contact cleared.

Suited up and ready to go, Leighton is handing out earpieces to the rest of our raiding party—Hunter, Hudson, Ethan and Hyland.

Theo and his team are on comms, with Brooklyn monitoring from the safety of HQ, much to her displeasure. Her husbands refused to compromise on this occasion.

"Here." Leighton hands me an earpiece. "Never thought I'd say this, but you look hot in bulletproof armour."

I slot it into place. "I'll take the compliment. Are you sure about joining us on this raid?"

"No way am I sitting behind a damn computer screen and listening to shit go south again. I'm sticking to you like glue."

"Sounds hot."

"It could be." He waggles his eyebrows. "Maybe I'll get to take that armour off you later when all this is done."

"If you like it so much, don't you want to see me in the armour and nothing else?"

His tongue flops out like an overexcited puppy. "Now you're speaking my language, Goldilocks."

"Alright, listen up." Enzo claps his hands at the front of the group. "The target's house is half a mile from here. We don't have a police cordon in place to avoid spooking her."

Everyone's loading up with weapons and gear, listening to his instructions. I unlock the case that carries my gun then strap it in the holster fastened around my thigh.

"We have reason to believe that Michael Abaddon may be holed up with the target. It's crucial that we capture this bastard alive."

Enzo looks pointedly at Hudson, who flips him off.

"You always ruin my fun."

"That goes for all of you." Enzo looks around the group. "Use force only if necessary. I want this to be a clean extraction."

Poking his head out of the nearby van, Theo is geared up in his headset. "I'll be keeping surveillance with the team."

I catch his eyes and force a smile on my face. His reassuring stare gives me the boost of strength I need to do this.

"Don't forget about me." Brooklyn's voice buzzes in our earpieces. "Enzo, bring my husbands back alive, or there will be hell to pay."

"You got it, wildfire. Let's move out."

We split into three groups, taking a darkened van each to blend into the early evening shadows. The rural rolling hills of Holcombe pass by in a blur with Hunter driving our van.

"Did you fill out that paperwork last night?" Leighton asks from the passenger seat.

"No, Leigh."

"Why not?"

I pull my earpiece out. "For starters, we were prepping for this last-minute raid. But I also still don't know which surname to take."

He removes his earpiece as well to give us a moment of privacy. "It's a big decision, especially with the book coming out next year."

"I thought you were about to convince me to publish it under Harlow Rodriguez."

"As much as I'd fucking love that, I don't think you should choose our surname."

"You don't?" I ask in surprise.

Leighton looks over his shoulder to face me. "There's still us with that name. My parents. Enzo has his aunt. We've got a family."

"So?"

"We have other people."

I quickly catch on. "And Theo doesn't have anyone."

"Exactly. Young isn't even his real surname. It's just what he was assigned when his parents abandoned him as a child."

"You don't think it would upset the others?"

"Why?" Leighton challenges. "Theo is our brother. You're ours. So it doesn't matter whose name you choose."

I want to melt into a relieved puddle at his feet. "Thanks, Leigh. I needed to hear that."

"I've got you, princess."

Hunter pulls into a small residential area, the thatched roof cottages all painted in mottled shades of white.

We pass the tiny shop and petrol station that captured Daphne's face and replace our earpieces to get ready for the final approach.

"This place is tiny."

"Perfect for hiding in plain sight," Leighton agrees.

Theo's voice whispers into my ear. "There's an old farmhouse on the edge of town registered under her false identity. Lots of land."

I don't need him to fill in the blanks. Michael's running his base of operations from somewhere. This is the ideal hideout.

We all congregate in an empty car park, surrounded by fields of corn and the distant spires of a local church. I climb out, following the two brothers.

"The house is over the back of this field." Enzo gestures into the distance. "We're going to approach as three teams to cover the perimeter and request their surrender."

"Request?" Hudson scoffs incredulously.

"We don't know who is in there. Could even be innocent lives. I'm not having anyone caught in the crossfire this time around."

Chastised, Hudson checks the various close-hand combat knives he keeps strapped to his gear and nods in submission.

"Look out."

Theo's voice follows the quiet hum of his drone zipping above us, offering a bird's eye view of the cornfield that reaches beyond our line of sight.

"If anyone makes a run for it, I'll call them out. We've got the whole team running surveillance. No one makes it out of our sight."

All prepared, we move in single file and dive into the deserted cornfield. The stalks have long since been stripped and cut down, leaving empty husks behind for the winter.

I follow Hunter and Hudson with Enzo at my back, keeping me sandwiched between walls of muscle. We move at a slow pace, approaching the shadow of a three-story house on the horizon.

"It's big," I whisper.

"Grade II listed property purchased five years ago," Brooklyn answers in my ear. "I've got the deeds up. She was a cash buyer."

"How did Daphne afford it?"

"Don't forget the husband," Theo reminds. "He left her a handsome sum, plus the property to be sold. Very convenient."

There isn't a single part of me that wants to meet this woman.

Even if she is technically another relative. The signs are all pointing towards her being a soulless psychopath like her brother.

"Focus up," Enzo growls. "Fan out, and get the place surrounded."

Emerging into the clearing that surrounds the wooden frame and wide, peeling porch of the farmhouse, there's a faint light emanating from inside.

Before we can take another step, the front door opens with an ominous creak. A shadowed figure emerges, her short, curved body lit by the light leaking out from inside.

"Don't move!" Enzo bellows. "The place is surrounded. We just want to talk to Daphne Portcastle."

Everyone has their weapons trained on the person, taking tentative steps against Enzo's command. I keep my weapon stashed and move forward an inch.

"Who are you?"

Creeping down the porch steps, her wrinkled face is revealed. "Don't recognise your own flesh and blood, girl?"

She's small, her back slightly hunched beneath the weight of the world. Her eyes are sharp and perceptive, scanning over the numerous weapons threatening to split open her skull.

"Took you long enough," she rasps, her voice low and grating. "I gave it twenty-four hours before you broke down my door."

Enzo keeps his gun raised. "You baited us?"

"Thought someone with a reputation such as yours would be smarter, Mr Montpellier. I've kept my face hidden for a reason."

Impatient and unable to read her lips, Hunter cocks his gun in warning. "Come out with your hands raised. We're not here to chat."

"This one can't even hear me," she snickers. "Why do you keep him around? For entertainment?"

"Enough," I shout. "Where is Michael?"

"Why don't you come inside and find out, Harlow?"

"Like hell." Kade steps in front of me in a protective stance. "She's going nowhere."

"Tell me..." Daphne smooths her plain shift dress, the golden crucifix at her neck front and centre. "Did you enjoy your visit with Giana?"

I swallow hard. "How do you know about that?"

"She's kept me a dirty little secret for all these years. I figured she'd cash in her last bargaining chip soon enough."

Something about this woman is causing my brain to stutter, overwhelmed by the scream of mental alarm bells. I've never seen her in my life, but somehow, the hiss of her voice is familiar.

"Come on," Daphne goads. "You really don't remember, do you? Michael always wanted an empty vessel for his will."

"I am not an empty vessel!"

"Did you really think he could come up with all of this alone? My brother is a smart man, but not even he could bring down an empire of sin without help."

Months of terror, violence and rampant destruction burn bright in the flickering embers of her eyes. She's proud. Fucking giddy with satisfaction. He did have help, after all.

From her.

His puppeteer.

"Our sister never quite understood the work we are doing here." Daphne touches her crucifix. "She cowered away from getting her hands dirty. The Lord doesn't condone such disloyalty."

Dread is slamming into me, over and over. Thick, cloying, suffocating waves of dread. We're missing something.

"If you hurry, you may still be able to say goodbye," she taunts. "He isn't quite done yet."

"What are you talking about?"

She cackles. "Stupid child."

"I've heard enough." Enzo advances with his gun. "Get down on your fucking knees before I put a bullet in you."

Hands raised, she follows his instructions with a maniacal grin on her face. The moment he slaps a pair of handcuffs on her, I take off in a run.

"Harlow!" Leighton yells.

But my feet are already thumping up the porch steps that lead into the farmhouse. I can hear the others following as I duck inside the living room, warmth emanating from a lit fire.

Empty.

Moving deeper into the house, darkness welcomes me home. The furniture is all antique and probably older than me. Wooden crucifixes hang from the walls, nailed into place over ugly wallpaper.

"Archived blueprints show a root cellar beneath the first floor," Brooklyn recites quickly. "There's access in the kitchen."

"Harlow." Hudson stops me. "Please let me go down first. I'm not letting that bastard touch you again."

I gesture for him to go ahead, and he nods, taking the lead into the kitchen. Dingy cabinets and peeling linoleum match the rest of the strange, antiquated house.

Beneath the adjacent staircase, there's a triangle-shaped door leading down. Weak light spills up from whatever lies beneath us.

"Theo," I say into the earpiece. "We're going into the cellar."

"Be careful," he responds.

As we begin to descend, off-key humming is the first sound that warns me we're entering the devil's lair. I recognise it without needing to see my uncle's dead eyes and leering grin.

The whisper in my head steals the relief I should feel, knowing we're about to end a whole year of emotional anguish. He's here. It's over, and yet the victory rings hollow.

It's too easy.

There's no way they could have known about my visit to see Giana. Not unless they had inside knowledge or it came from her.

Yet the dread persists. Spreading. Infecting. Metastasising into a terminal cancer that rots the flesh from my bones.

"Holy shit." Hudson's voice echoes up the staircase. "Harlow, stay the fuck upstairs!"

But it's already too late. I'm chasing after him and running straight into the arms of cold-hearted inevitability. The time has come.

Thudding down the last few steps, I'm slapped in the face by a familiar scent from my past. Blood. Litres of it. Copper perfuses the thick, dusty air inside the root cellar.

Hudson stands a few inches from the base of the staircase, his gun raised and trained on a figure perched in the corner of the dank room. The first thing I see is his mouth stretched in a smile.

"I was wondering when you'd show up," Michael says casually, as if greeting an old friend. "I'm afraid you're too late for the show."

His usual pressed robes are stained, the fabric covered in dark, sticky splotches. Red splatters mark the dog collar peeking out at his neck, the droplets congealing on his crucifix.

"The family ... all together again." Michael swoops a hand around the cellar. "Reunited at last."

The useless lump of organ that lives behind my ribcage stops, stutters then explodes into shards. I can't move. Blink. Breathe. My feet are glued to the floor as I take in the awaiting sight.

"Giana?" I whimper.

It can't be her. She's hundreds of miles away, locked in a high-security prison with twenty-four-hour supervision for her own protection.

And yet I'm staring into the dead, glassy eyes of my mother. Her mousy-brown hair is sticky with blood and clumped together. Mouth slack. Limbs stiff. Body naked.

The symbols that carve a violent path of scars into my own body are mirrored perfectly, slashing her twisted, limp body and adding to the congealed puddle of blood staining the floor.

"She didn't last long." Michael chuckles. "Your record remains unchallenged, darling niece. I was curious."

When I screw my eyes shut and shove them back open, the view hasn't changed. This isn't a dream. It isn't even a nightmare.

She's dead.

Butchered.

Gone.

Reality blurs as everyone moves around me—apprehending Michael, cuffing his hands behind his back and beginning to beat the ever-loving shit out of him.

None of it matters. Not their relief. Nor his satisfaction. All I can feel is the widening pit of nothingness in my chest as I stare down at my dead mother.

A soft pair of hands lands on my arms and pulls me back into someone's chest. They're stroking me. Whispering. Shaking. It doesn't break the numb mist that's taken over everything.

"She was a filthy fucking whore!" Michael screams, his veneer of calmness dissipating. "May she rot in hell with my useless wife."

His voice cuts through my shock, and I find myself shrugging the pair of hands off, landing next to Giana in a puddle of her blood.

"No," I choke out a sob.

She's cold. Waxy. Lifeless. The only colour on her skin is from the shocking slashes of crimson sliced into her with unimaginable rage.

"Harlow," the voice in my ear coaxes. "Medical help is on its way. I need you to talk to me, beautiful."

"She's d-dead!"

"Who is dead? What happened, angel?"

Taking Giana's hand in mine, I can hardly see through the ribbons of tears soaking into my face. All I can hear is what she said to me in the prison. I couldn't find it in myself to even give her a response.

I'm sorry for so many things, Harlow. But I'm not sorry for bringing you into this world. I'm proud of the woman you've become.

I left in tears then, unable to fathom the entirely foreign need I'd felt to throw my arms around her and share a single moment of love with the woman who gave birth to me.

"Harlow!" Theo shouts down the line.

"It's my m-mum. He killed her."

SCÈNE DU
J.ROSE

CHAPTER 26

Leighton

Queen – Perfume Genius

Standing at the back of the press conference room, I watch Enzo and Hunter artfully perform for the sea of reporters. My brother has even dug up an old smile to offer the room as the BSL interpreter translates their questions for his benefit.

Sitting on their left, the well-dressed, pompous hide of the superintendent herself, Natalie Hart, has made a rare appearance. Her perfect blonde hair is slicked back in a severe bun.

"I would like to take this opportunity to publicly thank Sabre Security for their hard work and determination."

Even I can see that Enzo's working his ass off to hold back a sarcastic remark. He was ready to lynch her not too long ago.

"Thanks to them, the most heinous, violent serial killer this country has ever seen will now face his day in court."

To my dismay, the room breaks out in a round of enthusiastic applause. The journalists that have spent the last year making our lives a living hell are now singing our fucking praise.

No.

I'm done.

Turning to leave the room, Enzo's response makes my feet halt.

"We still have a long way to go in this investigation. Michael Abaddon was aided by a co-conspirator and still has many supporters at large who need to be apprehended."

That's when the sea of questions begins. None of them knew about Daphne's involvement before now. Abaddon had a mastermind all along, operating in the shadows.

"Can you account for the presence of an inmate from a high-security prison being found dead at the scene?"

I have to glance back and relish the embarrassed look on Natalie's face. That particular failing has nothing to do with us.

"We are actively looking into how Giana Kensington was able to escape from Bronzefield," she answers curtly. "I have commissioned a full investigation into their security measures."

As the roar of questions begins again to vie for their attention, I sneak out of the room. I don't need the events rehashing. The memory is burned on my mind well enough.

We won.

But it cost … everything.

Outside the entrance to Sabre's HQ, there is relative peace for the first time in months. No one can quite believe the silence.

Accusatory placards and screamed curses vanished overnight, leaving only a gaggle of praying lunatics behind as they beg the Lord for his protection.

The moment the first headline was published to reveal Abaddon's capture, the world stopped caring. Their fear was the only thing causing them to give a shit.

We don't think about the suffering of others until our own lives are caught in the crosshairs. It's easier to move on. Forget. Give up. That's more convenient for everyone.

Until that threat reaches our shores and we pretend to have a moral compass for those five minutes of fame. Those people never wanted justice for Abaddon's victims.

We did.

Now we have it.

But that victory is far from the sweet release we were promised. Instead of relief and jubilation, all we have are handfuls of the still-burning embers of our lives, sacrificed to reach this moment.

Back upstairs, I return to our temporary apartment. There's been talk of going home to our abandoned London house that's sat empty since we left, but we haven't had the time to organise the move yet.

"Harlow?" I step inside.

"Shh." Theo's voice hisses from the living room. "I've just got her to sleep."

On the L-shaped sofa that dominates the airy space, he's working on his laptop with one hand, the other stroking Harlow's tangled hair.

She's curled up in a ball next to him, her eyes closed, and a brand-new journal gifted from Jude trapped in her arms.

"Did she take one of those tablets Richards gave her?"

Theo nods. "Took some convincing."

"She hasn't slept since we got back from Holcombe." I look around the messy room. "This will do her good."

Abandoning the email he was attempting to type with one hand, Theo glances up at me. "How's the press conference?"

"As you predicted. The reporters are kissing our asses now that we have Abaddon in custody. That bitch Natalie is loving it."

He scoffs bitterly. "She'll be lapping this up for months and claiming it as her victory."

"You bet."

Sitting down on Harlow's other side, I run a hand over her curled spine. She's in the foetal position, cuddling her journal for any semblance of comfort while unconscious.

I get better than most why Giana's sudden death has ripped the carpet out from under her feet. Loss isn't something that follows any man-made rules.

We can mourn things that we didn't even know we needed. Including the idea of a person. I grieved for months behind bars for the privileged life I'd so carelessly tossed aside.

She didn't love Giana.

Not in a normal sense.

But that didn't mean she wasn't still her mum. Without even a shitty, imprisoned bitch of a person to fill that void, it's just another empty reminder of everything Harlow will never have.

"Fuck, Theo. How do we fix this for her? It's killing me to watch her go through this."

"I don't know that we can," he admits quietly. "She's still in shock. We just need to be there for her until she comes back."

"And what if she doesn't come back?"

Looking down at Harlow, he nods with a strange sense of certainty. "She will. I've never met anyone stronger than our girl."

Wincing in her sleep, she shifts and almost wakes up. Theo hushes her, stroking the hair from her face until she relaxes again.

"Even now she's fighting back," he jokes. "Can't even make her sleep when she doesn't want to."

"I blame Brooklyn. She's a bad influence."

"Speaking of, she brought over two trays of lasagne for us. Extra burnt. I think we're being punished or something."

"God, I am not eating that shit."

Chuckling, he returns to looking at his laptop screen. I peer over Harlow's lightly snoring body to look at the live video feed he's studying intensely.

"Has Abaddon moved at all?"

"Nope." Theo sighs. "Been in the same position praying for the last three hours. His sister too."

The live feed of the detention cell holding Abaddon is crystal clear, allowing for no misinterpretation. The psycho is sitting cross-legged on the floor and happily praying in his cell.

"He's still refusing to speak to anyone." Theo catches himself. "Well, anyone but Harlow. It's the only thing he's asked for."

"Enzo still hasn't told her?"

"Not yet. She's fragile right now, and letting this bastard rub his latest kill in her face will only make it worse."

The no-more-sane sister, Daphne, is sitting in an almost identical position as she follows the same routine in a completely different cell. Their actions are identical.

"What about Daphne?"

Theo shakes his head. "Nothing."

"Goddammit. We need to know who is still out there doing their dirty work. This isn't over yet."

"We're trying, Leigh."

"Clearly not hard enough!"

My slightly-raised voice causes Harlow to stir again, and this time, her eyes flutter open. The usually crystal clear, aquamarine depths are muddied with exhaustion and bloodshot from crying.

"Sorry, princess. Go back to sleep."

"Leigh? You're back."

"Nice work," Theo mutters.

Cutting him a glare, I take hold of Harlow's elbow and gently pull her onto my lap. She snuggles into me, her lips brushing my throat.

"You need to sleep, baby."

"I'm fine," she whispers. "Is the press conference over?"

"Not yet. Hunter and Enzo are holding down the fort. They've even got a BSL interpreter in so he can take questions."

I can hear the smile in her voice.

"I'm sure he's loving that."

"Quite the opposite. Hunter looked bored to death and like he wanted to get the fuck out of there. His days of playing boss are long gone."

She points over towards the kitchen. "A letter from the hospital came. Hunter told me to open it while he's gone. His surgery has been scheduled for six weeks' time, right after Christmas."

Anxiety spikes through me. "Shit. So soon? That isn't great timing with all this crap still going on."

"It's a relatively simple procedure, so it shouldn't be an issue," Theo explains. "The recovery time is about a month before they activate the device to see if it worked."

"And what? He can hear again?" I question.

"No," he answers.

"I don't understand."

"The device receives sound from the environment and sends electrical signals to the auditory nerve for the brain to then recognise and process."

"What's that in English?" I sigh.

"It isn't normal hearing." Harlow cuddles closer to me. "He'll need months of speech therapy to learn how to interpret the sounds."

I'm sure my brother considered none of this when he made the decision to get the surgery. Even after all this time, he's still looking for some damned miracle cure that doesn't exist.

I rub circles on Harlow's back. "Did you speak to Foster this morning?"

"No, I haven't called him back yet. I can't face him."

"You have to speak to him sometime, Goldilocks. Talking to him may actually help."

"Help what?" she snaps. "Nothing about this can ever be fixed. Talking or not. Giana is still dead."

"Maybe he wants to talk to you about a funeral," Theo chimes in. "Do you want to say goodbye?"

She sniffles on my chest. "I don't know what I want anymore. Losing her was never supposed to hurt like this."

"When do our hearts ever do what they're supposed to?" I reply gently. "You're allowed to hurt and mourn her."

"Like she mourned me?"

Pulling free from my embrace, Harlow struggles to climb to her feet. She hasn't changed out of a borrowed pair of my sweats and Hunter's t-shirt that we wrestled her into upon returning.

Beginning to pace the living room, she ignores our favourite show, *Friends*, softly playing in the background. Angry tears are leaking from her eyes. Theo stops me before I stand up and intervene.

"I thought I'd be happy once Michael was behind bars, but instead, I feel empty. It won't bring anyone we've lost back."

"But it will stop anyone else from getting hurt," Theo points out.

She slows, offering a nod. "I guess so. What's going to happen now that we have him in custody?"

"He's been charged with twenty counts of first-degree murder, including Giana's death, and for kidnapping Candace. That's potentially twenty life sentences."

"Twenty?" I frown at Theo. "Weren't there more?"

"They aren't willing to discuss charges for the mass suicide or copycat kills until he talks or we have evidence. There's no proof."

"That's complete crap!"

"I don't make the rules."

"Then we need him to talk." Harlow turns to face us both. "Those people deserve justice too. It's not their fault he used them."

Exchanging a silent conversation with Theo, I wave towards her, encouraging him to spill the beans. She doesn't need our protection.

"What?" Harlow demands.

He clears his throat. "Abaddon has said that the only person he'll speak to is you. He's been silent ever since."

Wringing her hands together, she resumes pacing on the silver-threaded rug but remains weirdly calm.

"You don't have to do this," Theo reasons. "We have interrogators who are trained to get information out of people. Let them handle it."

"No. It has to be me."

"Beautiful—"

"I'm the only one who understands how his mind works. I can get him to admit what he did. We need those charges to be added."

"He's going to be behind bars until the day he dies no matter what happens," I supply. "Why does it matter?"

"Because," she cuts in. "They were his victims too. Their families need closure."

Realising she's got me beat, I back down. I don't give a shit what we have to do. If she needs this to feel better, we'll damn well do it.

"Okay. Then talk to him."

Harlow gapes at me. "You're seriously on board with this?"

"If you want to do this, then I think you should. Only you can know your own mind. All I care about is your feelings."

"I want to do it. No, I *need* to do it."

"Then we'll make it happen," Theo agrees. "We all want closure, angel. For you and everyone else."

Knuckles rapping on our front door breaks the moment, and I get up to answer, squeezing Harlow's arm on my way past. Pale-faced and antsy, Oliver waits on the other side.

"Is Harlow here?"

I hook a thumb over my shoulder. "She's okay. Nobody else got hurt during the raid."

"I need to see her."

"Dad?" her voice calls.

Stepping aside, I let him bounce past me in his haste to reach her. Harlow doesn't even flinch when he almost tackles her, and she's swooped off the floor in an emotional reunion.

"I was so worried about you," he rushes out. "We weren't told about the raid until it was all over, and the news broke."

"It happened so fast. We didn't want to worry you."

"I'm your father, Harlow!" He sets her back down. "I'll worry about you until the day I die, and you need to understand that."

When he realises what he's said, Oliver blanches. She takes his hand and pulls him back into another hug.

"I'm sorry, Dad."

He deflates. "Me too, love. When I heard what happened… I didn't know what to think or feel."

"She's dead. He killed her."

"Did … did she suffer?" he dares to ask.

When Harlow can't even fathom a response, Oliver breaks down. He looks as confused by his feelings as Harlow does. They hold each other through the tears and shaking.

"I know she hurt both of us so much, but no one deserves to die like that," Oliver croaks. "Not even her."

Finding the strength to separate themselves, Harlow guides him over to the armchair next to the sofa. The life drains out of him as he slumps into it.

"I spoke to her husband," he admits.

We all tense up.

"You did?" Harlow exclaims.

"He reached out to me a few hours ago. Seems like a decent bloke. He had the consideration to call me himself."

Harlow perches on the armrest. "Foster is a good man. I know he'll see to it that she's laid to rest properly."

"What about the kid? Ulrich, is it?"

"I can't imagine what he's thinking right now." Her hands move to cover her face. "I saw him a few weeks ago. He said that he misses his mum."

Sensing that this conversation needs alcohol, I retrieve the emergency bottle of whiskey that Brooklyn also delivered with her terrible food offerings.

Harlow and Theo each accept a glass while Oliver declines. He looks in better need of a good night's sleep than hard liquor.

"I think you should call the kid," Oliver suggests.

"Why? I can't offer him any comfort."

"You can," he encourages, squeezing Harlow's knee. "Just the sound of your voice will let him know that he's not alone."

Harlow's head falls. "All he wanted was his mum back. Regardless of what everyone else said she'd done."

Reaching over to take hold of her hand, I let our fingers curl together. "That's why he needs you. No one else can understand what that feels like."

With a final sigh, she submits. "I'll call Foster back and ask to speak to Ulrich."

Disappearing to make the phone call, she's still holed up in her bedroom when Enzo and Hunter return from the press conference. Enzo takes one look at us then pours himself a glass of liquor.

"That woman is an insufferable piece of shit," he grumbles. "I never want to work with her again."

"That good, huh?" I snort.

"Natalie is still down there taking credit for the entire investigation and acting like this is some grand victory for us all."

Crouching down next to the glass fireplace, Hunter hides his face in his hands. None of us have slept much in the whirlwind since the raid.

"Harlow wants to go into the interview with Abaddon," Theo interjects. "She's agreed to get him to talk."

"What?" Enzo explodes.

I hush him with a waved hand. "This is her call. She wants answers, and keeping this shit from her is pointless."

"I wasn't going to keep it from her forever." He deflates, knocking back a mouthful of whiskey. "I don't want her anywhere near him."

"What's the worst he could do?" Theo challenges. "Not like he can butcher or hurt anyone else. We're in control now."

Somehow, that sentiment doesn't ring true. None of us believe it, even if we're not willing to admit that. Abaddon handed himself to us on a gold fucking platter, and I don't trust it.

Several drinks in, and with Brooklyn's terrifying lasagne warming in the oven, Harlow rejoins us from her bedroom, eyes swollen from more crying.

"Did you speak to him?" Oliver asks.

She bites her lip. "Yeah, he answered. Giana's body is going to be cremated next week. Nothing fancy."

Walking into Enzo's arms, she brushes her lips against his and crawls closer to snuggle up.

"Are you going to go?"

"I think so," she answers me. "Someone should be there."

"We'll all go," Enzo decides.

"You don't have to do that."

"Trust me, it's not for her." He pecks the top of her head. "We're going to be there for you, little one. No one else."

We all chime in our agreement, even Oliver. I personally think the world is a far better place without Giana's sick brand of evil in it, but if Harlow needs us, our feelings are irrelevant.

Leaving Enzo's embrace, Harlow retrieves the open hospital letter from the table and brings it to Hunter. His throat bobs.

"What did it say?"

Rather than answer, Harlow encourages him to take it himself. Hunter sighs and slides the letter out of the ripped envelope to read.

His gaze scans over the printed text, and the smile that blooms on his lips is so fucking happy, it actually hurts to see that part of my brother reappearing.

"Six weeks," he recites. "This is it."

Despite everything—the pain and bloodshed still boiling at our feet—we all toast to that. If hope is what he needs, then we're not going to take that precious commodity from him.

"There's something else I wanted to talk to you guys about," Harlow begins nervously. "Changing my surname."

Everyone sits a little straighter.

She glances over to Theo. "I wanted it to be yours before all this happened. Please don't hate me, but I think I need to be Harlow Kensington now."

"You know, pulling out your earpiece doesn't stop me from being able to hear you," Theo replies with a wink. "Doesn't work that way."

"Leigh!" she chastises.

I spread my hands in surrender. "You're the one who started the conversation. I didn't think he was listening."

Her cheeks flush pink. "You're not upset?"

"Of course not," Theo offers. "Leighton said it himself... You're ours, regardless of what a piece of paper says."

"But why Kensington?" Enzo questions.

She fiddles with the hem of Hunter's oversized t-shirt that she stole to wear. Wearing our clothes comforts her.

"I thought that I wanted a new identity, but I was wrong. I want to honour the girl who survived that cage."

When he thinks no one is looking, Oliver subtly swipes under his reddened eyes. Harlow takes one look at him and chokes up.

"This is the start of my future," she says assertively. "Leticia Kensington lost everything."

"And now?" Oliver asks.

"Now Harlow Kensington is going to give it back to her."

SCÈNE DU RISE
I.DOSE

CHAPTER 27

Harlow

Chokehold – Sleep Token

Shaking out my hands, I stand frozen on the other side of the interview room. It's one of the secure, soundproof rooms on the same floor as the detention cells, complete with metal walls and floor.

On the other side of that steel sheet is the man who kidnapped and tortured me. Raped and murdered my friends. Brutalised countless victims. Tore the country apart and … killed my mother.

No pressure.

"Are you ready for this?" Theo checks in.

He's sitting on the other side of the two-way mirror with Hunter and Kade. All three of them are poised to watch the interview, with Enzo opting to accompany me for security.

"Yeah." I smooth down my blue sweater and plain skinny jeans. "Let's do this."

"Don't let him get into your head," Kade advises, his hand poised to take notes. "You're the one in control. Not him."

"I've got this."

Theo looks over the different feeds on his laptop. "Hudson's next door interviewing Giana's assigned guard from the night she escaped."

"You hauled them all in?" I ask.

"All five who were on duty that night, plus Bronzefield's head of security and the warden. We're interviewing them all."

"Doing the superintendent's dirty work for her again," Enzo grumbles. "Come on, Harlow. Let's get this over with."

Hunter smiles reassuringly. "Go get him."

With a deep breath, I pass Enzo, who scans his badge to unlock the door before setting foot in the lion's den. The room is cold—bitingly so. It leaches all the life and sustenance from my veins in a second.

Seated on the other side of a steel table, his hands cuffed to the centre bar that separates the two sides, sits my uncle. He wears a grey jumpsuit, and for the first time ever, no visible crucifix.

"Harlow," he rasps.

"Michael."

"First name basis now, huh?"

"We are family, after all."

I take a seat in one of the chairs, and Enzo settles next to me. The gun strapped to a holster on his hip is very much visible but remains safely out of Michael's reach.

In stark comparison to the last time I saw him, my uncle looks on the verge of collapsing. His skin is tarnished with purple and green bruises, swelling his beaten face to almost twice its size.

Hudson and Enzo did a real number on him when they first slapped those handcuffs on. I don't remember a lot of it, just the unhinged cackle that Michael unleashed as they beat him.

"How's dear old Mum?"

I restrain myself from flinching. "You know full well how she is."

"I thought you'd be happy, darling niece. She deserved to be punished for what she did to you. Are you not pleased?"

"I never asked for this."

"You didn't have to." His smile widens. "The Lord tasked me with cleaning the earth of all its sinners. I am only fulfilling his will."

"Killing countless innocent people, butchering vulnerable women and murdering anyone you come into contact with isn't God's will."

Settling back in his chair, he strains against the handcuffs. "You're weak, Harlow. It's such a disappointment. I raised you to be better than that."

"Raised her?" Enzo spits.

Michael's darkened green eyes slide over to him. "Ah, he speaks! What are you here for, Mr Montpellier? Her guard dog?"

"I'm here to finish what I started if you try any clever shit with us. I'll happily pulverise the rest of your face. You can even choose which bones I break first."

"Charming." Michael snorts in derision. "You've aligned yourself with such *wonderfully* sadistic people, Harlow. I'm proud."

"Cut the crap. You asked to see me." I gesture around the room. "I'm here. So let's talk."

Trailing his cold eyes over me, Michael takes time to catalogue every last change. It's like he's seeing me for the very first time. I don't move, refusing to flinch under his gaze.

"When you survived the little present I left for you in Wales, I realised that the Lord has greater plans for your suffering."

"Give me a fucking break," Enzo mutters, staring up at the ceiling.

"Death was not enough to punish you for deserting me," he continues, ignoring him. "That would be far too quick."

"Is that what this is?" I hiss angrily. "Punishment?"

"This is the result of your selfishness. You never should have left your cage. This wouldn't have happened if you did as you were told."

"Enough," Enzo snaps. "Tell us about your co-conspirators. Where are they? Who is the copycat killer?"

"Harlow." Michael sighs dramatically. "Please muzzle your attack dog. I'm growing tired of his disobedience."

Rising to his feet, Enzo's on the verge of grabbing his jumpsuit and strangling Michael to death until I rest a hand on his thigh.

"Go stand in the corner. I've got this."

"No. He isn't to be trusted."

"I'm not telling you to leave us alone. But I can't do anything with you on the verge of killing him for the whole interview."

Cursing colourfully, Enzo smashes his chair backwards and escapes to the corner of the room, resting a hand on his gun.

"You really do have them wrapped around your finger, don't you?" Michael chuckles. "How did I raise such a filthy little whore?"

"You didn't raise me. Period."

His amused gaze hardens. "I saved you from a life of sin. I gave you the Lord's light! And this blasphemy is how you repay me?"

I lean closer across the table. "You tried to break me. Surviving you is the greatest thing I'll ever accomplish. I saved myself."

"You ungrateful slut. All those years… wasted!"

"Because you failed. That will be your legacy. Failure to complete your mission. Do you think God will forgive that?"

He moves so fast, I don't have time to lean back out of the danger zone. His forehead smashes into my face with a resounding crack, and pain explodes across the bridge of my nose.

"Demon whore!"

Flashing across the room as fast as his muscled weight will allow, Enzo has the barrel of his gun shoved against Michael's throat before

I can swallow the blood pooling in my mouth.

"You dare to hurt her!" he thunders in a terrifying voice. "I'll cut your goddamn hands off and make you choke on them for touching her."

"Do it!" Michael yells. "Kill me!"

The door to the interview room blows open as Enzo shoves his gun between Michael's open lips, intending to penetrate his throat with it. Kade and Hunter bound into the room.

"Enzo! Stop it!"

"She's bleeding," he snarls animalistically. "This motherfucker made my girl bleed, and I'm going to bury him for it."

It takes both of their strength to wrestle Enzo away before he can fulfil his promise and cover us all in Michael's splattered brains.

Enzo manages to knock the wind out of Hunter with a well-placed elbow and breaks free from Kade's grip.

"Enzo," I entreat.

That's when he stops.

"Go. We need him alive."

"Harlow—"

"I have this under control! Go."

Head bowed, he submits to my command and grumpily storms from the room. Hunter spares me an eye roll, gesturing for Kade to follow after him.

He disappears then returns a minute later with a handful of tissues. I accept them and banish Hunter to the corner of the room, holding the tissues against my bleeding nose.

"Interesting." Michael watches the whole thing. "Do you keep them on their leashes at night too?"

"You're on very thin ice," I say nasally. "I'll forgive that if you tell me what I want to know. Who is the copycat killer?"

"Me."

"You couldn't have been in three places at once. Give us the names, and then we can discuss what happens to you next."

He rattles his handcuffs again. "Listen to me, you stupid child. I am everywhere. The Lord has granted me a devoted army of believers, and my will inhabits them all."

"You're insane."

"And you even speak like the devil now," he spits back. "You'll rue the day that you dared to venture from the path I gave you."

"Was murdering your wife part of that path? Or brutalising your sister? Torturing your niece? Trying to impregnate innocent women before killing them? The only devil here is you."

Absorbing the verbal blows, Michael slumps in his chair. His eyes turn down, and his mouth presses into a tight line.

"My bloodline is cursed, Harlow. From the moment that nameless whore birthed me to Rosetta losing our God-given child. I took you from Giana to prevent the same thing from happening."

"You wanted to raise me as your own. But then why kidnap, rape and butcher all the other women? Why end their lives?"

"Because someone had to protect the innocent from their poisoned blood!" His spittle hits the table. "All of those sluts deserved to die. They failed in their one purpose. I was protecting the world from their sinful ways."

The worst part is, he actually believes what he's saying. The lunacy is written into his DNA and perfuses every part of him with divine certainty.

He can't feel empathy. Regret. Guilt. The cycle of violence has repeated over and over, across the decades, fuelled by his own ingrained hysteria that no amount of begging could dig out.

"I never stood a chance, did I?"

He looks up at me. "What?"

"All this time… I've hated myself for being unable to protect those women. I've blamed myself. But I didn't stand a chance of stopping you."

"I enacted God's will!"

But I've already tuned him out as something fundamental clicks inside of me, and the whole world shifts. Even after everything, I still carried that survivor's guilt with me.

I don't need to anymore.

It … wasn't my fault.

None of it was.

Pulling the tissues from my nose, I ball up the blood-soaked material then breathe in the most incredible sense of vindication for the first time since I escaped his hellhole.

"I can forgive myself," I whisper beneath my breath. "It wasn't my fault. It was all his."

"Stop it." Michael convulses in his chair, desperate to escape. "Don't you remember Laura? The world knows what you did."

"I saved her life," I reply softly.

"You killed her!"

"No. I saved her from a slow, painful death. I gave her dignity in her final moments. I'm done taking responsibility for your guilt."

Standing up, I take one last look at him and walk away. He will never divulge his secrets. The more air we give him to breathe, the longer he will continue to spout his hateful lies.

"Harlow!" he screams for attention. "This isn't over. You only caught me because I wanted you to."

I look over my shoulder. "You think we don't know that? Look around you. There's nothing you can do from here."

His smile is dripping with vicious delight. "Wait and see. I warned you about defying me. Your punishment will be my final act."

The farther I walk away, the louder his soulless screaming becomes. It bounces off the walls and attempts to pierce my skin, but I refuse to give it power.

His reign is over.

We're in control now.

Hunter follows me out, his hand circling my wrist. "Are you okay? We need to take a look at that nose."

I brush him aside with a shake of my head. The door to the interview room slams shut, finally silencing Michael's madness. Enzo, Kade and Theo are watching with matching proud expressions.

"What?" I stare at them.

Leaving his laptop, Theo takes two strides then smashes me against his chest. "You are the most incredible human being I've ever had the pleasure of meeting."

"Um, thanks?"

His lips seek mine out, and we share a fast kiss. My head is spinning from the events of the last ten minutes, and their behaviour is freaking me out even more.

"Way to go, Harlow." Kade gives me a high five. "That was fucking brilliant, watching you tear him down."

"I didn't do anything."

"Yes. You did." Enzo steals me and kisses my forehead. "Only you can get beneath his skin. He's coming apart at the seams."

"But we didn't get a name."

"We will," Theo reassures.

Bursting into our area kept separate from the interview space, Hudson is wild-eyed with triumph. He grins at us all.

"I've got him. Two of the guards have admitted to slipping Giana a dose of sleeping pills with her evening meal and breaking her out."

"They drugged her?" Enzo repeats.

He nods. "Both of them were paid well by a third party. Sounds like one of Abaddon's foot soldiers."

"Probably acting on behalf of Daphne," I fill in. "She's the one funding this entire thing and planning it all."

"The brains to the brawn." Kade laughs without humour. "How the hell did we miss her all along?"

"We overestimated Abaddon," Enzo answers grimly. "He's mad as a box of twats, but even a deadly weapon needs guiding."

Despite the thick tension in the room, everyone bursts out laughing. Theo has to wipe stray tears from beneath his glasses.

"Mad as a box of twats?"

Enzo frowns at him. "You haven't heard that before?"

"I can't breathe," Hudson splutters.

Flipping us all off, Enzo mutters something about getting a coffee then escapes the room to cool off. We're still laughing when he's gone.

"I want to talk to Daphne."

Everyone quickly sobers up, and their attention fixes on me. Repeating my words for Hunter to decipher, his eyebrows knit together.

"Why?"

I tap my forehead.

"Because you don't remember her," he guesses.

"*No,*" I sign back.

"You've done enough, sweetheart."

"He's right," Theo agrees. "She's a spiteful old cow. You don't need to put yourself through that as well."

"I want answers. When I have them, I can finally close this chapter of my life."

With a sigh, Hudson holds the door open for me. "I'll take you.

Pre-warning… She's just as crazy as her whack job brother."

"It's a wonder I ended up even half-sane."

"Fucking miracle."

With Hunter trailing after us, we move to the next room down the silent corridor. This floor is kept off-limits to only those with the highest security clearance in the building.

Hudson scans his badge to let us both inside. Warner and Tara are manning the observation side of the room while Ethan attempts to interview a silent Daphne behind the tinted glass.

"Harlow?" Warner looks up at me. "Jesus. You're covered in blood."

I wave his concern off. "Just a misunderstanding. I'm fine."

"She's gonna have a crack at Daphne," Hudson explains. "We've got the two guards admitting involvement in Giana's escape on record."

"In that case, be my guest. This one won't say a damn word."

After Hudson opens the door for me, we filter into the room. Ethan backs away at Hunter's command and allows us to step into the walled-off interview area.

"I wondered when you'd grace me with your presence." Daphne snickers to herself. "Good to see you again, Harlow."

With her silvery hair pulled back in a no-nonsense ponytail, she looks significantly better than her beaten-up brother, though their grey jumpsuits match.

"I see you've spoken to my brother." Her eyes catalogue the blood on my sweater. "You should know better than to provoke him."

I take one of the seats. "Let's keep this brief. You're going to prison for a very long time. This is your last chance to save yourself."

"Save myself?" She laughs.

"We know you both had help. Give us the information we're looking for, and it will work in your favour."

"I don't need any favours from you, little girl."

"How did he do it?" I ask with narrowed eyes. "I understand about Giana. She couldn't protect herself. But how did he break you too?"

"I didn't need breaking," she snarls at me. "The Lord chose me. When I found Michael, I was lost. We saved each other."

"By killing innocent people?"

"By doing God's bidding! That useless wife of his certainly wasn't strong enough to do it. Look at you. She failed to keep you tamed."

"No, she spent a decade making every second Michael wasn't beating me a living nightmare. But I know now it wasn't her fault. She only did what he wanted her to do."

Daphne breaks down in hysterical laughter. "You really don't remember me, do you? Who do you think kept Rosetta in line?"

I can feel Hunter lingering behind me, keeping close enough to prevent any further attacks. His warmth at my back injects strength into me.

"I was there every step of the way," Daphne explains with a satisfied glint in her eyes. "The truth was staring you in the face all along. You're just too stupid to see it."

Our gazes locked, that awful, rushing sense of realisation filters over me again. It's in her eyes. Those sinister green orbs. The flash of them glowering at me through cage bars penetrates my mind.

"You're lying."

"So forgetful," she taunts.

"I won't let you manipulate me."

"What purpose do I have to lie? My work on this earth is done. I want you to know how much of a failure you are."

"Michael worked alone!"

"He found me long before our mother passed on. The Lord brought us together to enact his will."

The more she speaks, the more that sense of disjointed realisation increases. I can feel the truth in her words on an intrinsic level.

Her smile takes a dangerous edge. "He wanted to keep you at home. It was my idea to put you in that cage. Pain is the only way to cleanse a heathen's soul."

"You were there."

"For every single beating," she confirms. "Who do you think stopped him from killing you when Adelaide bled to death?"

This time, I can't suppress a shudder. I thought I was going to die that night. He was seconds from crumbling my bones to dust as punishment for his own failings.

The rush of returning memories stings like needlepoints slicing into my skull. I can still see Michael beating me limp and useless while his body was covered in hot, slick blood.

"There it is," she goads.

Her voice was there that night in my semi-conscious haze. Interrupting his violent assault and warning him that the work was not yet done. He wasn't allowed to kill me.

"I've been the voice in the back of your mind all this time." Daphne sneers. "You'll never dig me out. Never."

"I … remember." I gulp down a bubble of vomit. "You're the one who started it all. You killed Kiera."

"He needed a push." She shrugs it off. "Didn't she scream so beautifully, though? Full of such desperate, delicious fear."

"She was my friend," I choke out.

"Kiera was a demonic whore. She got exactly what she deserved. But still, you didn't learn. We had to bring more girls in to teach you."

The flashes come thick and fast. I watch the memories play out on a mental movie screen—Michael carrying in unconscious women, one after another, imprisoning them in the cage next to me. All while

Daphne watched on.

My mind forgot her.

Locked her out.

The greatest monster of all.

"And it was you who saved him from the house where you held Candace before help arrived. You helped Michael escape again."

Daphne sits back, satisfied by the horror painted across my face. "There she is. Still a scared little pup, locked in her cage."

I scrape my chair back, unhinged by the explosive realisations rocking every inch of me. I'm done. She doesn't get to hurt me again.

I'm not going to be her victim for a second longer. She's admitted to every charge we needed, and her sick pride will be her undoing.

"That's where you're wrong. I was scared then. But I will never be afraid of you again."

"We'll see about that."

"You're going to die behind bars. That's your reward for all you've done. Enjoy living the rest of your life in a cage."

"Your threats mean nothing," she combats. "The rapture will reward me. While you burn to death, I shall rejoice in my salvation."

Turning my back on the monstrous darkness that's preyed upon me since I left my cage, I let the mental walls slam down on every drop of sickness she indoctrinated me with.

A scared little girl was thrown into the cage she created. But a strong, powerful, unbroken woman is walking away from her now.

She failed.

And I fucking won.

ve spring
With Major League Ba
engage Paul White
players getting
eded change
SCENE DU
LOOSE

CHAPTER 28

Harlow

Drowned In Emotion – Caskets

It feels fitting to breathe the same air that began this journey for me as I say goodbye to my mother. The fresh, salty coldness swirls in my lungs and keeps the grip of grief at bay.

Croyde is beautiful in the late November sunshine—cool and crisp, with the silence broken by squawking seagulls flying overhead.

"We have a team of agents holding the media at bay." Enzo rests against the side of the SUV. "They won't get close."

"Are there many?"

"All the usual suspects. Everyone wants a glimpse of the funeral, but they aren't getting one. We'll protect your privacy."

Looking away from the sea, I peer up into his amber eyes. He's cleaned up for today, taming his long black hair and squeezing into a well-fitted, charcoal suit and black shirt.

"Shall we go in?"

I bite my lip. "I don't know if I can do this."

He takes my hand and squeezes. "We're all here with you, baby.

Every single one of us. We will get through this together."

"You didn't have to come. I know how all of you feel about Giana and what she did."

"That doesn't matter to me," he interjects. "All I care about is you. Fuck my feelings. Fuck all of our feelings. Yours are all that matters."

Reaching up, I cup his scruff-covered chin. "I love you so much. You've saved my life every single day just by being you."

His eyes crinkle at the corners as he offers me the same gentle, understanding smile that first calmed me in the hospital when we met.

"I think I loved you the moment I laid eyes on you, screaming your damn head off. I knew you were a fighter. You've shocked the shit out of me ever since."

"Well, I do my best," I joke.

"And I fucking love that about you."

Our foreheads meeting, I breathe in his ever-present woodsy scent. I'm not sure how I lived two decades of my life without his constant, unshakeable support at my side.

I'll spend the rest of my life being thankful that I never have to find out. I doubt I could tear Enzo from his permanent role as my protector, even if I wanted to.

"The others are waiting inside the crematorium. We can stay out here for as long as you want, though."

Pressing a final kiss to his lips, I release him then step back. "Let's just go in. The sooner this is done, the sooner we can go home."

"I'm so ready to get back to our actual house." He smooths a hand over my loose, curly hair. "I've missed it."

"Not as much as Lucky has, I'm sure. I never thought we'd see it again for a moment there."

"We still own the other house if we need to get out of London again," he adds. "It needs some serious repair work first."

"Do you still want to stay in the country?" I ask nervously.

Enzo wraps a strong arm around my shoulders. "I want to go wherever you'd prefer. But if I'm being honest, there's nothing left for me here."

"What about your family?"

"There are such things as telephone calls and aeroplanes, little one. It's not like it would be goodbye forever. We'll see them at our wedding."

"Our what?" I splutter.

He holds back a laugh. "Got you. Although it's gonna happen, sooner rather than later if I have anything to say about it."

Unsure of how to respond, I gape at him. "I think you're losing it."

"I'm fully sane, angel. And if you think I'm not going to put a ring on your finger and a baby in your belly when you're ready, then we need to have a serious talk."

With a single finger slid under my chin, he closes my mouth that's flopped wide open.

"Move it. People are waiting."

I clear my throat. "Right. People."

We leave the parked SUV with the other vehicles, taking the winding cobbled path along the country lane. The crematorium is set outside of the town on a quiet, grassy hilltop overlooking the sea.

"What about Sabre?"

"What about it?" Enzo claps back.

"You've spent years of your life building it from the ground up. Are you willing to just walk away from it and never look back?"

"In a heartbeat." He sucks in the ocean air like he's taking his very first breath. "I don't want fame and fortune. I don't even want a career. I just want a happy fucking future."

My throat catches. "Me too, Enz."

"Then that's exactly what I'm going to give you. Dirt bike rides, white sand beaches and endlessly happy fucking futures."

Before we enter the crematorium, I pause to kiss his stubbled cheek. "It's a deal."

Enzo's arm around me is the grounding force I need to step inside. The crematorium is a small, plain building with cream walls and dark wood pews lining the carpet. The simple coffin resting at the front of the room is on a platform, surrounded by open velvet curtains.

The guys offered to act as pallbearers, purely for my benefit, when we realised there was no one else to do it. We opted for simplicity instead. This entire service is a mere practicality.

On the left side, Sabre has turned out to support me. The entire Cobra and Anaconda teams are present, along with the rest of Brooklyn's husbands—Eli, Phoenix and Jude.

Hunter, Theo and Leighton stand in their places in front of them, deliberately putting themselves in my direct line of sight.

The other side features only three people in the unlikeliest of collaborations. My father, Foster and Ulrich. I'm sure Giana would have a meltdown at seeing them together in the flesh.

Wiggling out from underneath Enzo's arm, I give everyone a grateful smile and take the space next to my father. He immediately pulls me into a tight hug.

"Hey, love."

"Hi, Dad. You okay?"

His breathing is unsteady against my head. "I'm fine. You sure about this?"

"I want to be here. But you don't have to stay."

He kisses my temple before releasing me. "I need some closure too. You're not doing this alone."

Looking down the aisle, I briefly catch Ulrich's eyes, but he quickly looks away. His cheeks are stained with freshly fallen tears that punch me straight in the chest.

Foster manages a small, tense nod. "Harlow."

"Hi. Thank you for arranging everything."

"Of course."

At the front of the room, a grey-haired officiant takes his place. The service is simple and to the point. No emotional speech or words of comfort. When he's done, he opens the floor to us.

"Ulrich?" Foster prompts. "Do you want to say anything?"

My brother stares resolutely at his well-shined shoes, unable to lift his head. The tears silently drip down on the thick carpet. When his dad touches his shoulder, he flinches and bolts from the pew.

"Ulrich!"

Ignoring the shouts of his name, he runs back down the aisle between the pews and breaks out of the back door. Foster murmurs his apologies then chases after his son.

The slam of the door closing breaks the heavy, awkward silence. No one knows what to say. When my dad nudges me in the side, I look up at my mother's coffin, and resolution settles in my gut.

"Someone has to say something for her."

The weight of the entire room watching me doesn't sway my decision. I take the vacated spot at the front and face everyone, my hands scrunched into tight fists.

"I … wasn't planning to do this. Frankly, I wasn't sure I'd be able to attend at all. But even someone as flawed as Giana deserves better."

Hunter meets my gaze and holds it. He refuses to look away or leave me up here alone.

"She was my mum. But not in any of the ways that mattered. Instead, she was responsible for the darkest days of my life."

I force a breath into my lungs. The tears I expected never come. Emotion is gathering in my throat instead—thick and cloying.

"I'm not going to stand here and pretend like she was perfect or even a good person. But Giana was human. Flawed, messy and so very imperfect. For that, I'm willing to forgive her."

Turning away from them all, I approach the coffin. It bears an inscribed plaque but no flowers or finishing touches. My palm strokes the smooth wooden surface before I trace the letters of her name.

"I forgive you, Mum. What happened to you wasn't your fault. You're forgiven, and I want you to find peace with Grandma Sylvie."

Glancing back at my dad, I find him breaking down in tears. Theo gives me a nod then goes to his side to support him in my place.

"We're ready," I tell the officiant.

With silence encapsulating us, a button is pressed and the curtains surrounding the coffin close. The last remaining pieces of Giana Kensington vanish from sight.

Still, the tears don't come. All I feel is a weirdly light sense of relief. In my mind, I can see her, green eyes narrowed and lips pinched in one of her grimaces.

That changes as she stares back at me on a mental plane. Instead, a smile emerges. Soft and accepting. The version of her I always imagined overtakes the truth.

She's at peace.

Forgiven and free.

Maybe I can be the same. All of us can walk away from this battlefield, bleeding and scarred, but we're still alive to tell the tale. Perhaps we'll even find a shred of hope in it to warm our souls for the road ahead.

Stepping down from the platform, I walk straight into Hunter's open, tattooed arms. He tucks my head beneath his chin and rubs circles into my back.

"That was perfect, sweetheart."

The warmth of two more bodies at my back crowds me. I recognise Theo's scent—peppermint and well-loved book pages—and the hum of Leighton's voice.

"We're proud of you, Goldilocks."

"Your words were beautiful," Theo adds. "Just like you."

When they release me, I'm pulled into another hug from Brooklyn. She kisses my cheek and doesn't let go until Enzo laughs at her.

"You can't rush hugs," she snaps at him.

"Come on, wildfire. Let my girl go. We have places to be."

"She was my girl first, Enz. Hoes belong far, far before bros."

I gently push her away. "Enough, the pair of you. Let's get out of here."

Filtering out of the crematorium, we return to the lash of salty sea air. I look around for any signs of Foster or Ulrich but come up empty.

From here, I can see the cluster of camera vans and baying reporters being held back by our security detail in the distance.

"Where's Foster? Can anyone see him?"

Leighton stops at my side. "He's probably giving Ulrich some space. Want us to have a look around for them?"

"Please. I don't want to leave without saying goodbye."

He disappears with Theo and Enzo to search around, leaving me with Brooklyn and her men while Hunter and my father frown at the crowd of reporters.

Phoenix is halfway through a rant about choosing his latest hair colour when Leighton shouts my name, silencing us all.

"Over here! Quick!"

Legs pumping, the windswept landscape around me becomes a blur. The thud of several people at my heels accompanies the sudden roaring of my heartbeat.

Tucked behind a service building at the back of the crematorium, Leighton is waving us down. We reach him then race behind it to find Theo crouching down in the gravel.

"Oh God!" I screech.

Crumpled and unconscious, Foster's bleeding steadily onto the ground from a nasty gash on his forehead. His mouth hangs open as his eyelids refuse to lift.

"He's breathing." Theo lifts him into his arms. "We need an ambulance. He's got a bad head wound."

My eyes trace the droplets of blood to a nearby brick, lifted from a pile discarded at the back of the building. It's been tossed aside, still covered in slick blood.

"Someone hit him." My heart explodes into horrified butterflies that make my chest ache. "Where is Ulrich?"

"He wasn't here when we found him," Leighton replies.

"Shit! Did he do this?" Enzo exclaims.

"No," I cut him off. "He wouldn't do this to his dad. That kid's already lost one parent. Someone must have taken him."

Leaping into action, Enzo grabs his phone and calls down to the security team protecting the funeral, demanding they begin searching.

"Split up," Ethan barks at his team. "They can't have gone far. We were only inside for ten minutes."

Clutching my impossibly tight chest, I battle to remain calm, but I want to scream and rave at the top of my lungs. Ulrich is innocent in all of this. If he's hurt… I don't know what I'll do.

"Harlow," Brooklyn murmurs. "Take a breath for me. We're going to find him."

"Who would take him? Why?"

That's when reality hits.

I can hear him whispering straight into the depths of my mind, even from his secure cell hundreds of miles away in Sabre HQ.

This isn't over.

Your punishment will be my final act.

"It's him!" I scream hysterically. "Michael has him."

Theo pulls me into his chest. "Calm down, angel. He's locked in a cell with twenty-four-hour surveillance. Ulrich isn't with him."

"No. This is his people. His army. They're still doing his bidding, even without a master. You know Michael wanted us to catch him."

Looking down at me, his eyes are flecked with fear that vindicates my panicked rant. I know I'm right. The game is still on, and this is just his next move on the chessboard.

Well, checkmate.

He doesn't get to win.

Not while I'm still breathing.

SCENE DU 1er
J.ROSE

CHAPTER 29

Hunter

Vaccine – hometown & young

I t's funny how the silence can sound so much louder than the world itself. Even amidst a chaotic scene that plays out like I've sitting on the mute button, I can feel every last frenzied shout and scream.

Harlow's loudest of them all. She's pacing up and down in the police station, tearing at her hair and demanding updates every second. This destructive behaviour hasn't stopped since we arrived several long hours ago.

Up. Down.

Back. Forth.

Step. Step.

The sounds are still there, even if I can't hear them. That's the strangest thing of all. Their existence isn't conditional on my hearing. The world turns on its own just fine without me.

But I won't allow it to.

I want to exist.

Our worst fears were confirmed when Theo located traffic cam footage of a green estate car careening away from the funeral at breakneck speed. They quickly stopped to swap cars with two others and derailed our tail.

They took advantage of our security detail being overwhelmed by shouting journalists. Enzo fired the agents that allowed Ulrich to slip past on the spot. Too fucking right.

After taking over the small village police station, Theo and Kade traced the paths of three identical vehicles. All using fake registrations and heading in totally different directions.

That's where things went wrong. With a well-oiled system of matching green estate cars working in harmony, we followed the wrong vehicle and lost our targets in a decoy chase.

Licence plates were changed, and the trail went cold. We're now searching for a needle in a haystack as Harlow and Foster become increasingly worried about Ulrich.

Enzo stops at my side, his entire frame carved with the same building tension we're all feeling. I nudge his shoulder and lift an eyebrow.

"*Nothing*," he signs back.

"What about traffic cams? CCTV? We've got the most advanced facial recognition software in the whole fucking country."

With a head shake, he dismisses our best assets. All the fancy tech and money in the world still can't plug the inevitable gaps that people with enough determination can exploit.

The wound on his head stitched and bandaged by paramedics, Foster is looming over Theo and Kade, watching their every move. His face is a mask of raw terror.

Harlow was right.

This was all part of the plan.

We know that Abaddon still has an underground network of

supporters—the Angels of the Abyss—across the country that he's painstakingly built over the last few months.

Daphne was the tip of the iceberg, and her location was given to us wrapped in a red fucking bow. We've been playing by his rules all along, facing setbacks at every turn.

But it can't end like this.

We won't allow it.

Regardless of my feelings towards Giana and her scum of the earth relatives, Ulrich is an innocent child. I'm not prepared to sacrifice him to another one of Abaddon's sick games.

Enzo gestures toward the other side of the room, asking for me to take over with Harlow while he picks up an urgent phone call. I unlatch my tightly-folded arms and approach the hurricane of emotion.

She fists handfuls of her hair then tugs sharply, falling back into old patterns that haven't emerged since before we fled the country in a broken mess.

Approaching slowly, I take hold of her wrists then tug until she releases her hair. Harlow's anger-filled blue eyes look up at me, demanding answers that I'm powerless to give her.

"You don't need to do that," I murmur. "I've got you, sweetheart. We're going to find Ulrich."

Her lips move too fast, spilling out a rush of panicked words that I can't keep up with. Cupping her cheeks, I encourage her to slow down and recognise the two words she hisses out.

"My fault."

"No. This is on us. They shouldn't have had the chance to get anywhere near him."

Her lips quirk in a pained smile as she mouths back, "Can't … keep … all safe."

"I can fucking well try. If Abaddon dies, then his army dies with him. He's too dangerous to be kept alive."

Harlow's hand presses against my chest. "No."

"What prison can ever hold someone as powerful as that? He's far more than just a man now. He's become an idea, and we need to kill that idea to end this."

Gaze hardening, she shakes her head and frees up her hands to sign. "*Prison.*"

"You think that'll stop him from doing this again?" I scoff.

When she tries to escape my arms and walk away, I tighten my grip, cradling her against my chest. She can hate me all she wants. Not all of us have the luxury of a moral compass.

This is the last time he will be allowed to fuck with my family. I have no regard for what the right thing to do is. Killing Michael Abaddon will be my final act as Sabre's director.

More hours pass, and the tension in the room reaches a breaking point. Theo's scoured traffic cams covering every main road out of Croyde and identified our perps, all wearing ski masks.

There are no identities to even attempt to trace. These assholes are ghosts, enacting the will of a madman from afar. Not even we can counteract such mindless delirium.

On another laptop screen, the live video feed of a camera is strapped to Ethan's bulletproof vest. He's stepping through darkened rooms, searching the empty space with his flashlight and gun.

He took one of the SUVs a couple of hours ago to drive from Croyde to Holcombe, intending to check if there's any activity at Daphne's abandoned farmhouse.

Each room is declared empty one after another, killing our latest theory. Not a soul in sight. The rest of his team has taken a police helicopter to Tregaron in case our targets have returned there.

Nothing.

Not a damn lead.

As the dawn light rises, we've progressed to the cracked vinyl sofa in the corner of the police station break room. Harlow finally passed out, head pooled in her father's lap as he strokes her hair.

"Coffee?" I ask him.

Oliver shakes his head.

"Stay with her. She needs to sleep for a few more hours. I don't like how pale she is."

Even in the middle of this growing disaster, he can't help but roll his eyes at me. It's not every in-law relationship that the boyfriend can boss his girlfriend's parent around, or even be more protective than them.

Back in the main office, Theo miraculously holds his eyes open and scours the depths of the internet for any mention of Abaddon.

Our perp is a hot topic in online traffic, so there's a small chance we may find his supporters conspiring from the anonymity of the internet.

Brewing myself a cup of tea strong enough for the spoon to stand up in, I take Theo a black coffee and pat his shoulder. Again, he signs back that goddamn word that I want blacklisted from the English language.

"*Nothing.*"

"There has to be something," I insist. "We can't go another day like this. Harlow's on the verge of losing her mind in there, and Foster isn't much better."

The man in question is pacing up and down just outside the window, his headful of dark hair and glasses bobbing past every second or so while he smokes a cigarette.

"Keep looking. All we need is one strike of luck."

Scribbling on his notepad, Theo tilts the page for me to read.

We need to speak to Abaddon. He knows where they're hiding.

"Absolutely not. We cannot trust that monster."

What else do you suggest? They're already a step ahead of us. We need to play this smart.

Pinching the bridge of my nose, I attempt to battle the rising migraine threatening to take me out of action. Stress always triggers them to return.

"There has to be something. We've got all this evidence and not a single scrap of it correlates. That can't be possible."

Theo grimaces as he writes back to me.

He's perfected the art of making people disappear without a trace over the last decade. We will never find Ulrich alone.

If I still had hair to fist, I'd be following in Harlow's footsteps and ripping the whole lot out in frustration.

"Just keep looking."

He doesn't watch me storm away, unable to disobey my directive. The intelligence team is working hard back at HQ following the same steps, and for hours now, there's been nothing.

This isn't working.

But working with Abaddon is exactly what he wanted all along. He's trying to leverage us, using Ulrich's life as the bargaining chip. We don't negotiate with serial killers.

Sliding my phone from my pocket, I pull up the conversation with Brooklyn, safely tucked away in London for her own protection.

Hunter: What's Abaddon doing?

It only takes her a second to reply.

Brooklyn: Been sat in the middle of his cell praying since Ulrich vanished. Hasn't eaten or slept. It's like he's waiting for something.

Dammit. He's waiting for us to cave and give in to his no doubt psychotic demands. We should've seen this coming.

> **Hunter:** He's baiting us. Be careful. Don't go anywhere near him.

> **Brooklyn:** Phoenix, Eli and Jude are here. Call when you have news. Look after Harlow.

> **Hunter:** I will.

Enzo grabbing my shoulder startles me back to the busy room. Exhaustion and weariness have been replaced by alarm. He quickly signs an explanation.

"*Message.*"

"From whom?" I demand.

"*Army,*" he signs back.

We run back to the crowded table full of maps, laptops and documents. Theo is connecting his screen to a projector, offering us a wide-screen view of the video that's been uploaded to the internet.

Harlow races into the room, bleary-eyed and rumpled. Capturing her mid-stride, Enzo traps her between us so we can keep her calm.

With the Cobra team joining us, the room becomes crowded. Foster returns, stinking of cigarette smoke, and Theo hits play. His laptop automatically generates subtitles.

In the video, four figures are dressed in identical robes to the ones that Abaddon once wore. Their faces are concealed behind smooth black masks, adorned with Holy Trinities painted on.

"We are the Angels of the Abyss. You have taken our messiah, and we won't stop until he is safely returned to us."

Hudson's teeth are bared in a snarl, his fist banging on the table.

Beside me, Enzo stiffens and clutches Harlow even tighter.

"The child has been born of cursed, demon blood. We will sacrifice his life to honour our Lord unless you submit to our demands."

The camera pans to the left, skipping over cracked, mould-covered brickwork to find a set of rusted iron bars. Behind them, a shivering, curled-up ball rests on the damp floor.

Ulrich.

Harlow writhes between us, desperate to throw a fist into the screen and release her frustration. I pin her in place by her arms.

"Our messiah knows where to find us. Searching is futile. You have twelve hours before the ritual will commence."

The message ends, and even I can tell that it leaves deathly silence in the room. Foster is turning a very dark shade of purple as he stares at the wall where the image of his son was projected.

Twelve hours. We can waste it searching for the ghosts who have slipped through our fingers or align ourselves with a vicious murderer in order to save an innocent life.

This is it.

The rapture has arrived.

Slipping free from our embrace, Harlow begins to shout and rave, demanding immediate action. I know instinctively what she wants.

Her brother, alive. Regardless of the price. It's taken us years to track Abaddon down, and now that we've got him, he's playing his final hand to escape his sentence.

"We cannot surrender Abaddon," I announce. "He will butcher more innocent lives, and that will be our fault."

She rounds on me and signs, "*My brother.*"

"There has to be another way."

"*No,*" Enzo speaks and signs.

Staring at him, defeat burns in the pits of his hopeless eyes. I simmer with anger.

"We can make that sick son of a bitch bleed and beg for death until he reveals their location. I'm not playing his games. Not like this."

Even saying it aloud, I know it won't work. That man doesn't feel pain or regret. He's as empty as his false idols.

Grabbing a handful of my shirt, Harlow gets close to my face so I can't mistake her words, laced with desperation.

"*Can't ... lose ... too.*"

"We can't give Abaddon what he wants. Do you want more women to die like your friends?"

Her distraught expression fractures further. "*No ... choice.*"

Everyone in the room is on her side, waiting for me to crack. Even Enzo nods in reluctant acceptance. I know what he's thinking. We follow Abaddon to these lunatics then blow them all to hell.

If it goes wrong, we could lose them all. We'd be breaking every remaining rule in the book by taking Abaddon from our custody and using him in a prisoner swap.

This will end our careers. There's no coming back from this. Stomach twisting, I crumple beneath the weight of the world. At least we'll go out with a bang.

"Fine." I sigh, feeling an inappropriate smile rise. "Fuck the rules. Let's go find the kid."

SCENE DU R
LOOSE

CHAPTER 30

Harlow

Burn Down My House – Architects

Moonlight illuminates the suffocating darkness, offering glimpses of light. Midnight strikes, and the dawn of a new day doesn't relieve the pressure sitting on my chest, determined to strangle me.

Theo's hand is slowly turning white as I grip it hard in my lap. It's taking all of my strength to sit in the helicopter without moving. I want to throw myself from it to escape the man sitting opposite me.

Michael doesn't need a headset to communicate. Ankles and wrists handcuffed with a chain between them, his wide smile drips with anticipation, and his eyes refuse to stray from mine.

"Bearing east," Enzo announces from the cockpit. "The coordinates are taking us to a remote village on the Scottish border."

He's flying one of the three helicopters taking us to our destination, following the instructions that Michael was more than happy to give once we submitted to his plan.

This won't be a simple trade that allows him to disappear into the night. I know that Hunter will put a bullet through Michael's skull long before he allows him to escape and hurt anyone else.

"Stick to the plan," Theo advises from his seat next to me. "The Cobra and Anaconda teams will move first to circle around. Then we'll bring Abaddon in with Hunter and Enzo."

Sat on my right side, Leighton is adjusting the straps on his bulletproof armour. "Don't leave my damn sight, Harlow."

"We're walking into a trap," I point out.

"A trap isn't a trap if we know it's coming."

"Then what is this, Leigh?"

His dark brown eyes meet mine. "This is a showdown."

Even though being in Michael's presence should reduce me to a sobbing, terrified wreck, I take each of my guys' hands and stare straight ahead without an inch of fear.

He stares back.

Lip curled.

Eyes hard.

No matter what happens next, Michael won't get to take another innocent life. Ulrich doesn't belong in the middle of this mess. Giana already died for her so-called sins, and I won't let her son do the same.

As the miles tick by, the atmosphere in the helicopter thickens. Anxiety dances in the air, and we clutch each other a little harder. We have no idea what we're walking into.

"I'm flying a drone over the area ahead of us," Theo says into his headset. "Detecting a huge heat signature."

I look over at the tablet in his lap, relaying the data. "What does that mean? People?"

He shakes his head. "Not necessarily."

Opposite me, Michael starts laughing. Deep, belly-vibrating laughter that bounces around us despite the roar of the helicopter.

Leighton tenses in his seat, holding himself back from pummelling his face into an unrecognisable paste that won't get us anything in return.

"I think…" Theo hesitates, frowning at the screen. "It's fire."

My heart freezes into a lump of ice in my chest. With Michael staring at me without saying a word, his voice still manages to slither through my mind. I vocalise the words he used to repeat out loud.

"In flaming fire, we will inflict vengeance on those who do not know God and those who do not obey the gospel of our Lord."

Michael watches my mouth move with satisfaction, his silent nod a recognition of his agreement. We're not walking into a hostage situation.

No.

This is a war zone.

As the helicopter begins to descend with the other two accompanying us, darkness fades, but it doesn't lift entirely. Instead, a warm, orange glow overtakes the night sky, belching ash and smoke.

"We're going to need the fire brigade," I whisper into the headset's microphone.

"Already alerted them," Theo responds. "But we're descending into thick woodland. It's going to take time for them to arrive."

"Holy fucking shit," Leighton curses. "Look."

Leaning over his black-clad shoulder, I gape at the awaiting sight. Thick, impenetrable trees smother any hint of life. But instead of luscious greenery, there's a canopy of flames.

The woods are on fire. Burning, razing, almighty fire, spreading in all directions. The flames reach so high, they kiss the atmosphere and engulf us in smoke. Blackness swallows our line of sight.

"Fuck!" Enzo curses.

Careening through the ash clouding the air, we swoop low and all strain against our belts, preventing us from falling out of the sky. A column of heat rises and causes the temperature to spike.

Into the darkness we go.

Down. Down. Down.

Emerging in the mouth of hell, there's a tiny break in the flames and thick woodland. Enzo aims for it, guiding the rest of the convoy to relative safety.

We touch down in an adjacent field with an inelegant thud, barely making it without crashing into something while lost in the smoke. Enzo rips off his headset and takes a breath.

"Everyone out. We're here."

Packing up our stuff, I hop out of the helicopter into the acrid air, trying hard not to cough. Hudson and Kade appear to help Enzo remove our prisoner safely, leaving me to locate Hunter.

Beneath his bulletproof vest, all-black combat gear and multiple layers of weapons, he's hardly recognisable as the gentle, sweatpants-wearing man I've come to know beneath his harsh exterior.

We all look like soldiers going into war, unsure if we'll make it out alive. Michael has driven us to the point of no return and left us with nothing but insane choices.

"Not a goddamn word," Hudson barks as he wrestles Michael out in handcuffs. "Play by our rules, and you may live to see tomorrow."

All he can do is laugh hysterically. Michael's mind has fractured, and beneath the still-visible bruises that mar his face, his madness is palpable. He's waited years for this very moment.

"Alright, listen up." Enzo gathers the teams together. "You all know the plan. Nobody makes it out, including this son of a bitch."

With a snarl, Hudson slams Michael back into the side of the helicopter again, attempting to knock the laughter from his lungs.

"We will find them and locate the kid," Enzo continues. "As soon as we have a visual, the Cobra and Anaconda teams will advance from the west to close the perimeter."

Kade nods, a hand resting on his semi-automatic gun. "Affirmative."

"We'll do the exchange, and that's when we make our move. I want them all apprehended. Dead or alive. They cannot be allowed to escape with the suspect."

"Great plan," Michael chokes out between laughs. "Can't even honour your word. The Lord will punish your deceit."

"You don't need a tongue to be exchanged," Hudson hisses in his ear. "Shut up, or I'll cut it out to keep as a fucking trophy."

"Keep each other safe." Enzo raises his voice above them. "Remember your training. Stay focused. Every single one of us walking in there is coming out alive. Understood?"

Everyone chimes in their agreement with varying degrees of optimism and apprehension. Even Ethan and his hardened team look afraid of the unknown facing us.

"We see this through, and the first round of beers is on me tonight." Enzo summons a weak smile. "Move out."

Whispering goodbyes and clasping hands, Hudson, Kade and Brooklyn's replacement, Hyland, take off first. Ethan and his team follow, leaving us to approach head-on with Michael.

Hunter takes over, grabbing his shoulder and shoving him forward. "Where are we going?"

Michael gestures ahead towards the north. Right into the path of the raging fire. "This way."

"One wrong step and I'll blow your brains out without hesitation," Hunter threatens. "Start walking."

Keeping in a tight formation that leaves no one exposed, we creep forward into the burning midnight hour. Michael leads a path through the smoke, grinning the entire time.

We should be thankful that his supporters don't seem to give a shit about Daphne. Like every other woman who's come in touch with Michael, she's outlived her usefulness and been discarded.

The closer we get to the forest fire, the hotter it burns. Heat lashes against my face, stinging and searing until my eyes stream with tears.

Michael bears left, skirting around the flames and leading us farther from safety. Keeping their guns up, Leighton and Enzo press into my sides, leaving nothing exposed.

"There's some activity ahead." Theo checks the tablet in his hands, connected to the drone overhead. "Signs of life."

"How many?" Enzo barks.

"I can't tell. The fire's messing with the drone's surveillance program. All I can tell is there's something going on."

Terrifying, unknown something. Scruffy jaw tightening, Enzo nods and crashes the back of his gun into Michael's skull.

"What are you planning?"

"My people understand the concept of loyalty," he snarls back. "They're earning their passage to the heavens while the rest of you will be left to burn."

"I'm sure God appreciates you setting his bloody forest on fire." Leighton laughs bitterly. "Makes total sense."

Michael throws him a vicious look. "This earth must burn before it can be reborn. I will be here to lead a new generation of humanity."

"He's even more unhinged than before," Enzo mutters. "We're going to take great pleasure in executing every last one of your people in front of you."

Unbothered by the threat, Michael continues with stilted steps, his ankles still imprisoned by the cuffs connecting to his wrists.

"We're in position." Kade's voice hums through our earpieces.

"There're some abandoned buildings along the west side."

"Copy that," Enzo answers. "Ethan?"

"Approaching now," he replies with a crackle. "Nothing here. Just fire and ash. This thing is getting out of control."

"The authorities have been informed." Theo tucks the tablet under his arm. "Backup is on its way."

When the outline of a crumbling building rises on the horizon of a large clearing, our hackles rise. The nearest town is miles away, leaving ruins to fall into disrepair amidst the thick trees and shrubbery.

"Grant me your strength, Lord above," Michael calls out. "I am your loyal servant, and here lies my offering to you."

"Eyes sharp," Enzo orders.

When the first figures emerge, cutting through smoke with their painted masks in place, all guns rise to meet them. My horror intensifies as even more appear.

One after another.

Dozens of them.

We're surrounded on all sides by even more people than we anticipated, all dressed in their matching black robes and homemade masks. The sight of them makes me sick. He's indoctrinated them all.

"My angels," Michael calls out gleefully. "Your messiah has returned to reward your efforts."

Enzo butts him with his gun again, creating a gash that oozes fresh blood. "Silence. I have no qualms with gunning them all down."

"Save me!" Michael screams regardless.

Inching forward, the crowd of people shows no fear of the countless weapons trained on them. They're protected by their beliefs. This is their holy war, and we're their lambs to slaughter.

In the light of the rising fires from the forest, we meet on opposing sides of the battleground. Us, drenched in darkness, and their matching outfits lit by the glow of orange light.

That's when I spot it.

The towering pile of wood.

Sickness rises up my throat and threatens to erupt. Leighton curses, and Theo almost runs into the back of me. Hunter and Enzo are the only ones remaining even remotely calm.

Behind his trained puppets, Michael's ultimate revenge lies in wait. He's determined to wipe the last speck of his bloodline from this earth. Not even Giana's death sated him.

"I warned you," he says over his shoulder. "You had the chance to join me. This is your punishment for throwing God's grace aside."

Secured to a tall wooden post around which branches and logs are gathered, Ulrich is secured to it with tightly bound rope. Tied. Gagged. Tear-stained and petrified.

Oh my God.

He's going to be burned at the stake in front of us. It takes Leighton's arm barred across my chest to stop me from attacking Michael, even if it would provoke his people to do the same.

He isn't locked in a cell, awaiting to be exchanged. I'm staring at my brother on the verge of a public execution. They're planning to burn an innocent child alive for their messiah.

"Stop there," a voice calls as one steps forward. "Surrender, and we will let the boy go as promised."

"That isn't how this is going to work," Enzo shouts back. "Release the child now, and we won't kill your leader in front of you."

Michael breaks out in loud laughter. "You think I am afraid of death, sinner? Do as you please. My legacy will outlive me."

Enzo bares his teeth, desperate to sink a bullet into him. "I'll kill you in front of them if need be. This ends tonight."

"Then do it!" Michael shrieks.

Realisation of his plan settles in my mind. To him, this is the end of his mission. The culmination of all his hard work. The world is burning, and his angels are in place.

He can die safe in the knowledge that they will continue slaughtering on his behalf, even as he walks into the sunset to join his twisted false god in the burning heat of hell.

"Enzo, no!" I grab his shoulder. "Kill him and they set that bonfire alight. We have to follow their rules."

Silently communicating with my eyes, I urge him to remember the reason we came. We can still pull this off. Our teams are in place and ready to strike. None of them are making it out of here.

"Why don't you take your masks off and face us yourselves?" I yell at the crowd. "Only cowards hide their faces."

Grasping their masks, glowing with the symbol that adorns my body, one by one, they begin to pull them off. My breath catches, and the guys curse colourfully around me.

They're just normal people. Average men, women and even a couple of teenagers. Michael has captured them all. Bent their minds. Beaten. Manipulated. Warped and broken.

The ultimate cult.

Hidden in plain sight.

"Whatever he's told you is a lie," I try to reason. "You can still walk away from this. You don't have to follow his orders."

"The messiah has saved us from a life of sin," a young woman drones in a lifeless voice. "We have cleansed ourselves before God."

Enzo cocks his gun. "This is your last chance to walk away. All we want is the boy. I don't want to kill you all, but I will."

"And we would happily die for the cause." A man steps closer, drawing a knife from his robes. "Give us what we want."

I duck my head to whisper to the others listening on the line. "Be ready. This is going to get ugly."

"We're in position," Kade responds.

"Now!" the man roars angrily, his face contorted with devilish rage. "Give him to us, or we light that bonfire up."

"Enzo," I beg desperately. "Just do it. Give him to them."

With a sigh, Enzo unlocks Michael's handcuffs. The moment he's free, he takes a big, deep inhale, stretching his arms above his head.

He turns to face me. "I warned you this would end in blood, Harlow. The rapture is here, and your time is at an end."

"Give us Ulrich," I demand.

"That child is the last of my cursed bloodline. He must die like the rest of you." Michael turns away. "Arise, my angels!"

Moving in a flash, more masked figures emerge from the smoke rising on all sides, tearing through the flames like demons escaping the mouth of hell. We didn't clock any of them.

"Incoming!" Hunter screams.

All hell breaks loose. Enzo takes aim and guns down two of the approaching shadows at the same moment Michael launches himself into Leighton to tackle him aside.

The pair collide and tumble, punching and screaming at each other. I pull the gun from my thigh holster and almost unload a round into Michael's head when a robed-blur smashes into me.

"Advance," I hear Kade scream in my ear. "Get the fucking kid!"

A pair of hands wrap around my throat, grappling to choke me to death. I lose grip of my gun in the melee and fall back on my training, bucking to shake off the masked attacker.

When the blast of a gun being fired cracks through the night, warmth washes over me, hot and sticky. Hunter stands above me, splattered with gore as he offers me a hand up.

He snatches my gun from the ground then hands it back. "Get to your brother!"

With the fire inching closer throughout the woodland surrounding us, the battleground is bathed in hellish light. Robed fanatics descend from all directions, colliding with the teams appearing from the west.

Scanning past Enzo and Leighton caught in their own fistfights, I catch sight of Ulrich at the centre of the unlit bonfire. Someone stands at the edge, a burning branch in hand.

"Ulrich!" I scream.

His gaze finds me amidst the madness.

"I'm coming!"

That's when the bonfire erupts into flames. The stench of burning fuel permeates the smoky air, and I can see him screaming around the gag in his mouth.

Breaking out into a run, I duck past whizzing bullets and flying fists, my attention focused on one point. Someone tries to tackle me, but Hudson appears, easily cutting them down with a knife.

"Go," he shouts at me. "I'll cover you!"

Without hesitating, I continue to duck and weave with him on my tail, slicing apart more obstacles. Michael's unhinged angels have the advantage of numbers, but they're sloppy and untrained.

In front of me, Kade is locked in a bloody fistfight, his gun lost in the chaos. Fists flying and flesh slapping with the landed blows, he hammers his opponent into the ground.

Passing him, I screech to a halt at the edge of the bonfire, surrounded by violence. Smoke fills my lungs and silences my screams of Ulrich's name. He's lost inside.

I can't see past the thick black ash and smoke. On the verge of throwing myself in to try to reach him, a figure emerges from the darkness, and his strong arms wrap around my waist to pull me back.

"Not so fast." His hot breath lashes against my ear. "I want you to watch him burn before I feed you to the flames as well."

I buck against Michael, his wrinkled but muscled arms trapping me in a vice. No one responds to my wails for help. He's snuck through the smoke to hold me back from Ulrich.

"Stop this!" I scream at the top of my lungs. "You can have me, but he doesn't have to die!"

"Everyone must die, my darling niece. We will begin again with a clean slate and no more filthy sinners poisoning this world."

"Ulrich! Ulrich!"

"He's going to burn in hell with his whore of a mother," he spits in my ear. "Just like you will once I've butchered every last person you love while you watch."

Keeping his iron grip on my body, Michael spins us around so I have an undisturbed view of the violence devouring us all. My men are lost in the war zone of bullets and blood.

I can't see anything. The fires have created a burning hot prison all around us, and smoke muddies my line of sight. The wails and screams are the only indication of life amidst the haze.

"Watch them die for their sins," Michael taunts. "I tried to warn you. I tried to *save* you. This is all your doing."

A flash of steel slicing through the smoky air catches my eye, eliciting a pained bellow. Nearby, Leighton's face is blood-stained, his mouth hanging open on the agonised syllable.

The knife is buried deep into his shoulder, forcing him to halt his attack on the man trapped beneath him. I howl his name, but it's silenced by the roar of noise drowning everything else out.

"If only you'd stayed safe in your cage." Michael drags his tongue down my cheek. "My perfect little girl. It pains me to do this, but you've left me no choice."

"Pain," I gasp through my tears. "You don't know the meaning of the word. No one has ever truly loved you. You're alone, Uncle!"

"Alone." He chuckles. "But victorious."

"Not yet."

Losing all sense of control, I buck and fight against him, throwing myself around in an attempt to escape. Michael evades every last attempted punch, his iron-clad grip refusing to relent.

I have to watch as blood is spilt, and flames reach the point of no return. We're trapped on all sides, and the bonfire is raging behind us. I can't see if Ulrich's alive.

My spirit breaks. Shatters. Implodes. Violent rage slips into my bloodstream and expands, dissolving all intentions I had of granting my murdered friends the legal justice they deserved.

They will have justice.

God's justice.

Fire and fucking brimstone.

Managing to sneak a hand underneath my armoured vest, I feel for the small blade I stashed inside. It slots into my hand, and Michael howls when I bury it deep in his side.

We fall together, and I'm crushed beneath his weight, blood seeping over me. He wrenches the knife from his side and howls like a crazed animal at the sight of red.

"You fucking whore!"

The knife comes curving towards me, intent on slamming into my chest to pierce my heart. I manage to lunge at the last second, dodging the blow and rolling across the ash-laden grass.

Michael follows, slicing and stabbing, seeking a single blow to stop me from sliding away from him. We tangle together, and my fist connects with his face.

Taking advantage of the brief second of distraction, I pull the blade from his fist and redirect it up into his chest. The knife slips into his breastbone, and he screeches like a banshee.

"You took everything from me!" I pull it out and stab again, harder this time. "I won't let you take them too."

Bleeding everywhere, Michael pushes through the pain and launches another frantic attack. His forehead crashes into mine, causing stars to burst behind my eyes and blur my vision.

"Enough!" he shouts.

Punching me in the jaw hard enough to rattle my teeth, he prises the knife from my hand then takes aim. The slash of the blade parting flesh in my arm barely registers, though he leers in satisfaction.

The pain is inconsequential to the terror twisting my heart into a knot. I can't see any of my men. Michael has got me trapped, and the knife is firmly grasped in his bloody hand.

"You're an ungrateful slut," he lashes, slicing my arm with a long stab. "I should have killed you the moment I saw you."

"Yes!" I scream back. "You should have! I won't let you hurt anyone else!"

Jabbing my fist into his throat, he falls back, the air knocked out of him. I desperately search around, but the hazy air carries only grunts of pain and the sound of fists hitting flesh.

The bonfire behind me is a blazing inferno. I can see the huge wooden structure at the centre burning. Ulrich's body is just visible, still untouched by flames, but quickly running out of time.

"Ulrich!" I yell. "Hold your breath!"

Michael finds his feet then attempts to throw himself at me again when the glow of piercing, bright lights illuminate the disaster around us. He freezes, peering up into the sky.

It's as if the heavens have opened, and God's light is pouring down on us all. Michael's face is a mask of open adoration, his hands raising in a frenzied prayer.

"I'm here, Lord! Your servant!"

When the hum of spinning rotors accompanies the bright light, his smile fades into a stunned glower. Four helicopters break through the haze, their powerful lights smothering us all.

I spot the letters on the side.

SCU.

Ladders fall from the side of the first helicopter, allowing multiple bodies to descend into the battle. The flash of bright green hair is the first thing I see as Phoenix makes an appearance.

A familiar voice shouts through my earpiece. "I told you motherfuckers not to leave me at home!"

In the cockpit with a pilot lowering them to land in the clearing, Brooklyn leans out of the window, searching for us. She releases a spray of bullets from her gun and shouts our names.

All four helicopters have reinforcements climbing down from them. Phoenix lands on his feet in the clearing, with a furious-eyed Jude jumping down from the ladder a second later.

He takes one look at me, bleeding and semi-collapsed, before making a beeline straight towards me. Michael screams in anger, his body failing him as he slips and slides on the blood-slick grass.

"Get away from her!" Jude bellows, deftly weaving through the night with deadly ease.

Running straight at Michael, he throws his arms at his waist, then the pair goes sailing through the smoke. Jude slams him back into the ground, and they both roll, grappling for control.

"Jude!" I shout in a panic.

Clutching my screaming arm, I find my knife then battle to stand back up to help him. Phoenix appears at my side and hangs the gun from his arm to offer me a hand.

"He's fine!" he shouts. "Where are the others?"

"I don't know!"

"Shit!"

Shoving past him, I run towards the bonfire, begging for another sight of my brother. Phoenix follows, attempting to stop me from approaching the stench of fuel and flames.

"Harlow, wait!"

I ignore him.

Ulrich needs me.

Bolting around the back of the structure, I spot an opening where the wood has collapsed so the flames are lower. Phoenix roars but can't stop me from taking a running jump into the fire.

The world vanishes.

Only the fire exists.

Swimming through the devil's flames, searing pain licks at my skin, cooking my hands. Pain doesn't stop me. Not even as I feel my skin pop and sizzle.

I push onwards, clambering over fire-slick piles of wood. Numbness spreads over me, and my lungs scream in protest against the onslaught of smoke stealing all of the oxygen.

"Ulrich," I choke on a sob.

His head lolling forward, Ulrich is unconscious in a cloud of acrid smoke. Every second is pure torture, the few inches between us protected by an ocean of fire that I have to wade through.

Move, Harlow.

Fucking move.

With the voices in my head roaring to life, I dig deep to find the courage to take a jump. Piles of burning branches crack beneath my feet, almost dropping me into the pits of the bonfire.

When I lay my hand on the rope holding my brother prisoner, I position the knife in my shaking hand and begin slashing. It's barely working, my nerves exposed by melted skin.

Slash. Stab. Saw.

Tears burn my sizzling cheeks. When the rope finally breaks, Ulrich's small body slumps straight into my arms. I almost drop him as I fight to remain balanced on a blackened plank of wood.

"Ulrich! Please …wake up."

His heavy lids twitch and he moans. "Harlow."

"Hold on."

With the last vestiges of my strength, I throw us both back through the flames rising ever higher. Michael's rapture consumes us both, and we tumble through acid and pure agony.

Falling.

Falling.

Falling.

My shoulder impacts with something hard. We roll in a tangle of limbs, hitting the ground with Ulrich still cradled in my arms. The moment we're out of the fire, I feel someone grab my ankle and pull.

"Harlow! Breathe!"

But I can't do it. Not alone. My lungs aren't responding to me, and the air is clogged in my ash-filled throat. Eyes glued shut, I hold on to Ulrich in my arms and let the world fade.

I did it.

Ulrich will live.

Nothing else matters. If I was only meant to leave that cage in order to save his life, then I've prevented another lost childhood. More pain. Suffering. The endless cycle of violence.

My vision darkens. The world begins to wink out of existence, but at the last possible moment, I hear something. A shout. Bellowing my name in sharp tones of panic.

Lungs on fire, someone blows clean, pure oxygen straight into my mouth. Over and over. Pumping. Squeezing. Inflating. The purest essence of life fills me up and escapes my gasping mouth.

Eyes opening despite the endless stream of tears, I roll onto my side and cough until there's nothing left in me to give. Someone is braced over my body, trying to pull Ulrich from my arms.

Blue eyes.

Dirty blonde hair.

Familiar smile lines.

"I'm here, love." Dad holds the oxygen mask against my face. "I'm not leaving you. I need you to breathe."

My father is here.

Saving me.

I'm safe.

With the mask pressed back on my face, I gulp down the air, letting someone else take Ulrich from me. It's all I can do to suck in each agonising breath and hold it in my searing lungs.

More bodies in uniform stream from the helicopters, and when another face swims into my line of sight, I question whether I'm dead already. He's disturbingly familiar.

"I've got him," Sanderson barks, a medical kit slung over his shoulder. "Evac is five minutes out."

He looks at me, and our eyes connect for the first time since the hospital bed I woke up in last year. His smile is tight but filled with awe, unlike the obnoxious lash of his voice tormenting me before.

"You're going to be okay, kid," he tries to comfort. "We're here with backup. Try not to move too much."

"The g-guys," I splutter.

"Harlow—" Dad begins.

"S-See them…"

"They're okay, love."

Sliding an arm around my shoulders, he lifts me enough to have a look at the carnage around us. The clearing is littered with bodies, some writhing in pain and others still as the SCU takes control.

Bright lights flash, and uniformed figures tackle the blaze. God's fury fights back, lashing them with heat. The fire can't spread farther as it's pelted with water cannons.

The last few fights are being broken up—armed agents pulling apart robed madmen and their vicious clawing. I watch as Ethan is rescued by an SCU operative, his face covered in blood.

"Harlow!" a voice yells.

Broad shoulders are running towards me faster than a freight train. Enzo. He's followed by Theo and Leighton, both limping badly and supporting each other. Leighton's clutching his bleeding shoulder.

Enzo skids to a stop then falls to his knees on the grass next to me. I've been dragged several metres away from the still-raging bonfire to a place of relative safety.

His eyes race over me, taking in the burned skin of my hands and neck, which were unprotected by thick fabric. I know it's bad. I can't feel my extremities, and the pain has vanished into numbness.

"Fuck," he spills out in a panic. "You're …. fuck! We need an ambulance."

"Three minutes out," Sanderson retorts. "Good thing you called, Montpellier. You owe me for saving your backside."

Enzo spares him a glance. "Took you long enough."

"You're welcome."

"You c-called the SCU?" I choke out.

His face softens in a worried smile. "Always good to have a backup plan, just in case. Even if it is this asshole."

"Pleasure working with you too," Sanderson mutters, stepping aside so Phoenix can get a look at me.

"Next time you're planning to run headfirst into a blazing fire, give me a bit of warning," Phoenix tries to joke, even though his terror is obvious.

"I'm sorry, N-Nix."

"You're okay, Harlow. Just breathe. Help's coming."

Beneath me, Dad is trying to offer comfort in any way he can. He's struggling to find an unburned place to touch me. The areas that weren't covered by my protective gear are all crisped.

Enzo pulls a wedge of bandages from a laid out medical kit and applies pressure to where the blade slashed through an opening in my armoured clothing.

"Where the hell is that ambulance?" he shouts.

"One minute out." Sanderson drops another medical bag at his side. "I'll bring them in. Don't move."

"D-Dad."

"I'm here, Harlow." He smooths a hand over my charred hair. "You're doing good. Keep breathing."

At my side, Ulrich suddenly wakes up with a pained splutter, pushing the oxygen mask away from his face. He wrenches his eyes open and looks over at me.

"Hey," I sob through my mask. "Got you, little man."

His bloodshot eyes fill with tears. "H-Harlow."

Phoenix hovers over him, taking over Sanderson's position. "Put this mask on for me, kiddo. Nice deep breaths."

Surrendering to the mask placed back on his face, Ulrich returns to lying on his back. His hand reaches out to clasp my wrist. If I could feel my hands, I'd hold him too.

Rotors spinning above us, the fourth and final helicopter lands. Brooklyn and Eli climb out together, both appearing petrified of what they'll find on the ground.

Through the light of the bonfire, I can see her reunite with her husbands. Everyone is converging around us. Jude and Kade run straight for them, and the four collide in a tangle.

"Where is Hudson?" Brooklyn yells.

"H-Hunter," I rasp.

"Shh," Enzo hushes. "They're coming."

With a group of firefighters appearing to tackle the bonfire behind us, three outlines stumble past them through the smoke. Michael's slumped frame is trapped between two lumps of muscle.

He's still alive.

Barely clinging on, his entire body soaked in blood from our fight. He can't walk alone, too weak to even hold his own head up. But Hunter and Hudson refuse to let him get away that easily.

"I caught him about to blow his own brains out!" Hudson shouts. "Does that mean I get a medal or some shit?"

The pair throw Michael on the grass a few metres from us. His hard green eyes are glazed over, like he's been hollowed out at the core by a swoop of God's hand.

Empty.

Defeated.

Gone.

His angels are dead while his mission floats in the destroyed embers that settle around us. Michael failed. The slump of his body carries that defeat with each unwanted breath he takes.

Hunter delivers a swift kick to his ribcage before he turns to face us. The moment his eyes land on me, his face changes. Euphoria flicks to horror in a split second.

"Harlow!"

The darkest shade of rage filters over him. Hudson breaks his reunion with Brooklyn and the others to guide them over to us, until everyone is settled around us.

"It's … over?" I grit out.

Brooklyn falls at my side, her belly protruding from her clothes. "It's over, Harlow. Christ. What did you do?"

Almost hacking up a lung in a coughing fit, I stare up at her. "I c-couldn't let … s-someone else die."

Cheeks wet with flowing tears, she strokes my hair from my face, her face lit by steadily increasing blue lights. An army of people are arriving as the fires rage on around us.

Metres away, Michael groans in the most exquisite sound of pain. "N-Not over… W-Won't stop."

Face twisted in an animal-like snarl that matches Hunter's predatory expression, Enzo ducks low to brush a kiss on my forehead, above the oxygen mask keeping my lungs going.

"I'll kill him for this."

"No," I wheeze out.

"Look what he's done to us all. He deserves to die in agony."

Leaving me in my father's lap, Enzo rises to join his best friend. The pair of them stare down at our enemy—defeated and alone, abandoned by God and the drones he created.

"This is for every life that you've ruined." Enzo takes the knife that Hunter offers him. "You'll never hurt my fucking girl again."

Before he can sink the knife into Michael's black heart, I scream as loud as my damaged lungs will allow. He freezes at the last second, restraining himself long enough to look back at me.

"Living is h-his … punishment." I wrestle the mask aside with my good hand. "Death is too m-merciful."

Enzo's eyes briefly sink shut. "Please, Harlow. You know what he's done."

"I-I know."

"Then let me fucking do this!"

"I r-remember." I take a shuddered breath. "M-Make sure he does t-too."

When Enzo fails to move, held prisoner by indecision, Hunter kneels down next to him and prises the knife from his grip. It has to be him. Our leader. Our protector. The man who kept us together.

His gaze is fixed on me, but it's filled with the knowledge of all we've sacrificed for this defeat. All of us. In so many ways. There isn't a single member of our family emerging unscathed from this.

"You're sure?" Hunter checks.

With a final burst of energy, I nod back.

"Then I'll give him a nice little reminder instead."

Straddling Michael's crumpled body, Hunter hovers the knife over his face. The tip of the blade circles his eye socket in a slow, cruel tease, eliciting a thin stream of blood.

"I hope you live a very long, healthy life and look in the mirror every day. I want you to remember this moment."

Phoenix covers Ulrich's eyes to make sure he can't watch as Hunter sinks the knife deep into Michael's cheek. His screams ricochet around us in a beautiful, perfect harmony.

Hunter holds him beneath his weight, carving with slow precision. There's no emotion on his face. No pleasure. This is the final task on his list to be ticked off before we find our freedom.

"You're going to look in the mirror every single day for the rest of your life and remember this. You. Fucking. *Lost*."

We all watch the expert curve of the blade, slashing the triangle across the entire length of his face, from ear to ear. Michael's shrieking reaches a fever pitch as Hunter begins to cut the external circle in.

The Holy Trinity.

Father, Son and Holy Spirit.

"Your God has abandoned you," Hunter spits into his butchered face. "Failure will be your legacy. You couldn't complete your mission, and you never, ever will."

My own scars burn, knowing the pain that their inception brings. Only this time, that symbol will be etched on Michael's face forever, unable to be hidden or removed.

A constant, infallible reminder. For every woman he raped and carved up, he will see that same symbol scarred onto his flesh.

"Your ritual is complete." Hunter finishes his work with a flourish, parting flesh and muscle, skin and blood.

Bright blood is seeping through the deep wounds, flashing sickening flaps of skin and gaping soft tissues that will never be pieced back together. Now we match.

In life.

In death.

Into the forever.

The wails of my barely conscious uncle mourning his destroyed face are the last thing I hear. My eyes sink shut, safe in the knowledge that my friends have the justice they died for.

SCENE DU
J.ROSE

CHAPTER 31

Leighton

more than life – Machine Gun Kelly & glaive

"**I**'d like to petition to bulldoze this waiting room."

Sitting next to me, his laptop unopened and coffee discarded, Theo stares up at the ceiling. His blonde curls are ruffled from sleeping across the plastic seating all afternoon.

"Seconded," he mutters.

"Really?"

"I'm sick of the sight of it too. You know, there's a scene in this book I just read—"

"Theo," I cut him off. "If you're going to talk about books, I'm going to leave you in here while I knock it down."

He glowers at me. "It wouldn't hurt you to pick one up and expand upon your three single brain cells."

"I didn't see you complaining about the pizza I ordered you last week. Only a genius would think to combine anchovies and olives."

"Or a psychopath."

"Well, let's ask Richards. He'll make that judgement."

Sitting on the other side of the hospital waiting room with Brooklyn asleep on his shoulder, Richards is staring at the magazine in his hands. He insisted on coming down when Enzo called him.

"I can tell you the answer right now." Theo picks up his cold coffee then drains it with a wince. "Certifiably insane."

"Ouch. No more pizza for you."

"Thank God for that. I'm surprised we haven't gotten food poisoning already."

Both emerging from freshening up in the bathroom, Enzo and Hunter retake their creaky plastic seats opposite us. I try to reach for my water bottle and hiss in pain as it pulls my bandaged shoulder.

"Idiot," Hunter curses. "Just ask for help."

I gape at him as he passes me the water bottle. "He really doesn't get the irony of that after the last eight months, does he?"

"Don't start a fight now," Enzo grumbles, folding his arms. "At least give it twenty-four hours since our last firefight."

Lapsing back into silence, we all anxiously watch the doors that lead to the intensive care ward. At this point, we might as well move in here instead of returning to our empty London home.

Harlow and Ulrich were airlifted here after being stabilised in a hospital near Carlisle in the early hours of this morning. We've been waiting for an update since then.

The doors to the waiting room open, emitting Oliver and Foster with hot drinks in their hands. Weirdly enough, the pair have stuck close together, supporting each other in their fear.

"Anything?" Oliver asks worriedly.

"Not yet," Enzo grunts. "What's taking them so fucking long?"

"They're looking after her, Enz," Theo tries to comfort him. "She's in good hands."

"The only hands I want her in are ours. I don't trust anyone else as far as I could throw them."

"We aren't doctors." I roll my eyes. "Sit your oversized ass down, and be bloody patient for once in your life."

With a curse, he sinks back down into his seat, haggard and exhausted. None of us have slept, although my parents dropped off clean clothing after taking Lucky for us.

The past twelve hours have been a whirlwind of hospitals, helicopters and cordoned off smoking wreckages. None of it feels real. We've got a lot of shit to process.

"She's going to be okay," Oliver says, mostly to himself. "I cannot lose her again."

Foster clasps his shoulder. "Harlow's tough as nails. She's going to pull through."

"I just got her back. We haven't had enough time together."

"You're going to get all the time in the world," Theo reassures him. "The burns were localised to her hands and neck."

Oliver's face pales further.

"Good work," I whisper. "You freaked him out even more."

"Why is it my job to make people feel better?" Theo replies quietly. "You're the damn people person. Not me."

The doctors come to retrieve Foster first. Ulrich is stabilised and awake. He sustained minor burns on his arms and a nasty case of smoke inhalation, but he will make a full recovery.

My parents make a reappearance as evening settles, bringing food for everyone and setting up camp with Richards and Brooklyn in the corner.

Hudson and Kade are held up at HQ, managing the fallout along with our unexpected allies at the SCU, but Phoenix, Eli and Jude soon arrive with updates and more food.

"Abaddon has been detained in Belmarsh along with Daphne."

Phoenix pauses to kiss his wife. "After surgery, that is."

"They did what?" Brooklyn snarls, a hand on her burgeoning belly. "I'll go and fuck his face up again myself."

"Let me rephrase that," he adds to appease her. "Surgery to make sure the son of a bitch has to see that mangled mess until the day he dies. He's under medical supervision but stable."

Satisfaction fills me. As much as I would've liked to see him dead and buried, Harlow was right. This victory is far sweeter. His one purpose in life has been taken away from him forever.

He will serve the rest of his life behind bars, tormented by the knowledge that he did not complete his mission. God has forsaken him, and he will forever bear the marks of that failure.

That gives me the smallest smidgen of comfort, though I fucking hate what it's taken to get us here. We all fought for our lives, but Harlow was the one who sacrificed everything to save her brother.

She won that fight.

For all of us.

"Belmarsh, huh?" Enzo chuckles happily. "Neither of them will ever get out of that place. It's literally hell on earth."

"Fitting, then," Oliver chimes in with a smile. "They're both where they belong."

"Anyone need coffee?" Eli asks, taking a group order to hydrate us all. "Be right back."

"I'll come," Phoenix says.

The pair disappear to fetch everyone's drinks, and Jude takes the vacated seat next to Brooklyn, ducking down to kiss her belly first.

"The country's on fire with everything that happened, but it's contained," he reveals. "Kade and Hudson are managing it."

Face thoughtful, Enzo stares down at his hands in his lap. The knuckles are swollen and scabbed over, much like the rest of us. No one escaped without at least minor injuries.

By some miracle, we suffered no casualties on our side. Both teams emerged bloodied and broken, but still in possession of their lives. Perhaps God is watching out for us.

"How many of Abaddon's people were arrested?" Theo asks.

"Twenty-eight. Another nine are dead. The ones who were captured are giving up more names in a bid to save themselves."

"Not so loyal, after all." He snorts.

"More like rats fleeing a sinking ship," Jude agrees. "Hudson is coordinating the arrests with Ethan and some dick called Sanderson. The superintendent's managing the media like she does best."

"Taking all the credit?" Enzo supplies.

Jude shrugs. "Surprisingly not. That scene was a literal bloodbath. There's a lot of unanswered questions, and she's taking the brunt of it for the time being."

That's a change. We're usually the first ones to be thrown to the wolves. After all of this, it seems we've earned her allegiance. Even if it is temporary at best.

"Just got an email from Harlow's publisher." Theo sits straighter, eyeing his phone. "Apparently, pre-orders of her book have quadrupled in the last twelve hours."

"Jesus Christ," Oliver swears. "She's lying in a hospital bed right now."

"And becoming a millionaire," Theo answers. "Everyone's calling her a hero for what she did. The world wants to read her book."

That woman has given every single scrap of herself to this fight, trauma be damned, and she's going to be rewarded for her bravery. If that isn't hope in action, then I don't know what is.

"What happens now?" Hunter asks aloud.

We all look at each other, none of us knowing how to respond.

Sabre may connect our family, but Harlow is the glue that allowed us to find each other again.

"I'm done," Enzo says flatly.

Hunter nods, reading his mouth. "Me too."

Looking between them both, Theo's face is impassive. "Sabre represents the last thirteen years of your lives. You'd walk away? Just like that?"

Enzo nods without hesitating. "Yes."

"And do what?"

"Anything. We've done our duty. It's time to pass Sabre on to the next generation to take forward. I can think of the perfect people."

"Who?" I frown at him.

Enzo's eyes stray over to the corner of the room where Brooklyn's accepting a steaming cup of tea from Eli and kissing him firmly on the mouth. He gives her a secret smile, ruffling her ashy blonde hair.

His one hand clutching his phone, Jude is keeping up with the developing situation and exchanging whispers with Phoenix. Despite leaving Sabre, both are well-versed in managing disasters.

"The Cobra team has proved themselves time and time again." Enzo's voice thickens with emotion. "I can't think of anyone better to take Sabre from us."

He's actually serious. I can tell by the look on my brother's face that they've already had this conversation. The pair of them are united in their sheer exhaustion.

"Hudson and Kade will burn the place down within a week." I laugh under my breath. "But I'm totally on board."

Arms folded, Theo considers it for a moment. "We could go anywhere. Do anything. Whatever the hell Harlow wants."

I cross my fingers and pout. "Please let it involve that awesome seafood restaurant in Costa Rica. My stomach is begging you."

Enzo jabs a thumb at me. "We can leave this one here and go find a hot, sandy beach to bake ourselves on."

"Hey!"

"Obviously, Sabre would crumble without you." He winks at me. "Seeing as you work *so* hard for us, Leigh."

"I happen to have a great work ethic."

"It's truly next level."

I glare at him. "I'm glad you agree."

Hunter clears his throat. "We need to stay here for my surgery and recovery, but after that, I'm happy to go basically anywhere."

Enzo squeezes his forearm then signs back, "*Of course.*"

"While you're all busy making plans..." Brooklyn's voice interrupts us. "I'm going to be squeezing a baby out in a few months. You ain't leaving me here alone with these bastards."

"Your husbands?" Enzo laughs.

"Yes. They'll drive me insane." She points a finger at him. "You have babysitting duty too, Uncle Enz. No excuses."

"Ah, hell."

"Harlow's going to be busy with the press tour for her book," Theo interjects. "And Hunter will need months of speech therapy after his surgery to relearn how to communicate."

Enzo groans. "Looks like we're here for a while, then. But I want a holiday, and we're not moving back to London. I want out of the city."

Ending our conversation, the female doctor who took Harlow into the ward exits through the sealed doors. We all fall silent as she scans over the waiting room, packed to bursting with people.

"There certainly are a lot of you here." She chuckles in amusement. "Harlow is a lucky girl to have such a big family."

Enzo shoots to his feet. "What's happening?"

"She's stable and awake," the doctor confirms. "We intend to perform surgery to attach a skin graft to her right hand. She has severe third-degree burns there, but the left hand is only second-degree."

My gut twists with worry. "What about her neck?"

"Also second-degree. She will have some scarring. The team has done their best to treat the wounds. Overall, this is a good outcome."

Everyone breathes a sigh of relief and slumps, hugging each other for moral support. Theo quickly translates the update to Hunter in a text message as all four of us gather in front of her.

"She's a little groggy from sedation," the doctor warns. "Don't keep her up for long. We need to hold her for a few days to monitor her lungs after the smoke inhalation and for any signs of infection."

"Wait," Hunter says. "Oliver should go first. She'll want to see her dad."

Enzo slumps in disappointment but reluctantly agrees. With a muttered thanks, Oliver follows the doctor into the ward. It's another nail-biting half an hour before he reappears.

His eyes are misted with tears. "She wants to see you guys."

Clapping his shoulder, Hunter passes him first and leads us into the intensive care ward. Harlow's room is the last door on the right. We pass Ulrich's room, where he's quietly murmuring to his dad inside.

Stopping outside Harlow's room, we all freeze in the cold clutches of fear. It was hard enough seeing Harlow get hurt before. This is going to be far worse.

"Come on," Hunter orders sharply. "Our girl needs us. Grow some goddamn balls."

Nice to see my brother has made a very miraculous reappearance in time for our collective near-death experience. And here I was thinking he'd finally mellowed.

Filtering into the calm, low-lit room, the beep of a heart monitor accompanies the drip of fluids and drugs being fed into the bandaged angel in the bed.

Harlow's eyes are closed, her lips parted and breathing steadily. Thick, bright white bandages wrap around her throat while her hands are gauzed and immovable at her sides.

"Princess?" I murmur.

Eyes flicking open, two devastating blue jewels land on all four of us. Beneath the burns, bruises and scratches, she summons the same hopeful smile that first ensnared my heart and refused to surrender it.

"Hi."

That's all it takes. The distance between us vanishes as we all crowd her, fighting the urge to scoop her into our arms. Multiple needles and IV lines feed into her arms and body.

"You're awake," Enzo rasps, overcome with emotion. "Fuck, little one. I thought we'd lost you for a moment there."

"Like hell," Harlow says in a wispy voice. "It'll take more than that to get rid of me."

Bowing his head, he hides his face in the crisp white sheets of the hospital bed. The shake of his shoulders tells us enough. Hunter rests a hand on his best friend's shoulder to comfort him.

"You did so fucking good, sweetheart," he whispers in awe.

Harlow's mouth twitches in a grin. "I love you."

He can read those words well enough.

"I love you," Hunter echoes. "Never do that to us again."

When her glassy eyes flicker over to me and Theo, she whispers for us to come closer. Theo moves first, his days of being able to maintain a safe distance relegated to the past.

"Are you in any pain?" he asks gently.

"I'm okay. Can't really feel anything at all." Her throat catches.

"Where is Ulrich? Is he okay?"

"He's fine, angel. Just down the corridor."

Lips pinched together, she can't stop the fat tears from rolling down her cheeks. "I thought he was dead. I thought—"

"Enough," Theo hushes her. "You saved his life."

"Then … nothing else matters. It was worth it."

With the three of them crowding her, Harlow looks up at me last. Somehow, I can't cross the final space holding us apart. I'm terrified that if I blink, she'll be unconscious and bloody in that field again.

"Leigh," she croaks.

Still, I can't move.

"Come here."

"You could have died," I force out.

"But I didn't," she combats in a barely audible whisper. "Please, Leigh. I need you too."

Staring at the woman who went from being a stranger to a friend to my entire fucking universe all in one goddamn year, the final wall around my heart collapses.

One that I didn't realise I still held in place after going to prison and losing everything. She's dissolved all the defences I built up in myself to survive and showed me a better way to live.

My feet pull me over to the bed where I bury my face in her stomach, amidst wires and dripping tubes. A finger sticking out of her gauze-covered hand strokes over my earlobe.

"Your shoulder?" she murmurs.

"Fuck my shoulder." I look up at her, my own face wet with the stupidest of tears. "I'll take a knife for you any day, Goldilocks."

"R-Romantic."

A pained gasp slips past her lips, and we all flinch, shifting backwards. She squeezes her eyes shut and shakes her head.

"Don't leave me here alone. I can't… I don't want to be alone."

Enzo smooths her hair back to softly kiss her forehead. "Never, little one. Let me get the doctor to come check your meds."

He slips out of the room, leaving us to hold her close. Harlow can't stop now that the tears have started to flow, her hiccups fading as Hunter strokes her hair and whispers in her ear.

"Where is h-he?" she stammers.

Theo draws circles into the unburned skin of her arm. "Prison."

"He's alive?"

"Yes."

Her tear-filled eyes reopen. "Good."

When the door to the hospital room opens again, we expect to see Enzo running back in with a harassed nurse or doctor. Instead, Ulrich's nervous smile comes through the door.

"Harlow?" he asks in a scratchy voice.

The tears stream down her cheeks even faster. "Ulrich."

He limps into the room in his small hospital gown. I move out of the way so he can take my spot at Harlow's side. Ulrich reaches onto his tiptoes to plant a very gentle kiss on her cheek.

"Hi, little man," she rasps.

"You're okay." His bottom lip wobbles. "I thought… I didn't know if you were okay. Dad told me to leave you alone to rest."

"You don't need to do that. Ever."

Ulrich sniffs, trying to maintain composure but struggling. "This is all my fault. I shouldn't have run away. You're hurt."

"Stop." Harlow winces as she tries to move too much. "None of this is your fault. All that matters to me is that you're here. Safe."

"Because of you."

Wiggling her only two unburned fingers, she encourages him to link up with his little digits, connecting the pair without causing her any pain.

"What are big sisters for?" she whispers.

Resting his head on her chest, Ulrich holds on tight and slams his eyes shut, afraid that, at any moment, she may disappear on us. I think we're all feeling the same way.

If I could take a photo of this moment and ship it to those two sickos rotting in Belmarsh for the countless life sentences they must now serve out, I would.

Instead of violence and death, this right here is their everlasting legacy. A brother and sister, united not in death, but in life.

Love has prevailed in the end.

That's our mission complete.

ve spring
players getting
ec change
With Major League Bas
ngare Paul White
SCENE DU CRIME
J.ROSE
482

CHAPTER 32

Harlow

Outro — M83

"Leigh! I can open my own presents."

Sitting cross-legged next to me on the floor, he shakes the wrapped present in his hands and frowns, deep in contemplation. I poke him in the ribs with my scab-covered left hand.

"I think it's a book," he muses.

"Leighton Rodriguez! Stop it!"

He laughs, passing it over then hunting for more presents beneath the Christmas tree. Hunter went overboard this year, even more so than he did last year.

The moment we moved home almost three weeks ago, he was out furniture shopping with Enzo to furnish our old home in time for the quickly approaching holiday season.

The giant fir-scented beast is a monstrosity that had to be cut to fit under the high ceiling. It looks like Christmas threw up on it with ornaments, tinsel, lights and all manner of festive crap.

Leighton was like a kid on a sugar rush as he overloaded the branches with decorations and made us suffer through *Home Alone* for the second year running.

"Leigh," Theo snaps as he strides in with a steaming coffee. "Stop winding her up."

He shoots me an innocent smile. "Sorry, Goldilocks."

"You're a shitty liar."

"Guilty as charged."

Taking the present with my good hand, I try to unpeel the Sellotape with my bandaged right hand pinned against my chest in a sling. My fingers fumble and fail.

After the surgery to attach a skin graft a little over two weeks ago, I've begun the slow recovery process. It promises to be a long road, but we're not unfamiliar with having to persevere.

I was relieved to finally be released from hospital after a week in intensive care following the fire fight, though the surgery and several rounds of antibiotics knocked the life out of me.

Coming home to the familiar, welcoming warmth of our abandoned house in outer London was worth those sleepless nights in a hospital bed. Lucky and her over-excited tongue definitely agreed.

"I can help," Theo offers.

"Thank you. I can't get into it."

"This is from me anyway," he admits shyly.

Making space for him next to me on the thick carpet, he lends me a hand and tugs the paper until it rips down the side. Pulling the rest off, the most stunning set of books is revealed.

"Ooh," I coo.

The covers are made of plush, gold-embossed leather in a luxurious shade of red. Engraved letters lined with filigree carve out the titles of the matching set, all with illustrated spines.

"The complete works of H.G. Wells." Theo's cheeks are covered in a dusting of pink. "First editions. I know you love early sci-fi."

"You're kidding," I breathe.

"Found them earlier this year in this tiny antique bookstore on the street behind the underground station."

"And you kept them all this time?"

He shrugs it off. "I was waiting for the right opportunity."

Moving slowly, I curl an arm around his neck and pull his lips to mine. He kisses me back passionately, his tongue sliding between my lips to touch mine in a teasing whisper.

"Alright." Enzo's voice barks. "No live sex shows on Christmas Day, thanks. We have guests on the way."

Striding into the room with Hunter and Lucky hot on his heels, Enzo distributes breakfast sandwiches. It's still early, the sun barely risen in the sky, but Leighton woke us all up like a big kid.

"Thank you," I whisper onto Theo's lips. "I love it and you."

He pecks the tip of my nose. "Always, angel."

With everyone settling around the Christmas tree, I eat my sandwich with one hand and watch the two brothers exchange gifts. Leighton gets Hunter an air horn, joking that he can use it after his surgery.

The prank doesn't go down well, and Hunter gets him in a headlock, intent on strangling his younger brother until Enzo breaks the pair apart with his wrapped gifts.

"What the hell are these?" Theo eyes a pair of socks with tiny pink crabs on them. "Seriously, crabs?"

Enzo barks a laugh. "Just thought you'd like a reminder of getting food poisoning in Costa Rica and puking your pretty little guts up."

"You are such an asshole."

"I've been called worse. I'll take the compliment."

Enzo unwraps his gifts, unimpressed by the bright green

gardening gloves that Leighton dedicates to his upcoming retirement from Sabre. He's going to get a sandwich thrown at his head any moment now.

When Theo picks up the thin, wrapped rectangle beneath the tree with his name on it, Hunter and Enzo both tense up.

"Um, Theo." Enzo stops him from opening it. "That's from all of us, but Hunter was the one who made it happen."

Theo looks at Hunter questioningly.

He rubs the back of his neck. "Consider it an apology for the way I've treated you over the last six years. I hope it answers any questions you have."

"Questions? About what?"

"Just open it," Enzo demands.

Biting his lip, Theo tears into the present and pulls out a thin manilla folder. As he flicks it open and scans over the paperwork inside, his face drains of colour, mouth falling open without a word.

"What is th-this?" he stammers.

"Your family," Enzo supplies. "We know that you grew up without any answers, and Hunter wanted to give them to you."

Shuffling forward, I look over Theo's shoulder at the paperwork. It looks like Hunter hired a specialist private investigator to look into Theo's childhood and how he ended up abandoned in foster care.

"My parents were missionaries in Rwanda," he reads aloud. "It looks like I was sent here as a refugee in the early '90s. That's why I had no identity on record."

I cover my mouth with my good hand. "Shit, Theo. What happened to them?"

He swallows hard. "Looks like my mother was killed during a riot. Someone must have taken me and gotten me out of there."

Hunter clutches his cup of tea close. "Our investigator has been compiling information for almost six months."

"We think that we've found your father," Enzo adds hopefully. "He was caught up in the civil war and had no idea what happened."

Eyes red behind his glasses, Theo looks up. "You found him?"

Enzo nods. "He's still living in Rwanda. Teaches at a local school and works for a foreign aid charity. He stayed, hoping he'd find you."

"This … can't be real. I have a family?"

When they nod again, Theo removes his glasses to hide his face in his hands. I rub his shoulder in a silent, comforting circle.

"I have a family," he repeats.

When he looks up again, his dismay has disappeared, and hope rises to the surface. The biggest smile breaks out on his face.

"I wasn't abandoned, was I?"

Enzo grins back. "No."

Overwhelmed by emotion, he throws himself at Hunter. The pair crash into a tight, emotional hug, and I meet Hunter's eyes as his chin lands on Theo's shoulder.

I raise an eyebrow.

He smirks. "I still have some tricks up my sleeve."

Breaking apart, Theo returns to studying the paperwork. I can see his energy rising from here—eyes jumping from side to side, fumbling through the documents with his trembling hands.

"Does he know about me?"

"No," Enzo admits. "But our investigator found his address and contact information. We thought we'd leave the rest to you."

"I'm gonna need a minute."

Giving them both grateful smiles, Theo leaves the folder on the coffee table then slips outside into the falling snow for some air. Hunter watches him go apprehensively.

"Did I fuck up? Was it too much?"

I tap his arm to gain his attention. *"Perfect."*

It's a tense ten minutes before Theo returns, looking a lot calmer. He sits down and takes a gulp of his coffee, his eyes still on the file.

Leighton claps his hands together. "Shall we show Harlow her present? I'm dying over here."

"Wait, my present?" I repeat.

Four identical, excited stares land on me.

"Oh, Christ. What the hell did you guys do?"

Enzo offers me a paw. "Let us show you."

Taking his roughened palm, I let him gently guide me up. His arm circles my shoulders, careful not to disturb the light bandages still covering the healing, second-degree burns on my neck.

The other three follow us through the house that feels a little alien after all our months apart. I still remember the day I set foot in here, trembling and afraid, feeling completely out of place.

Back then, I had no idea that this house would quickly become my home, and the strangers who brought me here would be my family.

I wish I could go back eighteen months and tell that terrified girl she would become a strong, independent woman, strengthened by the love and support of men who would sacrifice it all for her.

We made it.

Scarred but alive.

Toeing on my Chucks, Enzo makes me laugh by kneeling down to lace them for me so I don't need to move or hurt myself.

"I can lace my own shoes, Enz. You did teach me."

"If I had my way, you'd never lift a finger again for the rest of your life. Be glad I'm letting you walk at all."

Holding my laughter in, I snuggle into his side and follow him out into the steadily falling snow. The driveway outside our modern Victorian mansion is covered in a thick carpet of white.

There's another vehicle parked in front of the high security gate, covered beneath a huge white sheet and adorned with the world's biggest purple bow across the bonnet.

"Um... Whose is that?"

"Yours," Theo whispers in my ear.

"I can't drive!"

"We're going to continue your lessons once you're healed up," Leighton says with a wink. "You were doing really well before."

Skipping ahead of us, Hunter grabs hold of the sheet and tugs. It's pulled off to reveal a dark-red, armoured SUV with beautiful black rimmed wheels, tinted windows and matte accents.

"Is it a fucking tank?" I can't help but blurt.

"Well, the glass is bulletproof," Enzo reveals. "You know, just in case. There's something else you should see on the back."

Following him over, I pitch my voice low. "Do I need bulletproof glass to drive around rural London?"

Leighton bumps my shoulder. "He'd put you in a bulletproof glass house if he could. This is a fair compromise."

Gathering at the back of the car, there's a black frame stretching across the rear with a tow bar. A shining, silver dirt bike is fixed to it.

I freeze on the spot. "No way."

Enzo crouches down to study it. "Bought it myself from an old friend in Oxford. It's a custom bike just for you."

Gaze skipping between them, the car and the bike, I'm lost for words. This must have cost a small fortune. All for me.

"This... Guys, it's too much!"

Leighton's arm finds my waist as he kisses my temple. "Nothing is too much for you. We're gonna spoil you like the motherfucking queen you are."

"Smooth," Theo mutters.

"Smoother than you, four-eyes."

Slipping past them, I approach the car to peer through the window. The inside is full of luxurious black leather and sleek control panels with a dark tortoise finish.

I feel Enzo at my back, crowding me.

"Do you like it?"

"Like it? Enz, I love it, but you shouldn't have spent all this money on me."

He slowly turns me so my back is pressed against the car door then smacks his lips on mine, careful not to disturb my healing wounds.

"This is just the beginning of us spoiling the hell out of you. Better get used to it. You've got the rest of your life to spend like this."

Then his lips are on mine again—attacking, demanding, nipping and biting. All I can do is let myself be consumed by the indomitable force that is Enzo freaking Montpellier.

When the security gate beeps and begins to slide open, he very reluctantly releases me. Hudson's Mustang purrs as it manoeuvres past us.

"Let her go, you animal!" Brooklyn shouts from the window.

Flipping her off, Enzo lets them drive past and kisses me again. Slower this time, with silent tenderness, whispering secrets to me through the gentle stroke of his lips.

"I promised you the world, Harlow," he murmurs into my mouth. "Now I'm going to give it to you."

"What if I don't want the world? What if I only want you four and nothing else?"

The corner of his mouth hooks up. "You already have us, come hell or high water. This is our happy fucking forever, baby."

I press my forehead against his.

"Fucking forever."

†

With the Christmas dinner spread out across the table, we somehow manage to cram our houseful of guests into the space. It's a tight squeeze with some creative organisation.

Della and Ben are at the head of the table with Enzo's aunt, Hayley, and my father completing the set of parents. Brooklyn and her husbands take the entire right side of the table.

Enzo orders me to sit down, refusing to let me carry a tray of golden roasted potatoes even in my good hand. When he swats my butt with a pair of oven gloves, I relent.

"Harlow!" Hayley pats the empty space between her and Brooklyn. "Come sit here, darling."

I slink over, wrapping my arms around Jude's neck from behind and pecking his cheek on the way. He gifted me a whole set of matching, personalised journals for Christmas.

When I take a seat, Hayley pulls me into a cuddle, being careful not to hurt me. Her thick, glossy black hair tickles my jawline.

"How are you feeling, *querida?*"

"Tired," I answer honestly.

"You're still on pain medication?"

"Here and there. Some days are easier than others. But I'm slowly getting there, a step at a time."

She brushes her thumb over my cheek. "I'm so glad. The thought of these boys almost losing you breaks my heart."

"That's not going to happen," Brooklyn chips in. "I'm not dealing with this lot alone."

I cuddle into her side next. "I still can't believe you're having a little boy. What happened to female solidarity?"

"Technically, the male is responsible for the part of the DNA that decides the baby's sex." She scoffs. "So blame them."

Phoenix fists bumps the air, his hair dyed bright red in honour of the festive season. "You know it, firecracker."

"I wouldn't have minded either way," Kade says while stabbing a roasted parsnip. "Maybe we'll have a girl next time."

Choking on her mouthful of non-alcoholic wine, I have to hammer Brooklyn on the back so she can suck in a breath.

"I'm sorry, next time?"

Kade glances at her with a crooked smile. "Yeah?"

"There's going to be a next time? We're not even done with *this* time yet, and it was a fucking accident!"

"Language," Hudson scolds. "There are parents present."

"I happen to be on Brooklyn's side here," Della says. "She's the one who has to give birth. You lot have it easy in comparison."

"Thank you, Della!"

Surprisingly, neither Ben nor my father disagree. Both simply look at the guys next to Brooklyn and nod in confirmation.

"See," Della says smugly.

"Turkey time!" Enzo calls over the ruckus. "Stop debating, and shut up for the toast. That includes you, Leighton."

"Ah shit," he curses from the stereo, where he was fiddling with the Christmas music. "Fine, I'll turn it down."

With everyone gathered in their places and taking seats, Enzo steers Hunter to his seat at the head of the table then sits down on his left side.

Still standing, Hunter clears his throat. "I just wanted to say that I'm glad we're all here together to celebrate Christmas as a family."

Smiling up at his son, Ben raises his glass in a toast. Everyone follows, their eyes still on Hunter, who picks up his filled wine glass.

"We've been to hell and back this year," he continues. "All of us.

But we've still lived to tell the tale. For that, I'm thankful. I love you all."

Leighton makes a fake throwing up noise. "Spare us."

Grabbing his fork, Enzo jabs it into Leighton's hand until he's yelling in pain. He retracts the fork and pins him with a glower.

"Listen to your fucking brother before I serve your severed head instead of the damn turkey."

Hunter lifts his glass with an eye roll. "Merry bloody Christmas, folks."

We all clink our glasses together in unison.

"Merry bloody Christmas!"

Dinner is a messy affair of veiled barbs, arguing over Christmas cracker jokes and Hudson arm-wrestling Leighton for the last turkey leg. The former wins, almost breaking Leighton's arm in the process.

When Brooklyn raids our cupboards and returns with a jar of pickles, everyone gapes at her. Enzo locates the peanut butter she was looking for and smiles as she dips the pickles in it to satisfy her craving.

"S'good," she moans.

"I think I'm going to throw up," Phoenix announces.

Smacking him upside the head, Eli smiles encouragingly at his wife. "Eat whatever you want, baby girl. I'll go buy more if you want."

"Suck up," Hudson mutters.

Brooklyn points a pickle at him. "You should be taking notes, Hud. Eli wins husband of the week. Congrats."

Green eyes twinkling with mirth, Eli grins at her. "Does this make me top of the leaderboard, then?"

"Not so fast," Kade jumps in. "I'm still ahead with five points. Gotta work harder than that, Elijah."

With all of the food devoured, everyone moves to the living room to watch Hunter's favourite Christmas movie. I catch Theo slipping outside again and quietly creep after him with Lucky at my side.

The door clicks shut and we're both immersed in the falling snow. It's coming thicker now, coating everything in a crisp winter wonderland. I follow Theo's footprints to the middle of the lawn.

"Theo?"

He startles, a slip of paper in hand. "Oh. Sorry, I just needed some breathing room. It's loud in there."

"Want me to leave you in peace?"

"No. Come here."

Stepping into his arms, we both watch Lucky zipping up and down the garden, attempting to catch the snowflakes melting on her tongue. Theo chuckles when she flops on her back in frustration.

"What's on the paper?"

"That investigator got a phone number for my father," he mutters, holding it tight. "It was in the file."

"So what are you thinking?"

"I don't know, beautiful. I've spent my entire life thinking that I was abandoned and left alone with no family. But it was all a lie."

Snuggling closer to his slim frame, I cradle my head in the crook of his neck. "I'm so sorry, Theo. You didn't deserve that."

"It's no one's fault. I'm just struggling to wrap my head around the idea of having a real family."

"You know… I struggled when I found out about Giana and my father," I admit, shivering in the cold. "It didn't feel real."

"How did you cope?"

"You guys helped me. I wasn't alone in it, and neither are you. Whatever you choose, I'll be here every step of the way."

His breathing is short. "I want to know him so badly, but I'm terrified of opening my heart, only to be disappointed."

"If you don't try, you'll never know. Can you live with the knowledge that he's out there without contacting him?"

"I ... don't think I can."

"Then call him," I encourage. "You've got nothing to lose and everything to gain."

"Stay with me?" Theo pleads.

"I'm not going anywhere."

Standing in the swirling snow, I hold his shivering torso tight as he dials the number. Theo hesitates, taking a breath for courage before hitting the call button and putting it on speakerphone.

It takes a moment for the line to connect for an international call, then the ringing begins. Over and over. My heart rate rockets higher with each second until the line cuts off without an answer.

"Fuck it," Theo growls out. "What am I doing? I don't need him in my life. I shouldn't even be calling."

"Hey, slow down. It's an international call. He's in a different time zone too. Just try one more time, and then we can go inside."

Reluctantly, he repeats the process again. The ringing starts, and I hold my breathing, silently pleading to God for a Christmas miracle.

The line clicks.

"*Muraho.*"

"Uh," Theo splutters, panicked. "Hello?"

"Who is this?" The voice switches to English.

"I'm ... uh, looking for Horatio."

"This is him. Who might I be speaking to? You're ringing up a hell of a bill calling me from a British number."

I squeeze him tighter, silently willing him to be strong. Theo sucks in another laboured breath then clears his throat.

"My n-name is Theo. Well, Theodore Young."

"Hello, Theodore Young. Listen, I'm running a busy school here. I don't have time for cold-callers. Whatever you're selling—"

"Dad?" Theo croaks.

Horatio stops, the line going deadly silent. For every wordless second that passes, Theo's shaking increases. I hold on tighter.

"Who… Who is this?" Horatio repeats.

"I think my name used to be Noah. Before … everything. That's what the paperwork says, at least."

Come on, I internally beg.

"Noah?" His voice breaks. "Is that… Oh God. Is that really you?"

"Yeah," Theo rasps. "I'm here."

"Son," Horatio begins to sob. "You're alive. I've been looking for you for over twenty years… I thought…"

"I was dead," he fills in.

"What are you doing in England? You're not in Rwanda?"

"I haven't been since I was a toddler. It's a bit complicated. I just found out that I have a family."

Horatio sucks in a shocked breath. "It must have been… Christ, twenty-five years since I last saw you."

"Yeah," Theo confirms. "I'm twenty-nine now."

"My boy. You're still alive."

"I'm here, Dad."

Breaking down, his father openly cries, and it doesn't take long for Theo to join him. I press a kiss to his cheek then step away, giving him some privacy as I slip back inside.

Hunter is waiting in the doorway, his nose almost pressed against the glass. He's freaking out over his present. I pull him into my arms and hold him close to silence his worries.

"I just wanted to give him something to show how much I care," he admits roughly. "I've treated him like shit since Alyssa died."

Leaning back, I move my lips slowly for him. "She would be

proud."

"Mad?" he guesses.

I bite back a laugh. *"PROUD."*

"Ah." Hunter's face softens in a smile. "I hope so."

Raising my left hand, I sign out a question. *"Surgery? Ready?"*

He shrugs, but I can see the excitement humming beneath his tattooed skin, covered in his usual delicious, pressed white shirt. I've missed his smart outfits, even if I love his sweatpants far too much.

"As I'll ever be. I need to go in for the pre-op in a couple of days. Should be home by New Year's, though."

Sliding the phone from his back pocket, I unlock it then pull up the notes app to tap out a longer message.

No matter what happens, your family will be here for you. Successful surgery or not. Deaf or not. We're here, and we aren't going anywhere.

Kissing my lips, he rests our noses together. "You saved us all, Harlow. I'm not sure how I can ever repay you for that."

Hand lifting to his back, I trace out the only words I'll ever be able to respond with. I didn't save them. We saved each other, night after nightmare-filled night, through thick and thin.

Hunter chuckles in my ear.

"Yeah, sweetheart. I love you too."

SCENE DU RIEN
J.ROSE

EPILOGUE

Harlow

Two Years Later

Dog Days Are Over – Florence & The Machine

Staring into my clear-blue eyes, I take advantage of the final seconds of silence. My shoulders are squared. Determined. Lips stretched in a smile of anticipation. Stomach flipping with nerves.

The person looking back at me would be unrecognisable to the old Harlow. She's the result of turmoil and bloodshed, a scar-laden phoenix who found the strength to rise from the flames and rebuild.

She's a person I can be proud of.

After all these years, I finally love myself.

It took the dismantlement of my uncle's underground empire to find peace. Watching him and Daphne being found guilty on multiple murder charges set me free from the final bit of their control still buried in my mind. They're both serving life sentences and will never see the light of day again.

The thud of Enzo's footsteps is unmistakable. I'd recognise his authoritative thud even with my eyes shut. Slipping into the small dressing room, he ducks beneath the door frame then straightens.

"Little one?"

I turn away from the mirror. "Enz."

His crisp charcoal suit is form-fitted and brings out the glow of his tanned skin, complemented by his fire-lit, amber eyes. The Australian sunshine we've spent the past eighteen months living in agrees with him.

"Fuck, baby," he curses. "You look incredible."

"It isn't too much?"

"You're kidding, right?"

Stepping farther into my dressing room, his eyes scan over my floor-length gown, the deep purple silk hugging my curves in all the right places. Brooklyn helped me choose it.

My now short, mousy brown hair brushes my shoulders in perfect curls, revealing the twisted scar tissue that marks my neck and throat. I don't care. Let the world see my scars.

They've gotten me here, to this exact moment. Minutes away from stepping on a stage in front of hundreds of people and flashing cameras. I'm walking in there as myself—on show and unapologetic.

Enzo's hand finds my lower back, running a thick finger up the length of my spine. "I want to take you back to our hotel room and tear this flimsy piece of silk from your body."

"I could get on board with that."

"Pretty sure you have something important to do first. We didn't fly ten thousand miles to hide beneath the covers. I miss the ocean breeze already."

Leaning back into his warmth, I savour the final seconds of silence. "Enjoy the moment, Enz."

"Trust me, I intend to. Leighton's taking advantage of time off from building his company and getting wasted out there."

"So he should. He's been working day and night on the marketing firm. I still can't believe we're in New York. None of this feels real."

Enzo's chuckle is throaty as he spins me around to find my lips. "You're the one who's brought us here, baby. I am so fucking proud of you."

"I know, Enz."

"We're all out there waiting for you at the front. I can't come on stage with you, though."

"It's okay." I kiss him again. "I can do this alone."

His gaze burns bright with pride. "Of that, I have absolutely no doubt."

With a final kiss, he leaves the dressing room, then I face myself one more time. Around my neck lies a thin gold chain, holding Giana's wedding ring at my clavicle.

I briefly touch it and whisper up to the heavens. "I hope you're watching up there, Mum. We made it."

Before I can start crying and ruin my makeup, I take a final breath and make myself leave the safety of my dressing room. There's an assistant waiting in the corridor to direct me.

When the hum of voices reaches my ears, I have to steel myself. I've faced far more terrifying things than this. Journalists. Television interviews. Conferences. Public speeches.

But this is a culmination of everything. All the hard work and hours I've poured in to the last two years of my life in the wake of leaving Sabre and England behind.

"Ready, Miss Kensington?"

I steel my spine. "I'm ready."

Standing at the back of the stage, I overlook the packed ballroom. Hundreds of faces fill the round tables, dressed in their fineries and awaiting my arrival. I can see the guys from here.

Hunter and Leighton are bickering like usual, gripping their champagne flutes. Enzo appears, stopping to kiss the top of Brooklyn's head before taking his seat next to Theo.

Brooklyn's eagerly watching the stage, bouncing not-so-little baby Logan on her lap. He's grown so much since his first birthday several months ago, taking after his mountain-like fathers all seated around him.

"Dad," I hum to myself. "Where are you?"

My anxiety builds until I spot him at another table with Della, Ben, Hayley, Foster and Ulrich. They're all here. My entire family has flown to the States to watch this huge moment.

Tapping the microphone at the front of the stage, the silver-haired president of Columbia University calls the room to attention.

"When I first read our next prize winner's book, *From the Ashes*, I was moved to tears. I can assure you all here tonight that this is no easy feat after the years I've spent doing this job."

There's a rumble of laughter.

"I was moved by the candour of the author and the magnetism of her raw, unfiltered honesty, even in the darkest of narratives. But more so, I was left with something far more precious... Hope."

Della's already sobbing her eyes out. My father has to pull her into a hug while Ben searches for the tissues stashed in her purse.

"It gives me the utmost pleasure to introduce the winner of this year's Pulitzer Prize for non-fiction, Harlow Kensington."

Everyone is on their feet, applauding and beaming up at me. I focus on my feet—one step in front of the other, like every other day of my life. Pushing forward. Breathing. Living. Even in the hardest of times.

When I do manage to look up, they're all there. The purest of souls at the very front table, all four of them wolf-whistling, even if it is inappropriate in front of this crowd. They couldn't care less.

Having an out-of-body moment, I accept the president's outstretched hand and shake. He hands me the certificate that never once entered my mind when I published my book late last year.

My name is there, etched in fine, curling calligraphy. The person I was made into, and the surname I left behind. Both versions of me melded into one, emerging from the chrysalis I hid in for so long.

Hugging the framed certificate, I hold it at my side and face the room. Tears burn my eyes just seeing my father's incandescent smile, filled with so much pride, I don't know how he's holding it all inside.

"Good evening, everyone," I speak into the microphone. "I want to thank Columbia University for this incredible honour. This means more to me than I'll ever be able to express."

As the applause dies down, everyone takes their seats, all eyes on me. The flash of cameras still bothers me, but I've trained myself to get used to the sense of vulnerability.

"*From the Ashes* was never meant to be published," I admit with a laugh. "These journals were written for one person. Me. I needed to make sense of a lot of things that happened to me while in captivity."

Meeting my eyes, Hunter nods for me to keep going. The huge smile on his face has to hurt, framed by long hair that he's regrown.

"I published this book not for fame nor publicity. My aunt and uncle's trials last summer brought me enough of that. I needed something good to come out of all the pain they put into this world."

Looking down at the certificate, my throat clogs. I take a moment to find my voice again.

"For a very long time, I thought I was alone in a cruel, uncaring world. That I wasn't loved, and I couldn't survive the abuse and bloodshed. That broken person desperately needed hope."

Passing Logan off to Eli for a cuddle, Brooklyn wipes the tears from her face, holding my gaze as she mouths her encouragement.

"I found it in the love, care and affection of the family I never thought I needed and had no intention of finding. They gave me the strength to rebuild my life, each painful step at a time."

His eyes shining bright, Leighton pouts his lips then blows me a kiss from across the room. Uncaring, I reach up a hand to capture it for everyone to see. The cameras go wild.

"I hope this book gives those who read it the truth they're looking for. That survival is possible. Hell, finding the courage within yourself to actually live is possible. There's always hope for a new beginning."

Touching the necklace around my neck again, I feel the first tear spill down my cheek.

"This prize doesn't belong to me. I would like to dedicate it to the eighteen women who died at my side and the countless others who perished in the fight that followed."

One by one, I list their names. Every single last one. All those who lost their lives and will never get to tell their stories. I will spend eternity speaking for them and honouring their memory.

"Their voices were silenced by hatred and evil. My message is simple... In their honour, we must live with love in our hearts, forgiveness within our reach and hope in all that we do. Thank you."

To another roar of applause, I pick up the certificate and head for the set of steps leading off the stage. Hunter rushes forward to meet me at the bottom, sweeping me off my feet.

I hide my face in his neck. "Did I do okay?"

"You did perfect, sweetheart. I heard every beautiful word."

Placing me back on my feet, the circular metal disk attached to the implant in his head is visible in his hairline. He doesn't always catch everything, but I know he was determined to hear my speech.

Guiding me back to our table, I'm overrun by people. Of course,

Brooklyn's the first to lay her hands on me. I'm smothered into one of her lung-squeezing hugs as her tears soak into my face.

"Fuck, Harlow. I told you not to make me cry."

"Sorry." I smile into her neck. "Couldn't help myself."

Releasing me, she hands me off to Theo and Leighton. The pair trap me in a sandwich of muscle and aftershave that makes me want to do things definitely not appropriate for the public.

"Good job, angel," Theo whispers in my ear.

Leighton kisses my scarred neck. "Fucking perfect, princess."

Their sandwich doesn't last long. Enzo snatches me from between them and boosts me into the air, even as I squeal in front of the entire room. He spins me in a circle before dropping me back down.

"You are the most beautiful thing I've ever seen," he says gruffly. "And I'm really done sharing you with hundreds of people."

"Come on." I laugh. "Let's get out of here."

†

I shouldn't be surprised that Hunter took the liberty of hiring an entire restaurant for our brood to descend upon. We take over the whole place, popping champagne and exchanging hugs.

My father summons the attention of the room with a tap on his glass, silencing our family. We all turn to look at him.

"I just want to thank everyone for being here to watch this moment." He turns to me. "Harlow, I am so incredibly proud of the person standing in front of me. You blow me away every day."

"Dad," I croak.

"Don't *Dad* me," he corrects with a grin. "I know the last two years haven't been easy for you, but you've made it through. This moment is a monumental accomplishment."

With champagne flutes clinking together, everyone toasts his words. Brooklyn has to scold Phoenix to stop him from feeding champagne to baby Logan. Eli smacks him for extra good measure.

"I believe there's something else we should be toasting tonight," Dad says innocently. "And with that, I'll hand this over."

"Hand it over to whom?" I laugh.

There's a tap on my shoulder, and I spin around, every single part of my body freezing in sheer, utter shock. While everyone was focused on my father, the four guys snuck behind me.

"Oh my God."

Every single one of them is resting on the carpet with one knee bent. The rest of the room disappears as I gape at their faces.

"Um, guys?"

Leighton beckons me over first, taking hold of my hand. "Harlow, we've been waiting for the right moment to do this."

"And arguing over it a lot," Hunter adds.

"But we've decided that it's time." Theo smiles up at me. "And what better moment than this, in front of our whole family."

"I voted for the beach in Brisbane," Enzo grumbles.

Silencing him with a glower, Leighton strokes his fingers over the twisted, mottled skin of my hand. He's smiling like a complete fool.

"We want forever with you," he says simply. "And even that won't be enough, but it's a start."

My breathing stops. "Leigh."

"Will you marry me?"

Vision blurred with tears, I nod numbly. "Yes. I will."

After he's pulled me into a hug, Hunter takes my hand from his. I'm pulled along the line before I can take a breath.

"I spent a year in speech therapy to hear those damn words for myself," he reveals. "Will you marry me, Harlow?"

"Yes. Of course, yes!"

Pulled into his chest, his mouth finds mine. I can feel his brother at my back, trapping me between both of them and their lips. Enzo breaks us apart with a deliberate cough.

I'm passed off to him, his huge height bringing us to eye level even with one knee pressed into the carpeted floor.

"You are my heart and soul, little one. I promised you forever, and this right here is it. Will you marry me?"

"God, Enz. Don't you know the bloody answer?"

"I'm a selfish bastard, and I want my own yes."

Kissing his mouth, I whisper into his lips. "Then yes."

He manages to keep the kiss to a parent-appropriate display of affection, but I can see the fire burning in his eyes. I lean close to whisper under my breath.

"I meant *yes, sir.*"

"You'll be saying it again later around a mouthful of my cock," he replies quietly enough to disguise his words.

Choking on a breath, I face the final person. Our entire story has been a beautiful case of better late than never. Theo was the last piece of my heart to slot into place, but he's the one who completed me.

"Beautiful girl, I didn't know I was lost until I found you." His smile is wry. "Turns out, I wasn't alive at all. Not until the moment you entered my life."

Reaching into the pocket of his smart trousers, he pulls out a velvet ring box. Theo pops it open to reveal a stunning, heart-shaped diamond, encased in smaller diamonds on a white gold band.

"Will you marry all of us?" he asks.

I fall to my knees so we're nose to nose, cupping his cheeks. "I will, Theodore. A thousand times yes."

He slides the ring into place then steals the last kiss. It feels so right on my finger, a physical representation of the bond that's tied us all together since day one of this wild journey.

Our relationship has been tested at every turn. Even after Hunter's successful surgery, surrendering Sabre to the Cobra team and leaving to start our lives abroad in the bright lights of Brisbane.

But while everything changed, the very fabric of our lives warping and transforming into something new, one thing remained the same.

Us.

It's always been us.

Our family.

From Leighton setting up his marketing business and Hunter taking a sabbatical from all paid work to recover properly, to Theo landing a contract working for the Australian government in cybersecurity.

Even Enzo got what he wanted after years of longing, finally setting up a chop shop. The tiny, family-run business is right on the Gold Coast. My father helps him during his regular visits every few months.

With the ring in place, our family engulfs us. I'm showered in hugs and kisses, tears and sobs. Hayley is a happy wreck as she reaches onto her tiptoes to kiss her red-faced nephew.

When my father pops the next bottle of champagne and begins to shake the hands of his future sons-in-law, I take a step back from them all to watch my family celebrate as one.

In the back of my mind, Harlow Michaels still lives. Watching her crazy, beautiful, wonderful life unfold from within her rusted cage. Awaiting the day she'll find the strength to break free and run.

"We did it," I tell her. "We survived."

And what a beautiful fucking life we're living.

THE END

SCENE DU NS

PLAYLIST

God Save Me – Genosky & Promoting Sounds

Who Are You Fighting For? – Gina Brooklyn

Let The Right One In – Boston Manor

THE ONE YOU LOVED – The Plot In You

1x1 – Bring Me The Horizon (ft. Nova Twins)

Living In Colour – Tropic Gold

The Day That I Ruined Your Life - Boston Manor

Half-Life – Essenger

Bad decisions – Bad Omens

Who Do You Want – Ex Habit

heartLESS – You Me At Six

Pirate song – mehro

HOPE – NF

WHO I AM – Parker Jack & Chyde

Foxglove – Boston Manor

Aura (Reimagined) – The Brave

Homemade Dynamite – Lorde

Misery Business – Paramore

Lost In The Moment – NF & Andreas Moss

Overgrown – Mountains of the Moon

Devil in Her Eyes – Bryce Savage

Sad Day – FKA Twigs

Everything Once – Hotel Mira

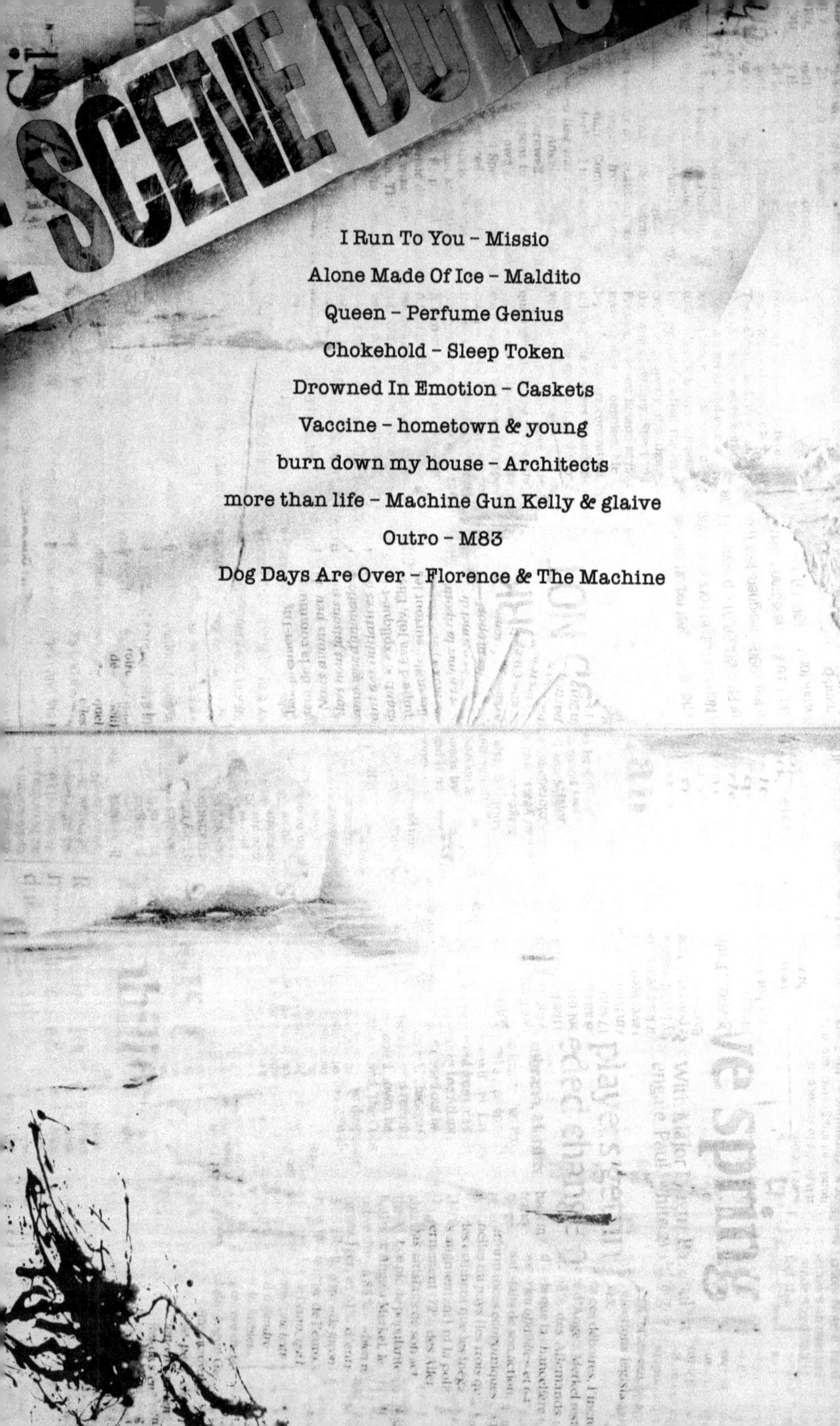
SCENE DU N
I Run To You – Missio
Alone Made Of Ice – Maldito
Queen – Perfume Genius
Chokehold – Sleep Token
Drowned In Emotion – Caskets
Vaccine – hometown & young
burn down my house – Architects
more than life – Machine Gun Kelly & glaive
Outro – M83
Dog Days Are Over – Florence & The Machine

WANT MORE FROM THIS SHARED UNIVERSE?

If you loved Brooklyn and her merry band of psychopaths, check out their completed stories in the Blackwood Institute trilogy—a dark, why choose romance set in an experimental psychiatric institute where monsters walk among us and nothing is quite what it seems.

https://mybook.to/TwistedHeathens

https://mybook.to/SacrificialSinners

https://mybook.to/DesecratedSaints

Follow Willow's story as she flees an abusive marriage and takes refuge in the small mountain town of Briar Valley, assisted in her hunt for justice by Sabre Security.

https://mybook.to/WBWF

https://mybook.to/WWTG

ACKNOWLEDGEMENTS

Wow. I'm struggling to believe that I'm actually writing these words. The end. Harlow's story is done and dusted after a whirlwind year of living in the Sabre Security world.

Harlow's character came from a very well-concealed, vulnerable part of myself that needed to be heard. A victim, broken and bruised, but also capable of rebuilding herself into someone she can be proud of. I've grown with her character, and I hope that you have too.

If you've experienced trauma, know that you are loved, seen and able to live the life that you want. Your pain isn't you. Take those wounds and use them to strengthen yourself.

You're a warrior.

Cherish that fact.

Let's dive into my usual list of amazing people who made this book and whole series a reality. The list continues to grow.

To Eddie, my love and soulmate. There's nothing else to be said. I love you with all that I am, and I always will.

To my girls – Lola, Kristen and Lilith. All three of you are my rocks and provide me with so much love every single day. You deal with my anxiety, tears and self-doubt, even when I can't do it myself. I love you guys.

Thank you to my team for keeping this chaos rolling – Julia, my PA, Kenzie at Nice Girl Naughty Edits, and Kim for proofreading to make my baby shine.

And a massive thank you to everyone on my dedicated street and ARC teams for being there to support me. I appreciate every single one of you. Not to mention Savannah at Peachy Keen Author Services for being fabulous in supporting me with another book release.

Finally, I want to thank you – the reader. You've stuck with this story through thick and thin, witnessing Harlow become a badass and finding her inner strength. Thanks for your trust and support. It means so much to me.

Over and out.

Stay wild,

J Rose xx

ABOUT THE AUTHOR

J Rose is an independent dark romance author from the United Kingdom. She writes challenging, plot-driven stories packed full of angst, heartbreak and broken characters fighting for their happily ever afters.

She's an introverted bookworm at heart, with a caffeine addiction, penchant for cursing and an unhealthy attachment to fictional characters.

Feel free to reach out on social media, J Rose loves talking to her readers!

For exclusive insights, updates and general mayhem, join J Rose's Bleeding Thorns on Facebook.

Business enquiries: j_roseauthor@yahoo.com

Come join the chaos. Stalk J Rose here…

www.jroseauthor.com/socials

NEWSLETTER

Want more madness? Sign up to J Rose's newsletter for monthly announcements, exclusive content, sneak peeks, giveaways and more!

www.jroseauthor.com/newsletter

ALSO BY J ROSE

Buy Here: www.jroseauthor.com/books
Recommended Reading Order: www.jroseauthor.com/readingorder

Blackwood Institute
Twisted Heathens
Sacrificial Sinners
Desecrated Saints

Sabre Security
Corpse Roads
Skeletal Hearts
Hollow Veins

Briar Valley
Where Broken Wings Fly
Where Wild Things Grow

Standalones
Forever Ago
Drown in You

Writing as Jessalyn Thorn
Departed Whispers
If You Break

www.ingramcontent.com/pod-product-compliance
Lightning Source LLC
Chambersburg PA
CBHW070337170726
48291CB00001B/78